ARTIST
IN RESIDENCE

SIMON BILL

artist in residence

Copyright © Simon Bill 2016

First published by Sort Of Books, 2016; an earlier version of this book,
Brains, was published by CABINET II

No part of this book may be reproduced in any form without permission
from the publisher except for the quotation of brief passages in reviews.

Sort Of Books, PO Box 18678, London NW3 2FL

Typeset in FF Hertz and Sun to a design by Henry Iles

Distributed in all territories excluding
the United States and Canada, by
Profile Books
3 Holford Yard, Bevin Way, London WC1X 9HD

336pp

A catalogue record for this book is available from the British Library

ISBN 9781908745576

eISBN 9781908745583

Printed and bound in Great Britain by Clays, Bungay, Suffolk
on Forest Stewardship Council (mixed sources) certified paper.

ARTIST
IN RESIDENCE

a novel

1: her diary

26th July
This is the first time I've ever been here. I am alive for the very first time. All of this is new. I am sitting in this room which I know is my room with my pen and paper planning this new day. I know this is my room where I live and have a bed a table and two chairs. One chair is for sitting at this table and the other is an armchair. I am writing my plans for when I leave this room later on today.

And here's another extract, this one also chosen at random.

14th Oct
This is the first time I've ever been here. I am alive for the very first time. All of this is new. I am sitting in this room ... etc. etc.

It makes no difference because she's been writing more or less the same thing every day since she recovered consciousness, almost three years ago. She was in Belize, this tiny country in Central America, and she contracted a rare viral illness. She collapsed without warning, having displayed no other symptoms, and went into a coma that lasted nearly seven weeks. One day she woke up and said she was hungry, and to begin with she looked set to make a full recovery. There were some problems with her memory,

5

but that's quite common following a long period of unconsciousness. Actually, though, these problems were caused by brain damage, and she's probably going to be like this for good. The scans carried out at Gray's show she has markedly focal damage to the hippocampus in both halves of her brain. (The necrotic tissue left by this pathology would be phagocytised – eaten – by specialised brain cells called microglia, the brain's housekeeping cells, leaving, in this case, a pair of identical bilateral cavities.)

What this means is that she will never be able to hang on to any new information for more than fifteen minutes or so. She can remember things from her life, apart from the few months just before her illness, and she can learn new skills if they can be taught within the fifteen-minute window, but she will not be able to recall that she has these skills. So if, say, you were to teach her to balance an orange on the crooked elbow of her right arm and then snap the arm forward, so that with her right hand she catches the orange before it flies across the room, she would be able to repeat it. But if you show her the trick a while later and ask her if she can do that, she'll say no. If then urged to try it for herself, she would be surprised to discover that she could. She knows how to do it but she doesn't know she knows.

2: at a private view

EMILY IS ONE OF THOSE PEOPLE I've met since I accepted the post of artist in residence at the Norman Neurological Institute at Gray's Hospital. I first heard about this from a friend I was talking to at a private view at Black Hole Gallery. We were looking at a series of cibachrome print photographs of celebrities' thumbs, and he told me about this residency that was coming up. I decided it might be an idea to try for it because of my financial situation at the time. My paintings weren't selling, and the people at my gallery, the gallery that 'represents' me, were losing interest. They'd look uncomfortable whenever I happened by, and I was being offered advice on how I might change my work to make it a bit more appealing for collectors – maybe my paintings are too big? (They *are* too big. I've given myself a ridiculous storage problem with my weekly output of at least two ten-by-twelve-foot abstract paintings.)

I was talking to this person – not a friend at all really – only because I didn't dare trying to mix with some of the more successful people in the room, and I needed to be seen talking to somebody; otherwise I'd have been standing there on my own. He's the kind of artist that works in art's public sector, with its grants and subsidies and residencies and fellowships. I've not really had much to do with this kind of thing before because I thought I could operate successfully in the more glamorous commercial sector, working with international collectors and continental art museums and so on. (It's two different ideas about art. Not two distinct camps, because in practice there's a lot of overlap, but the

7

public sector is generally hostile to painting, particularly abstract painting, because it has nothing to say about sociopolitical issues. I worry about that myself sometimes. How, for example, could I have done all those tormented self-portraits when the news was probably full of dying children in some Third World death zone? I was only about eighteen when I was doing those paintings of myself, in anguish, but still. If what I was doing was suffering, what did I think those children were doing? It's not the ethics that bother me so much as the logic of it.)

I didn't think much of my chances of getting this residency, in a hospital, having to act like I care, but I was, frankly, desperate. The bank and the credit card firm were after me, and I had to stay on my toes to avoid all those people I'd been borrowing money from – a tenner here and a tenner there.

My 'friend' wrote down some details about the residency while I considered, and decided against, trying to borrow money off him. He used the back of a private view invite, and next morning, searching rigorously for enough change to buy cigarettes, I found it scrunched up in my hip pocket. I decided not to bother with it, and then, about midday, having thought a lot about my situation, rang up for an application form.

Surprisingly (to me anyhow) I made it on to a shortlist of five artists. The application form was a lot less work than I'd feared. I've looked at, and binned, dozens of application forms for residencies and grants and fellowships. (Susan used to leave them around for me to find. She was concerned that my poverty and isolation might be affecting our relationship, and she felt that if I got some sort of job this might help. This is before she hit on another, elegantly simple, solution to our problems, which was for us to

8

stop seeing each other.) I had been expecting a document as thick as a glossy magazine, with plenty of baffling, jargon-heavy questions, and big blank spaces looking for qualifications and project outlines, allowing you to continue on a separate sheet. With this one, though, the space where I was supposed to say how I felt my practice could benefit from the Institute's clinical environment had room for an answer not much longer than that question. I still sweated over what to write – this really isn't my field – and I was not confident when I sent it off, filled in in biro, all dog-eared, but it must have been OK because I got shortlisted. Me and four other artists.

And then, having been asked to go in for this interview, I seriously considered not going, because I felt quite sure that all the others were going to be experienced and skilled interviewees. As well as being arrogant I'm actually quite timid. I'm not comfortable being questioned.

3: turning up for my interview

WHEN I ARRIVED AT GRAY'S, half an hour early for a twelve o'clock appointment, I was dressed in my private-view outfit (that is, the only clothes I had that weren't all covered in paint), and carrying the two books I needed to get me through this – a London *A to Z* and the illustrated catalogue from an exhibition of late de Kooning paintings. I always carry an *A to Z* because I have no sense of direction. You'd think 'sense of direction' was just a figure of speech, but I know there is such a faculty because I don't have it. I get lost all the time, even just going down to the shops. If I happen to enter a familiar street from an unfamiliar direction I won't recognise it for a while. When I finally do figure out that, Yes, I know this place, I won't be able to orient myself correctly – knowing which way I go now – because I've entered from the wrong angle. I wander around London like a tourist with my *A to Z*, looking up and down, checking street names in the index. It's a wonder I've never been mugged.

The de Kooning catalogue was for my prepared speech about creativity and Alzheimer's.

I was early to allow for orientation, and a quick drink if it seemed necessary. Gray's isn't one building. It's more like a kind of postmodernist shanty town. It's an incredible mixture of buildings all crammed together like bottles in a crate, so you'll get two of the more considered buildings – The So and So Clinic, and the The Such and Such Centre – both spoiled by having a crude breeze-block oblong built in between; or you'll get a nice Georgian townhouse squashed between two sheer concrete structures like enormous filing cabinets. Older parts get corralled by car parks, or a wagon circle of Portakabins. They can't expand the site of the hospital because it's in the middle of London, so it just gets more and more cramped every time they have to accommodate some new branch of medicine, with new things getting built on top of, or through, or actually inside other things. In the spaces between these buildings they've got some landscaped areas with low-maintenance raised shrubberies, and lawns crisscrossed with muddy 'desire-lines' – the routes people actually take to get from A to B, instead of using the paths. Basic needs are catered for: several fast food outlets, a hairdresser's, a florist, newsagent, chapel, even a pub.

Dominating the whole place is a massive tower block, Gray's Tower; the Norman Institute occupies its top floor, flanked by a weird cantilevered shelf-like projection. The roof above it is festooned with all kinds of technological rigging, aerials and dishes and whatnot, put there to keep pace with developing communications, and there was a plume of yellowish smoke that must come from the basement incinerator, where they burn all their hospital stuff.

The ground-floor foyer was like a Channel ferry, with its swirly carpet, screwed-down seating, and a reek of *croque monsieur* from one of the food concessions. I went looking for the lifts, but having misread or misunderstood a sign found myself in the A&E department, entering with a shove through a pair of swing doors and departing on the back-swing. I had another try with the signs – surely one of them must point to the lifts? – and this time found the toilets. I sat in a cubicle for a spell to calm down, and then went outside again to smoke a cigarette.

There were quite a few other smokers out there. One of them jerked his head at me: 'Awright?'

I jerked my head back at him: 'Awright?'

I thought he was leaning on a mike-stand, but it turned out, looking at him, to be the thing for his portable drip. I psyched myself up a bit, smoking quickly, allowed my eyes to go out of focus, and rushed back into the foyer. Ignoring the signs, I made an inspired dash through a flotilla of occupied trolleys, leapfrogged a wheelchair user, and halted right by the lifts.

It had taken me forty minutes to get from the main entrance to the lifts, and I was late. This made me feel better (because I might be *too* late, and they might send me home again). I pressed the button, waited calmly, got into the lift on my own, and went straight to the top.

4: the Institute

THE TOP FLOOR HAD MUCH BETTER AIR. The lift doors opened and that queasy hospital atmosphere gave way to a lovely waft of new paint and furniture smells. I went over to the reception desk and spent some time telling the classy receptionist, very busy with her hair and nails, what I was there for. Me being late wasn't a problem because she didn't know what I was on about, and seemed not to feel that dealing with me, in reception, was any part of her responsibilities as a receptionist. I asked her if she would mind trying to find out if there was anyone who did know. The lift doors opened behind me and someone else came over to the desk. He tried to speak to her while she got on the phone to see if anyone knew what I was there for, and she ignored him. She seemed to be taking a while. This other guy, another artist, and me, looked at each other and rolled our eyes. He was younger than me (I'm thirty-seven) and his clothes were better, but I felt no hostility towards him. Presently she put the phone down and said that someone would be with us in a moment (and I didn't mind about her undisguised contempt because it wasn't directed at me alone – and also because one of the things I'd been doing in the toilet was drinking vodka).

Two more artists got out of the lift: young women, with laptops. We told them that them being a bit late was fine, apparently, and that we were still waiting for someone to come out. The last artist arrived. We explained the situation to him, he nodded, and we waited.

It took me a little while to figure out what was wrong with this, but then it dawned on me: if we were all there at the same time, and the interviews were going to take at least half an hour each, then some of us were going to have to wait around a lot, *lot* longer. I nearly said something, but then saw they'd all worked it out already. They were *clearly* annoyed.

We were all standing there, waiting, and I started to take in my surroundings. The Institute was all really nicely done, I thought. They've used a good architect. The use of hardwood in the finishing gave it a Scandinavian feel, and the lighting was ingenious because you couldn't see where the light came from: there was just this fresh, Nordic light. The timber finishing added to the smell of newness, and even the sounds felt designed, filtered through some kind of soothing baffle system. This reception area seemed to be at the hub of a cartwheel or panopticon arrangement, with numerous broad corridors fanning out from it.

A door opened, somewhere up along one of those corridors, and we all turned to watch as a small woman walked towards us. She was moving at a smart pace, like a little torpedo, with her cropped salt'n'pepper hair and a neat grey suit, but it still took a while for her to reach us, and walk right past. She opened a door beyond the reception desk and disappeared. I doubt she'd even seen us, and the closing door made no sound at all. I looked at the door handle and recognised its design, very simple and quite beautiful, from pictures I've seen of the Wittgenstein house in Vienna.

One of the applicants started tapping her nails on the desktop. Some long minutes later we were approached by another, much rounder, woman, in no particular hurry, and this was 'Michelle', who apologised for having kept us waiting, and started to take us on a guided tour of the Institute. Nobody had said anything to us about any guided tour. I didn't mind about this apparent lack of organisation and breakdown in communication, but the others did. One of

14

the young women, the nail-tapper, wanted to know what was going on? She was here for her interview. At twelve. Michelle, not at all bothered, explained that we were going to have a guided tour of the Institute, followed by interviews at half-hourly intervals. There were some protests; everyone except me. The young woman argued the longest, and then left. Michelle watched her go (and about then I noticed that my friend, the guy who told me about this thing, wasn't among us. It's possible he wasn't shortlisted, but it also seemed quite possible that he never applied).

With one down, and the odds looking better, the other applicants agreed to be taken on this tour, but they weren't happy about it. Apparently they had other things to do that day. As the tour commenced they were all on their mobiles rearranging meetings. Not me, though. I haven't got a mobile.

Leading us up one of the corridors, Michelle began to tell us 'a little bit about the Institute itself'. It opened, just over a year ago, thanks to a very substantial endowment from the Norman Foundation, an organisation set up shortly before his death by the 'billionaire philanthropist' (she did actually call him that) Mr Conrad Norman. The Foundation's mission is to support neurological and ageing research. The Institute is its principal beneficiary. At present they have a core staff which includes their director, Dr Nancy Prabhakar, one resident neurologist, therapists, the technical staff and, of course, administration (and Michelle smiled very slightly there, because 'administration' meant her). The Institute is both a working clinic and a centre for research in neuroscience and its related fields, and offers a comprehensive range of facilities to scientists from around the world. There is, however, only one visiting research scientist working here at the moment. An eminent neurochemist from Atlanta called Owen Madden.

(I don't really follow current affairs, but it did definitely ring a bell when she mentioned Conrad Norman. Huge in pharmaceuticals. Or armaments. There'd been a lot about him in the press a while back. Something to do with him leaving all his money to some wacky cult, and his son, or his daughter, being unhappy about this.)

Michelle was showing us rooms now. We had emerged from the corridor, at last, into a spacious and luxurious waiting room, or living room. Actually, she told us, it's the Day Room. The banquettes, armchairs and coffee tables had all been carefully selected in keeping with the rest of the decor. There was a widescreen TV that you heard through earphones secreted behind little panels in the seating. There were water coolers and coffee machines. There were glossy magazines arranged on all the tables.

One wall of this huge room was just glass, and on the other side of the glass was a broad balcony or terrace, and the sky. She took us across to this giant window and held a plastic disc against a small box on the adjacent wall, which caused a single ten-by-ten-foot sheet of glass to pop fractionally forward towards us, and then slide sideways over its neighbouring sheet, with a faint hydraulic hiss. Having ushered us out onto the balcony, she closed the glass door behind us by holding the plastic disc against another small box on the outside wall. The balcony didn't seem as well maintained as indoors – there were weeds and shredded blue plastic bags on it. Maybe it's run by a different department. Peeking over the balustrade it felt like we were in a hot-air balloon, and I realised we were standing on the brow of the Tower's jutting shelf-like structure, with nothing beneath us. Michelle didn't seem to have anything to say about this. She was just showing us the view.

Walking back through the deserted Day Room, we were told about the clinic's inpatients. Although there are many patients being treated for the more common neurological conditions – Parkinson's, Huntington's, Alzheimer's, stroke, motor neurone disease, epilepsy, multiple sclerosis, etc. – the Institute specialises in the treatment of rare, even on occasion unique, conditions of the brain. There are twenty-four rooms for inpatients, whose condition is both rare and severe enough to render them helpless in the outside world. The former stipulation has kept numbers down (just one at present), but they are hoping to have patients transferred here from other hospitals.

We saw one of the MRI suites (they have a lot of them here), and it looked to me like an ideal vision of the future, with a gleaming white device like a giant Polo mint under a pulsing purplish light. Guided along another corridor, lined with regularly spaced doors like a hotel, numbers 1 to 24, we looked into a typical 'Guest Room'; actually an inpatient's room. Very nice. Big bed, TV, en suite bathroom. The only thing that wasn't great was it didn't have any windows.

Moving on, we passed some offices with their doors ajar, nice offices, were shown the IT suite, and from there to the Activities Room; and this, we were told 'is the very best-equipped facility of its kind in the whole of the UK, which offers our patients the opportunity to engage in interactive activities'. There didn't really seem to be all that much to see in the Activities Room. Or, at any rate, not much activity. Loosely deployed amongst the ranks of spotless new worktables, perhaps a dozen or so patients were sitting around not doing anything. I took them for patients, although, with the exception of the odd unusual posture, a tremor, or rigidity of expression, their symptoms weren't particularly obvious (certainly not to *my* untrained eye).

Michelle's claim that the room was unmatched in its provisions for craft activities was easy to believe. In fact, if anything, it was rather *over*-provided, because a lot of the equipment was just left standing in crates, untouched. For example, lined up along one side of the room was a brand new full-sized loom and next to that a state-of-the-art multi-speed electric potter's wheel and a programmable kiln (I've seen an earlier model at Central Saint Martins). Beside that was a printing press, of a design that Caxton would certainly have recognised, but newly hewn from close-grained blond wood.

One patient, a very old man, was sitting right next to a jigsaw and ignoring it. Not a puzzle, but an actual jigsaw; the type of saw that they use to cut complex shapes in sheet materials, this one being a modern reproduction of the traditional kind that looks like an upside-down pennyfarthing and is operated by a treadle. Possibly he would have liked a jigsaw puzzle to help pass the time, but he was expected first, if he wanted one that bad, to make it himself.

There seemed an assumption that this was the sort of thing we, as artists, would be especially interested in, so we lingered a while, adding to the air of inertia and listlessness. The other applicants clustered by the door looking obviously bored (contemporary artists are not usually very engaged with craft), and I might have too, if I had not noticed, among these patients, with their tremors and their tics, a young woman – a Pre-Raphaelite muse, sitting very still, her wide and innocent eyes upturned; pale, fragile hands loosely clasped in her lap, a cape of tawny hair descending from the pink centre parting to enclose her narrow shoulders. She looked like a flower child from some stock footage of the 1960s, or would have done if the wires from her earphones hadn't been visible.

As I stood there and gaped, a physically substantial and authoritative member of staff moved across the room, and, looking sideways at us, with open scepticism, she asked Michelle, in a soft Jamaican accent, 'Is this them?'

'Yes. Interviews in half an hour, Jade.'

Jade sighed: 'OK. I'll be along.'

'Brilliant,' said Michelle. And then she startled me by asking suddenly – 'All done?' Since I was the only one of the candidates not looking at their phone or laptop, I found I had been appointed, by default, as our temporary spokesperson, on this issue at least. So I said, 'Yes.' And as we were bundling through the door out into the passage beyond, I leaned back to catch a last look at the Pre-Raphaelite beauty, with her unearthly composure, as still as a waxwork.

5: I have to wait

BACK IN THE DAY ROOM we were left on the empty banquettes to wait for our interviews. I wondered if we were going to talk amongst ourselves, maybe about that huge loom, but two of them opened their laptops, and the third sat opposite me checking his mobile. I couldn't imagine what it was they were doing; how they were so busy.

There was a selection of glossy magazines fanned out on the table in front of me. I picked one with a good-looking cover (nervous again now) and began flicking through it, letting everybody know I didn't care. (Why do I still behave as if someone's watching me all the time? At my age.) After a few minutes of this mime it began to register with me that I didn't understand what I was looking at. None of the words or pictures made any sense. Whilst the form was familiar – lush photography accompanied by text in various fonts – the content was entirely alien. I'd heard of this happening to people, and knew it meant I was going to faint. I closed the magazine and looked at the cover, hoping for some kind of clue, a bit of known reality to hang on to, and I nearly laughed when I saw its title. I looked up at the man sitting opposite me, still fiddling with his mobile. It's OK. It's not me. It's this! The magazine was called NEURON, a neuroscientist's trade mag. It'd certainly fooled me, with its fashionable graphics and sumptuous photography. Naturally I'd assumed it was a fashion magazine, or a style magazine. Who'd have thought anything so recondite could look so sexy?

The image on the cover looked abstract – a blurred close-up of some costly iridescent fabric; or maybe a firework display pictured without any skyline to give scale and perspective. I checked the caption at the foot of the contents page, to see what the image on the front cover was, and my feeling of relief faded a little. The picture on the front was 'a front dorsal section through the lining of the lateral ventricle of the adult rodent forebrain'. I looked up again, and thought I caught the man opposite looking at me. I bet (I thought) he knows about this. He's no expert but I bet he's done some research and preparation. The PA system came on just then, announcing itself with a tiny click, and the first applicant's name was called for interview. She closed her laptop, gathered her belongings, stood, and walked off. I made a mental note of the direction.

Returning *NEURON* to its original position amongst the carefully fanned-out selection of glossies, I tried the next one that came to hand. This was *Molecular and Cellular Neuroscience* (*MCN*). It seemed somehow friendlier. I looked at the pictures first. A lot of these were stunning. Luridly pigmented, and rich in associations. Something that looked to me like the kind of marbled paper used for old-fashioned bookbinding, except suffused with an unhealthy glow, and marked with little black arrows. A series of near-identical portraits of a luminous fried egg laid out in a grid pattern, similarly marked and annotated. Skeins of colour-saturated wool dragged across a black velvet curtain by a mad kitten. Stained-glass windows designed by a tripping monk. Something that looked like purple sprouting broccoli, except obviously microscopic, and alive. These images were ravishing and, to me, incomprehensible (and I thought that that added something to their allure, because it made them full of promise).

With more time to fill, and needing to keep occupied, I started to read. I checked the contents page again, looking for a way in. 'Sites of Neuronal Differentiation in the Embryonic

Zebrafish Forebrain' looked promising. I was tickled by this 'zebrafish'. Was it some spliced monstrosity, or just a type of fish? I skimmed the introductory remarks and plunged in somewhere about the middle of the text – 'the nMLF is located along the ventral boundary of $pax6$ ...' – and I gave up there, and looked at the pictures. Very beautiful.

I leafed through the magazine a bit more, scanning for clues or glimpses. There were quite a few references to animals – besides rats and zebrafish (what are these?), there were cats, dogs, monkeys, mice, mutant mice, a kind of fly called drosophila, squid, lampreys, kittens, crayfish. Most of this didn't really touch me. I have no very strong views on any issue, including animal rights (although I did wonder what they were doing to those kittens). Among the adverts, most of them for laboratory research equipment, there were a few I thought were quite funny. 'FISH ELECTRIC ORGAN TISSUE' in big letters, with lightning zigzags all round it. 'Powerful Antibodies – you'll be AMAZED how powerful an antibody can be!!!'

There was also an ad for something called an Animal Behaviour Photobeam Activity Monitor, like an aquarium, with laser beams crisscrossing its interior, that they put lab rats into. The advertisement said it was bulletproof.

6: how my interview went

THE PA SYSTEM MADE ME JUMP. It sounded as if someone had crept up behind me and shouted my name. I gathered my stuff and set off in the right direction (noted earlier), and came to a door with a circular window, like a porthole. I could see four people sitting at one end of a big oval conference table with bottles of water, pens and sheets of paper in front of them. I knocked and went in. One of them looked up, said Hi, and asked me to take a seat. After some quick thinking I took the seat next to them marked by a fifth bottle of mineral water.

From then on it all seemed to go quite smoothly, given that I had no chance of getting the job. First they introduced themselves. Ben – the young resident neurologist, rugger player's build, posh, enthusiastic. Jade – the abundantly physical West Indian therapist I'd just seen in the Activities Room (showing no signs of the impatience I suspected she was feeling about having to be here when there were other things that needed doing). Hilary – pasty-faced, neurotic; London Arts Board. And Conrad – dark, sullen, and weirdly ageless, like a really huge toddler; he looked familiar.

Hilary got the ball rolling by telling me about the residency's mission statement, its emphasis on a performative outreach facilitation, and asked me how I felt I, as an artist, could benefit, and benefit from, the Institute's environment through this project, and what my key measures and output objectives were? My reply used most of the words she'd just used, but in a different order. Stupid cow.

Jade asked me how I thought I would cope working with people with neural deficits, and if I'd had any kind of experience that might be useful in this regard? I told her that, although I've had no professional experience in this area, I do have a younger brother who's deeply autistic. He's not the mildly autistic type of autist, with all kinds of exacting behaviours, and a talent for mental arithmetic. He's deeply autistic. He can't use language at all, and he can be quite violent. I didn't say any more about this because it was all stuff I'd got from a TV documentary, and I hadn't bothered to watch the whole thing. Jade didn't ask me any more questions. I guessed they got one each.

Ben asked how my practice as an artist related to neuroscience? Now this was the question I was ready for, with my de Kooning catalogue.

It's to do with something that happened when I was an art student. I was sitting in my space looking at reproductions in a catalogue. (In art schools back then you got a 'space', a squalid cubicle divided from its neighbours with eight-by-four-foot sheets of plywood.) One of the tutors, a painter with a brief spell of success in the mid-'eighties under his belt, came in and stood looking over my shoulder for a bit.

'You know he had Alzheimer's when he did those.' He wandered off again.

I didn't know anything about Alzheimer's but I was (still am, in fact) a big fan of Willem de Kooning. One of the key Abstract Expressionists, his work was the last word in real Painter's Painting. In fact he's frequently referred to as 'the last great painter'. Jackson Pollock was the greater innovator, but he really only had a couple of great years. Up until 1950 he was a more or less competent plodder; no obviously outstanding talent. He found his métier, the dripped and splattered field of action, and then, having produced a dozen or so masterpieces, got self-conscious about it, and got stuck. De Kooning, on the other hand, with his big, luscious, slippery, oily brushmarks, managed to straddle the divide between traditional easel painting and the extemporised field of action painting, and he kept at it, without putting a foot wrong, for decades.

I read the catalogue essay, not something I normally bothered with, and found some mention of an illness, problems with his memory, but the condition wasn't named; it was only in there to make a point about the artist's struggles with adversity, him being indomitable and so on. I looked around a bit. There was nothing in the college library. Eventually I found a book in a charity shop, *Coping with Alzheimer's*, a text which made very free use of the bullet point. I looked up the symptoms. First you have these warning signs:

- development of intense suspicion and fear of others
- inability to follow through on projects, such as tending a garden, sewing, or organising an event
- the onset of depression
- sudden onset of drinking bouts in a person not previously given to drinking
- outbreaks of irrational rage
- unbelievable stories of bad things done by others

Those are some warning signs (and we all have days like that, don't we?). And they are not very different from the symptoms of Alzheimer's disease, which may include:

- decline in personal hygiene
- staying in bed for long periods for no reason
- becoming fearful or anxious for no apparent reason
- having domestic accidents, such as leaving pots burning on the stove or leaving appliances on

- showing inconsistencies of memory or behaviour
- hoarding one kind of food, such as eighteen tins of beans, or eight sacks of oranges
- mood changes unrelated to external events

(Again, we all have days like that, don't we?) What happens in the next phase of Alzheimer's is dementia. You become demented. They don't know what causes it – it may not have a single cause – but what's actually happening is that your brain is dying. The worst thing about this is that your lucidity kicks in and out, at least in the stages leading up to dementia, so that you are able, in moments of clarity, to watch yourself die – when your brain dies, *you* die. The book mentioned another condition with symptoms similar to Alzheimer's, but with a clear cause. It's called Korsakoff's syndrome, and it's caused by drinking too much. Willem de Kooning certainly drank. He's supposed to have been a bottle-of-whisky-a-day man.

I found a few other things. A question and answer interview in the course of which de Kooning apologises for his occasional forgetfulness, and an account of his later years by one of his studio assistants; his daughter, I think. This didn't give much away either.

Looking again at those late paintings I tried to spot the giveaway signs of deterioration and dementia, and I couldn't see any. I tried to discern robotic unsubtlety or ham-fistedness, but the late work, whilst it is not amongst his best, is still full of invention – odd compositional tricks and balancing acts; an acute sensitivity to the unpredictable push and pull of improvised abstraction. Not the mindless repetition of a rote-learned formula. It still looks fresh. This from a man who can't remember his own name, and needs to be washed, dressed and fed.

Of course, by the time the illness had kicked in, an illness that's notoriously difficult to diagnose even in ideal conditions, a lot of the symptoms would have been invisible. De Kooning had become an emperor of the art world; a millionaire baby with lots of people to do stuff for him. There was really no opportunity for him to demonstrate his inability to shop, or keep up to date with household paperwork. Odd sleeping patterns, bouts of drunkenness, depression, strange outfits, irrational outbursts; all of this is fine in an elderly millionaire genius. The disease may have been quite advanced before anyone even noticed. And, anyway, no one had any reason to start noticing that Willem was losing his marbles if he was still producing one or two masterpieces a week, at half a million dollars a bite.

27

By the time Alzheimer's (or Korsakoff's) had become an unmistakable fact, it had already been years since he'd had to do anything for himself – clean a brush, stretch a canvas, meet a client, sweep up. All you had to do to get a prime de Kooning was park the old boy in front of a prepared canvas with one of those famous long-handled brushes in his hand, and watch him go.

I found all this quite unsettling. I sat in my space, looking at my own heavily wrought, man-sized improvisations, and they seemed to have gone blank. What does it mean when work like this can be produced by an automaton, with no conscious sense of past or future? A painting monkey. A cash machine.

That tutor wandered into my space again and found me sitting in exactly the same position as before, looking at the same page of the same catalogue. 'You look as if you haven't moved for a week.' We had a laugh about that, and then we talked about what it means that de Kooning could do a de Kooning even when he didn't know that was his name. I can't recall any of this tutor's exact words or arguments, but his take on the subject was quite clear, and made a big impression on me. To him de Kooning's work was in no way compromised by the fact of its having been produced by a man with less than the full amount of brain, because de Kooning was a genius. A genius was, for him, a kind of vicar, a conduit for some greater force. Art comes *through* an artist, not from him. It comes from somewhere else. Aesthetic quality has a metaphysical guarantee. The fact that de Kooning could do great paintings whilst on the brink of dementia, could reach out and tap that great resource from his little cell of blankness – no past or future; no sense of a world outside – just goes to show it.

I had problems with this view. Could you be demented all your life and still be a genius, or did you have to have been normally lucid and competent at some stage? Also, how come, when the guy's aptitudes were being deleted one by one, the last thing to go was his aptitude for making great art? You'd think it would be the first thing to go (and, having looked into it since, I know that nobody knows how come).

I had these quibbles, but in the final analysis, when all was said and done, I found that I had to believe him, because what he was saying tallied with an experience I attached a great deal of significance to. It's a feeling I sometimes got when working on my big, improvised abstractions; a sense of total rightness and inevitability about a mark, or deployment of colour, that feels as if it comes from elsewhere. (I attached significance to this feeling even though, come to think of it, I *knew* it to be unreliable as a guide to quality. So many times I had finished something, feeling that way about it, fully confident of its value as a work of art, and then, weeks later, had another look and thought it was crap. And there were artists I knew who spoke of this experience in relation to their own works of art, and this stuff of theirs, I knew, was *all* terrible crap.)

I was just beginning to enjoy myself with this interview, really warming to my subject, when they started looking at their watches. I had expected the final question to come from Conrad, since it was his turn, but to judge by his facial expression, totally bored, he perhaps didn't have one. Jade asked one more instead:

'One more question. Can you work a loom?'

'No.'

That might have seemed like a bad way to end, but then I very much doubted any of the others could have said yes to that question. I left, and, still rattling with adrenaline, celebrated a job well done by getting pissed on my own in the hospital pub.

7: another private view

I BUMPED INTO MY 'FRIEND' AGAIN a few weeks later at a private view (a recent Goldsmith's graduate showing protective headgear made out of shortcrust pastry, at the Terminus Gallery). He was standing close to, not actually in, a group in which were mixed some of the art world's established and emerging talents. That's where I was standing as well.

I told him my news about getting that residency he'd told me about, glossing over the details of how I'd found out.

In fact, I'd more or less given up hope of it, particularly since I'd had a chance to review my interview performance, the way I'd handled the questions: I'd started out being facetious, then I'd lied, then I'd gone on about my art school experiences. However, having heard nothing for almost a month, I finally rang them up (I didn't check my emails because I didn't have a computer, or an email address). I got the receptionist – I recognised her voice – and told her what I was ringing for. She didn't know what I was talking about, thought I'd got the wrong place, and needed to be persuaded to go and see if there was anyone else who knew anything about this. She couldn't just put me through, apparently. There was a very long pause during which I occasionally heard muffled voices, somewhere away from the phone. With a scratching and fumbling the phone was eventually picked up, and Michelle said: 'Yes.'

'Oh, hi. I was ... Hi, I'm ringing to see if I got the residency. I don't know if ...'

'Yes.'

'Yes?'

A sigh. 'Yes.'

'Oh. Great. I've got it, then?'

'YES.'

After I'd hung up, a bit stunned, I realised I needed to ring back. I didn't know when I was supposed to start or anything. Maybe that was up to me? And when do I get the money? The money was very important. I was too embarrassed to ring back right away, so I decided to leave it until the next day. That at least would give me a chance to come up with some kind of plan, since I was getting the feeling that I'd be required to use a bit of initiative with this.

8: slide talks

I THOUGHT I'D BETTER BEGIN with a slide talk. Slide talks are one of the staples of art education. They are almost never interesting or valuable, but they do have the advantage, particularly for a nervous speaker like me, of being conducted in the dark, and often from a position behind your audience. (I've done dozens of slide talks in my career as occasional and temporary lecturer in art schools up and down the country: Plymouth; Reading; Hull. Usually you just do one day's teaching, consisting of a slide talk and five or six individual tutorials. The students don't vary much. Two main types. There's the uppity student and the withdrawn student. The sociopaths and the bed-wetters.) So when I rang up the next day, and managed to get through to Michelle, I told her I would do them a slide talk. She said she'd pass it on to Ben. Apparently it's Ben I'm supposed to liaise with from now on. She didn't have any information at all about my money.

Next I rang Susan to tell her I'd got a residency, like she'd wanted me to, but when she finally picked up she didn't seem that pleased. 'Oh—' she said flatly, when she realised it was me. In fact me *again*. Apparently I'd rung up the night before to tell her I'd got a residency. First at 8.30ish, then at 9.30ish and 9.45ish. Then nothing until about 3am, and again at about 4am. I guess I must have had a few drinks to celebrate. To celebrate the fact that I was starting to get it together a bit more.

My 'friend' at the private view had listened to my good news – then he told me his. His new project. He's doing a piece about global capitalism. He's found an isolated council estate near Bradford, which is served by one shop only: one corner shop for about three thousand people. Its most popular line is White Lightning cider. His project, for which he has found substantial funding, is to buy the shop's entire stock and remove it to a secure warehouse. There is considerable support and enthusiasm for this project in the area, particularly from representatives of local arts funding bodies and one amazing local character. He's the guy that owns the shop. There's going to be a webcam installed next to the shop's CCTV, broadcasting live for one day from the empty shop.

I'd drunk three bottles of free private-view beer by the time he finished telling me about it. I asked how much funding he was getting from Northern Arts Funds, the Arts Council, and the webcam people. It was much more than I was going to get for my year's residency.

9: slide talk

I ARRANGED A DATE WITH BEN. I'd actually hoped to make an appointment with him to discuss the residency as a whole, but he seemed quite busy, so we just fixed a date for me to do my talk. I selected thirty slides, thirty paintings from my substantial oeuvre of meaty abstracts. Hundreds of them. (It always surprises me when I review my output of the last fifteen years as a professional artist: the sheer quantity of paintings, each one with its own history, its own archaeology of gestures and assertions and revisions, each one a record of multiple overlaid thought processes. I amused myself for a while, making new pictures by holding one slide over another and viewing them at the window. I tried it with three slides, adding more knots and veils and meshes. Then four, then five. With six, the result was just dark.)

I arrived thirty minutes early at the Institute, with my slides. I hadn't prepared anything to say about them. It's best just to say whatever comes into your head. Sometimes you find your extempore speech is an exact replica of the last one you did, right down to the pauses and coughs. Sometimes, though, you think of something new to say.

The receptionist, following some energetic pleading, gave me detailed directions on how to find Ben's office, and I learned a little more about the building's layout as I toured the place, hoping to get to Ben's office by accident. I passed the MRI suites more than once. I got back to reception several times too, each time from a different direction, but always doubled back on myself so that I wouldn't have to pass the receptionist again. I was just passing those MRI suites for about the seventh time when I spotted Ben at the other end of a very long corridor, and he was walking towards me. He was too far away to say hello to without actually shouting, so I waved and smiled in a way that could last until we'd got to within hailing distance.

I don't know why I hated Ben so much to begin with. I suppose because of him being younger and better-looking than me. I couldn't stand his uncomplicated sense of well-being, his tan or his tiny little ears. Or perhaps it was because I take an instant dislike to pretty well everyone I meet. (There's that joke, isn't there, about taking an instant dislike to someone to save time, but actually it only saves time in cases where you'd end up disliking the person even if you'd approached them with an open mind. In other cases you've wasted time, because you've had to traverse a larger portion of the spectrum between love and hate. And you never know how much time you've saved or wasted, because when you take an instant dislike to people they generally take an instant dislike right back.) At last—

'Hi!' he held out his enormous hand. I took it, and he really shook hard, crushing my fingers and yanking my shoulder. I knew he was going to do that.

'All set? Great.'

He took me to the room we were using for the talk, another large meeting room, with an oval conference table. I asked him where the slide projector was? They didn't have one. He thought I'd be bringing one. I should have thought of this. Why would they have a slide projector? You do all that kind of thing digitally now. Ben wasn't put out. He looked at me for a minute, said 'Hang on,' and disappeared.

I'll hang on then. I sat down and waited, for quite a long time. Tum-ti-tum. Tum-ti-tum. I didn't dare go to try and find him. I looked out, poking my head around the door as if the room would vanish if I actually stepped out into the corridor. I was hoping to be able to spot the toilet from there, but all I could see were closed doors with no signs. I needed to go to the toilet. I went and sat back down at one end of the conference table, and waited, tapping my feet, and ticking my tongue. A man looked in.

'Is this it? I wanted the art lecture.'

'Yes. Ben's just gone to find a slide projector.'

'Oh right.' He came in and sat down, a powerfully built middle-aged man I immediately took to be a cab driver, or possibly a pub landlord. Or a plumber. I asked him if he knew where the nearest toilet was. His directions got me there and back with no problems. He was sitting patiently, midway along the table.

'You the artist, then?'

'Yes. Yes, that's me.'

'What kind of work do you do, then?'

This can be a tricky question. You don't want to presume too much knowledge, but then you also have to avoid sounding condescending.

'I'm a painter. Abstract paintings.'

'Oh yes.'

That was OK, I think.

'I paint myself.'

Oh no.

'Monet.'

'You like Monet?'

'Marvellous stuff.'

He'd been to Monet's garden at Giverny with his wife. He's built a small lily pond in his back garden, and he does paintings of it, in the style of Monet. We talked about Monet for a bit. He knew a lot. More than I did.

Now then, he seemed alright to me, but he obviously wasn't a doctor or administrator, and he couldn't be working here in any other capacity – porter or maintenance – because he'd just told me he was retired. I had to ask.

'So you're ...? Are you ...?'

'Outpatient. Neural deficit.'

'What's that?' I'd only heard the term once before, during my interview. He has a neural deficit, and it's called prosopagnosia, which is a condition in which you lose the ability to recognise faces. It's a result of brain damage. Limited and localised brain damage. Everything else, he can see fine. Just faces he has a problem with.

I had to think about this. Does he just see a blank space in place of facial features, like looking at a wig stand? Or does he see a kind of generic face, recognisable as a face, but not as a particular face? Why can he recognise everything else but not, apparently, even his own wife? And what causes it?

'Stroke. I didn't even know I'd had a stroke. Just thought it was a headache. There's nothing they can do about it, but I still come in every week for my tests with Ben. It's not actually that big a problem. I can usually tell who you are by the voice and the build. And I already know what my wife looks like. Heh heh.'

Is she very ugly then? I didn't say that. I said we should do a lecture about Monet (thinking ahead about the residency, you see).

Ben got back with a slide projector, and a group of people tagging along behind.

'I've rounded up an audience for you. Got this old slide projector from the hospital. Didn't say what it was for. They hate us down there.'

There were seven of them, including the cabbie bloke. 'Hello, Colin,' said Ben. Seven including Colin. One of them I recognised from the Activities Room; the Pre-Raphaelite muse, very lively now. She came straight over and asked if she knew me. I said I didn't think so. It threw me a bit, her suddenly coming up and talking to me like that. She was so nice, with her long, copper-coloured hair, big copper-coloured eyes, a wide smile, and a pair of amazing tits under that sweater. My favourite kind of build. Slim body, big tits. I doubted she would have noticed me in the Activities Room that time because she was into her music, and I definitely hadn't met her before outside the Institute. Maybe at a private view, when I was drunk? No. I'd have remembered.

'I don't think so.' She was staring at me, and smiling. A great big smile.

'Oh,' she said, and went to join the others taking seats around the table, still smiling, still happy.

Between them Colin and Ben got the projector set up and helped me load the carousel. Colin got the lights.

Usually when the lights go out I just start talking, no problem. This time nothing came. It then struck me, for the first time, that without an informed audience, an audience that will know who you're talking about when you cite your influences – ally yourself with one school of thought; distance yourself from another – there's actually almost nothing to say about an abstract painting. You can't talk about subject matter because an abstract painting shouldn't have it. It's not a picture of something; it's a thing in itself.

We sat in the dark, staring at the wall against which was projected, life-sized, one of my paintings, with its lines and spirals, blotches, edges, fields, points, chromatic emphases and junctures, fizziness and weight, trajectories and full stops. I could remember everything about painting it. The slight nerves you get when it's just white. The first few marks, a bit shy about the mess you're making on that perfect field. The feeling of dawning recognition, as if you were not making something, but uncovering something that had always been there. It all going wrong, becoming flaccid and empty, and the sudden turnaround following a bout of painterly recklessness, after you'd practically given up on it. To me it was the site of a primal drama, a struggle for existence. It would look to them, I thought, like a scruffy sort of a pattern on the wall.

I fiddled with the focus, playing for time, and then, still stuck, started to tell them the date, medium and dimensions of each piece. Some artists do all their talks like that. Date, Medium, Dimensions. Date, Medium, Dimensions. Once, when I was a student, I was at a talk like that, and I fell off my chair. I wasn't asleep. I'd actually been bored off my chair. Normally by now I would be talking of mid-period de Kooning and late Picasso, some little-known Rothko drawings; 1960s hard-edged abstraction; what Malevich was up to in 1917. I clicked through the slides, telling them the date, medium and dimensions of each piece. The medium and dimensions were always the same. The date is the only variant. It was quite hot in there. The only sound, apart from the sound of me repeating myself, and the click and whirr of the projector, was the sound of someone in the audience scratching themselves, really putting a lot into it.

'If there are any questions or comments, please ...' Please. Feel free. Anyone.

Colin rescued me. 'That one looks a bit like a Monet.' And, d'you know? he was dead right. A darkened horizontal field punctuated with smeared blobs and splats, like ice cream dropped on the pavement. Or waterlilies. Colin went on to tell us about something he'd been reading the other day about Monet, which is that he believed he was painting the world as we really see it, prior to any ordering or classification – here is a table, there is a tree. What he painted was not objects in the world, but patches of light, coloured shapes that we have learned to recognise as objects. Ben kind of snorted. I thought he was going to say something then, but he didn't.

Having been kick-started by Colin's intervention I managed to keep talking until all the slides were finished, and then asked again for questions and comments. Ben switched the lights on.

'Yes. You have a question?' It was the girl. She'd put her hand up as if we were at school.

'Do I know you?'

It took a moment or two, but then the penny dropped. This'll be to do with a neural deficit of some kind.

'No, I don't think we've met?'

'Emily,' Ben told me.

'Emily. Very pleased to meet you, Emily. Anyone else?'

The moment's pause made us all very conscious of the noise of that scratching, which had actually been going on pretty much throughout. We all looked at the guy. It was beginning to get frantic, like someone who knows he has a small explosive device secreted about him, and he can't find it, and it's about to go off. Although everyone was watching him, there was no sign that they found it at all offensive or surprising, this orgy of scratching. It was, I guessed, another neural deficit, this one with symptoms resembling those of some awful skin condition. They all just felt for him. The poor guy was scratching himself to pieces. He didn't look as if he could take much more, and then with an 'Aha!', and a soppy grin, he began to slow down. Scratch Scratch ... Scratch ... Scratch aaaand Scratch.

He looked up at me and explained: 'I don't know where to scratch. I know I've got an itch but I don't know where, so I have to scratch until I find it. Somatosensory cortex, they think.' He tapped the side of his head with his finger. His face and the backs of his hands were crosshatched with parallel red weals.

By way of winding things up I asked Ben, with whom I'm supposed to liaise, if he had anything to say, and he made a little joke. 'They look a bit like the illustrations in NEURON magazine.'

He was dead right. My abstract paintings resemble pictures of something. Pictures generally represent things that belong within a certain range of scale – that between an ant, say, and a mountain. Men and women and houses and trees and apples and tables and chairs. Anything bigger or smaller, a weather system or an amoeba, a galaxy or a subatomic particle, looks abstract to us (when some breakthrough in cosmology or biochemistry is announced in the media, there will be pictures of this thing, and for all I know it could be a picture of a bogey). Things like that never have horizontals or verticals in them. We are very conscious of horizontal and vertical. We would constantly bump into things and fall over if we weren't. Also, such things, the minute and the gigantic, need to be seen at a certain distance in order to be visible at all. Seen too close, things are just background; field not figure.

I thought all that in the microsecond between Ben's remark and my going 'Tee hee' to the little joke. Sometimes you can think a lot in a very short space of time. It just flashes up on your screen, a whole map, from nowhere. I was pleased with this little insight, and grateful to Ben for it, and this gratitude caused my knee-jerk antipathy towards him to dissolve. I stopped hating him and liked him instead.

10: a chat with Ben

I ASKED BEN if he had time for a coffee in the Day Room, so we could liaise? Yes, sure. He had a 3funding meeting, another one (he rolled his eyes) but he had time for a coffee and a chat. He picked up the slide projector and carried it under his arm ('Got to get this back – I nicked it') as we strolled to the Day Room, just around the corner, as it happens.

I was going to ask him about all the patients I'd just met, to break the ice, and because I was very curious, but Colin was sitting right by the coffee machine, on his own in that great big room. He looked up, and smiled at us (recognising us by the clothes and build) and went back to his paper. I asked Ben about the scratching man.

'We think it's a problem to do with his somatosensory cortex. That's a part of the brain that has a lot to do with your sense of touch. It's like a neural map of the body, with areas of cortex corresponding to areas of your skin ...' he tapped the side of his head, indicating the approximate location of this map, 'but we're not sure. He had a fall at work and then started getting these symptoms. If he gets a cut or anything, he can tell where it is by looking, but itches ... drives the poor guy crazy. It's quite unusual.' While he was talking, we both started to scratch.

'And Emily,' I said. 'How about her? Fit, isn't she?' I didn't say that, but he smiled, and I thought he thought so too. He filled me in on her condition. The viral encephalitis contracted in Belize, the gaps in her head. I then felt a bit ashamed, but I'm not sure if that was just because I thought he could detect the lust in my voice. I was ashamed to be seen exhibiting lecherous feelings towards a person with deficits, and I was shocked by her condition. Fifteen minutes (or thereabouts). What kind of a life is that?

She looks happy enough, even though she seems to know she has no memory. She remembers that. Or else why would she keep asking (every fifteen minutes or so I now realise) if she knows you?

'I know,' said Ben. ' We don't understand it, but cases are rarely clear cut, and it's a young science. The term "neuroscience" was only coined in about 1970.'

Another thing. What the fuck was she doing in Belize? Its just a swamp, isn't it? Where they train the SAS. Ben shrugged. She'd been a patient when he started at the Institute. The first, apparently.

'But Belize. Who goes on their holidays to Belize?'

'She had work there. Was there something specific you wanted to ask?'

He was looking at the clock, so I thought I'd better ask what I do next, as artist in residence.

'Well, it's up to you.'

'Really? For a whole year?'

'You probably know more about it than we do.'

'But if you don't know what an artist in residence does, why am I ...? I mean, what ...?'

'It's one of the conditions of the new funding package that we have an artist in residence. And a writer in residence. Got to go now. I enjoyed your talk. Very interesting.' I didn't get a chance to ask him about my money. I watched him go and then, noticing Colin again, sitting not far away with his paper (reading doesn't seem to be affected, either), went over to him and sat down.

11: a chat with Colin

'NICE HERE, ISN'T IT?' said Colin. 'Beautiful job they've done. Bit austere for my taste – needs some pictures – but lovely work.'

We talked about building and decorating. Colin's worked in all the trades, and I, like a lot of art school graduates, have worked inexpertly in some. We found we'd both been had with the same building site practical joke. A classic. What happens is that one day you can't find a favourite tool, a particular filling knife or gloss work brush or whatever. You ask around but no one's seen it. You spend the rest of the day complaining about the way people borrow your tools without asking and don't put them back. The punchline is that a few days later you get sent a picture of your missing tool lying on a sunbed in Barbados, or propped against a palm tree or, for maximum effect, nestling in an amazing bronzed cleavage. I've actually always hated practical jokes – humour for people with no sense of humour – and this one struck me as particularly senseless, because in a way it can't help but backfire. It reminds everyone, not just the victim, how shit the job is. Colin and me were in agreement on this point.

'Fancy a pint?' said Colin.

'I can't at the moment. I'm a bit … until I get paid for this, and I don't know when that's coming through.'

'Don't worry, ' said Colin.

12: a drink with Colin

ME AND COLIN WENT to the hospital pub. I stopped protesting, offering to get him a good drink next time and so on, after the first five or six pints. I think he even loaned me the money for a taxi. When I searched my pockets the next day, I found what must have been the change from a twenty, and a bar menu with detailed notes for a lecture on Monet written neatly on the back. Productive evening. I was completely fucked so I spent the day in bed, thinking about Colin and Emily and the scratching man, with their neural deficits.

I did a little experiment, looking at one of those celebrity magazines Susan left here, and trying to imagine not recognising Madonna or Victoria Beckham. He doesn't just see a blank space. He can see individual features, tell brown eyes from blue, big noses from small, the same as anyone else, but still he can't recognise it, the whole thing, as such and such a person. Looking at pictures of celebrities at a film premiere I could begin to sympathise with his difficulty. They all try really hard to look alike. All the women want the same body, and the faces are all generically ironed out and unified. Hair colour does differ from person to person, but without adding a thing to their individuality, because they all change their hair colour the whole time. Perhaps Colin just sees the generic, average human face.

I wondered if his deficit has had an adverse effect on his ability to empathise with others. Perhaps he feels like early European explorers would have done in their first encounters with the peoples of new continents. We must all look alike to him, and he has no ability to gradually discover differences that had been invisible hitherto. The perception of others as undifferentiated does seem to lead to a dehumanised view of them. (And maybe, in a different way, that's my problem too. The only distinguishing characteristic I really care about is that of being me.)

I tried to see, or imagine seeing, what Colin sees when he looks at you. Looking at a picture of some other plastic celebrity event (in another of Susan's magazines), I tried noticing the difference between seeing a face and seeing anything else. I tried noticing the difference between recognising someone and not recognising them. To me faces in a scene seem contiguous with it. Not distinct, as a visual experience, from seeing a dress, or an item of furniture. With Colin's blindness being so specialised, its scope so particular, you'd expect faces to be somehow distinguished from the visual field they sit in, like the blue outline surrounding movie actors in front of old fashioned back projections. The face is highlighted, I guess, in the sense of it being salient, but that, surely, is a semantic difference, not a visual one. It's not seeing, it's reading, and reading is something you do next, after seeing. It's something that requires an additional effort, an act of will. And also it's something you have to learn to do. To see a page of writing is not automatically to read it. Seeing a word can, come to think of it, sometimes be like seeing a face. The word FUCK, in big letters. Or DANGER, or GENTS. Reading these words does feel like just *seeing* them. It happens, as far as you can tell, immediately; punctual rather than sequential.

Is seeing a kind of reading? Is this raw data, the visual world, actually a text we can speedread? We assemble the bits of information in our heads to make a picture. Looking around my room, with my peeled, hung-over eyes, it seems unlikely. It's all so revoltingly *detailed*. If I could mediate or edit it, I bloody well would. My room really is a shithole. I guess I've let things go a bit since me and Susan split up. I must have a bit of a tidy sometime.

Without looking or getting up I grabbed an old Monet book from under the bed (knocking over a capless vodka bottle and flooding an ashtray). I flicked straight to the back; the late works, dozens and dozens of waterlily paintings. Most of them are huge panoramas intended to occupy your whole field of vision. Monet's idea about painting the world 'as we really see it', as patches of colour, seems like a way of anticipating the deterioration of his eyesight as he got older. The waterlilies are all a blur, creamy smudges on a dark ground, and yet are clearly recognisable as waterlilies. With his eyes the way they were in later life he probably couldn't have told the difference between a waterlily and the face of one of his children without some kind of contextual clues – where did I see it? was it moving? did it make a noise? Monet's problem was in his eyes, not his brain, but he and Colin must share some reasons for liking waterlilies.

13: think about Emily

I THOUGHT AGAIN ABOUT EMILY. She had been in my first thoughts that morning. I'd tried to imagine her naked while I had my morning wank but couldn't get a fix on her – what kind of nipples? – so resorted to an old reliable wank fantasy that generally does the trick.

I thought now about Emily's condition; the sort of world she must be in. It seemed to me, increasingly as I thought about it and tried to imagine it, like a living Hell, as if you'd been put down a hole in the ground. A world of utter claustrophobia. No horizon.

Then again it would, I suppose, have the advantage of constant novelty, like the goldfish who always thinks he's just moved into a new bowl. This would explain her apparent cheerfulness. It's all new to her. Everything has novelty value. Her state is enviable in a way. We would all like to be able to live in the moment, like children do, supposedly.

She's lost a lot of what makes our lives: the stuff that isn't right there to hand – memories, of course, but plans too; a sense of the future. All she can do is enjoy the moment. That's if it *is* enjoyable. How about pain and misery? How does she cope? What gets most of us through the bad times is the knowledge that things have been better in the past, and can get better again in the future. For her, any kind of unhappiness must be like the deepest depression, a condition in which your assurances to yourself that it can get better don't ring true any more. You can't imagine that possibility.

That must be why they keep her there and look after her. There's all the practical stuff – she'd be hopeless in the outside world – but there's a question of humanity too. Allowing her to suffer any kind of unhappiness or discomfort of the sort we all cope with all the time would be cruel, because she wouldn't know, while it lasted, that there is anything else.

Does she get any visitors? Parents? Boyfriend? I tortured myself a little, trying to imagine her boyfriends, the men she used to go out dancing with, or to see a film, or to have a candlelit dinner together – gazing into each other's eyes across an untouched meal. I tortured myself again, giving my soul a Chinese burn. Emily before her illness, having sex with her boyfriend. Or boyfriends? Her natural, taintless enjoyment of penetration. (This is all rather sudden – all these strong feelings. Possibly I'm a little bit on the rebound here.)

But how would you get to sleep with her *now*? Building trust of that sort, where she'd be comfortable with you rummaging inside her pullover for one of those amazing bosoms, takes time. You need to develop a bond of trust. It might be possible if you just never went out of her sight during the entire courtship, however long that turned out to be, because that fifteen-minute window is more like a moving spotlight than a sequence of unconnected chunks of time. Even nipping out to go to the toilet could mean you having to begin all over again. Also, what does 'consent' mean in this context? Does the idea of consenting have any meaning at all for someone with her condition? If you forget you have consented, wouldn't that mean your consent had been withdrawn? So any sex would then surely be rape. It seems, when you think about it, that there are now no conditions in which it would be possible to have sex with Emily. It's as if her virginity has been restored.

What if you knew her before – before she got ill? As well as having lost the ability to form new memories, Emily has also lost a bit of her old memories, so there is a period of several months before her illness that she seems to know nothing about. But she can still remember most of the basic facts about herself. She does know about her life and her family and so on. So it's possible, in theory, that she had a boyfriend in that period who's now occluded from memory, and he'd turned out to be a real cunt, so she dropped him. She can't stand the sight of him any more, but she doesn't know that now. What if he visits her at the Institute, and he's been telling her he's still her boyfriend, and he fucks her in her room? I picture him walking off down the hall, zipping his flies and chuckling to himself. In my boiling imagination he has a blandly acceptable look about him, this terrible guy, but then, as he turns away from Emily, having tenderly kissed her goodbye, his face changes – it has a purplish flush, a leer, and is lit from below.

14: another private view

I FELL ASLEEP PLANNING what I was gonna do to that guy I'd made up, when I got my hands on him, and felt much better when I woke up, late afternoon. I decided to go out to a private view – an alternative space group show, in a disused petrol station in Hackney, called 'FUCK YOU, clASSHOLE'. Towards the end of the evening I found myself in a group with some rising stars of the art world. I must have been on good form that night, telling funny stories about my new job – that Activities Room! – feeling at home with these younger, more successful, better-dressed people. Such good value was I, socially, that I managed to get coked up – at some point everyone's little envelopes came out – without having to actually buy the stuff myself. I can remember sitting in a club, or possibly someone's house, talking to my public arts 'friend' (he'd got in there too) about Emily, or Susan. At one point I was in tears, I think.

15: thanks, Colin

I SPENT QUITE A LOT OF TIME with Colin over the next few days, so we could talk about our lecture. He saved my life did Colin. Not only did he lend me money – I wasn't getting anywhere with my phonecalls about my fee and the last thing I'd heard was I needed to invoice them – but he was a terrific source of information, gossip really, about the Institute. He spends quite a lot of time there, just hanging out and chatting to people. Besides learning a lot of useful stuff about the Institute I learned a lot about Colin. I got some more funny building-site stories – his dealings with hysterical clients and their hysterical interior designers; the job mate he used to have, who at the end of every job would invite the whole crew over to his house to have sex with his wife (they didn't all go); the job he had where they'd take turns to have a kip in the airing cupboard; the job mate he used to have who they all called 'Peas' – because he didn't like peas.

He told me a lot about his life outside work. His painting and gardening I knew about, but his sporting interests – I'd have guessed football, or golf (because of his clothes), or angling – turned out to be quite unusual. He does archery. He's learned to slow his heartbeat fractionally, to make for a steadier aim. This means he's less likely now to have another stroke.

The stuff about the Institute. Here's what I now knew about the Norman Neurological Institute. The NNI. Colin's take on things:

DR PRABHAKAR, THE DIRECTOR (the woman in grey I'd seen on my first day here, zipping across reception like a neutrino), he's got a lot of time for. Very clever woman. You don't see her much, particularly not lately, but she's not just the Institute's director, she's really its founder. It was her who persuaded Conrad Norman to put all that money into it, him practically on his deathbed at the time.

CONRAD NORMAN. A bastard and, towards the end, a nutcase. Like a lot of these characters, self-made billionaires that is, he became obsessed with his own mortality, death being the great leveller, and him not wanting to be level with anyone. Spent a fortune on all kinds of crackpot immortality pseudoscience. Got interested in neurology because he'd heard that even if nothing else gets you, your brain will pack up and die when you get to about a hundred. Also he'd heard about some research being done by some American neuroscientists into near-death and out-of-body experiences that seems to indicate the possibility of life after death.

There are three grown-up children: a daughter and two sons. The youngest, also called Conrad, who looks weirdly like a huge toddler, you see about the Institute sometimes. The other two (twins) are worse than their father.

BEN. Very bright young man. Seems to be under a lot of pressure at the moment but handles it well.

JADE. Lovely woman. Very caring. Would like to see her naked.

The Institute's premises. Beautiful work, especially the hardwood finishing, the lighting and the door handles.

The rooms with the MRI machines. Never seen them used.

EMILY. Lovely girl. Very bubbly. A real shame.

The other patients. He'll introduce me to some of them when we do our lecture. He's on friendly terms with quite a few of them.

THE RECEPTIONIST. They should sack her.

I got Colin round to my studio and showed him some of my paintings. It wasn't really his thing but I think he enjoyed it all the same. His first visit to a real artist's studio. It turned out he'd worked there himself, years ago when it was still a machine shop. He remembered how it's always much colder in there than it is outside, except in high summer, when it's much hotter.

16: slide talk

WE USED THE SAME ROOM as before to do our slide lecture. I'd got some obsolete transparencies from the library at Central Saint Martins. (While I was there I bumped into a member of staff I knew and he remarked on a change in my appearance; something different about me. I said that that was because the last time he saw me I was one of his students and I was nineteen.)

We were going to do the talk in two halves, with Colin talking about Monet at Giverny and me talking about Monet in relation to the history of abstraction, with particular reference to American painting of the 1950s and '60s.

As promised I got the chance to meet quite a few of the patients this time. Colin seemed to be friends with everyone, and knew all about them and their deficits. By the time we were all settled and set up there were about a dozen of them in the audience, with Jade there to represent the staff, in case anybody had any problems. Ben couldn't make it this time because he had a funding meeting.

Colin spoke at length and in great detail about late Monet, adding, here and there, reminiscences of his trip to Giverny with his wife, his retirement treat, so that it became a bit like holiday slide shows I remember from my childhood.

I could have learned a great deal if I'd been paying attention. Instead I spent most of that hour, sitting in the warm and dark, staring at Emily's silhouette. Her nose, lips and breasts, her lashes blocking out a little of the edge of each of Monet's widescreen projected lilyscapes. I could see her breathing and sighing. There was actually no need for her to sit that close to the screen. There was plenty of room, but no one asked her to sit back. They must all have learned to accommodate one another, with their peculiarities, in these little ways. A special type of etiquette is attendant upon those with a neural deficit.

At one point, just once in the whole hour, she moved. She reached out, or stretched her arm, as if she was about to pick a waterlily. She might just have been stretching. The room stayed quiet throughout. Just Colin talking, and the click and whir of the rotating carousel.

When the lights came on I recognised a few faces, and I saw that the scratching man was there, looking composed and normal. People stretched and yawned and looked at each other with sleepy smiles. I suggested we take a break in the Day Room before my half of the lecture. I had to wait for the rest of them to file out, moving slowly like afternoon cinema-goers, before I dared to stand up. The warmth and dark, my full bladder, and Emily's breasts in profile, had given me an erection.

Luckily the nearest toilet was a disabled toilet, so I could privately piss in the sink (it's a courtesy thing to use the sink when you've got an erection, or it just goes everywhere) and then catch up with everyone in the Day Room.

Walking towards them, I saw a man I had only seen from the right as he filed out with the others, who was turning from the coffee machine with two brimming coffee cups – *careful* now – revealing, as he turned, his other side, the left side of his head, which looked as if it had been caved in with a hammer and then sprayed with a flesh-coloured plastic coating. I looked away quickly, at the already seated group he was serving. Emily was sitting alone, smiling. Colin was perched on the edge of his seat, somewhere about the middle of the group, really enjoying himself. He was talking to a man and a woman, both blind, or partially sighted, their white sticks folded on their laps. Perhaps Colin was filling them in on the stuff they would have missed.

17: learning about visual deficits ...

I GOT THE BLIND COUPLE'S STORY LATER, pieced together from what Colin could tell me about them, and what Ben knew. Neither of them is blind in the usual sense. Their eyes are fine, but their brains are unable to process the information the eye receives. One of them, the woman, has severe, almost total, visual agnosia. I liked the image Ben used when he was explaining this to me. He said that to her the world looks like an exhibition of abstract art from another planet. She can see everything but recognises nothing. She can use her limited comprehension of the visual world, in concert with aural and tactile clues, to the extent that she's not helpless in a busy street or whatever, but without those contextual clues – cars are moving objects that make a car sound, etc. – she's lost in a world of abstraction.

The man's story is even worse. He doesn't know he can see and has lost for ever a part of the brain that does that – allows you to know that you can see. If you throw a punch, he'll duck. Throw a ball and he'll catch it. But as far as he's concerned he's blind. You'd think that seeing and knowing you can see were the same thing, but it isn't so. He can see, but only unconsciously, so that his seeing is merely functional, a motor response to light, like the photosensitivity of a plant.

18: ... and about Phineas Gage

THE MAN WITH THE CAVED-IN HEAD actually used to work downstairs, in Gray's Hospital, as an NHS mental health worker. One of his 'clients' had got on the roof of one of the buildings in the hospital, and he was saying he wanted to die and he was going to jump, et cetera. So, our man (who was a really caring person) was trying to talk him out of it, but then the client did jump. So he grabbed hold of this mental patient (or client) and got pulled over too. The patient fell into a skip full of bin bags, and he was fine, but our guy fell on some old-fashioned iron railings right next to the skip, and one of them pierced him clean through the skull. It went in below the cheekbone and came out the top. It didn't kill him (obviously), and apparently he was conscious and actually talking to paramedics while the fire brigade was cutting through the bar with an angle grinder so that they could take him to A&E, iron bar and all. He underwent surgery to remove the bar from his head, and although he was badly scarred he seemed to make a full recovery. What, it turned out, had been damaged by the removal of that big chunk of his forebrain was his personality. The care and consideration that he had demonstrated at work had also characterised his home life. And now he's a real fucker. A horrible man.

From the point of view of the brain's evolution this demonstrates that damage to the more recently evolved parts of the brain, like the frontal cortex, is far less debilitating than damage to the older parts would be. Much less severe damage in an older part of the brain, nearer

the spinal column, would kill you, because the older parts
deal with basic stuff like breathing. If you look at a human
brain in cross section, from the side, it's a kind of diagram
of evolution, with our lizard ancestors represented in the
brain stem. Each level of accretion, building up to the fully
cortexed human brain, represents another increase in
sophistication, but the lizard parts don't change, because
they still do what they need to do – breathe and flinch and
defecate. Natural selection doesn't fix things that aren't
broke. So the more recent stages in human brain evolution
have been concerned not with mere subsistence but with
the addition of, if you like, more software (or peripheral
hardware). They have been about adding new refinements
– frills and extras – to an already functioning and self-
sufficient organ.

The man had been a good dad, a loving husband, a reliable friend, and so on. Now he's lecherous, loudmouthed,
a substance abuser of every substance, and has a violent
temper. His lack of compassion even affects his view of his
own former self. When people try to be sympathetic about
the incredible pain he must have suffered in that accident,
he looks at them as if to say, 'What's it to you?'

He's sly, too. They've been trying some behavioural
therapy on him, trying to get him to at least *act* as if he's
got some consideration for others. Which explains a little
episode I'd witnessed while we were having our coffee
break. He'd brought a coffee across for Jade, and placed
it on the table in front of her with a great show of good
manners, and then, without skipping a beat, had made a
grab for one of her gigantic breasts. Jade, who had been
sitting with her knees together and her arms resting in her
lap, had responded with a reflexive upward swipe of her
forearm, a blow so powerful and well judged it caused him
to strike himself hard on the bridge of the nose with his

knuckle. He veered off like a wasp, blinking and staggering slightly. Jade picked up her coffee and began to interest herself in the general conversation. (Jade knows him well and calls him 'Phineas', even though that's not really his name. Phineas Gage was a railroad worker in the States in the nineteenth century who had a tamping iron shot straight through his skull, and survived, but with similar catastrophic effects on his personality.)

A philosophical insight to be got from considering this guy's case (and Phineas Gage) is the identity of brain and mind – the identity of brain and personality. The person you think you are, and the person that other people think you are, is a product of tissue, not of your immutable and indivisible soul. Obvious, but still shocking when illustrated in this way.

Also it highlights an important fact about brain science, which is its reliance, even now, with all the in vivo imaging technology we've got, on accidents. Serendipity does not generally play the important part in scientific research that people like to think it does. (Science relies less on eureka moments than on repetitive grind. Scientific research is pretty much all slog.) For example, we had never suspected that recognising faces was a distinct process, requiring a particular refinement of the neural apparatus, until we got patients like Colin who'd suffered highly localised brain damage which destroyed that ability. To discover that kind of thing experimentally, we'd have to deliberately remove or destroy selected portions of the brain just to see what you can't do afterwards. We often don't realise the brain is doing something until an accident, or a disease, stops it.

19: slide talk

WE DRIFTED BACK TO THE MEETING ROOM for part two of the lecture, none of us really in the mood now.

I showed slides of some big 1950s American painting – Newman, Still, Rothko, Louis, Olitski – and, reminding them of a slide they'd already seen of Monet in the big circular room he'd had specially built to show the waterlily paintings, talked about the problem of scale. When does a picture become too big to register as an object any more, so that it's just a decorated wall, or just part of the background? How is looking at a white canvas different from just looking at the wall?

I could feel their lack of interest. Over their heads, possibly, but also my delivery was very flat. I had become subject to a kind of depression or weariness – it's a sense of defeat that afflicts me sometimes when I look at great art of the last century, and it's brought home to me that I, as an artist, have added nothing to the achievements of the past. I'm not really saying anything new. This feeling is best pushed to the back of your mind if you're going to do anything these days. The other option is to just not know about your antecedents. Ignorance can be a great enabler for creative people.

I've fooled myself, too. Several times I've come up with something, an innovation that was going to change everything, and then realised that it was somebody else's idea thirty years ago, or just not very good. (Once I was watching a cookery programme, and suddenly had a great idea for a new dish, brilliantly simple – Grilled Bread. You prepare one of our staple foods using one of our most basic cooking methods, and yet no one has ever thought of doing it before. Then I realised that's toast.)

The thing is, although innovation in art now seems impossible – all the big moves were made in the twentieth century and Warhol was the last great innovator – we are now so thoroughly hooked on the sensation of newness that we're prepared to see it in anything. We awake with a new innocence each day, all ready to be shocked and surprised by the same things that shocked and surprised us yesterday. (There are some, with a nostalgia for innovation, who see its future in the computer. That's certainly possible, but right now the computer has yet to achieve the transparency of an artistic medium. Computer art at the moment is like those pointless journeys made in early motorcars, just to experience the novelty of the conveyance itself. Or it's like visits to the first cinematograph exhibition – Help! A train! Future people are going to laugh at us, puffing around with our electric computing machines, thinking we've conquered the world.)

By the time I got to the stage where I was supposed to ask for questions, I think we all felt that my part of the lecture was a chore dealt with. They'd all really enjoyed Colin. My lecture had been spent on doubts and misgivings. It must have been very boring for them. I allowed gregarious Colin to take everybody back to the Day Room for more coffee and chats, while I took the projector to Ben so that he could return it to wherever he'd borrowed it from.

This was a good opportunity to ask him about something – I knew he was busy – without seeming to pester him.

20: Ben's brains

I FOUND BEN'S OFFICE by following very carefully (I made her draw a map) Jade's directions, stopping off for a quick drink on the way (sitting in a toilet cubicle with the projector on my lap, swallowing gin out of a Volvic bottle).

'You sure you've got enough brains in here, Ben?' There were hundreds of them in his office. Every horizontal surface was forested with them, all these furrowed brows – like herbaceous borders growing nothing but cauliflowers. Big ones, small ones; medium sized; actual sized.

'You've got enough brains in here for a brain shop. BRAINS R US. BRAINS U LIKE. SIMPLY BRAINS …'

'Oh hi. You like my collection?'

'Really amazing.'

And they were. He had brains made from practically every manufacturing material you can think of – Bakelite, wood, ceramic, papier mâché, rubber, resin, tin, bronze. Most of them were of recent manufacture, made out of plastic. There were degrees of sophistication, ranging from a brain made in China, that was just a solid lump cast in the kind of plastic they use for toy soldiers, to an incredible triple-scale multicomponent model. This had sections and areas individually cast in different kinds and colours of plastic, resin and Perspex, and a hardwood stand with a brass plaque on it: THE HUMAN BRAIN. Others were comedy or novelty items, like a brain jelly mould, a brain keyring, an inflatable brain, a rubber Halloween mask in the form of a giant brain, as well as numerous ashtrays and paperweights.

'How many brains have you got, Ben?'

'Nine hundred and sixty three. The best ones they make now are American, but a lot of the older ones are German.'

'They're not all for work?'

'Not really. I just like them.'

I liked them, too. Incredible things. And the pictures and posters he had everywhere. Some of them were in old-fashioned gilt frames, including a nineteenth-century hand-tinted engraving, with German text, all views and sections laid out in taxonomic rows like a lot of peeled bugs. He also had a lot of new posters Blu-Tacked to the wall, with imagery of the kind I'd seen in those neuroscience magazines. Quite garish and druggy. One in particular caught my eye. A thing like a Cyclopean squid creature, with dozens of tentacles or tendrils sprouting from either end of its body, in tacky green and purple.

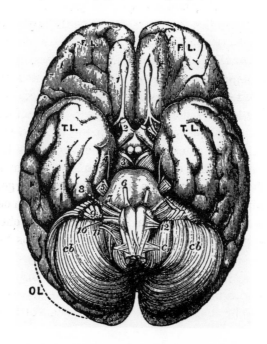

'What's that?'

'A neuron. You've got a hundred billion of those in your head, about.' (He gave this figure very confidentially, but I found out much later that, although that's what everybody says about the number of neurons, and it's the figure given in all the books, nobody seems to know who counted, or how.)

'You've got a hundred billion neurons with the potential to make forty quadrillion connections.' He wrote it down on a piece of paper to show me what forty quadrillion looks like. 40,000,000,000,000,000. Forty quadrillion. (I *think* that's right.) 'That's more possible connections in the human brain than there are atoms in the universe.' He had a lot more of this kind of thing.

'The external surface of the cortex is only about two square feet but if you were to open out all the neurons, it would cover three tennis courts (which isn't that big, but it's still a lot bigger than your head).'

I asked him what they do. He told me that they speak to each other. Billions of them speaking to each other all the time, even when you're asleep. They send messages around the brain using a kind of relay system. Each neuron has a nucleus, and on one side of this nucleus is a collection of tendrils called the dendrites. These collect information from other neurons. On the other side of the nucleus is the 'axon', which branches out and sends impulses to other neurons. Within each cell, information is sent from one end to the other in the form of a little electrical charge, like a fuse burning along the length of the cell. Between cells the messages are sent in chemical form, with special chemicals called neurotransmitters crossing the tiny gaps between one cell's tendrils, axons (axons sending), and another cell's tendrils, dendrites (dendrites receiving). Each neuron connects with up to a thousand other neurons. There are reckoned to be about fifty-three different neurotransmitter chemicals. (I've heard of some of these; serotonin, enkephalin, adrenaline, dopamine.) The neurons don't, for the most part, actually touch. The little straits between cells, across which the neurotransmitter chemicals are sent, are called synapses. (I'd heard of these too. I've heard of synapses.) So, what you've got is a chemical–electrical– chemical–electrical relay, with chemicals telling cells to fire more, or less, or no electrical charges (or action potentials or spikes), and electrical charges ordering different chemical cocktails across the synaptic cleft. On to the next cell or cells, and the next.

Everything you do requires a phenomenal amount of this intra- and intercellular activity. Think about chewing. Think about chewing without biting your tongue while you eat a sandwich. Your jaws and teeth are a very efficient and powerful cutting and grinding tool, and your tongue is a very soft and vulnerable lump of flesh. Every time you chew your food your tongue is doing a kind of complicated dance of death and yet it hardly ever gets caught. You hardly ever bite your tongue. There is a phenomenal amount of brain activity going on between the sensory and motor areas of the brain and the nervous system in the tongue and jaws, which allows you not to bite your tongue. An astonishing amount of to and fro going on. Millions and millions of dialogues and plans going on between brain and nerve and muscle to allow you to perform this simple task without even noticing. Walking and chewing gum simultaneously is a ridiculously complic- ated task. We're nowhere near coming up with a machine that can do it. We've got a machine that can play chess but not one that doesn't bite its tongue.

'And brain cells die, don't they?' That's something I knew.

'Between fifteen thousand and two hundred thousand a day in a normal brain. But it hardly makes a difference in the average life span.'

I didn't ask him how much that figure might be hiked by excessive alcohol consumption in case that alerted him to the smell on my breath.

Scanning the room, Ben's den, it looked as if he had summoned all those brains to a massed meeting. We were in an amphitheatre, with a congregation of brains organising itself in rows and tiers, brains facing this way and that, conferring and jostling, the little ones pushed to the front for a better view, or hoisted onto some convenient promontory – a pile of books or loose papers.

'What are those up there? Are they real?'

Up on the top shelf were two cylindrical jars being used as bookends, each containing a doughy, fraying lump. You bet they were real.

'They're incredible, aren't they? I got them from the hospital museum when they were closing it down. It was full of medical anomalies in jars, like two-faced babies, or babies with no legs. Most of the stuff went to the Wellcome Institute, but they didn't want these because the labels have fallen off and there's no record of how they came by them or who they were or anything. There's no obvious brain damage, so I don't even know how they died. They could have been donated by doctors or scientists.'

'From their own collections?'

'No, I mean from their own heads. After they died. That was quite common in the nineteenth century.' So they donated themselves for research, to advance medical science. And now they're bookends.

'Is it true you only use ten per cent of your brain?'

'No, that's rubbish. Thanks for the projector back.'

21: I shouldn't have said that

THAT WAS QUITE AN ANNOYING THING for me to have said, because it's the sort of thing people say when they don't think what they're saying (how or why would we have evolved to have a skull ninety per cent filled with filler?). To try and look less stupid, if only slightly, I advanced briskly to the practical matter I'd come to ask Ben about. 'Actually, there was something else. My studio.'

'*Studio* ...' he said, making the word sound as if he'd never heard it before, in any context.

'Normally when you do an artist in residence you get a studio. An artist in residence gets a studio.'

'Well, we haven't really talked about that.'

'No, we haven't.'

'I mean here at the Institute.'

The thing is I really needed a studio. I was about to get thrown out of my machine shop in Hackney – rent arrears, eleven months – and it was almost unusable in winter anyway. I had to wear all my clothes, all the clothes I possessed, under my overalls to go there in December and January. And then I could hardly move. My brushwork lost fluidity, too, as the paint became thickened with cold; like painting with fudge. Getting a studio with heating and an inside toilet was one of the things I wanted from this residency.

Just then there was a fumbling at the door, and Michelle shouldered herself in, arms full of files and papers, a biro behind each ear. She looked right past me,

'Ben—'

'Yes, I know. I'll be there in a minute.'

'—'cause you've missed the last two meetings, Ben.' She withdrew, letting the door shut itself. Ben looked at me, as if it was my fault, then went and opened the door again, and called after her,

'Look, Michelle, I'm dealing with something in here at the moment. A funding-related problem.' I couldn't make out what she was saying, but the tone of voice was there – dubious, put upon. She gave some kind of assent, and Ben turned back into the room, letting the door click shut.

'Studio ...' he said again, still trying it out. Testing its heft.

'Well, it wouldn't have to be a painting studio,' I said, picturing the paint stalactites and the ankle deep slurry of my studio in Hackney.

'It could be a drawing studio. Drawing, and uhrrm ... *research.*'

That could work well for me. I rarely got any real painting done in winter anyway. I'd tried working with a bottle of whisky at hand 'to keep out the cold', and nearly killed myself. A couple of times I'd passed out in my folding chair and come round at four in the morning, almost frozen to death. One such session put me in bed for a month, all alone. That was one of my bad times. I felt I was on safer ground suggesting a drawing studio. He couldn't possibly have any idea of the amount of mess I could make doing one of my drawings; generally an undisciplined assault on a giant sheet of paper torn from a nine-foot ream, involving a fantastic array of mark-making tools and substances (soot, snot, boot polish, crayons, jam), tearing, scraping, biting and stabbing. The look on his face, signs of something beginning to hatch, caused me to think that I had correctly guessed what his idea of a drawing studio might be. Me standing at an easel, or perhaps seated with an A3-size sketchbook on my lap, 'sketching' something. A vase. An orange.

I drove home my advantage with an idea I thought he might like. 'I could maybe do something with the patients there. Drawing classes or something.'

He liked that.

'OK, look. I think we could do something about that. I'll go and have a word with Michelle. Back in a mo,' he said, and ran out.

22: Ben's brains (cont.d)

BEN WAS GONE for about three quarters of an hour. I passed the time looking at all the brains around me – tum-ti-tum – taking the occasional glug out of my Volvic bottle. I tinkered with a brain.

When Ben returned, he practically leaped into the room, and handed me a cheque. 'I've had a word with Michelle and Nancy ... Dr Prabhakar, and you can use one of the Guest Rooms as a studio. We've hardly got any inpatients right now. And you can do drawing classes in the Activities Room. Michelle will find some patients you can work with. Once a week. Wednesdays OK with you?'

That was absolutely fine with me. A cheque. And the Guest Room. I could probably put a dust sheet down or something. I wonder if I could sleep there? Be better than my flat, I told him.

'Fine. Brilliant.'

'Great.'

'Good. Um ... do you think you could give me a hand with this? I'm sorry, I got a bit bored.' I'd dismantled one of Ben's brains; the big one. It was in a heap.

'Oh sure. Don't worry. See ... look, the pons, thalamus, hypothalamus and colliculi all go together like this, top of the medulla ...'

'Yeah. With you so far—'

'So that's your hindbrain and midbrain ...' a thing like a bean dropped out and he popped it back in '... pineal gland, then you put the cerebellum on here ...' It was like watching someone reassemble an automatic pistol after

71

cleaning it. Things clicking and slotting back where they belong.

'You put all the lobes of the cerebrum back together. The occipital lobe connects to the parietal lobe, the occipital and parietal lobes connect to the temporal lobe, the ...'

'... the leg bone's connected to the hip bone ...'

'What? Oh yeah ... heh heh. The occipital, parietal, temporal lobes all connect to the frontal lobe ...' It was a very satisfying thing to watch. It was a stunningly well-made model. Ben had had to sell his scooter to buy it. He showed me where the cortical map of the skin is; a long ridge running from behind your ear up to the top of your head, picked out on this particular model in irregularly spaced horizontal stripes, like a caterpillar.

'Each of those stripes corresponds to a part of the body. See, you've got one stripe for each finger and another for the thumb. The lips here – that's a wide stripe because the more sensitive parts take up more space in the brain. Up the top here you've got your neck, head, shoulders, then down there, where the two halves of your brain join, you've got your feet next to your genitals. You see, all physical sensations are actually going on in your brain. There's this guy in Arkansas who's lost a leg, and apparently he's been experiencing these incredible phantom limb orgasms when he has sex, and it might be because the part of the brain associated with his foot has nothing to do now, because it's getting no input, so it's started to respond to input from its cortical neighbours.'

'Just like when you're on your own, and you can hear them having sex next door, and it's really loud—'

'Except in the brain the neighbours having sex makes you feel as if it's you having sex.'

'—instead of making you feel lonely and depressed. So that guy with the itch is sort of not reading his body map.'

'Exactly. Possibly. Actually we're not sure we're going to be able to help that guy. We can't find any likely neurobiological causes for that thing he does, so it may be a psychiatric problem. It could be he's just mad. Of course, the distinction between psychiatry and neurology comes partly from the idea that the mind and the brain are distinct, even though, as a neurologist, I tend to think of the distinction as false, because the brain supports the mind. Or, they aren't the same thing, but you definitely don't have a mind unless you have a brain.'

So, if I've got this right, a pain in my hand is actually going on in my brain. Specifically, somewhere just above my ear. But I experience it as occurring in my hand. Wherever my hand goes the pain goes too, even though it's not really there. It's in my brain. The word 'where' seems to mean less when you talk to a neuroscientist, or at least its meaning comes with a lot of caveats and provisos. I started to experience an odd detachment from my body; a sort of intellectual highlighting of the slight numbness and remoteness caused by the gin.

'Would you like to hold a brain?' Ben was really enjoying himself now, and so was I – with a cheque in my pocket, a gin buzz on, and knowing that I was suddenly very popular with Ben because he'd been able to use me, somehow, to get himself out of some dreary obligation, and he could show off his amazing collection instead. I think I made a good audience. Of course I'd love to hold a brain.

This turned out to be quite a tricky operation, getting a large jar containing a brain in preserving fluid down off the top shelf. Ben stood on a chair, then with one foot on a lower shelf, leaning and stretching, pulled the specimen jar to the edge, me hovering beneath, looking ready. Yep … that's … OK got it … Oops! The liquid slopped about and the brain fore and afted itself against the sides. Now could you ...? Yep. OK. Holding the jar like a crown he shuffled forward to the desk, while I looked busy moving papers and stuff, ready for him to place the thing ceremoniously next to the computer.

The actual thing, when you see it up close, is a bit of a disappointment. Small and greyish.

'You'll need a glove. Hang on.' He looked in a couple of drawers and found a pair of Marigold kitchen gloves.

'There y'go.' I put on a glove and leaned over, all ready. He grasped the spherical knob of the lid, and with a *ta-daa!* flourish, lifted it off the jar.

'Weeugh! Jeezus. Fucking stink!' I reeled back and looked up at him. He was smiling at me, nearly laughing. OK, here goes. The thing was narrow enough to be picked up between thumb and forefinger, but I thought that would look irreverent, and girly somehow, so I slid my fingers underneath and scooped it up, holding it over the jar so that the foul preserving fluid wouldn't get all over me. It weighed about the same as a pint of beer.

I wanted to prod it, so I got Ben to help me on with the other glove. Spongy. Quite tough. I have actually eaten brain – a while ago when I was flush, at a restaurant popular with the art world that specialises in offal – and was expecting this to have the same kind of consistency, like a mousse, or cod's roes.

'They're much softer than that, really,' Ben explained. 'The fluid makes them rubbery. Also this one's shrunk a bit with age. The average brain weighs about 1,450 grams; three and a quarter pounds or so. This one's Broca. The other guy up there I call Wernicke. ' This is a neuro joke. Broca and Wernicke were nineteenth-century brain doctors, and each gave his name to a kind of aphasia.

'See here ...' he prodded the brain with a biro, 'if you had damage there you'd suffer from Broca's aphasia. You'd be able to understand what was being said to you but when you tried to reply it would come out all wrong. You keep trying because it's like that thing of having a word on the tip of your tongue. It's like that all the time. Really frustrating.

'And here' – he gave it another prod – 'is Wernicke's area. Now if that got taken out, with a bullet or whatever, you wouldn't be able to speak properly because you wouldn't be able to understand anything. Wernicke's aphasics hear all language as gibberish, but because they've lost comprehension altogether they think it's OK. They have no awareness of there being a problem. They seem to know all the words but not how to use them, so to them language is just an exchange of vocalisations. They have some basic awareness of language as a means of interaction, but they have no idea of there being any content to these exchanges. The Broca's patient will get incredibly frustrated because they know they're not doing it right. Wernicke's patients haven't got a clue there's anything wrong. You can talk to them for hours. It's like avant-garde poetry or something.'

'So that bit' – I prodded – 'produces speech, and that bit' – another prod – 'understands.'

'Not exactly. Put it this way: if you destroy Broca's area you can't speak properly, and if you destroy Wernicke's you can't understand, but that's not the same as saying Broca's area "does" speech, and Wernicke's area "does" comprehension. They're obviously both crucial to these functions but ... well, it'd be like saying the City of London "does" money. It does "do" money, but so do lots of other places, and the City does a lot of other things besides money. It's just very complicated. But the brain does do language. It does everything.'

The brain does money, language, wars, advertising, art, arson, astronomy, astrology, cookery, sarcasm, pedicures, parenthood, BarMitzvahs, jokes, furniture, spite. It does the Universe really, if you take the view that observation, cognisance, brings things into existence. The human brain is the part of the Universe that brings the Universe into existence by knowing it. We looked at the brain, the human brain, in silence for a minute.

'Can I have some of that gin?' said Ben. Secret drinking is one of the defining characteristics of alcoholism, but, as it turned out, I was clear on that score. Ben went and got some ice from somewhere, and some grapefruit and cranberry juice. We sat in his office drinking cocktails out of plastic cups. He didn't even mind me smoking, while I elaborated my idea for a drawing class.

23: my idea for a drawing class

THE THING ABOUT ME CONDUCTING a drawing class is that I've never been any good at representational drawing. I can't draw hands. Life classes had almost disappeared from art schools by the time I got there, but I have done a few, and found out that I can't draw things realistically, and I cannot look at a naked woman in a disinterestedly aesthetic way. Once, I was trying to draw this young girl from Northern Italy, who'd been posed on all fours, with me facing her vulva. She was a novice life model, just trying to make a bit of money to see her through her London trip. She kept giggling. My drawing looked like the kind of DIY porn that workmen will trace into the dust on their van with one finger – curly hair, two circles with dots in the middle for tits, curly minge, eyes and a mouth.

But if we did drawings of Ben's brains, no one would ever need to know. When you pull a brain model in half, the cross section looks like part of a paisley pattern, and I can copy patterns. The details of relative proportion are nothing like as crucial as they are in a hand. Also, being a cross section, it's all on a plane, flat, whereas a hand occupies all three dimensions. Neural space may be fantastically complicated, but a brain is just a roughly differentiated clod of tissue. A big walnut. A cabbage. A deflated football. A boxing glove. Much easier to draw than a hand.

Ben wasn't too sure, initially. He's very protective about his brains. He started to come round to the idea when I told him about the first Academies – how the students would spend years doing detailed drawings of plaster casts made from classical antique statues. Three months spent doing a god's nose, or a nymph's ear. He was reassured by this image of patient study.

'But I don't want any of my brains getting damaged.'

Ben must have decided to declare that day a holiday for himself. What the heck. Let's go to the pub. I learned some amazing stuff. A surprising amount of which stuck. I also found out something bad, and something puzzling.

The bad thing. Full of positive feelings about it all – the residency, Ben, Nancy Prabhakar, the Institute – I expressed my surprise and gratitude at having been singled out from all those fine candidates. Turns out I wasn't. They only offered the job to me because the others turned it down. The money wasn't enough. My interview performance, they had all agreed, stank. But they needed to appoint someone because of the conditions of their funding package, whatever that is.

The puzzling thing. At some point I asked him why he'd made that funny noise during my lecture. I had been saying something about Monet painting the world as we see it, as patches of colour, prior to the attribution of meaning or identity to things in the visual field.

'Well, for a start,' said Ben, 'the world is not coloured.'

24: another private view

I SAW MY DEALER a few days later, at a private view. I was hoping for some good news from him. 'Any news?' I shouted.

'Huh?'

'I said ... ANY NEWS?'

We were having trouble making ourselves heard above the racket of the art. A sound-piece by a Dutch artist entitled *me*. The recorded voices of a million people saying 'me', one after the other, at one-second intervals. It was a work in progress, with only 2,379 'me's recorded so far –and it was rumoured most were just the artist and her friends saying 'me' in different voices. When complete, the piece will last about eleven and a half days and will culminate in the sound of all million 'me's being played simultaneously, before an audience wearing ear protectors.

My dealer signalled we should go to the bar, set up on trestle tables outside on the pavement. I could already tell he didn't have any good news. I'd had hopes of a sale, after a protracted lean period. A German collector had been viewing images of my paintings trying to decide which one to buy.

'I'm really sorry. He said he likes your work but it's not right for his collection.'

We were queuing at the bar for our free beer.

'I see. That's ... How long since one of my paintings sold?'

'I don't know.'

'Yes, you do.'

'Fourteen months.'

There was supposed to be an abstract painting revival going on. Collectors were falling over themselves trying to buy every abstract painting they could lay hands on. But not mine. My work's position remained secure, undisturbed by any bandwagon-jumping opportunists. I took this news very well, though, because I'd been to see my other dealer earlier on that evening. Arthur, the drug dealer. Arthur does everyone in the art world. He had been quite surprised to receive my coded phonecall.

'Hello, Arthur. It's me. Are you ... OK?'

'I'm ... OK.'

'See you in a minute, then.' I was only downstairs, at the phone box. Arthur's one of the few people left in the art world who can still afford a loft space in Shoreditch. Beautiful flat. Arthur's doing very well at the moment. Apparently he used to be an artist himself before he got into this line of work.

'Haven't seen you in a while,' he said. I told him something that gave the impression I'd been kept away by the demands of my career, and not by not having the cash. I'd got Arthur at a good time today. He didn't have his scales around – 'lent them to someone and I can't remember who' – and he'd been taking drugs. He pulled a plastic bag full of drugs out of a shoebox under the sofa (obviously the police would never think of looking there), and then cast his eye about the room, looking for something, another thing, he'd misplaced.

'Look,' he said, 'have you got anything to put this in?'

I found an old envelope in one of my pockets and held it open for Arthur to pour some drugs into. It sounded like *sssssshhhhh* as it poured.

'Do you think that's a gram, about?'

'Yeah. Roughly,' I said, testing its weight in my hand.

I got out of there before he changed his mind, or found his mind. I had about half an ounce of cocaine in my pocket.

25: c(C)reationists

I OFFERED MY ART DEALER some drugs, before he had a chance to find someone else to talk to. He turned from scoping the crowd – hundreds of artists and art writers and art dealers bunging up a narrow street in Hoxton – and looked at me with newly discovered interest.

'A line? Yeah. Why not?'

He was mine for the night after he saw how much drugs I had. He was going to stay right by my side. Throughout the course of a long evening, a night and a morning, we were able to discuss my career a lot, at regular intervals. Why doesn't anyone buy my paintings? Is it the size, or the ragged improvised style? (I would sometimes claim, defensively, that this style was 'post-ironic'.) Perhaps they'd do better in Germany, or Belgium? I've been hearing good things about the Czech Republic. Is it the colours? Too much red?

'Maybe', someone said, 'it's because no one likes them.' This as we were entering a well-known designer bar in Soho, about 4am. After an evening's peripatetic schmoozing, with me now perceived as OK because of the enthusiastic attendance of my dealer, who's doing very well at the moment and is OK with everyone, we had settled into a small group. Seven or eight of us. My posse for this evening.

By half past five I was talking about brains. Or, more accurately, I was *going on* about brains. The five thousand gazillion neurons in the average human brain, covering several Olympic size swimming pools, connecting to every star and galaxy in the Universe. I was aware I was getting some of the details a bit wrong, but felt very confident of my ability to convey the spirit of the thing. I was saying a lot; enough for some of it to be spot-on.

I had paired off with my neighbour in our seated group, a woman my dealer represents, doing very well at the moment. I have her attention because she can see I have his attention, and she doesn't know with what currency that attention has been bought. She probably thinks there's some big career move in the pipeline for me. My interest in her is sexual and professional. She does Hilliardesque miniature watercolour portraits of people in the fashion industry, and I think they're shit, but she *is* doing very well at the moment.

I'm telling her all about neurons ...

'... they're doing it right now, in your head, billions of them flashing on and off, pulsing, electrical–chemical–electrical–chemical, and that's how you can do things like hold that glass and choose your clothes. That's how it all happens, Natasha. Hitler's neurons made World War Two, and Picasso's neurons made *Guernica*, and Einstein's neurons made ... you know ... relativity ...'

Natasha didn't find this as exciting as me.

'But I don't agree with that,' she said.

'How do you mean? What don't you agree with?'

'That's just all, like, *science.*'

'Yes.'

'But that's all just explaining things. I'm a Creationist.'

'Really? Are you sure?'

'Totally.'

'But, I mean Creationists are ... How do you mean, Creationist?'

'I just really believe in my creativity. Totally.'

'Oh right. Sorry. I thought you meant like those people in America, Bible Belt, who're trying to stop them teaching kids about natural selection and Darwin in school. I thought for a second you meant like those Creationists.'

'But that's just really fucking sexist.'

'Yeah, that's part of it, too. Creationists are right-wingers, definitely.'

'No, I mean like Darwin is just completely sexist. It's all about, Oh yeah, think what I think because I'm a man, and just explaining things. There's got to be something else apart from just science and conforming.'

All the cocaine in my system seemed to withdraw, like the tide going out, and I felt incredibly lonely. I was never going to get anywhere with her, anyway.

At dawn we were sitting, and sprawling, and lying about at my dealer's flat above the gallery; just the four of us now. Me, my dealer, and a couple who make work together – a recent addition to the gallery's stable. They were new enough to have no idea where I should be placed, how much of their time I deserved, and they were enjoying my company. Especially having dug in to my supply, and shown me how to take it through the eye (you make a solution in vodka, and use a shot glass like an eyebath). We were drinking sherry and smoking a spliff the size of a traffic cone, and I was talking about my career again.

'Why don't you do something else?' says Tina, lying on her back and staring at the ceiling.

'What, you mean – change my painting?'

'Just do something else. Do a video.'

'But I couldn't translate my subject matter to another medium. Painting is my subject. It's painting about painting. I'm a painter.'

'Have a different subject. Do something about brains.'

'Do something different?'

'Yes. Fucking good stuff, this.'

Another few lines and this idea began to develop. By mid-morning we had all attained a kind of homeostasis, the various chemical demands on our systems having levelled off with each other to produce an affective plateau, a condition approximating sobriety but feeling much better. We drank 'Portuguese coffee', instant coffee with sherry in it, and kicked a few ideas around.

'You could do a kind of performance thing. You go to private views and pretend to have a fit. You could have someone with you with a camera. Recording people's reactions.' That from Tina's boyfriend, Barry. Aiden. Karl?

'Nah. Been done. That French guy.' Oh yeah. That French guy who'd turn up at private views all over London, then at the Venice Biennale. By the time he started doing it at the Frieze Art Fair, everyone was sick of him. Two or three years ago.

'You could take photographs of people with brain damage and then ... um ... hang the pictures upside down, or sideways. Y'know. Like a different perspective thing.' We realised we'd all received invites for a show like that due to open next week.

'You could do something with those images of brain scans. You could have two side by side. One thinking about art and one thinking about ... something else.'

'You could do a massive sculpture of a brain out of wood. Call it *Blockhead.*'

'You could do a photopiece with someone called Brian holding a brain.'

'You could do a sculpture that's a brain on a turntable playing "Mellow Yellow" by Donovan, and call it *Donovan's Brain .*' My idea that, but no one else had heard of Donovan the singer, or the film *Donovan's Brain.*

'You could do something with those amazing films of people being given electric shock treatment. EEG ... EGG ... ETC?'

'You could show it slowed down. Or speeded up.'

'I saw this amazing thing where someone superimposed all these faces of hundreds of different people, and it looked exactly like Elvis. It was someone to do with neurology.'

'Where did you see that?'

'A science programme, on telly.'

'That means it's already been done, doesn't it?'

'Not as art, though.'

It had been done as art.

'That Japanese guy.'

Oh. Yeah.

There were a few more hours of this before we all fell asleep, more or less simultaneously. Karl fell asleep standing up, like a horse.

26: art therapy?

'WE'VE CHOSEN SOME PATIENTS for your drawing class.' This is Ben on the phone to me. Me on day three of recovery. I'm weaning myself back onto solids with tomato soup.

'Do I know any of them?'

'Yeah. There's Colin and Emily you know. There's those two severely visually deficited people …' – the Blind Couple, 'there's a hemi-neglecting patient, an achromatopic guy, a man who was blind until recently – he'll be interesting, there's a woman with Charles Bonnet syndrome, and there's this amazing Touretter. You'll like him. He's amazing. See you Wednesday.'

'Do I need to bring anything?'

'Well, paper and pencils, I suppose.'

'I've got to get the materials?'

'Well, we haven't really budgeted for it, you see.'

'It's only a few quid. You must have that.' They've got fucking millions. They've got a full-sized loom! You'd think they could buy some pencils. The fact is I was practically skint again. I'd had to weigh off a few people I'd run into at that private view, feeling big and generous about it, and now I was on the floor again. I sulked down the phone at Ben, and he started to give in.

'I suppose I could have a word with Michelle about it. It's a budgeting problem. We might be able to reimburse you. I'll see what she says. See you in the Activities Room, Wednesday.'

I put the phone down, feeling really depressed about the whole thing now. Why do they want sick people to do art anyway? What is art therapy? What's it supposed to do for you? I had a mental picture of myself supervising various craft activities, like the making of raffia-work placemats, or handmade greetings cards done with stencils. Helping a psychopath make a plywood pipestand in Broadmoor. Sure, it's good to do something with your hands. It helps keep your mind off things and gives you a sense of achievement. It keeps the darkness and despair at bay, which has to be a positive thing. Sometimes I think that's why I do it – all those hours in the studio. I pictured an art gallery full of placemats and pipestands. Quite a good idea for a show, actually.

There's this idea of 'expressing yourself', isn't there? Everything else you do fails, presumably, to express you. Walking, talking, eating, watching TV, having a wank. All these things are mute, inexpressive activities. I've seen plenty of so called 'Outsider Art' – the work of yokels and mental patients – and what seems clear to me is that, given free rein to express their unique and ineffable selves, people demonstrate only conformity skewed and inflected by ineptitude. It's not that I don't enjoy it, but I know I'm not accessing another reality through the art of 'outsiders'. It's an attempt to join the consensus reality, made odd, and, to a sophisticated audience, more interesting, by its failure to do so. The fact that there are people called 'art therapists', and art education officers whose job it is to explain Joseph Beuys to gangs of hostile teenagers, means that on some level in public life the idea of art is incorrigible. It's just meant to be good for you.

And because of that I have to buy paper and pencils out of my own money, which doesn't seem fair. Later on, feeling a bit better after my soup, I admit to myself that the only reason I've got any money at all (and there's another instalment coming soon) is because art is supposed to be good for you. Someone in a position of authority had decided that it would be a good thing to have an artist about the place. A good thing about doing a drawing class – maybe I should call it a 'Workshop' – is that I could give Emily some guidance while standing behind her, smelling her hair and looking down her front. Would she be able to learn how to draw? She might be able to draw quite well already. She might be able to draw hands.

I got round the problem of any needless expense by getting a roll of heavy-duty lining paper from a DIY shop, and filling a carrier bag with a variety of mark-making instruments from my studio – dozens of nearly spent marker-pens, charcoal sticks, oil pastels, biros. That way the students wouldn't feel inhibited using expensive art materials, and would feel free to experiment freely. If anyone just wanted a pencil, they must have loads in the offices.

There was no one in the Activities Room when I got there, so I dumped my stuff and went to the Day Room. (I only needed to traverse the reception area, past that woman, a couple of times.) What I saw, approaching my group of students across the big room, was something of a kind you'd expect to see outside the Pompidou Centre. They were all watching a juggler. Some fucking crusty. Nobody looked round or said hello when I arrived. This fucking crusty was doing some amazingly complicated juggling with oranges and croissants – they leave them in baskets by the coffee machines here – keeping six, seven, is that nine? – in the air at once with his hands, feet and nose. He'd bunched his dreadlocks at the top so that his head looked like a pineapple, and he was wearing a multicoloured patchwork breechcloth over his combat trousers, and a hessian cloak with leaves on it. He looked, I thought, like a tit, with his wizard jewels and bells.

Everybody was enjoying it, sitting there with their coffees resting on their knees, looking up at him at the centre of the little group. Colin was enjoying it. So was Ben. Emily was *really* enjoying it. He'd singled her out for his best stuff, making it look, at one point, as if he'd chucked an orange directly at her face, causing her to start back, and then hooking it out of the air an instant before it hit her on the nose. He halted its trajectory with his toe, flicking it from there onto the back of his right elbow, snapping the arm forward to slap the orange into his right hand, and then presenting it to Emily on his open palm, with a medieval bow. She bloody loved it. I, personally, cannot stand jugglers and crusties. Crusties, in my view, are a bunch of soap-dodging work-shy nitwits who go to Stonehenge thinking they're Druids, even though everybody knows that Stonehenge had nothing whatsoever to do with the Druids. Even if the Druids had gone to Stonehenge they certainly wouldn't have turned up dressed like that. Who is this person?

'Who's that?' I asked Ben.

'Stick.'

'Stick? I'd have him checked out if I were you. That may not be his right name. What is he? Is he the juggler in residence or something?'

'Stick? No, I told you about him. He's a patient. Tourette's.'

'I see. And is the juggling some sort of therapy? Is it to stop him swearing at people.'

'No, it's actually a symptom really. He doesn't swear at people. The Tourette's gives him these incredible reflexes. You don't want to play table tennis with him!'

No. I don't. He's got this expression on his face. This fucking *look*. And what this fucking look seemed to want to tell us was something along these lines – *I am a devil-may-care madcap fool, and a child of the Earth Spirit. Oh Yes!! I am of the Elven folk ...*

'Couldn't you teach him to swear at people instead?'

I'd have thought Ben would see eye to eye with me on this. I thought we had a lot in common after our session the other day. Maybe I was overreacting a bit because of Emily. She was looking lovelier than ever. And that's all it took to please her. A juggling idiot. Of course I could see the logic of it, with her attention span so attenuated. Fifteen minutes was plenty of time for 'Stick' to show her what he was made of; what a lovely guy he is. And here's me – complex, fathomless, infinite. A lifetime's work for any woman. I didn't stand a chance against a man who can juggle. He'll be all over her by the end of this lesson. He's going to sleep with her, and I, most probably, am not.

'I've brought some of my paintings for you to look at,' said Colin.

'Yeah yeah. Be with you in a minute, Colin.'

27: my drawing class

BEN HAD GOT THE ACTIVITIES ROOM all ready, with three tables at the centre of the room, and on each table was one of his brain models, the least treasured examples from his collection. (I noticed there was something different about that room now. An improvement had been made. All those huge craft things, the looms and lathes and pottery things and whatnot, had gone. That's good!) I started cutting off lengths of lining paper and placing them like table settings, with a crayon, biro or felt tip. I explained to Ben that I didn't want them to feel intimidated by the materials, and they should feel free to experiment. 'Look, I'll just go and get some pencils from the office,' said Ben.

Colin guided the Blind Couple to their seats – I don't know what the fuck they're supposed to do – and then approached me with his paintings. He seemed to have several in a Sainsbury's bag. This was a bad sign already. Far too small. Monet's waterlilies were generally painted more or less actual size, so that a picture of a pond would be the size of a pond. These, I could tell even before he opened the bag, were painted on the cheap canvas boards they produce specifically for the amateur market. (I've used them myself, but only ironically, as a way of underscoring my professionalism.) He took them out and laid them against the wall in a row. OK, I can see what he's done here. Basically what he'd done is interpret everything in the kind of shorthand they use in paint-by-numbers kits. The whole thing was rendered in coloured-in shapes, like a jigsaw puzzle with each piece a little area of flat, local colour. You could see a tremendous amount of work had gone into them. He'd drawn them out very carefully, every single leaf and petal and glint of light outlined. Then he'd coloured it in.

There's actually nothing at all wrong with painting like this if that's what you want to do. Or if that's what you mean. Painting like this has come to be associated with a Pop/post-modernist kind of alienation from the natural world. Monet's garden would be, according to this view, a hyper-real re-en-actment of nature. Colin was painting Monet's garden as a follower of Warhol would: someone who signals their removal from the possibility of free will within late capitalist hegemony – a world in which the subject is a construction of received taste – by just saying, 'Oh, I like it,' when asked to express an opinion on anything.

The stance is a response to this problem that's been around ever since artists began to differentiate themselves from craftsmen and courtiers. The craftsman will build a cathedral without asking whether or not God exists, or whether, if he does, a cathedral is really what he wants (Maybe we should be helping the poor or something?). A courtier, which is what artists like Velázquez and Rubens were, has the job of bolstering the status quo, being a pro-fessional flatterer. The problem is the artist's relation to money and power. Aren't we supposed to be against it these days? Or, if we're not against money, we must be against privilege and injustice. And then, if we are, why are we so utterly dependent on patrons, all of them unjustly privileged?

For the greater part of the twentieth century you just said you were a Communist, and that was fine, but by the '60s that didn't seem good enough. If you're a Communist, *how* are you a Communist? What are you doing differently because you're a Communist? The artist's financial depend-ence on a system of which he is supposed to disapprove continued to be a problem. It compromised his independence of spirit. The Warholian answer to this problem was simply not to answer it. You just drop any defences against prevailing standards and embrace them. You like popular things just because they're popular. The artist fulfils his role as humanity's representative to itself through a kind of exemplary acquiescence. Where Warhol scored over his followers was in making this craven attitude seem incredibly weird and unnatural, whereas in fact it's the norm. Acquiescence as a form of critique. Or you could say he brought us full-circle, back to being courtiers. Court jesters, licensed to poke harmless fun at our betters. So the kind of art that Colin's closely resembled (by accident) is trying to say something like: 'I can't like gardens because I'm supposed to like gardens, so if I do it's not really me liking gardens.' It's a post-Warhol lament for the loss of gardens.

I didn't have time to go into all this with Colin. But I found it hard to understand how he could have produced his pictures thinking they looked anything like Monet's. Maybe if he'd only seen them in reproduction. But he's been to Giverny and seen the real thing. He must know it's not the same. As someone with a good grasp of how things are made, able to look at something and reverse-engineer it, and leaving aesthetics aside, he must be able to see that Monet's paintings just aren't done like he paints. The marks that make up the plane of those Monets are applied with the whole surface attended to, so that it begins as a loose mesh, a frond here, a petal there, a swathe of shadow, with figure and ground worked simultaneously. Not coloured in, area by area, working from left to right. How could he be so blind, even to the point of ignoring common sense?

'Do you like Andy Warhol's work, Colin?'

'I quite like some of it.' Wary. 'I quite like some of the colours.'

I didn't pursue this. Besides his aspiration to be a kind of everyman Warhol is also weird and poofy. I could see Colin bristle at the mention of the name and I considered the possibility that the problem may have something to do with his visual deficit, but couldn't see how. I nearly asked him if he'd done any painting before his stroke, but decided not to. The thing is, in a way, there was absolutely nothing wrong with his paintings – I could see them looking OK in a show of contemporary paintings – but it obviously wasn't what he wanted to do. He wasn't doing what he thought he was doing.

'I can see these in a show of contemporary painting, Colin.' He seemed quite pleased. I don't know. It's possible his visual deficit has made him more sensitive to the sound of insincerity in people's voices.

When I looked round everyone was sitting at the table, holding their drawing tools (they'd all ignored the crayons and whatnot, and were holding pencils) like orphans in the workhouse waiting for their gruel. Everyone except 'Stick', that is, who was sitting with his chair tipped back and his feet against the table, balancing a felt tip on his nose, his arms out-stretched. Emily, I was glad to see, had removed her cardigan and hung it on the back of her chair. She had a tight T-shirt on. Those tits. Christ. She was sitting opposite 'Stick', and smiling at his 'antics'.

I'd never done anything like this before. (When I taught in art schools I'd see the students individually in their little spaces, traipsing from one shrine of self-indulgence and self-regard to the next, wishing I was allowed to use the cane, or a rolled-up newspaper round the head. This ... thwap! is for thinking you've suffered when you haven't; and this ... thwap! is for thinking you're original when you're not. And ... THWAP!! that's for not turning up till half past bloody twelve when I've got to wait around here from nine o'clock.)

I'd never actually taught a class. I stood at the head of the row of tables, as if I had something to say.

'Um. You. Thing. "Stick". Could you not do that please?'

'Sure Mr Artist. Mr Artiste. Mr AR-TEE-STAH!'

He kept catching Emily's eye, and she was giggling, activating her breasts. I'm going to have to kill that crusty. I'll take that carefree, happy-go-lucky cunt to a lock-up in South London and pour acid on him, after I've worked on him for a bit with lopping shears and a blowtorch. He exchanged another glance with Emily (another hiccuping quiver of the tits) as he noisily settled himself in line with the others. Then he started drumming on the table. Jesus Christ.

'Well, you've all got what you need. You have got what you need, haven't you?'

'Can I have a rubber?' says one. I didn't recognise her.

'A rubber. Yes I'm sure we can find one.'

'Why do you want us to draw brains?' Another stranger.

'Well, I'd have thought in the circumstances ... where we are. I'd have thought it was the natural choice of subject, really.'

Doubtful looks were exchanged, at least between the normally sighted. I didn't feel like getting into a discussion about it, so I asked them if they'd all like to just start, just anyhow they felt comfortable, and I'd talk to them individually as they worked. Colin, Emily and Stick got to work immediately. I realised some of the others would need a bit more guidance to get going. The ones who couldn't see. Actually Ben was talking to the Blind Couple already, and I went and joined them, looking like a teacher doing his job.

'Just a little experiment here, really,' said Ben.

'I can't do drawings, can I?' said the Blind Man, 'I'm blind.'

'Well I'm going to ask you to draw what you guess is there. Just see what comes.' Ben held out a pencil for him, and he took it.

'I don't need to guess. I know what's there. It's a model of the brain.'

It actually was only half a brain. A coronal section through the brain; that is, cut from ear to ear showing both symmetrical halves, rather than in profile from nose to nape, which would be a medial section. The Blind Man sighed, OK, and then began to roll his head around as if it contained one of those games where you have to get the ball bearings in the little holes. This seemed to prompt a guess about what he was supposed to be drawing, and he started to make marks on his paper. Ben turned to the Blind Woman and asked her to do the same. He held out a pencil for her but she made no move to take it, so he took her hand and placed the pencil between her fingers, the wrong way round at first. She didn't attempt to change its position, so he helped her out again – here, like that.

'I can't even begin to guess what it looks like. I can't remember what anything looks like.'

I tried to help. 'See if you can draw what you see here,' I pointed, 'in this area.'

'What area?' Oh yeah. She can't tell I'm pointing, can she. Ben had a better idea. He bent over and laid his head down on the table in front of the brain. 'Here.' She turned her head and lowered her chin a little, orienting herself towards his voice, pretty accurately as far as I could tell. 'Here.' Another tiny adjustment. 'OK. Draw now.'

We went and looked at what the Blind Man was doing, and I would say that it was a crude but definitely observed representation of what was in front of him. Not some guessed approximation of what a brain looks like. He'd got the centre parting and the layering of the cortex, like a geological cross section. If he'd really been guessing you'd have expected him to do something that looked like the more familiar side view.

'That's good. You've done it. It looks like what's in front of you.'

The Blind Man smiled, and carried on working, drawing fast. We stood and watched for a bit, and as he worked the image began to stray from the model. The thing got more and more elaborate until it came to resemble some kind of flower. It stayed symmetrical, but now looked like the fabulous creatures in Celtic manuscript illumination.

'OK, you can stop now,' said Ben. I thought that was a shame because it was starting to look really good. The Blind Man sat back and his smile gave way instantly to an expression of utter bereavement. Brilliant. We've just illustrated for him, perfectly, what he has lost. Fucking well done, Ben. You might have warned me, at least. It's going to take the poor guy months to come back from this.

'And how are we getting along here?' We stood behind the Blind Woman and had a look. Perhaps we should have given her a felt tip. She'd made a few very tentative marks. She was sitting with her pencil resting on the paper, her head tipped slightly back and her eyes wide as if she was waiting for a message from the spirit world – as if something would come through and the pencil would come to life in her hand.

'Not feeling very inspired today?' She smiled a bit at Ben's remark. She took it quite well really. I glanced across at the Blind Man and he seemed OK now. I suppose you just get used to it. 'How are you getting on, my love?' he asked.

'Not feeling very inspired today,' she said. They smiled at each other. I suppose they got together because of their deficits. They might have met here, Jack Spratt and his wife. She who can see everything but make sense of none of it, and he who can make some kind of crude sense of the visual world without being able, in any sense that you or I can understand, to see anything.

No wonder the Blind Man looked so bereft. He used to be a graphic designer, apparently. Mostly wallpaper. Very detailed stuff, which would account for the elaborations; the lappets, arabesques and curlicues he's added. There's no way of knowing exactly what he's getting when he sees something without seeing it but Ben reckons it's something akin to the impression you get of the shape when someone traces a letter on your back with their finger and you're supposed to guess what the letter is. What got him this way is a stroke. His eyes are fine, and the higher visual processing areas of his brain are fine, but the stroke has ruined communications between the two like a well-placed strategic terrorist attack, leaving only the primitive sub-cortical visual centres in working order. He's got all the equipment, but because of the destruction of one tiny but crucial neural avenue it's all useless now.

Ben's actually much more interested in the woman, because her case is, as far as he knows, unique. Total associative visual agnosia. Her world is made of those images of familiar objects seen from an unfamiliar angle or distance. There is a big puzzle about how she got this way. To get that kind of damage without collateral damage severe enough to mask this particular loss, a ruin among ruins, would be like removing all the plumbing and electrics from a house without damaging the walls or floors. The lesions are clearly visible in the scans they've done, but the only clue as to how they got there is her own account. She says she went 'blind' after being abducted by aliens. She tells a very detailed story about it, with descriptions of all kinds of weird probes and examinations. What's unusual about her tale is that all the attention is focused on the eyes rather than the genitals.

28: my drawing class – coincidences

SUCH ACCOUNTS ARE NOT TO BE IGNORED, but it's hard to know what they mean. It's tempting to find a link between this alien encounter she's quite certain she has experienced, and the view she now has of Planet Earth – everything looks 'alien' to her. But that's the kind of logic ufology experts employ. The kind of reasoning that finds indubitable links between the ancient Egyptians and the ancient civilisations of South America, because they both built pyramids, and links from there, via the inscrutable 'alien-ness' of the products of these cultures, to outer space. Another explanation of this coincidence is that if you have a great deal of manpower, a limited understanding of structural engineering, and wish to make a very tall and massive building, then you're going to come up with a pyramid, which is basically just a neat mound.

The thing about people who are interested in coincidences is that they don't believe in them. They think they happen for a reason, and they're right, but it's not the sort of reason they mean. A coincidence is a chance combination of events that seems meaningful but isn't really. We notice them because looking for significant relationships between phenomena is something we do all the time. It's called thinking. Coincidences are a sort of illusion. A cognitive illusion. (Optical illusions occur when the brain misapplies the rules of vision, and coincidences occur when the brain misapplies the rules of thought.) Finding meaningful connections where there are none even has a name – a condition called apophenia.

Coincidences don't indicate the intervention of an occult agency; actually, though, a total lack of coincidences would. An unseen force would have constantly to invigilate the teeming plethora of worldly events to make sure it never happened that two men named Keith, wearing red ties, both turned up for the same job interview; that nobody ever rang someone who happened to be thinking of them at the time; that lost keys never made their way back to you in any unexpected way; that no vegetable or wallpaper pattern or rock formation had Churchill's face or the Virgin Mary in it. This force would have to be the cosmic guarantor of singularity in all eventualities. No two distinct cultures could independently devise a system of mark-making to keep their records, or a viable seacraft, or the spear.

(In fact, taken to its logical extreme, a world without coincidence would have entropy as its natural order, and natural selection would be impossible. You couldn't even have two people with blue eyes; or even two blue eyes; or even two eyes. One eye in the whole Universe. God would preside over a Creation consisting of nothing but unique, and therefore immutable, acausal, entities. Total chaos. You'd have to bring in another God to sort it all out.)

There is a possible link with temporal lobe epilepsy. Some people think it's behind a lot of stories of alien abduction, because temporal lobe seizures can occur without the sufferer knowing, and cause hallucinations and 'lost time' episodes. The Blind Woman does have damage in her temporal lobes, but there's no history of epilepsy on her medical records, and any real link is difficult to establish. Another possibility would be that she's been struck by lightning, causing damage of the so-called 'Swiss Cheese' type.

The Blind Woman and The Blind Man were sitting opposite one another, smiling: the most normal-looking couple I've ever seen. The exaggerated normality of their appearance must be because that's how you're bound to look when other people choose your clothes and hairstyle for you.

29: paranormal Susan

THIS IS SOMETHING ME AND SUSAN used to argue about a lot. 'Why are you so negative and cynical about spiritual things?' she would ask. Whenever something happened that she approved of – something good for her, or bad for someone she didn't like – she'd say, 'That was meant to happen.' And I'd say, 'Meant? Meant by whom? And if that was meant to happen, Susan, how come these mysterious benign forces are never around when natural disasters and wars are happening?'

Her tidy bookshelves in her tidy flat said it all, really. She had a whole section devoted to healing and so-called 'metaphysics' (crystals and so on). The bulk of her personal library, however, was dedicated to her career plans: artist's monographs and catalogues arranged in alphabetical order; copies of *Frieze* and *Art Monthly* and *Artist's Newsletter* arranged in order of publication; many box-files containing paperwork related to applications for residencies and fellowships and grants. The shelves were actually labelled. Above the paranormal shelf – 'Mind, Body and Spirit' – was a shelf of 'Cultural and Critical Theory'. At times this combination of careerism and irrationality seemed to me to betray a mind at odds with itself; at other times, though, her pragmatism and her occultism seemed to form a chilling contiguity. When we were first going out, she used to tell me that mine was an ancient soul, and I took this as a compliment, but later on I began to think it was some sort of snide reference to the difference in our ages, me being nearly ten years older than her.

30: my drawing class – 'Stick'

I LEFT THE BLIND COUPLE WITH BEN, and began to walk around the tables, looking over people's shoulders, casting a professional eye over their work. Stick had settled down and was quietly busy, with his face nearly touching the paper and his left arm crooked around his work, as if he was worried his neighbour was trying to copy him. I wanted to go and look at Emily – sitting bolt upright and concentrating hard, like a model pupil. Her face in repose looked older, I thought. Standing behind Stick would give me the vantage point I wanted and prevent any suspicion of excessive eagerness on my part to 'help' her. Smell her hair. Try for a whiff of her breath. How would it smell in the morning? (I realise I'm being paranoid about this. Nobody could suspect a thing.)

'So, Woody, how are we getting on here?'

'It's Stick ... Wood, I like that ... heh heh ... Sticky Wood, like it like it ...' He was back with the drumming and bouncing around in his chair.

'Why are you doing a dragon? We're supposed to be doing brains today.'

'The dragon is the brain it drags through see it's connected there's all these connections Cone X Cone X it's a symbol it's my feeling The Brain yeh The Brain like all the CON-ECK-SHUNS I see you can't see because you're connected like the mafia the brain mafia that controls you and trying to gain control of me ...'

I stood and listened to this rubbish for about five minutes. I was, I gathered, some sort of instrument of the oppressor. Paranoid conspiracies could be another symptom of his condition – what is Tourette's, anyway? I thought it was just swearing – but I thought it more likely it was just a world-view he felt comfortable with. A lifestyle choice really. You're going to smash the system, then, are you, Stick, with your juggling skills? Twat.

He had Emily's attention again. She looked up and then quickly down again, with a smirk. She's on his side now. I'm the bad guy now, am I? You just have to dress up like a fucking cyber-jester or something to be a hero of the people. Emily must see through that, surely? She must have some sort of judgment, shrewd like a child or an animal, able to sniff out a phony. Some kind of sixth sense. She must be able to tell from one look at me – externally conventional in dress and manner, but different somehow – that I'm the real deal. I'm the counterculture. Not this buffoon. This worthless piece of shit. (This hyperperception of hers would not extend to any apprehension of my bad habits. The drinking and so on.)

'No, that's fine Stick. You carry on with your dragon. You express yourself. I won't stand in your way.'

I looked at Emily, her face looking older again, very businesslike, as she worked at her drawing, and I decided I wouldn't try to talk to her right now because I was giving out too many bad vibes, and surely she'd be preternaturally sensitive to a thing like that. My sweaty hostility. I put my mind to the task at hand: teaching people with special needs how drawing can help them.

I was doing this, leaning over and listening, and nodding while some bloke was explaining the problems he was having with the shading on his crappy drawing, when we were joined in the Activities Room by a tour group, a serious-minded, purposeful looking bunch of people. Men in suits. Women in suits. A few less well-turned-out individuals with clipboards and notebooks, one of them the woman from the Arts Council who'd interviewed me. Hilary. They drifted in, groups of two or three conferring about something, or just looking around. (Why do people always look at the ceiling when they first enter a room on a guided tour? There's nothing up there. It's not the Sistine Chapel.) Nancy Prabhakar brought up the rear of the group, besuited and intimidating, in company with a man dressed in a kind of hybrid style – a wealthy middle-aged Harley Davidson rider crossed with a successful architect, his shaven head, shades, bandana, and enormous tache worn with a Japanese-style black pyjama suit. He was bending very far forward to listen (Nancy was about half his height) as she made and emphasised some important point, clenching and unclenching her tiny fist, karate chopping the open palm of one hand with the other.

None of them seemed to notice us at first, even though there was nothing much else to look at in that gymnasium-sized room. They began to cluster at a point some distance from us, so that their conversation, their plotting, was audible only as a barely inflected monotone. The odd little laugh. Dr Prabhakar, still very engaged with that biker guy with the huge moustache, was helping strays into the cluster with a traffic policeman's slow rotating movement of the forearm.

I felt very conscious of the need to look busy. A time and motion study, perhaps. A visit from minor royalty.

'Who're they, Ben?' I said from the corner of my mouth, feeling a sudden declension or loss of rank. Ben ignored me and began, dead casual, to walk across to them. He's been expecting this lot. I could only see the back of his head but I could tell by the way his little ears hiked up that he'd started to smile. Big smile. Dr Prabhakar reached out her policeman's arm as he approached and held it at a point a few inches from the small of his back as she guided him through the group of tourists, making introductions. I couldn't hear but I could tell what was going on. 'This is Ben, our young ...' 'Yes, we're very lucky to have him on board ...' '... with us, how long is it now, Ben?' Poor bloke. Jumping through hoops.

I was enjoying this, sadistically, until I realised they were beginning to look across at me, first just one or two, then all of them, with Ben directing their attention; nodding as they looked first at him, then at me, then him again, then me again. With rising panic I braced myself for their approach. Ben, please. No, Ben. NO. (What's wrong with me? Why am I so frightened?) They seemed to lose interest in me for a minute, looking at a vent or light fitting, but then, all with their eyes on Ben, came forward in a rush. The group opened its flanks as it drew closer, adjusting itself to embrace the whole table setup. I saw that the Conrad guy was among them, with his unhappy face. He was heading for me – him and Dr Prabhakar and Hilary and some suits.

'So. You're our artist.' Conrad was no better at this than I was. Is he asking me a question or just describing me?

'Yes.'

'Good, good. I collect art.'

'And the patients are deriving a lot of benefit from this initiative.' That's Hilary. Her eyebrow ring looks very sore. Again I am able to help them out.

'Yes.'

'And this initiative is achieving its output objectives.'

'Yes.' I'm flying now. Go on. Ask me another. I've got all the answers. They seemed satisfied, however, and moved off to examine my students' work, leaning over their shoulders, a few whispered enquiries. Everyone nodded. Yes to everything. It's all fine here. That confirmed and noted, they were ready to move on. Dr Prabhakar led them out. I had not really caught her eye, or registered with her, and I was quite grateful about that. I guess I passed.

'What was that?' I asked Ben.

'Funding bodies,' said Ben.

31: I find out what's going on around here

LATER ON IN THE DAY ROOM, Ben was filling me in, bringing me up to strength on something that anyone with any sense would have figured out already.

'There's no money. Our funds have been withdrawn, at least until this court case is settled, and that could take years.'

Court case. I see. Colin helped me out a bit more.

'Don't you read the papers? No? Well, basically all the assets have been frozen because of the twins, Simon and Selina, disputing the circumstances of old man Norman making the endowment. They're saying, basically, that Dr Prabhakar got to him while he was not fully competent, mentally.' He rotated his finger next to his temple, indicating a loose screw. 'They're saying he had Alzheimer's.'

'He did have Alzheimer's,' said Ben. 'That's not in dispute. What the whole thing turns on is whether the condition was affecting his judgment at the precise moment of making the endowment. Alzheimer's sufferers can have episodes of temporary recovery, where they become quite lucid again for a bit. Admittedly, evidence about this is not the best kind of evidence because it tends to come from carers, who're usually the spouses or children, so there could be an element of wishful thinking there. It's probably just caused by natural fluctuations you would get in any-one's brain, healthy or sick, but they're going to try and argue in court that it was to do with the brain's plasticity. There's a popular theory about that.'

What happens, according to this theory, is that although the brain of an Alzheimer's sufferer is steadily dying, the functions of the dead parts can be taken over by other parts. The parts of the brain that aren't so busy, whose functions can easily be sacrificed, can be taken off one task and put onto something more important. So if, say, you lose the power of speech – some neural pathway that you need for speech has died – then another adjacent neural pathway that does needlework or something can be adapted to the more urgent task of speaking. In this way the brain can accommodate its losses, at least until that reserve neural pathway also is affected. The brain loses competencies, regains them, loses them again and so on, until there's nothing left in reserve, and dementia sets in.

Neural plasticity is a recognised phenomenon, particularly with stroke victims who can recover a lot of the capabilities that their brain damage has robbed them of, and also with some spinal injuries, and it is known to involve not only the rerouting of tasks through existing neural pathways, but also the growth of new 'processes' between neurons. Neurons can grow new connections. Add new wiring as well as adapt existing wiring. So the questions at issue in the court case will be: (a) Does neural plasticity counteract Alzheimer's symptoms? (b) Can the recovery of mental competence due to neural plasticity be said to be total, even if temporary? (c) Was Norman in such a stage of temporary remission when he made the endowment? Can a diagnosis be retrospective? Could anyone say for sure that Norman had Alzheimer's the day before the condition was diagnosed? Common sense says, Yes, of course, but the legal situation is more complicated.

(In another way there can be no doubt that the Institute owes its existence to Alzheimer's. Not a symptom of, but a result of the fear of. The Institute is all about Conrad

Norman hoping to buy a quick fix for his Alzheimer's. The desperate act of a frightened billionaire. That's why the whole setup is so lavish. Throwing a mountain of cash at the Grim Reaper.)

'So, there's no money,' I'm getting it now, 'and you're having to get funds from elsewhere.'

'Anywhere,' said Ben. 'That's all we do around here at the moment, and it's definitely not what I signed on for.'

'That's why I'm here, then.'

'A lot of funders like cultural output. Your position was a condition of this funding package we landed recently. Quite a small one, but beggars can't be choosers. Actually we've found it's a good way of attracting other funding. There are certain hoops you've got to jump through. They're never very happy about funding just scientific research. Not here, anyway. In America it's easier. I could have gone to Santa Barbara but this place looked so promising at first. It was supposed to be that you could do any kind of research you wanted – from neurobiology to neuropsychology – and have all the funding and facilities you needed. Too good to be true.'

'Didn't Conrad Norman want you to concentrate on Alzheimer's?'

'Yes, but the whole thing was set up so quickly that there was never anything very clear on paper about that. Just a commitment to research Alzheimer's with no conditions about how much of our resources we should devote to it. And Nancy knew that Norman's Alzheimer's would be advanced enough by the time we were up and running that he wouldn't know the difference. Actually it was quite a rapid deterioration. He was dead before the Institute opened.'

'I'm just window dressing, aren't I?' I'm catching on.

'You're the show pony. Actually it did really well today. I think they liked it. Nancy'll be quite pleased.'

I'm not sure what I feel about this. I'm here only because, to certain parties, it makes the place look good. And it could be anyone really. It's just the title or job description 'artist' they are after. On reflection I find that I don't mind it at all. I can't recall the last time I felt so sure of my role in life. I'm cosmetic.

'Doesn't Conrad Junior want the money back, as well?'

'I think he does but he feels bad about it so he's trying to help with alternative funding. He does have all these contacts, just from school and university he knows a lot of important people. I'm not really sure what Conrad wants, to be honest, but we need him on our side so we try to keep him happy – getting him on all these panels and committees. And that job for his girlfriend.'

'Girlfriend?'

'Reception.'

Thinking about the situation as it was being revealed to me, I was getting a sense of definitely increasing authority. I sought compliments to amplify this newly discovered sense of worth. 'Nancy liked it, you think? Dr Prabhakar.'

'We did do these patient activities sessions, with a lot of patients from neurology and psychiatry and geriatrics downstairs, but it didn't really work.'

'I'll say it didn't work. I saw one. When Michelle was showing us round, before the interviews.'

'Oh, that's right. You were there one day when we'd got all those patients in, and then we never had anybody who had any idea how to use the craft things. The looms and potter's wheels and things. Anyway, it's not because of that. It's to do with hospital politics. The neurology department hate us because they're supposed to refer all their interesting patients to us. Hospital administration love us because it's good for the hospital's profile. Quite prestigious. So the neurologists downstairs were being leaned on. Also we've got all this new equipment. Did have, anyway.'

'Did have?'

'We have *six* MRI scanners. Six! And then we didn't have any radiographers to operate them. Couldn't afford them, so five scanners will probably have to be sent back now.' (That would be why that loom and the pottery stuff and so on have disappeared already.) 'The only money around now is basic running costs. I'm only here because of out-sourced funding. All the money goes on maintenance. You know they repaint the entire Institute every three months? New carpets every six months. The twins want to keep the premises in good repair because they'll never be able to recoup the cost of doing it up like this.'

I looked across the Day Room and noticed that the balcony had been cleaned up, and there were potted plants out there.

'I heard they were thinking of turning it into a hotel,' said Colin, 'or a health club. Oh look, there he is. What a character.' Stick was juggling again, just for Emily. Twelve oranges. If Colin could see the fucking expression on Stick's face, he wouldn't think he was a character. He'd think he was a dick. But I'm not so bothered now. I feel some advantage has been gained now that I understand my role here.

I put my mind to the business at hand as artist in residence of the NNI and returned to the Activities Room to examine my students' work. Colin had been gathering everyone's work together, self-appointed class monitor, and he'd arranged it in a pile on the table. I had been very curious to see what Emily would do, and was pleased to find her drawing at the top of the pile, signed 'Emily'. It was head girl standard work. Very neat and, so far as I could tell, very exact. I couldn't tell how accurate it was because Ben had taken the brains back to his office; he was scared they'd get nicked or something. Emily's picture looked to me almost like a textbook illustration. The line was workmanlike. Nothing fancy or expressive, and no sign of anything having been rubbed out. It wasn't what I would have guessed she'd do at all. I was half expecting to see the borders decorated with flowers and kittens.

I looked through the rest of the pile. Some of it, like Colin's, was OK in a pedestrian sort of way. The Blind Woman still hadn't got anywhere. Actually I had to admit Stick's fucking dragon was the best. He'd got hold of all my defunct felt pens and crayons and his was the kind of uninhibited 'psychotic' regurgitation of imagery – swastikas, eyes, knives, etc. – that art therapists and 'Outsider Art' fans love to see. It's actually a style a lot of young artists have adopted lately. I wondered if Stick really was after Emily. It's possible I'm the only person in the world who would see someone so hopelessly impaired, so hospitalised, as a potential sexual partner. I surely am the only man alive, outside the constituency of internet cruising nonces, who could possibly entertain the notion of having a relationship with someone like that. Fall in love with her, and become convinced she can love me back. I'm not in control, am I.

I'm beginning to see the need for me to fucking GET A GRIP here, and concentrate on the two important matters at hand: my new role as the funding-friendly art therapy face of the NNI; and the new development in my career, as an artist who does art, somehow, about neuroscience. The manner of this 'about-ness' doesn't need to be made explicit. It can be about neuroscience without really having anything to say on the subject. I knew this from having read countless press releases for exhibitions 'dealing with' or 'addressing', for example, questions of female identity or of cultural difference. These issues, having been addressed or dealt with, remain pretty much there, and unchanged.

The main thing I have to do here is think of something about brains that I can put in an art gallery, that people who go to art galleries are going to like. First, of course, my dealer has to like it, and believe there's a market for it, otherwise he's not going to show it in his gallery. I'm a painter but I can certainly knock the painting on the head for a bit. I've got plenty of them there in storage if anyone wants one. This new departure is just what my career needs. It's needed it for at least fourteen months – since the last time anyone was persuaded to part with cash for one of my paintings. My work as artist in residence will be preparatory research for this reinvention of myself. And it's going to pay off with Emily, I'm sure. I need to communicate with her on some other level, unmediated and instantaneous, because first impressions are the only kind she can ever have. I've got to exude something. Good vibes. A feel-good factor, like a kind of spiritual aftershave. Positivity pheromones have got to be the way forward with a creature as primal and immaculate as Emily. It couldn't hurt if I learned how to juggle a bit as well.

32: another private view

I RAISED THE SUBJECT of this new departure of mine with my dealer next time I saw him, at an opening at his gallery: FRESH!, the gallery that represents me. Tina and Karl were having their debut show there that night and the place was packed, a big hit already. I'd seen the piece, a video installation, on the way in. The thing only lasted thirty seconds. They'd taken a small section from the footage of Kennedy's assassination – the part where the bullet hits and a hinged flap of skull opens up at the back of his head – slowed it down, and added some CGI so that it appeared as though Kennedy's head was hatching a fluffy yellow chick. The chick taps its way out of the President's skull, pauses to look about, then hops onto the back of the car seat. I watched it through a few times, it was on a loop, to make sure I'd seen the whole show, and then went looking for my dealer. I made slow progress, the place really was rammed, finding him eventually at a spot not far from where I was when I first started to look.

'GREAT SHOW,' I hollered.

'GREAT SHOW,' he hollered back. I had established contact and rapport.

'I was thinking about neuroscience again. You know. What we were talking about the other night.'

'Great title,' he said. He was thinking farther ahead with the project than I'd expected. 'Neuroscience' would be a great title, but we hadn't even discussed what the show would have in it yet. I still had my research to do. And I'd have liked to discuss other possible titles for the show. 'Art and Science' maybe. 'Vision and Memory' was another idea I liked. Our conversation got sidelined as people came up to kiss my dealer and congratulate him, while I stood and smiled; then it got postponed as more fans filled the gap between me and him, and I was out of earshot.

I found myself gratefully in conversation with my 'friend', telling him all about my new project. I was distracted only slightly by the film crew, nudging their equipment into the remaining gaps between gallery-goers. 'Don't worry about them. They're doing me for Swedish TV at the moment. Just carry on as normal. What were you saying?'

'Neuroscience,' I said.

'Oh yeah. Great title.' Everyone seems to know about it already. That made sense. My dealer's very proactive once he gets his teeth into a project. He's probably been telling everyone about it. A little prematurely for my liking, but I can't deny I'm pleased he's so much behind the idea.

I discovered, quite a lot later, having dug myself in very deep talking about my forthcoming show – probably called 'Neuroscience', but that's not really settled yet – that *this* show is called 'Neuroscience'. I'm already at a show called 'Neuroscience'.

Luckily I was able to resist the impulse to accuse anyone of plagiarism long enough to do a few calculations – How long does it take to get a show publicised? How far in advance of the opening do you need to get the cards printed and sent? – and review our conversations of the other night. Of course. It was always going to be called 'Neuroscience'. That's what we'd all been talking about, a lot of the time anyway. I realised that my memories of that night had been skewed by the assumption that we were talking about me the whole time. Now certain exchanges, apparent misunderstandings on their part, were retrieved and freshly comprehended. Crucial ambiguities in the use of the word 'you': 'you could', meaning not 'I could' but 'one could'. *One* could fake a seizure, or do a sculpture of a giant brain. I wished I had bothered to read the press release, or even look at the invite card. I need to stay on top of these things a bit more.

A later reassessment of this state of affairs, at home drinking gin from the giant, optic-sized bottle I keep, saw me through from a deep sense of humiliated reversal to a new resolve. My show about neuroscience wouldn't just be *called* 'Neuroscience'. It would be *about* neuroscience. My role, my position at the Institute, would be the crucible and the launching pad for my reinvention. I would research my subject thoroughly. Really get to know my patients. (I'm almost a doctor now, I decide, after a few tumblers of gin.)

From now on I'm going to be paying attention. I want to see the world through their eyes. What's it like for the Blind Couple? How does Colin really feel? Or the Scratching Man, or the Phineas Gage guy? And Stick. What's his fucking problem? What does it feel like to have Alzheimer's, or Parkinson's? Ben says music can cure the symptoms of Parkinson's, but only for as long as the music is actually playing. And I suppose with Alzheimer's you feel it most when you're not suffering its most extreme symptoms, and you can see what's happening to you. What's aphasia like? How does the world seem to someone with Wernicke's aphasia, where part of the condition is that you don't know you've got it? How does it feel to forget everything all the time? How does Emily feel?

33: the soul

THE NEXT FEW DAYS were spent marshalling the tools of my new vocation, as therapist and researcher. I got another cheque out of Michelle without too much difficulty. I bought some pencils and paper. I bought some books on the subject. Most of these began, I noticed, with an apology; an admission of the provisional and fragmentary state of brain science, even in regard to some quite basic stuff. For instance, I've sometimes wondered how quick are the effects of decapitation? but nobody knows. This I found quite encouraging. Ben had already told me it's a newish science. Closer examination of my small new library of popular science and textbooks got me scared, though. New sciences are still pretty fucking complicated. But Ben could fill me in on anything I might be unclear on. He'd enjoy that. I looked through my books for points of easy access, recognising things here and there that Ben had already told me about.

I looked up the hippocampus, expecting, crazily, to find an illustration somehow depicting Emily. Perhaps a section through her head with the missing parts arrowed or coloured in. They could show her standing naked, not a woman but an example of a woman, medically nude, with the sides of her head opened out to reveal her debilitating losses. The hippocampus is so called because *hippocampus* is Greek for 'seahorse', and a seahorse is what this part of the brain is supposed to resemble. I couldn't see it myself. It looked nothing like a seahorse, but I suppose early anatomists would seize on any fancied resemblance to

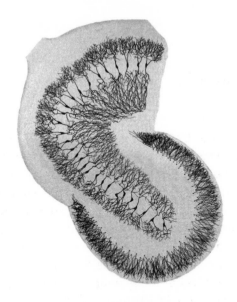

anything of the various bits of undifferentiated offal and gore they were trying to sort through. The hippocampus is one of the better understood parts of the brain, but it's still quite sketchy. One thing they do know is that it's a must-have piece of equipment if you want to be able to remember your life. It does something which is a necessary preparation for any information prior to its being stored elsewhere in the brain, as a memory (a bit like RAM you want to think, even whilst observing due caution about computer comparisons). It doesn't seem to be involved in retaining memories of skills acquired. If you've got a faulty hippocampus and you learn how to ride a bike at the same time as learning that it's called 'a bike', you'll still know how to ride the bike even though you can no longer recall what the thing is called. It also has something to do with spatial memory – directions.

Another baffling simile from those early anatomists is with the pineal gland. It's meant to look like a pine cone. It was thought by Descartes to be the seat of consciousness. Repository of the soul. He probably thought that because it's very small, and because he mistakenly believed that it's the only part of the brain there's only one of. And it's in the middle, more or less. Its smallness would help him out with the logic of his view that the soul, or consciousness, is a thing of the unextended world, and ought, therefore, not to be seated anywhere at all in space. There is no space in the unextended. That's what 'unextended' means. A small thing is in space, but not as much, you want to think, as a big thing.

Its singleness would support the idea that the soul is indivisible. It ought, as an abstract thing, to be able to be in two places at once, since it's really nowhere, but equally if it is anywhere at all it should be somewhere suiting its atomic uniqueness and authority. The seat of consciousness would be like a tiny throne, or maybe a pilot's seat, in the middle of your head. One feels intuitively that the place where the real YOU can be found is the head, maybe because the brain is in there, but more likely because the eyes and ears are there.

It does seem that that basic hunch of Descartes' is still being adhered to. We still want to think the soul is somewhere behind the eyes. I don't doubt it when I look into Emily's eyes. There is most definitely something there, even with so many of the vital components of selfhood having been deducted – memories and plans, continuity. There is enough there to fall in love with, and that is capable of loving you back. The loss of her hippocampi has ruined her ability to lay down new memories. She has lost the capacity to form 'episodic memories'. She is 'anosognosic', too. That is, she shows no awareness of her loss. Her world is complete to her. Or at least, for her sake, I hope it is. She must know something's up. Surely she has some inkling that things are not as they should be. I think I should be the one to level with her – reveal to her the full facts of a situation she must at least suspect, and she will tumble into my arms, shocked of course, but grateful to have been treated with the candour and respect she deserves as an adult woman. Then I'll be in there.

Unwilling to embark on anything like an organised program of self-education, I spend a lot of time 'researching' the same way a 1950s schoolboy would research sex with the aid of a dictionary, or a hypochondriac seeks explanations for a particular rash or swelling in the library's medical section. In this way I discover, among other things, that my lack of a head for figures – and it really is bad: I can't sing 'Ten Green Bottles' because it involves counting backwards from ten and I always get lost in the middle – is in fact a condition, called dyscalculia. There's nothing I can do about it. It may be related to my lack of a sense of direction. Or I may lack a sense of direction because I retain less than other people of an obsolete ability to sense electromagnetic fields. It's possible that all members of our species had this ability until quite recently in our evolution, but that now it is no longer selected for by the demands of our lifestyle, and it has almost disappeared. Birds have it, but we don't need it any more, because we no longer forage or migrate overland like Cro-Magnons or Neanderthals. If this is true, it means I'm slightly more highly evolved than other people, and must, therefore, refer to my London *A to Z* constantly.

Between research sessions, with a cup of tea or gin at my elbow, I also put in quite a lot of time trying to develop my juggling skills. I find that I have even less natural aptitude for juggling than for arithmetic. I should have bought a whole load of oranges to begin with, instead of purchasing them and juicing them against the walls and ceilings one by one, but after a few days and a few domestic breakages, lightbulbs and things, I sort of had it. I could do it successfully about one time in three. The orange is balanced on the right elbow. The forearm snaps forward and the cupped right hand describes a short arc at a speed slightly greater than that of the forward-propelled orange, so that it makes a rendezvous with the orange at the point of its greatest extension. The orange slaps neatly into the hand, which immediately rotates and opens to present the orange on the flattened palm.

34: another private view

'HEY, SUSAN! CAN I BUM A FAG?' Bum a fag? I *never* use that expression (I'm not some trust-fund boy who wants everyone to think he's working class). The reason for this forced matiness was that Susan was looking pretty fucking good, standing there outside the Sustainable Art Co., smoking a cigarette with her equally intimidating friend. If Susan had looked this good the first time I saw her, in the office at FRESH!, I doubt I'd have had the nerve to talk to her. She was their new intern at the time, and she was looking distressed because she'd been given the job of sorting out some administrative tangle no one in the office would take responsibility for. She was a recent graduate from Goldsmith's and seemed to have got out of her depth already. All the other staff were ignoring her as she sat blinking at the gibberish on her computer screen; and I was feeling pretty good about myself just then, because I was a recent addition to the FRESH! stable – all promise and potential. I went over and had a little chat and a joke with her. I expected her to be grateful and she *really* was. Plump little thing she was then. As it turned out it wasn't that long before my standing with the gallery began to slip (poor sales performance), but it was some time before Susan realised that was happening. Two years. We went out for two years, almost to the day.

Puffing on an American Spirit, with one eye half closed, she turned and looked at me, as if trying to put a name to the face. It had been a while since those drunken phone calls of mine and I sort of hoped she'd forgotten about that; or perhaps that she'd come to regard it as some sort of lapse. (I know. Why should she?) Her friend, similarly dressed, also turned to look, in a way that made me feel even less welcome.

'Oh. Hi,' said Susan. She took a packet of cigarettes out of her bag and handed it to me.

'Cheers.' I took one and lit it. 'These are healthier than Bensons.' I said that because (a) I wanted to let them know that I did actually have some cigarettes; I was just exercising choice here, and (b) I wanted to say something I knew Susan would agree with: she thinks American Spirit don't give you cancer.

'So ... what d'you think?' I was talking about the show we'd all just seen. I said it looking at Susan but quickly turned to her friend as if it was her I'd been addressing in the first place. 'What d'you reckon—?'

'Polly.'

'What d'you reckon, Polly?'

'Well, it's all just that whole thing, isn't it?'

I looked at her, and blinked. I'd been hoping for a little bit more than that. But that was it, so I nodded slowly. 'Yuh. Uh-huh.' At this point Susan seemed to have decided I'd suffered enough for now, so she asked how my residency was going.

'That's going really, really great, actually. Really amazing.' (Executed with a bit more sparkle and pep, this could have been a perfectly acceptable private view conversation.) I wasn't going away, so Polly asked me something about myself.

'Are you an artist?'

'Yes – I am.' And then, to give it a bit more beef, 'I'm with FRESH!, actually.' She perked up then.

'Oh right. They're a really good gallery. Susan used to work there.'

'I know. That's how we first met.' Not *where* we first met, but *how* we first met. The 'how' implies a bit of history, and

Polly picked up on it. She respects Susan, so I've come up a peg or two. She wants to know more now.

'What's your work like?'

I hate being asked that. All artists hate that question, because: (a) you feel they ought to know, and (b) it means you've got to describe it, and you're never quite sure how to pitch your description. With relatives and other non-professionals they just want to know if you do portraits, or landscapes, or weird stuff. But with Polly – who knows where she's coming from? What agenda is she bringing to this? She might be one of those people who think all painters are lickspittles and morons. I had a go at describing my work, and that seemed to deal with the subject adequately as far as Polly was concerned.

'Ah,' she said, 'I don't know it.'

'So...,' I said, 'are you two about to leave, or d'you fancy going to the pub for a quick drink?' Or are you going some-where better? *With* someone better. They looked at each other – What now? – and Susan took control.

'Well, there's not much to see in there, so OK.'

There was, in fact, nothing at all to see in there. The gallery was empty, because the artist (a well-known and respected figure) had come to an arrangement with a major collector whereby he would be paid not to produce any more contemporary art. They'd worked out a sort of tariff with a certain amount agreed for him not to do a drawing, another amount for him not to do a painting, and so on. (There were rumours that the whole project had run into difficulty because the artist was becoming more and more negatively prolific, not producing bigger and bigger works of art, and the cost was getting out of hand.)

'What can I get you ladies?' (I'm getting worse now. I sound like somebody's dad.) Pints for everyone, and a packet of nuts for Polly. Then I had a really great idea. Why don't I ask Susan how *she's* getting on?

'I'm doing the Wallenstein curating course.' Evidently I should know what that is, but she remembered that I never know what things are, so she told me.

'They take twelve young curators from all over the world. They get eighteen thousand applications a year, apparently.' I liked that 'apparently', as if she hadn't checked. 'The next session is in Stockholm. Then it's ... where's the next session, Polly?'

'Moscow. Then it's Sydney, then it's Seoul.'

'Oh my God!' laughed Susan. 'Seoul!'

'Seoul!' laughed Polly. They both laughed, and I looked from one to the other with an ingratiating smirk on my face, prepared to get the joke. Obviously I wasn't supposed to get it. I had absolutely no idea what was going on. I did, more or less, understand what was meant by a curating course. The sort of curator they were training to be isn't like the grizzled old codger who catalogues museum stuff. Curators are a new breed of art world professional. They get things done in this business – organising shows and conferences and 'events', writing catalogue essays and reviews and press releases; sourcing funds; spending funds. Jetting about between biennials and art fairs and symposia and Kunsthalles and Kunstvereins, busy busy busy.

I told Polly a bit about my residency at the Norman Neurological Institute. (Curators love residencies because they engage with the social. It's a chance for artists to get out there and meet real people, and tell them where they're going wrong.) I told her about Emily (trying, I guess, to make Susan jealous: not a flicker), and about my Drawing Workshops ('Workshop' sounds better than 'Classes'), and about Conrad Norman, who's some kind of squillionaire, and I've met him, twice.

'I know the collection,' said Susan. I'd actually forgotten Conrad had said he collected art. Susan knows all about it, though. In fact she's got a file on it. She's got files on all the major collectors.

'What's he like?' she asked.

'Rich and lonely.' I was repeating Colin's assessment here.

'Ah,' she said (and you could see that bit of information being stored away somewhere; a mental file marked 'Potentially Useful').

Feeling a bit more sure of myself (and, weirdly, having half forgotten that me and Susan used to go out, and that I was pining for her), I told them all about my idea for some sort of show. My curating project. I had been going to call it 'Neuroscience', but then Tina and Karl nicked my idea, so now I'm kicking a few other ideas around. Its exact form isn't really settled yet, but I know it's going to involve the Institute in some way, and the patients, in some way, and I've already opened discussions with my dealer at FRESH! about the whole thing. Then I started to tell them about neurons, and Phineas Gage, and agnosia – but their interest seemed to tail off again.

'Well, I'm really glad you're doing well,' said Susan. They left me then.

'Oh. You two off?'

'We've got this thing.' As she stood up she reached into her bag and pulled out a private view card.

'Here. You might be interested in this. It's a friend of Conrad Norman's. I think it's an old schoolmate of his.'

'Oh, right, cheers. Will you be there?'

'I shouldn't think so.'

'Oh, OK. Bye, then.'

'Bye.'

35: anterograde amnesia – Emily's diary

I SAW STICK ON MY WAY in to Gray's for the next Drawing Workshop. (It's a 'Workshop' now.) I was on a walkway, arriving at the hospital by yet another unfamiliar route, but in no great hurry because I'd allowed myself plenty of extra time so I could talk to Ben. Looking down I could see Stick in a hole. There are always a few archaeology sites dotted about the place at Gray's because of the constant renewal and rebuilding of the place. The developers always have to allow the archaeologists to look at a site before it's filled with a new centre or admin block, because this part of London has been inhabited for so long, but there haven't been any spectacular finds. Mostly thousands of clay pipes and animal bones and pottery shards. No golden shields. If they're lucky they find the post holes from an Iron Age hut or, if they dig deeper, the tooth of an extinct shark.

Stick was in this hole with a lot of other crusties, wearing a yellow hardhat atop his stupid pineapple head. I couldn't see what he was doing but he seemed to be doing it at an uncharacteristically measured pace. I wondered about the need for a hardhat on an archaeology site where there is, almost by definition, nothing above you. They can't have that many accidents on archaeological digs, surely. Maybe they get the odd miniature landslide or cave-in. At any rate it meant that Stick would not be bothering me today. This pleased me a lot. I felt readier than ever to do my job and pursue my research.

My mood was improved further by the sight that greeted me as I stepped out of the lift: Dr Prabhakar talking sternly to the receptionist, who looked as if she'd just been slapped. It wouldn't surprise me if she actually had been slapped. She's a tough woman, Dr Prabhakar.

I was still smiling about that when I found Ben, who took me to see my new studio; one of the Guest Rooms that's not being used. (Actually none of the Guest Rooms are being used at the moment apart from the one Emily occupies.)

Ben knocked on her door – Guest Room 1. 'I've just got to speak to Emily for a minute first.'

Emily answered almost immediately, as if she'd been sitting right by the door waiting. 'Yes,' she said. She said it not as a formality but as an affirmation. YES. Whatever it is, I'm in. She looked fantastic, with her hair still wet, but (alas) fully clothed.

'Hello, I'm Ben. I've come to see you today.'

'Come in, Ben. This is my room. Sit down anywhere. I've just been washing my hair.' I wasn't sure if I was supposed to go in too, but Ben seemed to expect me to follow him, and I entered her room, with its girl smells. Everything clean and nice.

'How are you today, Emily?' he asked.

'I'm very well, thanks. Actually ... this is a bit embarrassing. I'm not quite sure about something. I'm all at sixes and sevens today. It's just ...'

'Go on ...' Ben's smile was reassuring.

'This is my room, isn't it?'

'Yes.'

'Did I make an appointment with you? I'm not sure. What have you come about? Sorry ... it's just I'm a bit disorganised today.'

'I'm a doctor, Emily. I've come to see you today because you've been having some problems with your memory.'

'Oh, right. I knew it was something like that.'

'We've been doing a sort of test together. I've been asking you to keep a diary.'

I thought I could discern a moment's panic before she rallied, and furrowed her brow, her head tilted, trying to recall something that had momentarily slipped her mind.

'Test. Yes. I'm usually very good at tests and exams.'

Ben prompted her gently, 'I think I saw you put it in your desk drawer. Over there.'

Emily tried to open the drawer.

'Oh, is it locked?' Ben seemed puzzled. 'Is the key not there? Hang on. I've got the same sort of desk.' He made a show of searching his pockets, and found a small key.

'There you go.'

She unlocked the drawer and handed the key back. I suspected for a second this was going to be a trick, and there was no diary there, but she opened the drawer matter-of-factly and took out a standard stationer's diary, with the word DIARY embossed on the cover in gold, but no date.

'Ah!' she said – 'I'd probably forget my own head if it wasn't screwed on!'

'Don't open it just yet, Emily. This is part of the test.'

'OK, fine.' She looked at him, all attention. Tests. Yes. She likes tests.

'What I want you to do is the same thing we've been doing already ...' – Emily wavered a bit – 'which is this. I want you to open the diary at the next empty page – see the bookmark, there – and write an entry for today. Doesn't have to be anything much. Just anything that comes into your head about today ... a paragraph or so. But don't look at any of your previous entries. OK?'

'Just write anything.' She seemed a bit disappointed. 'That's it? That's the test?' She smiled at Ben, humouring him.

'I want you to make the entry in your diary, and then as soon as you're finished put the diary back in the drawer.'

'Yes, OK, fine.' She was getting irritated. Doctors. Christ.

'We're just going to do something now. Back in twenty minutes or so.'

We left with Emily looking at us incredulously, amazed now at our stupidity. Ben took me to see my allotted space, my studio, at the other end of the corridor. Guest Room 23.

'Emily likes to listen to music sometimes, so I've put you up here in case it disturbs you.' There's a laugh. I guess Ben has quaint ideas about artists and the conditions conducive to their creativity. Northern light and a Chopin piano sonata as mood music. In Hackney I've had complaints from my car mechanic neighbours about the volume of my music. I like to work late at night, listening to, for example, Napalm Death, Godflesh or, my all-time favourites, Ultimate God of Terminal Death. And I never listen to music on my iPod because (a) I haven't got one, and (b) I wouldn't use it if I did because I always think someone's going to sneak up behind me. I could see I was going to have to adjust some of my working practices. But that was on the cards anyway, now that my work is going to involve research, and study. Not a headlong charge into a giant canvas, wearing big boots, and completely covered in paint.

My room was identical to Emily's. They're all the same. They'd even made up the bed for me. I stood in the middle of the room and looked about me, beginning with the ceiling (why do we do that? You know there's never anything up there) and finishing my brief visual tour at the desk. I went over and put some books down. My own personal touch.

'You've been doing some reading, then,' said Ben. He had a look through my beginner's guides and introductions to the neurosciences, most of them dreck apparently, but one he tapped with his finger, approvingly.

'That's a very good introductory work. I still look at it myself occasionally. The guy who wrote it taught me. Amazing guy.'

I hadn't even looked at that one yet so I picked it up and flicked through to the author's photo at the back, and I saw that the guy who'd written it was the man with the gay biker outfit and outrageous moustache. Owen Madden.

'I recognise him. He was that guy the other day with Dr Prabhakar. The one who looks like a baddy from Tintin. Why doesn't he shave that fucking tache off?'

'He's actually done some very exciting work.' Ben made me feel ashamed of my facetiousness. I must learn to look beyond the moustache. I tried to redeem myself by asking about the nature of this work. Ben, previously so generous with his explanations – in layman's terms; spoon feeding me – was terse now. 'Neurogenesis. With Dr Prabhakar.' I didn't dare ask what that is. I'd try and look it up later, or ask him again when his mood improved. In fact his mood improved almost immediately. I guess Ben doesn't stay angry with anyone for long. He showed me stuff in my room – or studio, or study, or laboratory. Taps in the bathroom. Light switches here. Very good. I was about to ask him about 'neurogenesis' when he looked at his watch. 'Twenty minutes. We'll go and see how Emily's getting along.'

When we knocked, and she answered, it was the same routine. The immediate opening of the door, the energetic 'Yes!' Ben introduced himself again and we were invited in.

'So – how are you feeling then, Emily?'

'Oh, fine thanks. Very well.'

'Good, good. I've come to see how you got on. We've been doing a little experiment. A little test.' Again that discomfited look, wrong-footed, and the quick recovery.

'Yes, well, I enjoy tests. Sorry, could you just …? It seems to have slipped my mind. Did you make an appointment?'

'Well, I just asked you to make an entry in your diary. Nothing personal or anything. Just a few thoughts. Whatever came into your head.'

'Of course, Yes. I'm not sure ...' struggling again now. She began fiddling with her long hair (her copper-coloured hair), scoping the room for clues.

'Perhaps you put it in your desk drawer?'

Of course she had. She'd forget her own head if it wasn't screwed on. Ben asked her to open the diary at the latest entry, and wondered if she'd mind reading it aloud for us.

She complied with a sigh (her sighs), sceptical and a little exasperated. '27th October. This is the first time I've ever been here. I am alive for the very first time. All of this is new. I am sitting—' she stopped and looked up at us blankly, and then continued, '—I am sitting in this room which I know is my room for the very first time and I am writing out my plans for this new day. I know this is my room where I live and have a bed a table and two chairs. One chair is for sitting at this table and the other one is an armchair. I am writing my plans for when I leave this room later on today.'

She looked at us shrewdly, getting ready to see the joke. 'This is supposed to be my diary, is it?'

'It *is* your diary, Emily. You see the reason we've been doing these tests is because you've been having some problems with your memory.'

She thought for a moment. 'Yes, I know it's my diary. I recognise it now ... I think maybe ... I do seem to be having problems remembering things at the moment. I'm glad you mentioned that. You're a neurologist, aren't you?'

'That's right. Now I wonder if you'd mind doing something else for me. Would you just open the diary at random, any page, and read it out for me?'

'Sure...' She opened the diary and looked. She stared for a moment, frowned, and flicked to another page. She tried a few more. 'They all seem to be the same.' She turned a few more pages. She closed the diary and then opened it at the beginning, and began turning the pages slowly, her manner reminding me bizarrely of a man I saw once examining a porn magazine in the newsagents. She got about half way through, and closed the diary, and sat with it on her lap, her palms pressing on the cover. Her face looked older again, the way it had looked when she was concentrating on her drawing. Something occurred to her, and she opened the diary at the first page again, checked something, turned to the most recent entry, checked that. 'That's about two years I've been like this. Shit.'

I'd have been shocked to hear Emily say 'shit' a few a minutes previously, but it sounded quite consistent now with her sudden maturity. She was all grown up now, all of a sudden. She looked at Ben through narrowed eyes. 'Do you come here every day? I've been doing this every day?'

'Most days, yes.'

She stood up, so quickly it made me jump (Ben didn't move) and began to pace the room, raising her arms and letting them slap to her sides, stamping, and muttering, and swearing. Then she went and sat at the end of her bed, and cried, and cried, and cried. When her sobs had subsided enough, down to a hiccuping snivel, Ben told her something encouraging.

'Emily, listen to me. We're seeing definite signs of improvement. A few months ago you wouldn't have recognised that diary, even when I told you where to find it. In the drawer. D'you see, Emily? You needed to be reminded, but once you had been reminded you knew it was yours. You didn't need to be told about it all over again. That's a definite improvement.'

'Yes.' She blew her nose loudly, her face all red and puffy, and childlike again. She tried a brave little smile. Oh Emily.

She blinked at us for a few moments, and then seemed to remember her two years, and started to cry again. Ben just sat and watched, a benign, disinterested presence. He gave it a few minutes and then began to talk abstractedly, as if he was thinking aloud, about the clear signs of improvement we're beginning to see; a distinct upturn. He seemed to be carefully avoiding specifics at first, but then began to steer his monologue towards the business at hand. 'And of course there's Emily's drawing, which I understand is going very well. And you enjoy drawing, don't you, Emily? And she enjoys drawing ...' he seemed to be addressing me now, '... you've seen her work of course. You should see Emily's work. It shows a lot of promise. Emily's drawing. And, actually,' he checked his watch, 'it's nearly time now, isn't it? It's about time for you and Emily to go to the Activities Room for the Drawing Workshop. Did you forget?' He was looking right at me and his eyes widened a bit to indicate that, yes, it's your cue. You're on.

'Oh, yes. I completely forgot. I'd forget my own head if it wasn't screwed on!'

That was good. Ben continued.

'He's just as bad as you, Emily! What a pair.' What a thrilling thought. She and me. 'Did you forget about your drawing class? You always look forward to them so much.'

'It completely slipped my mind.' She's forgotten what she was crying about now.

'Well, he's got some drawing materials for you.'

I held up a drawing pad and pencil, hitting my cue again. Ben stood and moved across the room. 'Come along, Emily.' He opened the door for her, and she passed him, smiling a thank you, wiping her nose. 'I think I'm getting a cold ... runny nose.'

'See you there then, Emily. Activities Room.'

We stood in the corridor and watched her go. 'Is she alright to find it on her own?' I asked.

'Yes, she's fine. I'll just go and lock that drawer.' I wasn't fine. I followed her: shaken; moved; watching her arse for a few steps before trotting up beside her.

'Mind if I tag along? I keep getting lost around here.'

She seemed perfectly OK now. I realised, at this point, I had never actually really spoken to Emily before, and I didn't know what to say. I was keen to make a good impression now that normality had been restored, all brisk. It was difficult to find a way of talking that didn't involve making any explicit references to anything she would realise she had no recollection of. I couldn't ask her if she'd enjoyed that last class. Maybe that would be OK, though. She seemed to have some awareness that things slipped her mind occasionally. The gaps in her comprehension were explicable, and nothing to worry about. Where does she think we're going now? She knows we're going to a Drawing Workshop, but can't have any recollection of the one we've done already. It's possible she did some kind of amateur art class before her illness. That would explain her dull but competent work last time. And her purposefulness now. Her sense of continuity. She knows from the way Ben was talking about it that I'm something to do with it, and she probably has enough to guess that I'm not another student; I'm in charge somehow. I decided it was worth taking a small risk.

'I liked the drawing you did last time. I'll be interested to see what you come up with today.'

'Oh, thanks. What are we drawing today?'

'Same as last time. Brains.'

'Oh, I can draw brains.'

Emily's response seems immediate and natural even though she can't possibly recall having drawn a brain last time. She's got some kind of default mechanism in place that papers over the cracks in her internal account of events.

Like when you're in a group, all talking about a film you haven't seen, and you pretend you've seen it so as not to feel left out. You can easily fool everyone by picking up on what they've said already, and when you come up against some obvious gap you just say you were in the toilet when that bit happened, or something. That must be how those deluded conmen manage to get into hospitals and work there, for years sometimes, as doctors, when they don't know anything at all about medicine. Maybe just a few scraps of information picked up from reading or watching TV and confining their conversation to repetitions and generalities. Ignorance can easily pass itself off as humility or professional reticence. I've heard of some of these people actually performing operations. (Christ. How do I even know Ben's a real doctor?) Part of the gift for dissembling these impostors have is to do with their own deludedness. They must know that they're lying, but on another level they really think they're doctors. That's how all the great liars work. If they're confronted with clear and incontrovertible proof that they're lying, they feel wronged.

Emily's confident 'I can draw brains' is probably a defensive strategy, and at some level she must know that. (I'd lie more myself if I had anyone to lie to. 'Drinking? No. Well – just a couple.')

'You enjoy drawing, then?' I'm struggling already. I considered asking if she'd had any experience as a life model (it can't hurt; she'd forget it soon anyway), but I was put off by her air of head-girlish propriety and confidence.

Emily just smiled and nodded.

36: Ben conducts an experiment

THE ACTIVITIES ROOM WAS ALL READY when we got there, with three brains (different ones) set up on the tables, and most of the patients sitting at their places. A few missing – the Blind Couple, Stick – and some I didn't recognise. I asked Emily if she'd mind helping by handing out drawing materials to everyone. That way she knows I'm in charge. Colin came over – practically cantered – to help Emily help me, and he managed to elaborate and fuss the task in the way people do sometimes when they're getting older, chatting all the while. He seems to have a kind of paternal bond with Emily. (I'm sure it's paternal.) I hadn't noticed this before. I did a little sum in my head. She's, what, twenty-two?, twenty-three? And he's got to be in his late fifties. I couldn't figure it out exactly, but that's almost a big enough difference for him to be her grandpa. Of course he's going to feel protective towards her, especially as he feels his own powers fading. Colin, the great all-rounder. Probably a useful pub fighter in his day. Ben arrived late, and strangely dressed. He was wearing a blond wig and a shell suit. He was also walking oddly. All hunched and shuffling. He was looking up at Colin, through his curly fringe, as he took his time making his way across the room from the door to the tables. Colin looked at him. We all did.

'You'll have to do better than that, Ben, mate,' said Colin. Ben stood up straight, smiling, and I realised this must be part of some ongoing game, or joke, or experiment. Ben disguises everything but his face to see if Colin will recognise him. A pitiful effort. Even if he'd been wearing a mask, we'd all have recognised him. You can't disguise all that confidence and well-being. (Nor its reverse. You couldn't disguise it if you were unlucky and defeated.) Is that really the best he can do to test the limits of another person's perception? He's very bright, but maybe he lacks imagination. I could have come up with a better way of doing that, and I'm not even a scientist. Is that what neuroscientists really do all day – muck about? Or it might be just because things are slow around here at the moment, while they're trying to sort out their money problems. It had never occurred to me that something like brain science could involve practical jokes. I wondered why Colin seemed to enjoy it so much. Public schoolboys like practical jokes, and so do a lot of people in the building trades, but I knew Colin didn't. Probably he just likes Ben.

Having taken the wig off, and with the general hilarity subsided (Emily really laughed), Ben asked me to come and meet one of my students. 'You two should meet.' One of Ben's hidden agendas here, like taking me to Emily's room just now. This is Achromatopic Man. About Colin's age and size, but soft. His torso was like Colin's torso inverted, with all the breadth in the hip, not the shoulder. He was wearing a bow tie. He told me all about his deficit.

'Well, as Ben may have mentioned,' – he hadn't; go on – 'I've suffered a mild stroke, and this has had consequences, of course. I am now privileged to be the proud possessor of a condition known to all and sundry as "A-CHROMA-TOPSIA".' He made a big deal of enunciating the word, rolling the R in 'chroma', and pronouncing 'top' as 'DOP!', with a kind of rising yelp.

There's something typical Ben about this. What I see here is a very lonely guy, and I always try to avoid lonely people (possibly because I don't want to be tarred with the same brush). Ben just sees an interesting case. Achromatopic

Man is very keen to tell me all about it. Probably the only interesting thing that's ever happened to him.

'Achromatopsia is a form of colour-blindness. The fascinating thing about it is that it's not the usual type. It's quite exceptional. Trust me to be different!' He has an irritating way of talking. What his condition is, and in what way it's so unusual, he explained to me. It took nearly an hour. Ordinary colour-blindness is only partial, usually red–green, and it's caused by a problem with the cone receptors in the retina. Rods and cones. (I've heard of those.) Achromatopsia is total colour-blindness, and it's caused by brain damage somewhere at the back of the head. He tried to get me to touch the back of his head. I badly wanted to get away from him and I had to keep reminding myself of my new vocation. His breath was sour and he kept trying to touch my hand or my leg – but he *did* have an interesting condition.

There could be an idea for a show in this. 'Achromatopsia.' Great title. Also it struck me for the first time that although I am a visual artist, and vision is my trade, so to speak, I knew almost nothing about how it works. I suppose I felt that I had some kind of an intuitive grasp of what seeing really is, but, thinking about it now, examining the content of this putative 'grasp', I found that there really was nothing there beyond an ill-founded confidence. I was wholly ignorant of the subject of vision. What it is and how we do it.

37: how vision works

HOW VISION WORKS is quite surprising. Things you thought you knew or, at any rate, *felt* you knew, turn out to be wrong. It feels as if it all happens instantaneously and as a whole thing, but actually it's a process that takes time, and it's in bits. You get these diagrams in school human biology books where there's an eye shown in cross section from the side, and this eye has an upside-down miniature image of some-thing – a tree or a candle or something – projected onto the retina. So the impression given is that the eye is exactly like a camera obscura, and all the brain has to do is somehow turn the image right way up and then look at it. The brain, we are allowed to suppose, is just like a little man sitting in your head watching a screen with images on it. This idea is wrong in all sorts of ways, one of the main ones being that the eye doesn't collect images, whole and in full colour; it collects rather meagre scraps of information that the brain then uses to update or revise the 'internal model' of reality it has already stored. I'll get back to this.

The meagre scraps are collected by means of the retina. This is a sort of mat or sheet of cells – photoreceptor cells – which contain a chemical that reacts to light. This chemical reaction is then translated into the electrical and chemical language the brain will understand (a process called 'transduction'). This message goes from the retina into the brain through the optic nerve. The foundations for what will, at a later stage, become clear and conscious visual perception (an 'image') are established in the occipital cortex at the back of your skull. (That's why a heavy blow on the back of the head can cause blindness.) This is where the picture is roughed out. And here's one of the really counterintuitive things about vision. The information provided by the retina is sorted into abstract categories – form, colour and motion – and then each of these is dealt with separately along dedicated pathways and in their own dedicated areas. These are the V areas of the occipital cortex. V1 and V2 sort the raw material out (I'm simplifying a lot here) for the other V areas to deal with. V3 does form, V4 does colour and V5 does motion. We're not dealing with an image yet – we're dealing with the *properties* of an image, its basic components. This modular way of processing information is what computer people call 'parallel processing'.

Monet believed that the way seeing works is you see shapes and colours, and assigning identities and names to these blobs is a conscious thing you do after that, which we could choose not to do (and when painting, for example, a haystack, he was deliberately *not* noticing that it's a haystack). But we don't just see forms and colours, do we? We see things: cars and people and clouds and watches and thumbs and oranges – things that we can name and describe. To understand what happens beyond the V areas to make abstract properties like form and colour into coherent things, with identities and names, we need to go back to the eye and its capabilities.

As I said before, the retina doesn't collect images; it collects bits and pieces. There are two types of photoreceptor cells in the retina – rods and cones. Rods are like a wide aperture lens, specialised for collecting light across a largish area, so they are useful for vision in dim light. They are colour-blind. Cones are specialised for colour and fine detail. Rods and cones are not evenly distributed across the surface of the retina. The cones are mostly concentrated in a small area called the fovea. This means that only a very tiny

proportion of the visual field can be seen clearly and in colour. If you hold your arm out with your thumb up, it's about the size of your thumbnail. Tiny. This is quite surprising, because it normally seems like you can clearly see a lot more than that. So there must be something happening to *make* it seem like that. Two things, in fact: saccades and 'filling in'.

Saccades are tiny flickering eye movements. The eye flits about like a bumblebee taking little thumbnail-sized pieces of information every time it stops. Imagine going into a dark room with a Maglite torch, flicking it on and off a few times, and then having to describe the contents of the room. That's what you're doing all the time you look at things. 'Filling In' is the process by which these dots – these scattered jigsaw pieces – are joined up to make a picture. Images don't form in the eye but in the brain. Say you're looking at a table. The eye is capturing information that will allow you to surmise it is a table, but the eye itself still can't tell you it's a table, because the eye itself doesn't know anything. What has to happen is what's called a 'top-down' process. That is, the sense organ, the eye, furnishes these bits of information, the 'bottom-up' part of vision. The brain then interprets these bits, 'top down', and creates the picture of which they are most likely, given past experience, to be a part.

So, the image you can see is largely conjecture. The brain fills in the gaps between these thumbnail-sized spots of sensory information by drawing on past experience. A lot of what you see is actually memories. The so-called 'higher processing areas', beyond the V areas, are a storehouse of information about the kinds of things the eye is likely to encounter. First, general things about what you're seeing have to be established. Is it regular or wonky? Curved or straight? Moving or still? The brain's store of innumerable templates has to be searched to find a match for the data being offered, sifting down from the most general characteristics to more particular things. Having established that what you are looking at is disc-shaped (for example), the range of possible causes of this sense datum can include the moon, a plate, a ping-pong ball, a coin, a DVD, a cup seen from above, a hole drilled in a piece of wood, a Hula-Hoop, and so on and so on. When you are looking at things, you have to decode an array of these fragmentary clues of shape and colour and so on to determine, for example, is this, or is this not, a table? If the match is a poor one (perhaps other clues might indicate that it's too small to be a table, or too irregular, or even too squishy), then some other possibility must be tried out. It's a toy table, for example, or a sculpture, or a pouffe. You can only see things consciously, knowing that you are seeing something specific, *after* all that process has been gone through, and the brain has made up its mind about exactly what it is you're looking at.

The job of populating our visual world, without apparent effort – with so little sense of effort in fact that we think we're just passively registering things – actually involves an astonishing amount of to and fro between the brain and the eye. The brain has an encyclopedic store of possible things, and spatial relationships between things, plus a rational and economical set of rules for matching these possibilities to the bits of raw data it is offered, beginning with the general and ending with the particular. We don't see the world; we see what our brains can construct using raw and meagre sense data to update its own much richer 'internal model', like an archaeologist using a few shards and bones and ruins to reconstruct an entire civilisation. (Ben first explained this to me by saying it's a bit like predictive text: the brain completes images in a way that's analogous to your phone completing words. But having come up with this example to help me he then had to explain what predictive text was.) The world looks real and detailed because the brain is usually very, very, good at this.

38: interesting but unsettling

SOMEONE ONCE DESCRIBED the visual brain as a black box, with the sense organs being like peripheral plug-ins, and this mechanistic image conveys something of the disquiet all this can make you feel. When you look you seem to be in the light, but you're not; you're in your head. (In fact, you can tell it's not really a direct encounter with the light by rubbing your eyes in a dark room. You'll see flashes of 'light' because the neurons in your optic nerve will interpret any stimulation as light, even though it's just your fingers pushing it about.) Neuroscientists are fond of saying that the world is not coloured, because colour is just the subjective experience of differentiating between different wavelengths of electromagnetic radiation within the visible spectrum. Colour can be thought of as a way of colour-coding things where the brain has been obliged to invent colour in order to facilitate the colour-coding.

And another thing that is troubling about all this: the idea that things need to be recognised *before* they can be seen seems to imply that you could never see anything truly novel, which is very disturbing for me, being an artist. You'd never be able to see anything really new because if anything like that presented itself it couldn't find a match amongst the vocabulary of neural templates you have to apply to visual experiences, and so, I suppose, it would be invisible. It makes me think of the chimaera from Greek mythology. A fantastical creature with the head of a lion and the body and tail (I seem to remember) of a goat and a snake. (I think it has eagle's wings too, or maybe just eagle's talons.) The point is, it's fantastical but it's just a jumble of things we already knew about. Rather than adding to the world of possible things, it mixes up some that existed already. It's like a Bolshevik door handle or a flinty soufflé.

When you're an artist like me, you want to think you can come up with something the like of which nobody has ever seen. I think this is why my paintings are such a mess. I'm trying to approximate the primal soup conditions out of which entirely new visual life-forms could emerge. And the trouble is that this kind of mess is actually a recognisable style called Abstract Expressionism.

39: Ben was telling me something

I WOULD NEVER HAVE BOTHERED to find all that out if Ben hadn't introduced me to Achromatopic Man. He was teaching me something about why the world isn't coloured. Colours are added by the brain in visual processing to different wavelengths of light reflected from different objects so as to label them. Rather as if the brain had invented colour so as to be able to colour-code things, allowing us to tell unripe berries from ripe, or hot coals from cool. But saying that is merely to hint at the degree to which things we see aren't really there. They are mostly made of hypotheses: they are skilfully put-together guesses that mostly turn out to be correct. The main difference with colour is that these hypotheses can't be checked and either corroborated or refuted by other senses, particularly touch. So when you go to touch an hallucination, and find you can't, you can say with confidence that there's actually nothing there. But the hallucination of a red thing is, in a way, just as real as the redness of a tomato in your hand.

Monet's idea about the world being seen as coloured patches is a mixture of received scientific ideas (that must have had some currency at the time) and a wish for a kind of prescientific innocence. Making decisions about the type and identity of things is, according to this view, something conscious and deliberate, and it always happens *after* the pure act of seeing has occurred. (Whereas, in fact, and rather surprisingly, we decide what things are, and *then* we can see them.) Monet wanted the life of the senses and the categorising imperative of reason to be separate. Like thinking and feeling are supposed to be separate. The head and the heart. One of the things that makes the current view of how seeing works so difficult to take is that it rides roughshod over any such romantic distinctions. To see something at all, it turns out, is always to see it *as* something. Seeing is thinking. It involves a decision-making process, and nothing that hasn't been through that process can be seen. Indeterminate sensation is no sensation at all.

We know that what we see is made up of various different bits of information, processed along distinct neural pathways, but when you're actually seeing it doesn't seem at all like that, and we don't really know how that happens. It's called 'the binding problem'. How are all those bits bound together to form a seamless whole? Is it a gradual process, like the gathering plausibility of a well-told tale? Or is that sense of reality and contiguity some final addition to the assembled thing, like a stamp of authentication, or like putting a picture in a frame? Nobody knows.

I'm sure they're right, but contemporary theories about how vision works feel far from complete, because they don't seem to do justice to the sheer lavishness of the world I can see, with all its details, and all that lovely colour. Saying the world isn't coloured is something neuroscientists like to do, because colour is a feature that can't be verified or corroborated by any other sense. But to me, looking at it, the world is no less coloured than it is dark or light or striped or big or small or fizzy or fast; or anything else you can tell by looking.

Canaletto probably had a clearer idea of how seeing works, a hundred and fifty years before Monet. If you look closely at one of his scenes of Venice, you'll see that it's made up of a limited vocabulary of shorthand conventions. His way with crowds was especially brilliant. All the faces in one of his very convincing throngs are just dots of pink. And yet it seems to stir and hum like a crowd. It's the same with stonework, and waves, and clouds. His middle-distance figures, totally alive, are rendered with three or four calligraphic squiggles of colour. He probably had assistants whose job it was just to paint little pink dots all day.

40: it's not a problem

I SPENT A LONG TIME LISTENING to Achromatopic Man tell me all about his condition, and only interrupted him when he got onto the subject of his faith – what a comfort it is. (I knew he'd have a faith.) I asked if he missed seeing colours, and he said he coped (his faith), but also one effect of the condition is that you forget what colour is like. You know that you're colour-blind, but in another way you don't know, because it feels as if the world was always like that. You can't even imagine what it would be like to be colour sighted. I thought it was probably like trying to remember being happy when you're depressed, or being depressed when you're happy. You can recall how it made you behave but that behaviour is now inexplicable to you. It might as well have been someone else. Then again it must be quite sad in a way because, even though you don't really know what you're missing, you know you're definitely missing out on something – something that's generally agreed to be good. Colour.

I thanked him for his time, and telling me all about it (demonstrating, I felt, a commendable new compliance with accepted standards of professionalism and courtesy), and began to look at the work of the other students, giving tips and pointers here and there. I made sure to leave Emily till last. By the time I got round to her she had finished and was sitting with the drawing on the table in front of her, the pencil laid neatly beside it, her hands resting in her lap.

I couldn't think of anything to say about Emily's drawing. She'd been sitting facing a quite awkward three-quarter angle on a medial section of the brain, split front to back, which could have been made into an interestingly inscrutable image by a more gifted or imaginative person. Instead she had chosen to draw it as if seen in the standard textbook way, frontal view of the medial section, rather than in a way that acknowledged what was particular about her viewpoint.

41: another private view

'CAN I BUM A FAG, MATE?' asked Conrad. He was looking faintly nauseating, dressed entirely in slick black leather.

'A cigarette? Certainly, Conrad.'

We were standing outside an art gallery somewhere in West London, and for some reason I was being rather snotty with him. One of the points of my being there, after all, was to arse-lick, so God knows what I thought I was achieving with this attitude of mine (and I was wondering, not for the first time, just what the fuck *is* my problem?). I was lucky, though. Conrad didn't notice my pointed use of the word 'cigarette'. In fact, although Conrad knew he knew me, he didn't know how or from where he knew me (I imagine this is often the way of things with Conrad).

Another bit of luck was that Ben was there. I'd mentioned in passing that I was going to the private view of a show of paintings by an old school chum of Conrad's (Eton or Harrow), and Ben said that sounded like an idea, and did I mind if he tagged along? That suited me very well. Art galleries in Notting Hill belong to an art world that's almost entirely unconnected to the art world of Shoreditch. Different art, different personnel, different drinks, different everything.

Apart from trying to chat up Conrad (a long shot at best), my other reason for coming to this thing was the hope that Susan might be there, even though she'd said quite clearly that she wouldn't be. So, all things considered, Ben being along at least insured me against the strong possibility of another evening's isolation. Since it was obvious Conrad had no real notion of who I might be (perhaps we'd been at Eton together?), Ben wondered aloud how my Drawing Workshops had been going. My Drawing Workshops, at the Norman Neurological Institute. The NNI.

And so I said, 'Really great. Really, really great, actually.'

Something seemed to stir within Conrad then, and an idea formed. 'Aaahh. The Institute. Drawings. Uh huuh ...' He still couldn't place me exactly, so I reminded him of our short exchange when he'd come round on that guided tour with the funding bodies people.

'So,' I said, 'I gather you're a collector. In fact you told me so yourself at the Institute.' This was what I'd been hoping to talk to him about, and I was pleased with myself for having got to the point so quickly. I'd been wanting to say something about the possibility, since he was a collector, of him maybe collecting something by me; especially since we've got so much in common. I was prevented by the faint but unmistakable air of alarm that came over him the instant I mentioned him being a collector.

'Ah, well, this isn't a shopping trip today. I'm here to show a bit of support for an old mate. And, also, I bought the last exhibition he had here.' I think he must have thought that me and his old mate knew each other, us both being painters, and that I was trying to persuade him to buy the entire show – again. So my sales pitch about my own stuff had gone wrong already. That fuck-up took less than five minutes. I am terrible at this.

As we'd come to a dead end, Ben suggested we all go in and take a gander. Following Conrad through the door I took a good 'gander' at the blazon on the back of his squeaking black leather jacket. THE HELL FIRE CLUB it said, with fiery letters and skulls and whatnot. Once inside, I satisfied myself about three things: that although (1) Susan is nowhere to be seen (oh well), and (2) these paintings (in which the artist cack-handedly depicts his own martyrdom) are shit, there is (3) the fact that unlike private views in Shoreditch this one has uniformed waiters with trays of Champagne. They also had waitresses with trays of nostalgic nibbles – melon and Parma ham on a stick, mini-quiches and so on. The crowd, like the style of snacks, was redolent of times past – not just older than in Shoreditch, but actually elderly. I took two Champagne flutes (one for me and another for me, too) and went and joined Ben, who was standing seriously in front of the first painting nearest the door. He seemed to be planning to look at each one in order, consulting the relevant notes in the catalogue as he went. He was falling precisely in line with what other people seemed to be doing, copying the behaviour of a septuagenarian couple right next to him.

'Have you ever been to a private view before, Ben?'

'No, but it's exactly how I'd imagined.'

'I know. That's what's so weird about this private view. It's weirdly like how people imagine them.'

He seemed puzzled by this remark but, rather than pursue it, asked if I liked the painting we were stood in front of.

'Ben, it's shit. Obviously.'

'That's a bit of a swift judgment, isn't it? You've hardly even looked at it.'

'I don't need to look any more to be able to tell it's shit. I didn't even need to come in here to tell they're all shit. I could tell just from the guy's name. Public school boys never make good artists. They don't have the drive to do anything really creative. They're too comfortable with things.'

'Uh, huh. I went to public school, you know.' He didn't seem offended. In fact he seemed to be finding this funny. Of course, I had to admit then that private education doesn't necessarily disqualify you from being able to do anything worthwhile. Ben is, after all, definitely alright. Ben is one of the good guys. I handed him my extra Champagne, a bit warm now, and we moved on to the next painting – a self-portrait, entitled (for fuck's sake) *Torment*. After three or four more of these terrible paintings I began to suspect that Ben was taking the piss slightly, making the most of his unhurried examination of each painting so as to comically underline my obvious impatience and distaste – me huffing and puffing and tutting and cursing; him moving slowly crabwise around the room, furrowing his brow and nodding at the catalogue notes.

'Ben. I'm going outside for a fag.'

'Hmmn? Oh, OK.'

Conrad was standing uncomfortably (or so it seemed to me) next to a sinister-looking couple.

'Do you want a fag, Conrad, mate?'

'Oh, ta, mate. Have you met my brother and sister?'

Simon and Selina took this introduction not as an invitation to chat but as their cue to move away. They looked like vampires. If they get their evil hands on the Institute, then God help us all.

'So … Conrad. So, what sort of thing do you collect? All contemporary, is it? Or British modern?'

'Well, my father, Conrad, used to collect Impressionists, so I carried on with that for a bit, then I think I got a Miró, and then a dear friend opened this gallery and I bought quite a lot from here.'

Yep. The tortured genius whose paintings we've been looking at is also the proprietor of the gallery. And his dad, funnily enough, is the gallery's principal backer.

'But I've been thinking of going in a different direction with it, and luckily I met this marvellous young curator at St John the other night and she's offered to advise me on my collecting.' From his description of this young curator, and the fact that her name is Susan, I was able to deduce that it's Susan. *My* Susan.

'Oh, you know her!' said Conrad. 'She's really fantastic, isn't she?' Apparently he'd been at an artist's dinner and been very impressed by the fact that Susan had ordered the deep-fried brains. That's Susan the militant vegetarian who used to shout at me for eating bacon.

Ben joined us, having apparently had enough of a look, and I asked him what he thought.

'Fantastic, aren't they?' said Conrad.

'Very interesting,' said Ben.

'They are, aren't they. Very interesting,' said me too. And then, 'Hey, d'you fancy coming to the pub, Conrad? Fancy a drink?'

'Um, I won't actually. Got the old jalopy here.'

We all looked across the road at his astonishing custom-ised Harley-Davidson trike, and Conrad started pulling on his liquorice-coloured gauntlets.

'That's one helluva beast you've got there,' said Ben and, for the first time since I'd met him, Conrad looked happy, and I really wished it had occurred to me to say that. I had to work fast.

'Hey, Conrad, maybe we could hook up some time and maybe go to my studio and you could take a gander at my work? And then have a drink, maybe?'

Conrad's reply was muffled and qualified by the fact that he was walking away, backwards, and pushing his hel-met on as he spoke, but I thought it sounded like some sort of a yes. At least it definitely wasn't a no. It's a yes, I'm pretty sure of that.

Later on, in the pub with Ben, I was privately fretting about the nature of Conrad's relationship with Susan, while at the same time– as some sort of displacement, I guess – loudly abusing that gallery and those shit paintings. Which are, let's be clear on this point, shit.

'Well, I suppose I'm no expert – art's not really my thing,' said Ben, 'but they didn't seem so bad to me.'

'Ben, one of them was called *Despair*, for fuck's sake! The guy's dad owns half of Gloucestershire.'

'Well in that case why didn't you tell Conrad how you felt? Hmm?'

'Buy me another drink and I'll tell you why. In fact, I'll just tell you. It's because I'm a hypocrite.'

He bought me another drink. Cheers, Ben! The next morning, searching my pockets as usual, I found a neatly written list of handy neuroscience books, all of which I have now read and found very entertaining and useful. Cheers, Ben!

42: Trevor

STICK TURNED UP the following Wednesday but he was quiet all day. His hair and clothes still annoyed me but his behaviour was impeccable. Not a peep out of him. I spent most of the time with the newly-sighted patient, a Romanian immigrant called, apparently, Trevor. He was late because he'd had some kind of a fainting spell on the way in. Jade had been helping him off the community ambulance when he had this attack and had to be taken to A&E. He was OK, but they put him in a wheelchair because he was still a bit groggy, and Jade wheeled him in about half an hour into the session. Quite a task, this, even for a powerful woman like Jade. He weighs about twenty-six stone. He must have gone down like a collapsing smoke stack.

Regaining your sight is not such a straightforward process. There are always a lot of problems, and it can end disastrously. Trevor had been blind since he was about three and had got used to the idea that he was blind for life. It turned out that his problem could be rectified by a simple surgical procedure. At first he was thrilled, as you'd expect, but he found quite soon that adapting to life as a sighted person was very difficult.

His faint was a result of his new sightedness. One of the problems with suddenly becoming sighted is that you don't recognise anything any more. In your blind world you know all about cars and birds and buildings and telephones. You know how they 'look' in your world of tactile, auditory and olfactory information, but this blind person's picture of the world doesn't map onto the visual world. A dog's appearance is not a direct analogue of how it feels and sounds and smells. When Trevor opened his eyes for the first time after his operation, it was all just clamour and riot. He'd been blind for so long he didn't know how to see. You don't just open your eyes and see things. It takes long enough for a baby to be able to see things, and with Trevor there was not just the problem of getting the hang of a new ability; there was forty years' worth of old abilities to unlearn. Learning to see isn't just a matter of naming things – that's a cow, that's a chair. You need to master the basic grammar of visual recognition. Crucial to this is the difference between the sighted and the blind's conception of space. For Trevor it's all experienced as if it's right in your face. He often finds the visual world to be unbearably claustrophobic and menacing.

Recognition is essential to the spatial sense of a sighted person. You need to know what something is to know where it is; and you need to know where it is to know what it is. Alternating comparisons of possible identities and possible positions of things is a knack you need to master. The blind person does use comparisons to understand, but can only understand space beyond arm's length, beyond the immediate tactile space of the body, in temporal terms, as travelling times. A room is understood as the amount of time, or number of steps, it takes to walk from one wall to the other. Beyond that space is understood in terms of journey times, and the sounds and bodily sensations associated with different modes of transport. Cars going *Brrm-Brrm*. Trains going *clackety-clack*.

Trevor's faint had been caused by a kind of wrenching revelatory moment as he was alighting from the patients' bus. He'd asked Jade how high Gray's Tower is, just making conversation. She told him and, as he explained to me, he'd done a quick mental sum – adding the room-sized blocks or chunks that form the basic unit of his spatial awareness, stacking them in his mind, and then he had looked up at the Tower and was for the first time able to identify the thing he saw with the previously unimaginable number of spatial units he knew it to contain. Basically what happened is he'd realised how high the Tower was. His sense of height previously had been derived from dropping things occasionally, or tripping over. The height of a room he knew about by jabbing upwards with his stick. A staircase was understood as a sequence of movements. This realisation, suddenly becoming acquainted with what a sighted person means by 'high', or 'very high', had caused a rush of something like vertigo. Vertigo amplified a thousand times by the total novelty of this concept of height. The experience, I imagine, was something like it would be if you were staring up at the stars one night, wondering at their great distance and size, and then looking down found that Planet Earth had disappeared and there was an equal infinity of space beneath you.

I liked Trevor (it's not really Trevor – it's something like 'Trayvo' or 'Trivah'), and I had to take my hat off to him. If that had happened to me, I'd have screamed and shat myself as well as fainting. Fainting seems to be the bare minimum reaction to an experience like that. And I certainly wouldn't have gone anywhere near the Tower again. He's found life more and more difficult as space continues to trouble him, either crowding and bullying him with its clutter, or causing these shocking vastations. At his age, learning to identify and place objects reliably may never happen, because all the brain apparatus that would have been devoted to that task normally has been co-opted by his other senses, or has just atrophied. The brain works on a strict 'use it or lose it' policy (which is why, if you never think, you get more stupid).

161

Jade and Ben have been very concerned about Trevor because he's been getting more and more depressed. I'd have said he's not so much depressed as disappointed. Seeing turns out to be a poisoned chalice and a big fat letdown. Disorienting, exhausting, and scary. Every time he opens his eyes it's a psychedelic ghost train, or a bungee jump. He's actually taken to keeping his eyes shut a lot of the time.

I asked him what he likes doing. What keeps him from giving up completely?

'Food in England – iss fucking lovely.' He weighed less than twelve stone two years ago when he had his operation.

Ben and Jade had an idea that drawing might help Trevor. They sought my professional opinion. I thought it might unblock a few neural pipes, but drawing brains wouldn't be any good for him if the problem was to do with scale and recognition, because there's nothing about the shape of a brain that's very particular to its size. A thing of that approximate outline could be a cloud or a sultana.

I devised a drawing exercise more like a traditional still life, with two objects: a chair and an apple. I'd picked two things so he could make comparisons of scale. They were different enough to make scale distinctions easily, but still within the arm's-length range of scale that constitutes a large part of his spatial awareness. So that should make it easy for him to translate visual sensation into more familiar tactile terms – to move from the tactile register to the visual. They were also familiar objects, so he could compare appearance and feel (and taste). And there was a strong intuitive sense of the contiguity of shape and identity with these objects, which, I thought, ought to help.

It didn't really work. We left him for an hour with the chair, and the apple on the seat. But when we came back to have a look, he seemed to have been unable to properly understand what he was seeing. He'd drawn the chair and the apple separately, with the chair at the top of the page and the apple at the bottom. The chair was not the chair he'd been asked to draw, which had a curved steel frame and moulded plastic seat. He'd done a rectilinear stick chair – an idea of a chair. He'd made the apple the same size as the chair, like an illustration in a children's dictionary. What made it heartbreaking was the amount of effort he'd obviously put into it. He'd added a leaf to the stalk on the apple. And he seemed really pleased with his effort.

I felt so bad I went down and got him a *croque monsieur* and an apricot Danish from one of the fast-food places in the foyer.

43: studio visit

WE WERE SITTING IN A PUB. The sort of pub you'd imagine would go instantly quiet when a middle-class white person entered, but which doesn't because it's almost empty, and, anyway, nobody's bothered.

'Maybe he's not coming,' I said to Ben.

'Give him a ring,' said Ben.

'I haven't got a mobile.'

'*Really*? OK, I'll try him.' He dialled: 'Oh, Hi, Conrad, it's Ben, we were supposed to meet and I was just wondering ... uh-huh ... uh-huh ... mm-hmn ...'

This seemed likely to continue a while, so I went to the bar. When I got back it was still going on, with Ben nodding slowly and swivelling his eyes about – from the yellowed ceiling, to me, to the beer mat he was fiddling with, and then up to the ceiling again. Conrad seemed to be making detailed excuses for his failure to turn up. According to Ben, he'd been very enthusiastic about visiting a real artist's studio. Really quite keen. Not any more though, apparently.

'Uh-huh ... mm-hmn ... uh-huh ... OK, Conrad, well, never mind ... yes I quite underst— ... yuh ... yuh ... OK, then. OK. Bye.'

'Not coming,' I said.

'To be honest, I can't really see him being comfortable round here. I doubt he's ever set foot in Hackney. In fact, I think he may have actually turned up here and gone away again when he saw this pub. Perhaps we should have arranged to meet at the actual studio.'

'People can never find it because it's a bit inaccessible. Do you want to come and have look anyway? Since we're here.'

'Sure.'

My studio is just around the corner on the other side of these huge steel gates. Looking up at the razor wire with, for some reason, a brand-new pair of trainers dangling from it, Ben remarked that this seemed like the sort of place where people are taken to be wacked.

'It does look a bit like that, doesn't it. Except I don't think English gangsters say "wack". Here we go.' After something of a struggle I'd managed to get the second padlock open. There's a knack to it.

'My studio is just across the yard there.'

'Where?' He'd have to take my word for it because we were standing in near-total darkness. To fill time as I locked the gate behind us and started across the yard, I began to say something about the scrap metal business.

'The scrap metal business, OW!' I would have gone on to say that this studio space had been cheap when I took it on because the scrap metal market had been slow back then, and the landlords had been looking for a different sort of tenant, and the only other sort around was artists. But I'd hit my shin hard on some metal.

'You OK?' said Ben. 'That sounded nasty.'

'I'm in excruciating agony. In fact, OW! OW! OW! OK, that's better, just stay there and I'll get the lights.'

I took it nice and slow feeling my way to the studio door, and then took some time trying to get the padlock, which is another one you need a knack for. That done, I gave the door a huge shove, using all my weight, and reached round for the light switch. Click.

'Has your power gone?'

'No. Give it a second.' The strip light came on, and then went off again immediately. But then it came on. Off. On.

Off. And on, for keeps this time, and there stood Ben in the yard, in a pool of light, eyes wide and mouth gaping at what he could see through that doorway. 'Jesus,' he whispered.

'Come in. I'll make some coffee.'

I could see Ben had quite a few questions about the state of the place, and the first one he was able to articulate was this: 'How did these enormous paintings get in here? The door isn't big enough.'

'Ten-by-twelve isn't so big. I don't bring the whole thing in. It comes in in bits. I make the stretchers out of three-by-two timber, and then stretch the canvas. Then I paint the painting.'

More than half of this large light industrial unit was taken up with finished paintings. About the cubic volume of a single-decker bus. The next thing Ben had to say was a remark, rather than a question: 'There's paint absolutely everywhere.'

'It is a painting studio.'

'And do you ever actually sell these to people?'

'Have done, yes. Not that many, to be frank.'

Ben nodded, and I felt that perhaps he was thinking there's something really wrong with me; that perhaps I was suffering from some compulsive hoarding disorder. He may also have been wondering if he'd been wise in allowing me the use of a room at the Institute. I wanted him to understand that, although I'm sure he's never encountered anything quite like it, this is actually typical of the several thousands of artists' studios in Hackney and elsewhere. Since, though, this now struck even me as implausible, I didn't say anything else. I decided to act as if everything was normal. (I considered, and decided quickly against, telling him the story of an artist I knew who, working alone one night in one of these units, had got trapped under his own paintings and died. He'd pulled out the front one from a stack of ten- by twelve-foot paintings leaning against the wall, and the vacuum had pulled the next one forward too; like the domino effect, but pulling the one behind rather than knocking the one in front, so the whole lot fell on top of him. Oil paintings are surprisingly heavy.)

'It's freezing in here, and now I come to think of it there's nowhere to sit. Shall we go back to the pub, Ben?'

Later, Ben said that he doubted Conrad would have bought one of my paintings. I guess so. Thanks for trying though, Ben.

44: jealousy

STICK CONTINUED TO MAINTAIN a low profile over the next few weeks' Workshops. He'd just come in and draw, and chat to people, Colin mostly. His drawings changed, too. He was doing as he was told. In fact I came to miss the old Stick. His new drawings were quite dull and I missed having someone to hate, although my hostility could be quickly revived by any signs of intimacy between him and Emily. I'd see the pair of them, out of the corner of my eye, having conversations about their drawings. I'd be at the far end of the tables, advising someone to loosen up a bit and be more expressive with the charcoal, and I'd see the pair of them making comparisons, referring drawing to model, and drawing to drawing. Instead of looning and twitching about, Stick looked quite stern during these little conferences, with his ridiculous plume of clotted hair waggling as he looked and nodded, holding his chin, frowning. Yes, yes, that's a good bit there. Yes. But that bit's not so good. No ... At times I suspected he was taking the piss, acting like a comedy art critic, but then he seemed not to be doing that.

I did get a few panics – once or twice a day, when Stick would go and stand behind Emily and ask her about something – because of the way she'd turn and look up at him, smiling. Just that look with a little smile on her face was enough to cause a terrible surge of anxiety and fury. Because, as the weeks passed, and Emily continued to produce her capable but dull brain drawings, I still couldn't think of anything to say to her. That is, I couldn't think of anything that I could say, really, in the circumstances. May

I hold your breasts? You could lift one cup of your bra so that the bosom would be lifted too, before it spilled – plap! – into the palm of my hand. May I lift your skirt and press, with the tips of my fingers, the little cushion where your pubic hair stuffs and tautens the gusset of your knickers? I want to hear the faint Velcro crunch that would make. Can I see what your spit tastes like?

When I saw Emily and Stick together I was very envious of the naturalness of their exchanges – with me just stopping by once in a while at Emily's place to tell her it's very good, what she's doing. Yes. Very interesting. I discovered new areas of inhibition and timidity within myself. I didn't know where to look or how to stand, or what to do with my hands. Very often I'd find myself giving extra special attention to whomever happened to be sitting opposite Emily that day. A little look, or movement, or faint olfactory savour when I'd happen to walk past her could cause me to salivate.

On the way into the Activities Room of a Wednesday morning I would rehearse fifteen-minute scenes in my mind, beginning with a bright and positive 'Good morning, Emily!' and ending in cunnilingus, or her bent over the table with her knickers round her knees, her tits squashed against the drawing paper. The last second of the fifteen minutes being the instant of rear entry. After a few weeks of this, my morning greeting, 'Good MORNING, Emily!!', was beginning to sound, to me anyway, like the beginning of some kind of hysterical outburst.

45: professionalism – Zeinab

I WAS KEPT IN CHECK, and kind of grounded, by a growing sense of professionalism – my guided attention to Ben's 'interesting cases'. This linked to my reinvention as a whole new artist with a different career path. The Workshops were such a success – the funding bodies, whose representatives were regular visitors now, loved them apparently – that they became day-long exercises, generating reams of poor draughtsmanship. Great stacks of it. Despite Emily, and what she was doing to me, I was getting quite good at dealing with the patients, even getting a certain amount of proper satisfaction out of the pleasure they would take in their cack-handed efforts. After a few months I found I was even starting to drink less. I did come back from lunch pissed, but I usually wasn't pissed before lunch.

At first I would try and disguise the fact that I was a bit drunk in the afternoons by walking in perfect straight lines and enunciating clearly, but I packed that in pretty soon. Ben knew and didn't seem bothered about it. He even joined me and Colin in the hospital pub sometimes. Dr Prabhakar probably noticed when she'd come around with the funding bodies, but I was never required to do more than say 'Yes', or sometimes 'No', when questioned about outputs and so on. I was just there as an example of a good thing that the Institute does. They didn't want details.

And at least I was there on time every Wednesday. Years of compensating, even slightly overcompensating, for my poor sense of direction and my constant drunkenness has made me an excellent timekeeper and a natural for the life of routine from which these things, in fact my whole lifestyle, would seem to have disbarred me. Having learned something of apperceptive and associative agnosia, of blindsight and prosopagnosia, achromatopsia (that guy still gave me the creeps), of Phineas Gage and Broca and Wernicke and Tourette's, and recovered vision (Trevor seemed to improve as the weeks went by, and the drawing helped). The next revelations, of something called Charles Bonnet syndrome, were the kind of thing I took a routine interest in now. My attitude was becoming, as I say, more 'professional'.

In fact, our Charles Bonnet patient gave me reason to regret having got pissed at lunch that day. She joined us, at Ben's request, one afternoon – a flying visit. Her condition was interesting, and she was fit. I really wished, when I was talking to her, that I'd remembered to bring some mints for my breath, and that I didn't have to concentrate so much on speaking clearly. If I'd been on better form and in better shape psychologically I could have been in there – with Zeinab, the beautiful estate agent from Woking, with the scotoma. She was like an Asian version of Emily. Same build and long hair.

Ben got her to tell me all about her condition. ('You'll find this very interesting, as an artist.') You can see the scar on Zeinab's eyeball where it was pierced when she was twelve by some boys playing around with darts on the recreation ground. It caused irreparable damage to a part of the retina, leaving her with a blank patch in the lower left of her visual field – a scotoma. I was trying to look into her eye without breathing on her (I should stick to vodka at lunchtime, instead of beer).

Zeinab kept stopping to answer her mobile. She's very busy. She comes to the Institute occasionally only so that she and Ben can discuss possible coping strategies for the problem, because there's no actual cure. She sees these incredibly vivid hallucinations in her scotoma. A lot of the time it is just a dark patch like an inkblot, but then all of a sudden it will become a little screen for all these images, like an animated vignette. Pixies and elves and faerie folk, often involved in faerie folk ceremonies and processions. The coronation of a faerie prince attended by a host of sprites and goblins and glowing Tinkerbells darting about in the air. She quite enjoys these sometimes (at least when she's not working, which is actually almost never). But she finds them very puzzling. She can't figure out where they come from. She has no particular relationship with that kind of thing. Bedtime stories about pixies and elves were not a feature of her childhood. No picture books at all, in fact. Her folks are not particularly strict Muslim, not especially iconophobic. But there was no interest in pictures or in fantasy stories.

Charles Bonnet syndrome isn't rare but it's odd, so it's one of those things Ben can't leave alone. It's thought to be a result of the brain's attempt to accommodate, or compensate for, the fact that it's getting no activity in a certain part of the visual field. Zeinab finds it very distracting at times and she'd like to find a way of dealing with that, but it is livable with ('…'scuse me. Got to take this …').

It isn't well understood, but Charles Bonnet does seem to be an attempt by the brain to fill an anomalous gap. Because it's getting no input where it expects to find it, it seems to grab imagery from some enormous neural stockpile of imagery and use it to fill the scotomic blind spot. The brain hypothesises promiscuously about what's there, in the dark patch at the lower left of her visual field. In Zeinab's case it seems unable to take its cue from the content of the remainder of the visual field – hypothesising another desk in the office, or another passenger on the tube. (It's different with other patients, with different eye problems, who might, for example, hallucinate a thousand extra desks in an office big enough for only seven or eight.) It makes wild guesses about what's there, and then presents them to consciousness with total confidence – that is to say, clearly and vividly. With some Charles Bonnet patients' hallucinations there is an obvious, though not necessarily meaningful, connection with something in their lives. Some experience or wish. With Zeinab you want to think that she sees pixies because it expresses a wish; either the wish to have had a more traditional European childhood, or for a more idealistic adulthood. Or you could think of it as her brain secretly satirising her job – estate agents and their faerie tales or something. But when she tells you it's a fucking nuisance, and that's all, you believe her ('… 'scuse me. Got to take this call.')

I took advantage of the opportunity to go to the toilet and leak some of that beer away. I considered my chances with Zeinab. My new professional status would look good to her, I thought. An artist, but also clinical somehow. To do with the Institute in some capacity. A sort of consultant. I saw in the mirror above the sink that I wasn't looking too bad, either. I did always make the effort to shave and wear clean clothes when I did my Workshop. Checking my breath in my cupped hand, that didn't seem too bad, either. I had a quick wank to steady my nerves and returned to the Activities Room to ask her out, but she'd gone.

46: hemi-neglect

'SHE'S GONE,' said Ben. 'Just thought you'd be interested in Charles Bonnet.' He then pointed me towards an affable and lopsided lady patient in a wheelchair. Pauline is one of our 'borrowed' patients. We get them from the neurology department of the hospital downstairs to make up the numbers for when the funding people visit. I hadn't really noticed it with Pauline's drawings before, but she always does only one hemisphere of the brain, even when she's supposed to be drawing the whole brain.

I gave her some of my time. 'How are we doing today, Pauline?' (I'm sounding more like a real doctor every day.) Pauline's had a stroke and is now a classic 'hemi-neglecter'. She lives in only half the world. The right half. The left half of the world just isn't there for her. The clock goes one to six, or else all twelve numbers are compressed into the right half of the clock face. She eats half of what's on her plate, and will only dress the right half of her body.

Ben has been encouraging her to overcome this blindness to the left of everything by trying to get her to draw both hemispheres of the brain model in front of her. He'd place it in the right half of her visual field. (Contrary to what you may have thought, or what I thought anyway, it's not true that the left eye connects to the right hemisphere of the brain, and the right eye to the left hemisphere. It's the left half of the *visual field* that connects to the right hemisphere, and vice versa. The left half of the body, however, *is* connected to the right half of the brain. And vice versa. Hemi-neglect of the left half of things is caused by damage

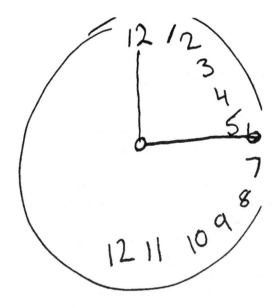

in the right half of the brain. But it ought to be possible to see the left half of things if they are within the right half of the visual field. This is hard to explain without diagrams.)

She was still drawing half a brain even though she could see the whole thing. Ironically she can only draw the damaged half. She ought to be able to see the left half of the brain model in her right visual field, but there seems to be an inability even to acknowledge the left of things. It's an ontological problem, exposed by the attempt to render anything that's vertically symmetrical. Butterflies, Rorschach inkblots, classical porticoes, faces seen from the front. Pairing has ceased to exist. No identical twins or big blue eyes in her world now. No mandalas or altarpieces. No full moon. She lives in a world where you wake up and reach out to the bedside table for your spectacle and denture. Put on your trouser and shoe. In the morning paper the page three girl shows you her tit, and the only cutlery on the breakfast table is knives.

After my disappointment with beautiful Zeinab, I wasn't really in the mood for Pauline. Colin came over and made a fuss of her, pretending to flirt with her and making her laugh – a kind of puff-puffing out of the corner of her mouth, as if she were smoking a crafty cigarette. I noted a degree of self-interest in Colin's behaviour here. He was enjoying her decrepitude, I thought. He's starting to feel his age and needs to demonstrate his own comparative vigour by behaving in a way that contrasts it with the debilitated condition of some of the other patients. Still, it very much brightened up Pauline's day for her, and put him in a good mood, too. Colin asked if I fancied joining him and Stick for a drink after work.

Since I'd had my eye on Stick, and Emily and Stick, I thought it would be a very good idea to have a drink with him – to see if I could find out what was going on there. Why's he behaving so well lately? Is it just that he was on something before, with all the juggling and looning about? Crystal meth or something.

47: The Canadian Volunteer

I DON'T KNOW WHY I kept going to that hospital pub. The Canadian Volunteer. There were plenty of other pubs nearby if you just went a little way beyond the hospital's boundary. It has no atmosphere at all. Not even a phony atmosphere: mock Irish or Dickensian. I was the only regular. You never saw any medical staff there. Most of the customers seemed to be the friends and relatives of patients, and sometimes the patients themselves, standing at the bar in their over-coats, with the J-Cloth hem of a hospital smock sticking out at the back, and no socks. Nobody ever really says any-thing about that, although it has generated a nickname for the pub – The Self-Harmer's Arms. I think I liked it because people only went there to get pissed; it was like a pharmacy for self-medicators.

By now, though, I had a favourite seat at the corner of a banquette facing the door, and I offered to get some drinks in while Colin and Stick got settled in my corner. The bar-man asked me did I want anything else with that? – pints for me and Colin, orange juice for Stick. Yes, I'd be wanting two pints and an orange juice quite soon, but let's get these dealt with first.

It turned out the reason Stick has been so subdued lately is that he's actually been subdued. Chemically. It's not that he was on drugs the first time I met him but that he wasn't on the drugs he needs to take to suppress his innate speediness. He only does all the juggling and bouncing about and juvenile wisecracking when he doesn't take his medication. He prefers it when he doesn't take his medicine, and it helps him professionally – he actually is a street entertainer – but he appreciates it can be difficult for other people to cope with, and so medicates himself accordingly. Out of consideration for others.

Colin wanted to tell us the latest he's heard about Simon and Selina's plans for the Institute. They're going to hire it out for some kind of neurology-based market research. 'They're going to use the brain scanner – the one they've still got – to test new products. Apparently they get you to sample the product, a biscuit or something, and then they do a brain scan.'

'How does that work, then? What does that tell them?' I asked.

'They can tell whether you liked it or not because it'll show on the scan.'

I'd seen scanned images of the brain, where the active areas literally light up, like satellite photos of weather systems. They do a lot of experiments like that where they get you to perform some task like counting backwards from a hundred, or memorising a meaningless sequence of letters, and the brain scan shows which areas of the brain were demanding most oxygen. You need oxygen to do anything, including think.

I didn't get it, though, with the market research. 'How does that tell them anything different from just asking if you liked the biscuit?'

'It's right in your brain. If they just asked you a question, you might lie.'

'Why would anyone lie about liking a biscuit?'

They thought that would be really funny to do that. That'd throw a spanner in the works. I thought it was just a classic instance of people getting overexcited about technology. Market researchers and people like that always want to claim some kind of scientific authority for what they do, so that it won't seem like such an amoral, time-wasting, phony-baloney job. Brain scanners are just what they've been looking for. An impressive piece of machinery – FMRI scanners are really fucking impressive when you see one – to endorse this claim of being 'scientific'. It's like those old-fashioned adverts, with a man in a white coat and carrying a clipboard to test a washing powder. Is this white shirt (a) clean, or (b) still dirty after you've washed it? We've got our best people on it. We should have some preliminary results through in about six months.

There seemed to be an instant's wordless communication between Stick and Colin at this point. You would say that they had 'exchanged glances' if you didn't know that Colin can't really do that. It was a little stir and a sigh in concert ... Oh dear. I wasn't taking this seriously. You see ... it's all connected.

48: conspiracy theories – it's all connected

'YOU KNOW ABOUT NORMERON, DON'T YOU?' said Stick.

'No. What's that?'

Apparently Conrad Norman's empire includes a secret weapons research facility in South America, called NORMERON, where they test chemical and biological weapons using indigenous peoples as guinea pigs.

'Yeah …? *Really*?'

'You may well be sceptical,' said Colin, 'but you don't want to take everything at face value. The American government has been sponsoring chemical weapons research for years—'. And, Stick wanted to add here, '—the British government is involved too. And the French. It's all part of the same organisation.' Stick is involved with a website that disseminates prohibited information about all this. Simon and Selina are part of it, just like their old man. Neuro-market research is part of it.

In fact, this was all starting to sound plausible. I didn't go along with the idea that there's some sinister elite at work, but I'd always had the feeling that there's a lot of really bad, heavy stuff going on that we don't normally get to hear about. Of course I had reservations. In a way it doesn't make sense just because every other Hollywood film and TV series of the last fifteen years involves a secret govern- ment organisation that's fucking things up for everyone. So I didn't see the need for us to whisper (Stick was leaning forward as he spoke, and he'd glance around once in a while, to make sure we weren't being overheard). But the idea that it was going on in South America somewhere gave it all a sinister plausibility. That's where they make snuff movies, and they have CIA-backed drug cartels. It would have to be there, or in some remote corner of the former Soviet Union. There is a connection there, I now discover. Conrad Norman wasn't his real name. That's an anglicisation of his real name, which is actually Normenkian, or Normokovski. It's all to do with something called the New World Order. This is a secret international organisation that meets twice a year in Luxembourg. Everything seems connected, part of some deranged plot to fuck up the world, because it actually is all connected. AIDS, SARS, the Spanish flu epidemic of 1917, all wars, genetically modified crops, the so-called 'space program'.

As the empties stacked up on the table between us (Colin, generous as ever), Stick elaborated the whole scheme for me, seeing now that I could be trusted. The death of Princess Diana was mentioned more than once. Child abuse; specifically 'Satanic ritual (child) abuse'. Cattle mutilation in Omaha and Nebraska. Alien abduction. What, just for example, did I think the Institute's role in all this was? (I didn't know – what?) Well, he wasn't saying anything definite, but what about the Blind Woman's alien abduction, Huh? No one else at the Institute took her story seriously. But they couldn't explain her condition, could they?

I was getting sceptical again now. 'It's no good hinting darkly at "so-called unexplained phenomena". You're saying, are you, that there is an explanation that we're not allowed to know? What is it then, d'you think?'

'Well, do *you* think it's a coincidence every time someone reports having been abducted by aliens they get a visit from certain people? Often they end up in a mental home.'

'Who says,' I say, 'that everyone who says they've been abducted by aliens gets a visit from "certain people"?'

'The abductees themselves. First-hand witnesses! And then of course nobody believes them because their testimony has been compromised.'

'Their testimony has been compromised because they claim to have been abducted by aliens.'

'Exactly!' Stick was very pleased with the way that point had been made so well, and he let me in on another *so-called* unexplained phenomenon. 'And how about Emily? Did she just "lose" her memory, or was it erased?'

'Erased?' I hazarded.

'Well we don't know, do we? That's my point.'

I looked at Colin. Surely—?

'Well ... ,' he said, and took a steady pull on his pint, '... it might not mean anything, of course, but she does get a lot of extra attention from Dr Prabhakar. So, you know. Food for thought.'

'OK, then.' I shifted forward on my seat. 'Does that mean there's an explanation for every unexplained phenomenon in the world, and the explanation is to do with the New World Order? Ay?' (Thinking back, I could have said something about 'apophenia', that condition where you think you can see meaningful connections in random data. But I didn't, because I didn't know about it then.)

'Well if "science" can't explain it ...' – and here Stick spread his arms and widened his eyes at me, inviting me to complete his rhetorical question, and answer if I could.

'If science (or "science") can't explain it ... what? I don't get it. Are you saying that science can explain it but just won't tell us, or science can't explain it because science is all nonsense?'

'They say they've got all the answers, don't they?'

'Do they?' (I'd always thought the whole point of science is admitting you *don't* know all the answers – otherwise they'd stop, surely.)

'They can't explain crop circles, can they?'

'Right,' I tell them. 'Maybe *they* can't explain crop circles, but *I* can because I've made one. I once spent a night in a field in Wiltshire, wrecking some farmer's wheat crop for him. I have *actually made* a crop circle.'

As it turned out Colin and Stick had both been visitors to the annual 'crop' of crop circles: Colin just the once, but Stick several times a year, every year, since the mid-90s. He can spot a fake immediately, he says. He has felt their power (Stick is psychically gifted), and he knows respected scientists who have recorded anomalous electromagnetic effects in crop circles. (Oh, we *like* scientists now.) What I did, or claim to have done, can have been nothing other than an act of desecration. I have sullied and defiled the crucible of resistance to the hegemony of the New World Order.

I knew now that I was in the company of at least one fanatic. I tried to reason with them, amusingly, I thought, by giving them an account of the logistics and *modus operandi* of doing crop circles.

49: **crop circles**

IT WAS FIVE YEARS AGO; five summers ago. Crop circles are an exclusively summer activity, for obvious reasons. I only went along for a laugh, really. An old friend of mine from art school days had persuaded me that crop circle hoaxing, or 'circlemaking', as its practitioners prefer (because 'hoaxing' would imply a distinction from some 'genuine' phenomenon), is a lot of fun. It is not. For one thing I wasn't allowed to take along the large bottle of whisky I'd thoughtfully purchased.

We met at six in the evening at a flat in Brixton. (A lot of circlemakers are conceptual artists from London.) We had to be briefed and tasked; each member of the four-man team. There were maps and plans to look at. There was a great deal of circlemaking banter and gossip. Triumphs of the season thus far were joked about. The team showed me pictures taken from light aircraft. One thing they hardly ever do these days is circles. They do fractals and mandalas. Spirals. Hallucinogenic mazes. There'll be recognisable imagery sometimes, much of it deliberately provocative; the disabled symbol, or the numbers 666, six hundred foot across. I was allowed a drink here, at base camp in Brixton, but when I picked up the bottle as we headed for the car they said, 'You're not bringing that'. I should have baled then.

A five-hour drive to Wiltshire, and more of their circle-maker humour: once there, another hour of driving around slowly, trying to find a good hiding place for the car, some-where near the chosen field – chosen the day before by one of the team on a recce. Then *another* hour's hiking cross country, with all the gear – that's poles and ropes, 'stalk-stompers', surveyors' tape measures. At the edge of the field everyone sorted out their own kit, and then they left me. 'Just wait here,' someone hissed at me in the dead of night, 'and don't make a noise; and don't stand up.' 'And ...' another of them, I can't see who, ordered, 'do *not* smoke.'

This was the worst part. The English countryside at one or two in the morning is as black as black can be. The circlemakers prefer to work on moonless nights. I squatted there with my stalk-stomper and stared up the narrow track they'd disappeared into. I would never be able to find the car again on my own. All I knew was I was somewhere in Wiltshire, in near-total darkness, with no watch, no money, not smoking, chilled to the marrow and quaking. All alone.

At times I thought I saw a procession of hooded figures moving along the skyline at the far side of the field. I knew very well that it must be the tops of a row of poplars swaying in the breeze, but knew equally well at other times that it was, actually, a procession of hooded figures. (If I'd known then what I know now about the way mood affects perception, I wouldn't have been so scared.) I had just made up my mind to take my chances with the barbed wire, and a long walk back to London, when one of the team broke cover in front of me.

'OK,' he beckoned, 'come on.' We walked for twenty minutes along a tram line – these fields really are massive – until we came to a flattened area they were using as base (this area later to be incorporated into the design) and he directed me to my task – 'stalk-stomping'. This was basically blocking in the areas they had delineated, 'drawing' in the crop by walking through it sideways, making curves by doing that while holding one end of a length of string that is secured at the other end, like the point of a compass. The stalk-stomper is just a four-foot plank with a rope tied to

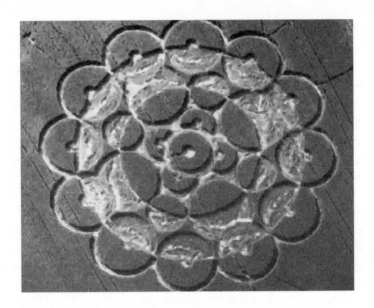

each end so that you can hold it against your foot as you walk forward into the wheat, shuffling along with the stomping foot always in front. The noise it makes is quite something when there are no other sounds. You think it's going to alert the whole of Wiltshire. Angry farmers with pitchforks and guns. SWOOSH, it goes. Every forward push into the wheat with your stalk-stomper. SWOOSH! and SWOOSH! and SWOOSH!!!. Three hours of that.

I regretted having drunk whisky earlier. I should have drunk lots of water like the others. I couldn't believe my luck when the team ambled up out of the thinning gloom – nearly dawn – and said it's done. My life away from this field had disappeared by that time, and I knew that this was all I had ever done, or would do, for all eternity.

'And is there any indication as to how these friends of yours are financed?' said Stick. I had not succeeded in lightening the mood. Colin was looking at me strangely, as if I had disappointed him somehow, and Stick was giving me a nasty look. That didn't bother me much, but the fact that Colin seemed to have cooled towards me, in that moment, was something I did not like one bit.

I knew what Stick was getting at, but I acted dumb. 'They aren't really friends of mine. I just know them. Or used to. And how d'you mean "financed"? It doesn't cost much to do crop circles. Stalk-stompers are cheap to make. Surveyors' tape measures aren't that expensive. Petrol money—'

'But you admit it is *organised*.' The word 'organised' very potent here.

'Of course it's organised or it'd be a mess. You've seen those things. They take a lot of planning. And the circle-makers are all experienced. Some of them have been at it for twenty years.'

'And have you ever asked yourself just why they do it?'

'I know why they do it. They enjoy it. I didn't, but they do. They fucking love it. They enjoy everything about it. Basically, they are nerdy art school graduates who work in special effects and model-making, and they just love solving unusual technical problems, and they enjoy having a secret identity. All the planning and designing. Sneaking around in the dark. They enjoy winding people up and making them think aliens have visited. People like you, Colin.' I was hoping that would make him smile. Nope. I even thought for a minute he was going to hit me.

Stick spoke up, attacking from a different angle. 'And what was the crop formation?'

'Formation?'

'The symbol in the crop. It's known as a "formation".' He smiled, a fake indulgence. Evidently I knew nothing of these matters. Nothing to get angry about. (He was very angry.)

'Actually I've got no idea. I just went along for the ride and did all that stalk-stomping.'

'So actually, what you're saying is you have no idea whether you did a crop circle or not. You could have been flattening the crop at random. You only *thought* you were making a crop circle.' He was quite right. You can't see what you're doing, and you probably couldn't even if it were light, because the things can only be seen from the air, or a hill.

'That'd be funny, wouldn't it? They were just winding me up, taking me all that way and then leaving me in the dark to freak me out, and then making me do all that stomping for hours. They were probably smoking and drinking behind a bush somewhere, and laughing their heads off.'

'No, no,' Stick was much less angry all of a sudden, 'I've heard of them doing that. They get someone along to "make a crop circle", and you go through the motions, like you did, and then they show you photographs of a genuine formation. It's a classic disinformation technique. Obviously none of the genuine formations could be made by humans. I mean, three hours!? It's been calculated that a genuine crop circle could not be made by humans, even using the latest technology, in less than a month.'

Calculated? By whom? He did have a point, though. The whole thing could have been a windup. But it didn't seem that likely. It's a lot of trouble to go to just to freak me out. Just me. But then the other alternative doesn't seem all that likely either. That the circlemakers have been doing night sorties into the fields of England, all summer long, summer after summer. Well, I just didn't know what to believe.

Stick, however, knew exactly what to believe, and had a *lot* more to say about it, speeding up now as his medication was wearing off. It was all quite simple. I had accidentally (or perhaps not) stumbled across two major parts of the New World Order's axis of power. The Norman Foundation and the 'circlemakers'. This may or may not be a coincidence. It may be evidence of the benign agency of an unseen force. Whatever the case, I am now in a unique position, as someone who has gained the trust of the New World Order, and who now understands their evil purpose, to subvert them. My mission, should I choose to accept it (and I'm being only slightly facetious here; this is really how it sounded) is to keep my eyes open, and my mouth shut. Whatever it is I'm supposed to do will become clear in due course.

As I stood to go for a slash, Stick began a discourse on the history of class war, and Colin was joining in with stuff about the Levellers, a proto-communist movement in seventeenth-century England. Sitting down again when I got back from the toilet, I was in time to hear them finish talking about what they were calling 'Britain's bloodiest battle'!

It fell, I believed, to me to raise a sensible objection or two, since Colin wasn't doing it (and why wasn't he taking *my* side here?). It was my responsibility at this point to make the voice of reason heard. 'Hang on! "Britain's bloodiest battle"? That's you and your crusty mates doing feeble class war protests and "subversive" graffiti, is it? Look,' I said, glancing quickly at Colin, and still finding no hint of support or approval, 'Stick, or whatever you're really called. I know you've made up your own nickname, and you're probably really called Tarquin or something. And all of this, what you're saying, is bollocks. It's nonsense. You're a moron. I'm off.'

I made it home using a means of transport well known to all drunkards. You set one foot outside the pub and the next thing you know you're outside your front door, trying to get the key to work. It's called the Drunk Portal.

50: a proper lunch

COLIN DIDN'T TURN UP the following Wednesday, so I thought I might see what it would be like to spend lunchtime in the Day Room with all the others (and, of course, Colin's absence wouldn't have had anything to do with my behaviour in the pub). I was surprised to see there was quite a nice buffet lunch laid on for us. Light snacks. Just right for someone like me, who can't take much in the way of solids at this time of day. I was helping myself to a prawn in batter, dunking it in the Thai sauce, when I was interrupted by the Achromatopsia Man. He was closing in on me at great speed, wagging a finger and shaking his head: 'Noo noo noo noo noo noo.'

'No?'

'Noo noo. These delicious condiments are not for the likes of us mere mortals, I'm afraid to say.' (Why does he have to talk like this?)

'I thought—'

'Oooh noo. These are for the visiting guests of Dr Prabhakar.' He meant the funding people. I wiped the sauce off the prawn with a napkin and put it back.

'Why don't you share some of my humble repast with me? I always bring far too much.' He was holding an enormous Tupperware box full of sandwiches and biscuits and stuff. I checked what he had in there, to make sure there was no egg, or tuna and sweetcorn, and decided to allow myself to be treated. A ham sandwich. At least I'd be spared the effort of having to think of things to say. By the time the A. Man had arranged our table and napkins 'like a little picnic', I already knew quite a lot about him. The situation with the old lady

190

he looks after, as live-in nurse and companion, is becoming very difficult and he's not sure he can cope much longer.

'… she's nearly ninety but she's quite the little minx sometimes and some of the things she says to me can be very hurtful.' The thing with their tablets seems to be coming to a head. 'I've not actually caught her *in flagrante delicto* stealing my tablets but I know it's her – of course it is. I do everything in that house so it couldn't be anyone else purloining them, and I know they're going missing because I have to keep a very strict record of my dosage in case I have another of my little accidents.' He needs his pills because of his depressions.

'You don't want to know,' he says. Then he tells me. His depressions and his 'accident'. He showed me the little notebook he keeps with its miniature hand-written drug inventory – types, dates and quantities. 'I don't even know why she needs to pilfer my medicine unless it's just to upset me. She's got plenty of her own medicine. She is very old.'

He is doing some kind of origami with the napkins as he speaks so I am able to look past him at what is going on around us without him noticing I'm not paying attention. Stick and Emily over there with their apples, talking between bites (Stick's revenge, evidently, for the other night, is courting Emily right in front of me, and doing quite well by the looks of it).

Meanwhile, the important visitors are beginning to cluster around the buffet table. They have wine. I can see Dr Prabhakar moving amongst them, small and neat, not eating herself, and stopping every now and then to make sure everything is OK … Yes? Try the prawns. She draws their attention to the balcony, a point of interest. They stoop and nod. Michelle is standing almost to attention by the little box that opens the sheet glass wall. Prabhakar gives her the nod and she holds the key-disc against the box, and a segment of the wall pops forwards and slides across. That certainly gets everyone's attention. Best thing they've seen all day. They are herded past Michelle onto the broad balcony, with their paper plates and wine glasses, and she closes the window behind them and resumes her state of readiness. Lovely out here. Almost like spring. They seem to be getting in the party mood, some of them enjoying the view, the women mostly, and others, the guys, clearly fascinated by that window. The incredible cost of it. Michelle still at her post in case any patients try to get out there. She seems to have the only key.

Nancy breaks away from one besuited group, goes up to the glass and mimes an instruction – *Michelle* ... Again! They love it. Michelle does her thing with the disc. The great glass sheet goes *CLCK*, and *sssssshhhhhhptah*; the guys are nodding slowly, and firming their jaw muscles at it – yep; that's a serious piece of equipment – and then closes again. Michelle to attention once more.

I can see that Emily is rather enjoying it too. Stick no longer has her attention. He tries a bit of juggling, nothing too showy this time. Just the three oranges while he sits beside her. She's watching the window to see if it'll do it again, and Stick switches to the elbow trick, trying to get her with that *slap!* of the orange into the hand. She is still distracted, so he takes one of her arms and moves it into position like a Barbie doll's arm, elbow crooked, back of the hand resting on the shoulder. He balances an orange on the point of her elbow ... Go on, have a go. Go *aaaarn*. Try. Her arm snaps forward and she gets the orange just right. She knows how to do this, and she's delighted. Stick looks up for a moment smiling, and catches my eye unexpectedly, and winks at me. I think. I think the cunt is actually winking at me. They carry on with this for a while. Slap. Slap. Slap.

51: my studio/study/office/room

BY NOW I'D GOT MY STUDIO – Guest Room 23 – just how I liked it. This turned out to be quite different from the way I had things at my other studio in Hackney (still not evicted: it's coming, though) or in my flat. Instead of making a mess of the place, I found I enjoyed making it into a busy but orderly place of work and study. On the walls were some of my favourite drawings from the workshop. My favourites weren't what you'd call good drawings, necessarily, but the drawings that best evidenced the condition of their authors.

The fact that they were registers of a set of symptoms, useful as diagnostic tools, was something I came to find aesthetically pleasing. So there was Pauline's halves of brains; the Blind Woman's minimal traces; Stick's Nazi dragons; the Blind Man's brain-to-wallpaper-pattern-morphs. I put some of Colin's earnest efforts up so as not to upset him, and some of Emily's because I loved her. I had none of my own work to put up (having managed to avoid demonstrating my own skills as a draughtsman) apart from some mono-prints I'd made using a brain model as a printing block. I'd got myself one of the cheaper Chinese-made ones, and it struck me, looking at the flattened intaglio face of its medial section, that I could use it to make a kind of potato print. I smeared the surface with acrylic paint and then pressed it to a piece of paper. It looked pretty good. The walnutty crenellations of the forebrain, the arched corpus callosum, the reptilian mid- and hind-brain structures – all quite clear.

I had also tacked up some relevant images from art history. I had a postcard of Rembrandt's *The Anatomy Lesson*, although the dissection in the picture has only got as far as the tendons in the subject's forearm. I don't even like Rembrandt that much, but it was a postcard I happened to have, and it seemed to say something about Art and Science. I also pinned up a favourite of mine, a print by Hogarth called *Superstition, Credulity and Fanaticism*. Abstract painters like me are supposed to disapprove of any narrative element in painting, but I'd always loved this picture. Probably because all the references are so topical that they were meaningless to me looking at it 250 years later.

In fact I'd only just realised the picture had a brain in it. Like a lot of early Hogarth it's so densely packed with imagery that it can look to a contemporary eye like some kind of hieroglyphics or heraldry, as legible as a foreign banknote. Having noticed the brain in the picture I broke with my habit of ignoring the explanatory text. It's intended as a satire on the Methodist movement. At top right you've got the Methodist preacher going berserk in the pulpit. (The word 'enthusiasm' was used in the eighteenth century to mean a specifically religiose kind of demonstrativeness; an excess of zeal.) His wig is falling off, revealing a shaven Jesuit tonsure. The point is – Methodists are just as bad as the Catholics for overdoing it. Next to him is a strange kind of hanging scroll, charting the degrees of excess in the preacher's ranting, rising from 'Natural Tone' at the base to 'Bull Roar' at the top, and above this chart (and completely departing from any pretence at naturalism) is the cartoon depiction of a disembodied mouth, a nose with a ring through it attached, and inscribed across the tongue of the open mouth are the words 'Blood Blood Blood'. Top left is a kind of chandelier in the form of a 'NEW and CORRECT GLOBE of HELL', with a screaming face on it, and the geographical features particular to Hell – Eternal Damnation Gulf; Bottomless Pit; Brimstone Ocean; Deserts of New Purgatory; Molten Lead Lakes; Horrid Zone; Parts Unknown.

The starving congregation occupies the centre of the picture, wedged together in box-like pews, and actually eating effigies of Christ – little statues with perfect semi-circular bites taken out of them; some kind of comment about religion and poverty. At the bottom left of the picture is a woman giving birth to rabbits. A litter of bunnies processes from under her skirts like Flopsy, Mopsy and Cottontail, and she is collapsed in some sort of ecstasy of parturition. This is about credulity. The woman who gave birth to rabbits was a part of contemporary folklore at the time, and Hogarth's point here is *some people will believe anything, won't they?*

The brain appears at bottom right of the picture as part of another scale of Methodist excess. This is the Scale of Madness, like a large barometer. At the top, Raving, then Madness, EXTACY, LUST, Love-Heat, Luke Warm, Low Spirits, Sorrow, AGONY, Settled Grief, Despair, Madness, Suicide. Madness both second from top and second from bottom. And, another anomaly, Settled Grief between Agony and Despair. You'd expect to find it before or after, not between. The brain forms the base for the madness barometer. I hadn't recognised it as a brain, for years, because it's the brain's ventral view: i.e. seen from beneath, with all its fussy internal organs showing. The antenna-like Olfactory bulbs. The clitoris-like Hypothalamus. The bulging Pons. The knobbish Medulla. The Cerebellum resembling, from this angle, both a pile of worms and a crab. I'd thought it was something Hogarth had made up, like those nightmare creatures in a Bosch painting. What adds to this impression is the fact that he's added an ear to it. One ear.

Bringing the wall displays up to date a bit, I'd pinned up some reproductions of de Kooning's breezy, untroubled late period abstractions. The ones he'd done when his condition had gone beyond the point of rendering him merely 'a little vacky' (his words: he never lost his Dutch accent) and had brought him right to the brink of total dementia.

52: my project taking shape

MY PLANS FOR AN EXHIBITION about all this were coming along quite well by now; the idea dictated quite naturally by all the sifting and sorting and arranging of material generated by my Drawing Workshops. It would be an artist/curator project, a total departure for me. I would just show all the drawings the patients have done. The whole lot. I had hundreds by now. I would just pin them to the gallery walls, floor to ceiling; and include the ceiling, too, if there were enough. Kind of an installation. Just call it 'Brains', I thought. And there'd be a catalogue with essays by art critics and neuroscientists printed side by side. Each page with two columns of text, scientists on the left and art critics on the right (this corresponding to the roles of left and right hemispheres in the brain). I might include some case histories and some illustrations from the literature, and I'd use some of those amazing FMRI scan pictures, in colour hopefully. (That digital colouring of the active areas is amazing, like those pictures that are supposed to represent your psychic aura, or life-force or whatever. Kirlian photography. I saw some reproduced in a Mind, Body, Spirit magazine. Susan's.) I could do some of the writing myself if the budget doesn't run to hiring a proper art critic.

I was spending a lot of time poring over the books from my growing Brain Library. At first I'd had these arranged on the shelves in alphabetical order by author, but as the library grew I developed a more informed, less arbitrary system. Arranged by subject – Vision, Memory, Motor, and so on. Actually the bulk of my books belonged to the looser category of General and Introductory. Owen Madden's book was very useful.

I had my minibar in case Colin should visit – stashed under the bed in case Jade or (God forbid) Dr Prabhakar should happen by. I could enjoy a cigarette in the en suite bathroom, blowing the smoke directly into the extractor fan. To begin with I would retire to my studio at the Institute on a Wednesday, after my class, often with Colin, or sometimes with Ben. As time went by, though, it became my habit to spend a good part of the week in there, with my studying, and lots of civilised drinks. A proper gin and tonic (no ice, unfortunately, but with a slice of lemon, and out of a glass), or a nice white wine. I would sit there and spitefully relish the thought of my former self toughing it out in Hackney. Cleaning his brushes in a melted icicle. Drinking instant coffee (the cheap stuff) with vodka (the cheap stuff, too) in it.

I would sit at my desk in the evenings with a book open in front of me trying to memorise all the names – fornix; basal ganglia; dendrite. I found it useful after a while to use Emily's drawings to help me out with my brain anatomy. I'd been looking through them one day, sniffing, licking even, and began also to name things. That's the hypothalamus I'm snogging. And here's the hippocampus, Emily's missing part. Since they were worthless as artworks, and she'd never know if they'd been defaced because she couldn't remember having done them, I started to use them as part of a memory test. I would write the names of the parts on her drawings and then check my labelling against the illustrations in a textbook. Doing this I got to know my way around the gross anatomy of the human brain.

At seven on the dot each evening I'd be alerted to the fact that the Institute was closed for the day by the muffled chorus of many vacuum cleaners powering up. There were two teams of cleaners, the Nigerians and the Romanians, who seemed to be in competition and would make as much cleaning noise as they could to broadcast the evidence of work getting done. Competing for the permanent contract, I thought; Simon and Selina behind that, probably. They were generally done by midnight and I rarely saw them.

Leaving, I would nod at the security guard sitting at the reception desk, one of the three living souls left here through the night. The others were Emily, and a nurse in a room somewhere whose job it was to look out for the solitary inpatient. I would sometimes stop at Emily's door and listen. I never heard anything because of the excellent soundproofing. I was always hoping for a little sigh, as she breathed out in her sleep, or the sound of a vibrator, like a moped in the distance.

I had pretty well mastered my routes to and from anywhere I needed to get to by now – the Day Room, Ben's office, the Activities Room – but would lose this acquired mastery sometimes after all my gin and tonics and nice white wines. Once or twice I didn't make it out of there until three or four in the morning, and on one occasion I ended up having to kip under a conference table in a room that the cleaners had left unlocked. The security guys never showed any curiosity about my funny hours, or my flat-footed step and fixed expression as I passed the desk. They'd glance up from a book or game, not at my face but at my chest, where I had my laminated security pass clipped on, and look down again with an 'alright', or just 'K mate.'

Colin hadn't turned up, and it had been weeks since our bad-tempered discussion in the pub about the Institute, and crop circles, and other shit like that. I was missing him. He'd been my principal drinking buddy, in the Canadian Volunteer and here in my studio, and I missed his funny stories, and telling him mine. We'd been talking about the possibility of me coming to see him at his archery club sometime. He does medieval archery, and sometimes they dress up in all the gear like the Merry Men. Colin in tights.

The thing is, though, I might have missed the old Colin I thought I knew even if Colin had actually been turning up, because I wasn't sure about him now that I'd seen he could be so suggestible. Frankly, I thought he should have taken my side about the conspiracy theory stuff. (OK, he was quite pissed, but still.)

53: another private view

'HELLO. WHAT D'YOU RECKON?'

'Susan! Well, it's just a French film, isn't it?' We were looking at the monitor in a darkened gallery space. 'Am I missing something here?'

'Yes. The subtitles are from a *different* French film. It's about performativity.'

You see, Susan will have bothered to read the press release, before she came here even. We watched the movie (or movies) a bit longer. 'OK,' I said, 'well, what I reckon is he's combined elements of two things to produce something that's not as good as either individually. I'm no cinema expert but this looks to me as if it was quite good before it got turned into a contemporary artwork.' How's that for provocation? Let's see what she has to say about that!

'Yes. I know. It's one of those sooner or later pieces.'

A 'sooner or later piece' was our private joke. We'd been at a private view during, I think, our first week together, and we were wondering why the glass hammer we were looking at was so annoying. It was annoying because doing a glass hammer is one of those ideas that a lot of people have, and then dismiss as too obvious. Then someone comes along and actually does it, because it doesn't seem so obvious at all to them, in fact it feels entirely fresh and resonant, and it's a success. And then all the people who've had that idea already and dismissed it as too corny get annoyed, because they could have had that success.

We both had had the idea of doing a glass hammer. And here we were now looking at something of the same sort that, Susan now informs me, has earned the guy a Turner Prize nomination.

'Hang on,' I said, 'the shortlist doesn't come out for months. How do you know?'

'It's my job to know things.'

'Yeah. I didn't know you knew Conrad Norman, actually. You never mentioned it last time I saw you.'

'I only met him the other night, at St John.'

'Oh yeah – you eat meat now.' I said this with some resentment, after the hard time she used to give me about it.

'Eating properly-sourced offal at St John's is a bit different from eating a kebab when you're pissed. And people do change, you know. Actually you've changed a bit lately yourself. You seem a lot more together now you're doing that residency. At that place—?'

'The Norman Neurologigacal Institute.'

'Did you just say "neurologigacal"?'

'Neurological,' I said, enunciating carefully this time.

'You seem a lot more mature and organised than you used to. You used to have the mentality of a twelve-year-old.'

'Uh-huh?'

'Now I'd put you at around seventeen, or eighteen.'

'Cheers.'

'You're very welcome.'

And this is all fine, really. Our relationship has been set where it belongs, in the past, and now we are two people with some history, and a shared sense of humour, and, it seems to me, a new respect for one another. This is great!

'I'm really getting into the Institute, actually. It's really interesting. You should meet some of the people there. You wouldn't believe some of it.' I told her all about my idea for a curated project there using the patients' drawings, and some things about Emily (not everything obviously), and started to tell her about how vision works, and what saccades are, and top-down visual processing. That last bit seemed not to interest her so much, so I got back onto the sort of stuff she was comfortable with, and even wondered if she'd like to get involved in my project, somehow?

What I suppose I was doing here was trying to give Susan the impression that I'm able to assist her career in some way (because curators love things to do with the disabled). Rather fortunately for me, she didn't jump at it. To be honest there wasn't really a lot of substance to my offer. She was, however, kind of interested in just the right way. That is, she had now formed the impression that I was sort of important these days. As an added bonus, when the time came for us to kiss goodbye, I found that I was not yet thoroughly and obviously drunk. Yep. I did good there.

54: Miss Havisham's lab

I GOT A VISIT FROM BEN one evening after work. I was at my desk in my study, with a nice glass of white wine and a book – Owen Madden's *Brains*: Chapter 6, Memory. I was listening to Radio 3, another new habit. 'Come!' I said when he knocked. (That's definitely new: 'Come!') Ben came in and plonked himself down on the edge of the bed, causing the ends of the mattress to lift off the frame – he's a big guy. He didn't speak, so I said something.

'You heard anything from Colin lately? He hasn't been in. You heard anything? I suppose he's OK ...?'

'Oh, I'm sure he's fine. He doesn't *live* here, you know. You got any more of that?'

I gave him a glass of wine. He looked, now I came to think of it, like shit. He even looked, actually, and very surprisingly, as if he was a bit depressed! I then discovered, having puzzled for a moment about what it was that seemed especially odd to me about that, that I personally was not depressed. Not at all! I knew there was something. You could always depend on Ben to furnish these insights, even when he wasn't trying. The recognition that I was actually in a pretty good mood a lot of the time these days, even despite the heartache, served to improve my mood again.

'What is it?' I said, from my position of emotional stability and centredness, seated at my desk.

'Just this place sometimes ... all the bullshit.' I understood what he meant, in a general kind of way. I told him about the prawn a few weeks ago, and he smiled a bit. He'd been in meetings with those people all week. He's had to spend a lot of time with Hilary from the Arts Council. Not from the Arts Council any more. Some kind of fundings freelancer now. I'd seen her around a few times, with a new eyebrow piercing looking like a silver-headed boil. 'My Christ she's boring.' That said with a lot of feeling. He's practically a broken man today. He never gets a chance to do the kind of stuff he came here to do.

'Have a look at this,' he said. 'Come along. I'll show you something.'

Turning left out of my room – I always turn to the right: I know what's to the right – Ben leads me along a lot of corridors, probably new to me, though identical to everything else here, so who knows? By the time we stop at a door, I judge us to have walked about half a mile. Almost certainly I've never been here before. As he's unlocking, he says, 'Have a look at this ...' reaching an arm around to get the light, 'Miss Havisham's laboratory.' A room the size of the Activities Room, with long white-tiled benches running parallel across its width, and huge sinks at intervals around the walls. Every available horizontal bit of space was occupied with boxes, all sizes. There are no cobwebs but I can see what he means. The place looks as if it's been got ready for something that's never going to happen.

'There's another two laboratories like this one.'

'What's in all these boxes?'

'It's all laboratory equipment. We've got machines here even I don't know what they do.'

They've got piezoelectric manipulators, patch-clamp systems, confocal laser-scan microscopes, microcannulas, optical filter changers, startle reflex systems, photobeam activity measurement systems, microcapnometers. There are syringe pumps, centrifuges, incubators, brooders. Hundreds of different sorts of pens and cages for rats, cats, chicks and monkeys. There are a lot of fridges, most still boxed, but a few taken out of their packaging and plugged in; they're full of antibodies and fish tissue. Crates and crates of testtubes, beakers and droppers. Cases of rubber gloves and protective goggles. Hundreds of boxes of neuroscience journals – NEURON, *Molecular and Cellular Neuroscience* (*MCN*) – some opened, and a few copies taken out. Ben puts copies out on the tables in the Day Room: out of date but they look good. Other boxes have just been dropped so that they've split and the magazines have spilled out of the cardboard like a disembowelling. Somewhere in here there's a box containing a machine that Ben definitely doesn't know the use of, and which cost almost as much as all the rest put together. Over there somewhere, under those rat mazes.

We were picking our way across the room, squeezing through and stepping over, Ben listlessly examining things as we passed, flipping the odd box to read the label, or turning it with his foot, '—hmm, well well', 'Didn't know about those', '... could have had a lot of fun with this', 'Tut'. Then he told me all about the Institute's purchasing policy.

'At first, when Nancy was putting all this together here she was doing it all properly, like you'd do it normally. She'd have these meetings with Norman or his people and she'd show them all the figures for budgeting she'd worked on. She was working twenty-hour days at one point, just on budgeting. She couldn't work out why they were never happy, so she did what you do and started cutting corners and finding ways to economise, and they still weren't happy. Then she twigged they wanted her to spend more, not less. The more she spent, the happier they were. So she ended up just going crazy with it. She went on a total shopping binge. You remember all that stuff in the Activities Room? The looms and printing presses and pottery kilns and things. Instead of ordering from the catalogues she'd just ring these companies up and say she wanted everything in their catalogue. Two of everything. Five.'

'Is it all useless, then?'

'Now it is, yeah, because we've got no one to actually work with it all. It could have been fantastic, having all this equipment, if we'd had some scientists as well. You could have done anything here. Any kind of research you wanted, and you could have followed a problem around from one discipline to another so you wouldn't have to see everything from the same angle all the time. You could have the chemists and the clinical practitioners working together on things. If Norman had lived a bit longer, we could have had the funding in place to run the labs, and there would have been nothing like it anywhere, not even in the States. That kind of freedom is unheard of, where you're not constantly having to justify everything and argue about money the whole time. Between all the ethics and the money it's impossible to get anything done. You never get really exciting work, like Wilder Penfield's stuff in the 'fifties, because those opportunities that he had just don't crop up that often. If you had all the money and a little bit more leeway about ethical practice, we could have been miles ahead of where we are now. It's only all the bullshit that's holding us back.'

55: Wilder Penfield

WILDER PENFIELD. I was a big fan myself. He's in all the literature. Great name. One of the things he's famous for is discovering the sensory cortex; that sausage of brain that goes from the top of your head to behind your ear, in which the whole of your skin is represented. An image I knew quite well, even before I'd looked at any books on the subject, is something called the Penfield homunculus. It's on at least two CD covers that I know of. It's a little man with all his proportions distorted so that the size of each part is commensurate with its degree of sensitivity. So he has enormous hands and lips. Nothing special about the cock, though.

Another thing Penfield is famous for is the method by which he made this discovery of the sensory cortex (and the motor cortex, right next to it). He developed a ground-breaking surgical procedure for treating epilepsy.

(You always think there must be something sinister about brain surgery, because of lobotomies. They did thousands of lobotomies shortly after World War Two. It was quite a craze, used to try and treat all sorts of conditions – psychosis; depression; various neuroses. The procedure was fantastically crude. They'd stick a scalpel up into the brain through the eye socket and then just slash side to side through the frontal lobe. Hence 'lobotomy'. The effects weren't all bad. There were patients suffering from 'unendurable thoughts' who reported some relief. But a lot of patients turned out like the Phineas Gage guy. It's a similar injury. They began to display 'inappropriate behaviour'. They would have difficulty planning. They never considered the consequences of their actions. They'd have an idea and just go right ahead and do it. The technique was devised by António Egas Moniz, who was awarded the Nobel Prize for Medicine, in 1949, and was later shot in the spine by a patient and paralysed. Not, actually, by a lobotomised patient, though.)

Penfield's procedure sounds just as scary as a lobotomy, but it was actually a lot better thought out and was used effectively on over a thousand patients with intractable epilepsy. First he'd give them a local anaesthetic and take off the top of the skull. They'd be conscious. Then he'd probe the brain with an electrode – a fine needle with a tiny electric current going through it. This doesn't hurt at all, because the brain has no pain receptors for itself. He would prod with the electrode and ask the patient if they could feel anything. The electrical current stimulates brain cells around the needle, and what he was looking for was the area, usually in the temporal lobe, from which the patient's seizures are generated. Before an epileptic seizure most sufferers experience what's called an 'aura', which is just the feeling that they are about to have a fit. (This can be very pleasant, apparently. A lot of patients look forward to it.)

Penfield would prod with his electrode and ask if the patient was experiencing their aura. If they were, then he'd found the problem area – a little cluster of cells which is the focus of occasional erratic electrical activity. This arrhythmic pulsing is what triggers the seizure. It causes a surge of violent and promiscuous electrical activity right across the cortex, like dropping a match in a box of fireworks. Once the site has been identified – the patient reports that they have the feeling that they are about to have a fit – it can be lesioned, or ablated. Just a tiny 'snick' with the scalpel. Then the top of the head is replaced and apparently you'd be walking around again in no time, with a big bandage like a turban. And usually there'd be a marked improvement in your condition, if not always a total cure. It does sound a bit drastic to take the top of your head off while you're conscious. Daunting for the patients, certainly. But it's not surprising so many consented to the procedure when you think that a lot of these people were having violent seizures every half-hour or so. You'd try anything. The technique isn't used as much now because they've got better anticonvulsant drugs, but it's still done. (So is ECT, another treatment with a sinister reputation.)

The way Penfield discovered the sensory cortex is that, when he was doing this operation, patients would often report bodily sensations in response to prods in particular parts of the cortex. They would say 'I can feel something touching my knee', or touching my buttock, etc. He found that there was a correspondence of parts of the brain to parts of the body, and that this relationship was stable and universal. Thus he was able to identify the cortical bulge or gyrus along which the skin is represented cortically. Also he discovered that the spatial relationship of the body parts in the cortex follows a different topography from the body itself. So, for example, in the brain the genitals are next to the feet. And the sizes are different, the shoulders in the brain being much smaller than the fingertip. He realised, in other words, that it was a map where things are measured not in inches or centimetres but in degrees of sensitivity. It is a spatial analogue of sensation. An aesthetic chart. The area corresponding to the lips is huge.

It was also this technique – prodding and asking, 'Anything there? No? how about … there?' – that gave rise to the other discovery for which Penfield has become renowned, this one a lot more controversial. Often patients would report not feelings but memories. They would find themselves reminiscing as a result of his surgical procedure. Here are some examples:

- a time of watching illuminated signs
- a time of lying in the delivery room at birth
- standing on the corner of Jacob St., South Bend, Indiana
- watching circus wagons go by, years ago
- hearing father and mother sing Christmas carols

A lot of the stuff they'd get in these reminiscences was just music. 'White Christmas'. 'Rock-a-Bye Baby'. The theme tune from a popular radio show. The controversy about these results has to do with something called the 'engram' – kind of a mythical beast in the neuroscience world, like Big Foot or the Beast of Exmoor. The engram is the physical repository of a memory. Put it another way, the engram is what needs to be physically, measurably different between a brain that has learned a certain thing and a brain that hasn't learned that thing. It's supposed to establish a connection between thought and matter, like Descartes' pineal gland. It has been thought in the past to be something like a cell, or a cluster of cells containing your sixth birthday, or losing your virginity. The idea is that Penfield had hit the engram for particular memories, and thus evoked them.

The theory, what Penfield thought at the time, is that we are all recording all the time like CCTV or a tape recorder, but that most of what we record lies forgotten somewhere; languishes somewhere in the brain's filing system because we don't need it, and it's not near any frequently travelled neural pathway. Out of sight, out of mind. And so what has happened with the probe is that this forgotten file, or tape, or disc, has been rediscovered because of the highly unusual circumstance of the brain being exposed and arbitrarily nudged and rattled. The engram has been discovered in a particular locale, just waiting there, doing nothing.

Current thinking about memory, about the brain in general, is hostile to this sort of straightforward localisation, and to the idea that memory is a passive, whole, and neutral record of events. The engram, if such a thing can be said to exist at all, won't turn out to be like a little nut or egg. It'll be something systemic and distributed – a product of the interplay of electrical, chemical and somatic components. (Proteins are very important, apparently.)

Memory, like vision, is now conceived of as a process, dynamic and constitutive of its object. It's not a record of events. In fact, when you remember something that happened ten years ago you're probably remembering not something that happened ten years ago but your most recent experience of remembering what happened ten years ago. And that most recent recollection is itself the memory of the recollection before that. It's like Chinese whispers. There are distortions. Penfield's patient's reminiscences could be the Ur-memories upon which those sequentially shifting recollections are based, but there's something fishy about their nostalgia that makes you suspect otherwise.

There is a suspiciously intuitive, sentimental appeal, too, about the amount of music in the reminiscences Penfield recorded. This could be something to do with the particular neural processes involved in remembering tunes as opposed to, say, names or skills: they are certainly all different things. They're all called 'memory' but the physiological processes that make them possible aren't the same. (Why is it easier to remember tunes than names of tunes? The aptitude for remembering tunes seems to have some links with arithmetic, or at any rate stronger links with arithmetic than with remembering names or faces. And the abilities to remember names and faces are, again, distinct from each other.)

It's certainly true that Penfield's patients wanted to call these experiences memories. They must have felt like memories, but then so does déjà vu, and we know that's wrong. The patients wanted them to be memories, possibly, because they felt good, and reassuring. Like a kind of value-inverted False Memory Syndrome, where instead of recalling episodes of abuse on which you can blame the fact that your life is fucked up, you have idealised memories. Perfect moments. Harmless pursuits. In most cases there's no really reliable way of proving one way or another if the recollections are accurate or not. Even if you really wanted proof, and it seems Penfield didn't, who's to say if you felt happy smelling the roses or roasting the chestnuts on a particular afternoon twelve years ago. What kind of evidence could be used to support or counter such a claim? My own evidence would be no good, based on a recollection elicited in such singular circumstances. And what could other witnesses give you? Trying to pinpoint a certain afternoon, years ago, on which nothing of note happened, and then having, maybe, got it right, trying to recall what kind of mood I seemed to be in.

The fact that Penfield didn't really examine this matter – whether or not these memories could really be described as such, if by 'memory' you mean the recollection of a real event, verifiable by other witnesses – doesn't mean he was being sloppy. Those reminiscences were a completely surprising result, and he didn't have time to pursue their implications *and* treat his patients. He was a doctor. Also, back then in the early 1950s, there probably seemed no reason to doubt or question the claim that a certain experience was that of remembering. Now, of course, we're beginning to see what a complicated thing memory is, and understand some of the ways in which it is not to be relied on.

Memories, actually, can be faked or installed. If you ask people to describe something they've seen, it's quite easy to add something to their memory of it. Say, a man running from the scene of a crime. You ask: What colour was his moustache? About fifty per cent of people will say they didn't see any moustache, but the other fifty per cent, after a moment's thought, will come up with a colour for the moustache you've just invented. From then on their memory of the event will include a brown moustache. And that doesn't mean only fifty per cent of people are likely to confabulate. Ask another question, and try the same planting of some element by suggestion, a limp or something, and a lot of people who wouldn't go for the tache will go for the limp. It's not that about fifty per cent of people are unreliable witnesses, it's that we're all unreliable witnesses about fifty per cent of the time. We all do it. It's part of how memory works.

56: so ... memory

MEMORY IS NOT A FAITHFUL objective record, and scenes from the past pictured in the mind's eye are not photographs. Just as optical illusions can expose the proper normal functioning of vision – its use of conjecture and salience – so the con trick of planting a memory exposes the normal functioning of memory. If you were to remember everything in clear detail and without any narrative embellishments or elisions, it would be impossible to get on with life. It would be too distracting. So-called 'photographic memory', the rare phenomenon of clear and total recall, is actually a handicap. People with that kind of memory just get swamped in mnemic junk, like keeping every single object you've ever bought in the house. Every single toothpaste tube and magazine. To work for us, memory needs to be not an *accurate* but an *enabling* account. It's annoying that you can't remember if you locked up properly, or turned off the gas, but just imagine if you could remember all that. Imagine being able to remember every single time you've turned the gas off. You'd go nuts. (There's evidence that the right hemisphere of the brain, the romantic, artistic half, has the job of configuring your memories and self-image into a meaningful whole. It tells you a story about yourself, because the bare facts would be too numerous, dull, confusing and, let's face it, depressing.)

Nobody doubts that Penfield's account of what his patients reported is accurate, but what it means is disputed, and probably undecidable right now. It'll be a long time before any more light can be shed on what those results mean, because that kind of surgery is much rarer due to the new anticonvulsants; and also, frankly, you probably wouldn't be allowed to do that kind of rummaging around in a living patient's brain these days. The consent forms for a thing like that would be a nightmare, probably undraftable in any form that would allow you to do the work and stay covered if anything went wrong. It would have to be a document that said, in effect, 'If we find anything interesting in there while we've got the old hood up, do you mind if we take a look at it and forget the treatment for a bit?'

Penfield took advantage of a unique window of opportunity: a surprise finding in the course of performing hundreds of near-identical operations on conscious and articulate patients, and no ambulance-chasing lawyers or accountants breathing down your neck. No wonder Ben's so envious. Penfield had the lot. The three Ls – Luck, Licence and Leisure. And successful treatment of his patients. It's going to be a while before those results can be pursued seriously. It'll probably have to wait until some other breakthrough in in vivo brain imaging technology comes along. Could be decades.

57: 'neurogenesis'?

BEN WAS PICKING ABSTRACTEDLY at the lid of a cardboard box, mourning, I believe, the loss of that kind of frontier spirit. We're all too busy watching our arses these days. No one's prepared to go out on a limb. And the thought of those tantalisingly uninterpretable results. Like opening the door to Tutankhamun's tomb and then closing it again because your torch battery went dead.

'Is that a mini-fridge in that box?'

He leaned sideways to look at the label. 'Yeah.'

'Can I have it? Not to take home. In my studio?'

'Don't see why not, as long as it doesn't leave the building. Simon and Selina are going to check the inventory at some point.' I lifted the box, which was quite heavy, and carried it back across the room to the door. That's as far as I could manage. 'Here ...' Ben took it from me and I opened the door for him. Not completely useless then.

Halfway along the second or third corridor Ben was showing no signs of effort, and I asked him about something I'd been meaning to mention.

'Have you ever heard of something called "NORMERON"?'

'Yeah, 'course. Nancy used to work there. That's how she met Norman in the first place.'

'Oh, right.' Not such a big secret, then. Ben suddenly registered something in my tone and smiled. 'You've been talking to Stick, haven't you.'

'So it doesn't make chemical weapons, then.'

'It's a biochem company – mostly nootropics. Smart drugs. Performance-optimising drugs.'

'Sounds like coke. Or speed.'

'They did actually use speed for years, as far back as World War Two.'

'They?'

'The US Army. And Air Force.'

'Sounds like it is to do with weapons, then.'

'No it's ... Norman has, or should I say Norman *had*, interests in other companies that produce missiles and whatnot. NORMERON isn't connected to that, though. It gets a lot of funding from the US Defence Department because they're always on the lookout for things they can use in all sorts of areas. They fund all kinds of research just because they've got these huge budgets and they want to make sure they get first dibs on anything new. Lots of stuff on the market now was developed with money from the American Army. All kinds of computer and communications stuff; medical stuff; fabrics; cars; sunblock; building materials; pens. You'd never get anything done without the Defence Department. So they're working on stuff to improve alertness and memory. Eventually it'll end up on the market, when they come up with something good. They're looking into all sorts of things. Adrafinil. Centrophenoxine. Melatonin. Gingko biloba.'

'Gingko biloba? You can get that in the health food shop. NORMERON isn't a secret, then?'

'The company's existence isn't a secret. It's mentioned on all the Institute's stationery.' I hadn't noticed that. 'And what it does isn't a secret. But obviously the details of any results have to be kept secret. Definitely. If they do come up with a really effective memory-enhancing drug, or something that keeps you awake with no side effects, it'll be worth billions.'

'Nothing like that so far?'

'I don't think they've come up with anything as effective as amphetamines, epinephrine or whatever. Matter of fact

I'm not sure they've come up with anything better than coffee. They were really excited about a drug called modafinil at one point, but they've published the results so it can't have been anything great.'

We had reached my room and I was examining my new acquisition.

'There's no ice tray in this.'

'It's a laboratory fridge. You don't need ice cubes in a laboratory.'

Oh yeah. I could improvise. Fill a plastic bottle with water and put it in the fridge. When it froze I could cut the bottle open and break up the ice in the sink.

'What's "neurogenesis"? You said Nancy and Dr Madden were working on it together. Is that another project?'

'It's not a project, it's a phenomenon. It's something the two of them were looking at ... really exciting avenue, actually. A bit of a long shot but the potential is massive. What it is ... you know the brain doesn't grow or repair itself once it's formed? There's only a fixed number of brain cells and when they're gone they're gone.'

'Yes.' I knew that.

'Well it turns out that's not true. The brain does produce some new cells in the ventricles and the hippocampi. That's what neurogenesis is. So Nancy and Dr Madden were working on that; working on something to promote neural stem cell division. It'd be like the ultimate smart pill. Because, even though the brain does produce some new cells – so we know it's possible – it doesn't produce anything like enough to make any noticeable difference to performance. Nothing in the order of hundreds of thousands, and it'd take billions to make any real difference.' He helped himself to a glass of wine, in a much better mood now.

'It wouldn't keep you awake, though.'

'Probably not, but it could improve your memory enormously. In fact it could improve the brain's performance globally. It could have applications in all sorts of areas. Depression, schizophrenia, Alzheimer's, drug addiction, degenerative diseases. Even repairing brain damage – stroke, head injuries ...'

'Conrad Norman must have been quite excited about that.'

'When he realised he had Alzheimer's, he was very excited indeed. NORMERON was just another company until that happened. Then when he realised someone working in one of his companies might be able to help him out with his Alzheimer's, he threw all kinds of resources at Nancy and Owen. That's why we're sitting here now. But I don't think he had a realistic idea of how long these things can take, even if you do have all the resources. It still might not come to anything. They've had some encouraging results with rats, but that's just one study. There are always encouraging results for something, based on one unreplicated study. It's like cures for cancer. There's always lots of amazing stuff in the pipeline. Some of it may turn out to be something and a lot of it won't.'

'Stick seems to have rather misunderstood things, then. Is it even in South America? It's probably in Wales, isn't it?'

'No no, it is in South America. Or, actually, Central America. Belize actually.'

'That's where Emily got her illness.'

'She was an employee, actually. She was lucky in a way, because if she'd have been working for any other sort of company out there she probably wouldn't have got such good treatment. If Emily had gone to any ordinary hospital in Belize she'd most probably have died, but she got taken to the clinic they run at NORMERON for the locals – it's sort of a goodwill thing. The staff are all volunteers from

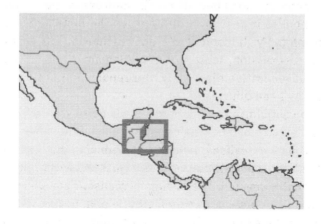

NORMERON, so as soon as they realised it was neurological they all knew what to do. You need to keep a very close eye on the vital signs with encephalitis, because they can change very suddenly.'

'That's irony for you. Getting a neurological condition in a place where it's all neurologists. Or is that a paradox? Or a *coincidence*?'

'One of those. Like getting knocked down by an ambulance. Which, actually, does happen quite a lot, come to think of it. It's not that surprising, though. Oncologists get cancer too. Anyhow, Nancy managed to get her coptered out after she'd stabilised. Yeah ...' He seemed rather to lose his train of thought then, and as he continued it was to fill me in about context, rather than any details. 'It's quite a strange place, Belize. Did you know it used to be part of the British Empire? Also, weirdly, it's where they invented chewing gum. And the racial mix is incredibly complicated for such a small place. It's mostly Afro-Caribbean, but you've got Creoles, Mayans of course, you've got Chinese, East Indians, Hispanics, you name it. There's even a group of Amish people who speak German! And a lot of poverty, so free health care is important. They do have public hospitals but they're a bit cash-strapped.' As he talked he was watching me go through my CD collection. 'You've got it very cosy in here,' he said. 'A real home from home.'

'Not really. You should see my home.'

'Why's that?'

'You shouldn't see my home. It's a toilet … Ah! Here it is.' I showed him a CD with the Penfield homunculus on the cover. Ben was quite surprised by this. He hadn't realised the image had got out into the world like that; into popular culture.

'Do you want to have a listen?' Why not? I thought. We've come this far together and found some common ground. Let's try with the music. I guessed his taste would be quite conservative, but when you like someone and you like a certain type of music you always want to introduce them and see if they get along, because your liking them both seems to imply a deep consanguinity. Maybe I could broaden Ben's horizons a bit, aesthetically.

He wasn't very polite about my taste in music, though. In fact, he didn't give it much of a chance. 'That's just a lot of screaming and noise. It's horrible. Turn it off.'

People can be highly sophisticated in one area but Philistines in others. I suppose I shouldn't have been surprised (and actually a bit hurt). Whilst I myself could be considered a cultured individual in some ways – I know a lot about painting and marginal rock music – I'm quite ignorant about a lot of things. There's just too much going on out there and I can't be bothered with a lot of it. Contemporary poetry, for example – whiny and incomprehensible. Contemporary dance – gymnastics and flopping all about the place, not interesting even when the girls are naked, with their flat muscle-bound titties. Modern Literature – I'll pretend to enjoy reading Burroughs, but you can't read more than a paragraph or two. Art films – not as good as good real films. Contemporary classical music – that actually *is* a lot of horrible noise. Nobody really likes that, surely. What else? Opera. *Jazz*. I've really got no interest in things outside my own area. Even with contemporary art, which is my bread and butter. I almost never watch the whole of an art video, or spend any time in an installation. Installations are things you have to climb over on the way to the bar.

58: love

THE CLEANERS WERE ALREADY going at it when Ben left, and I found I was in the mood for being in love. This is being in love as an activity, rather than as a condition to be experienced passively. And not for the first time. It has tailed off a bit in recent years, but being in love is something I've devoted quite a few hours to. There's not actually a lot to it. 'Activity' is putting it a bit strong. It's just the right kind of music, some wine (if you've got it), and thinking.

Emily is by no means my first love object, and I'm well aware of all the problems. I'm not stupid. My age, for a start. It's all very well mooning about with an aching heart when you're seventeen but I'm pushing forty and ought to have cut it out by now. Which brings us to the subject of masturbation (which I also ought to have stopped), which is connected to being in love as a kind of index. It's when you find yourself unable to conjure the loved one's image as an aid to wanking that you know it really is love, and not just lust or infatuation. Another problem is, of course, it *is* lust and infatuation. I scarcely know the woman. Given her condition it's debatable whether she can be known at all. Does a person whose consciousness leaks like a sieve have a personality? She's just an idea of something, isn't she? She's beautiful and unknowable and (for all sorts of reasons and in many ways, practical and philosophical) unattainable.

I'm very well aware that the long sexual famine I'm going through, in the middle of, or wherever I am with it, has a lot to do with all this. My sexual appetite has been transcended by some kind of meta-urge that doesn't even really have an object. Like a medieval monk. I'm in a condition defined by unrealistic expectation, and I know that, and it doesn't make any difference. I still feel like doing being in love. Obviously the aching and yearning and pining is an indulgence I'm allowing myself. (And me being a natural ascetic, too.) Part of the reason I need a drink to go with being in love is so that I won't feel embarrassed and self-conscious about it, even though there's no one here to see me, and nothing much to see if there were. Me in a chair listening to music and sipping wine, sighing.

I choose my music carefully. Nothing by Dethinstinkt or Katharghsiss. I go with one of my favourites for this kind of thing: noisy, but in a remote, oceanic way, with fragments of some half-remembered melody pulsing woozily in and out of consciousness, and a girl's voice, untutored, singing what sounds like a lullaby to herself, very deep down in the mix. It's called 'Spunk Bubble'. It is not called 'Spunk Bubble'. (Facetiousness: at a time like this. I can't even take *my own* feelings seriously.) It's called 'To Here Knows When' – the title is as meaningless and evocative as the tune itself. Oh, my aching heart. That girl's voice in the distance. You can never make out the words. I must have listened to this a thousand times (Emily's predecessors) and I've still got no idea what she's saying: the lack of comprehension tying itself up with an auditory trick of this piece of music, where you start to think the sound is coming from somewhere other than the speakers – behind you, or just outside the door. Emily is calling to me.

I play it a few more times and it doesn't work so well after a while, so I look for something else. Flicking through my CDs for something not to do with violent death, I make an inspirational discovery. I'd forgotten I had this. *Pink*

Floyd: The Early Singles. 'See Emily Play' – a song about some kind of Victorian ghost story child/woman. It's just right. Psychedelic. Remote. Innocent but spooky.

I listen to this many times. So many in fact that it too gets boring, and I find I'm sitting in silence and thinking not about the fantastical Emily – making daisy chains or whatever – but about the actual thing. Those boyfriends she must have had. Must have. And she must have gone to university, and she obviously had a job (she can't have been living on fairy dust, in a land of unicorns, like I'd been imagining she did). A job, somehow to do with NORMERON. It took her to their place in Belize, apparently. And she'll have parents …

59: conjecture, hypothesis and wild speculation

COLIN'S HER DAD, ISN'T HE? Of course! He'd be bound to have kids, a bloke like him, and he never mentions them. I'll bet he has loads of kids by all sorts of different women, and Emily is one. Or, probably, he *thinks* she might be one of them, but he doesn't know. *That's* how come he was so sympathetic to Stick, and all his mad conspiracy ideas. He thinks Emily, who might be his love child, is a captive here, or the victim of some secret experiment that went wrong. He's here to keep an eye on her, and he's made it all up about the prosopagnosia. After all, we've only got his word for it. It'd be easy to fake a condition like that. There's no really objective way of testing for it. A brain scan could show damage that might cause the condition, but it can't show that you actually have it. It'd be a much easier condition to fake than a lot of things where the physical cause isn't easy to spot. Faking acute schizophrenia, for example, would be a hell of a job, because you'd have to remember to keep up all these behaviours all the time, and be endlessly creative with it. So he's faking prosopagnosia so that he can keep an eye on Emily in secret. No wonder he's always making such a fuss of her. And he makes a show of making a fuss of the other patients just to cover himself.

This all makes perfect sense now. He's smart enough to do a bit of research and find out about an easily fakeable condition consistent with having had a mild stroke, and it's quite possible he did actually have the stroke. The pretence would have to be good enough to consistently fool a neuro-logist, because they'd all have to be in on it, including Ben. He must suspect that Colin is faking it, but isn't sure, so he's contriving these bizarre tests to try and catch him out. But that 'test' I saw proved the opposite. Ben coming into the room that time dressed up and walking strangely proved that Colin can recognise people from all the non-facial characteristics, even where there is an attempt (however feeble) to disguise those characteristics. And he's not afraid to show he can do that even though it casts doubt on his claim that he has prosopagnosia. So that thing of disguising everything but the face is not a test for faked prosopagnosia. But then maybe that's why he did it in such a half-arsed way. To lull Colin into such a false sense of security that he will even double-bluff, and act as if he is successfully compens-ating for the deficit of his dissimulated selective blindness. And all the while Ben is actually conducting very much more sophisticated tests, with the comical dressing up as a blind or feint, and none of us even notices he's doing it.

The entire Drawing Workshop could be a means of test-ing Colin. Ben is tricking Colin into demonstrating his lack of any deficit by getting him to draw more or less accurate pictures of the brain. It makes sense, because if we were drawing portraits Colin would smell a rat and just not attend the Workshop, because if he could draw faces he'd be found out. But brains have a lot in common with faces. They're about the same size, are laterally symmetrical and composed of a collection of distinct paired organs – two ears and two hippocampi; two temporal lobes and two eyes. And I'd thought the Workshop was *my* idea.

This, actually, is all seeming quite far-fetched now. A little bit fantastical. My mind may have become overstimulated. I know, I thought: why don't I just go and ask her? I can't ask Colin, because we aren't in touch just now, but Emily is just round the corner. She must know what she was doing at NORMERON down there in Belize, or if not that she can tell me about her life before all this happened. Her family and her job and those boyfriends. If nothing else it'll give us something to talk about. I'll go and see if she'd like a glass of wine. The cleaners were all done.

60: head in the fridge

COMING TO, THE NEXT DAY, was an experience of a type occurring so frequently in my life that it's got itself a kind of nickname. A label I use for it. I call it Head in the Fridge, and it's called that because of a recurring dream of mine. I think it's a recurring dream. It might just be the recurring memory of this dream. Anyhow, here's the dream ... I awake with a terrible feeling. I feel sure I've done something very bad, but I don't know what. I lie in bed and try to think – what did I get up to last night? It's all just beyond the liminal boundary of conscious recollection, and I need to bring it to the foreground because I know it's something serious. An hour or so of introspection (in dream time) yields nothing but glimpses and fragments. Oh yeah, so and so was there, wasn't he? And wossisname. We went to that place, didn't we? A blue coat or handbag got lost. Somebody shouting about soup ...

I'm getting nowhere with this, so I have to grasp the nettle and get on the phone and ask. I have to ring everyone I know I saw, and everyone *they* tell me I saw, and maybe try a few people I may or may not have seen. The long shots are going to be the most embarrassing but it's got to be done. So I ring people up, sounding dead casual, and after a bit of small talk, work my way round to asking '... was I alright? Did I ... *do* anything?' The first call is the longest because I'm being so incredibly casual – '... and your mum; how's she? ... Good?' – before asking if I did anything last night. But the phonecalls get shorter as I go. It's a morning's work, me not washed or dressed yet, but I persist because the feeling I've done something unforgivable is so strong. It isn't supported by any evidence from my friends – I may have got a bit mouthy at one stage, nothing more – which is actually quite frustrating, as if I actually *want* to have done something that puts me beyond the pale. I give up, having pursued every avenue I can think of.

So, not satisfied exactly, but having done my best, I decide to have a cup of tea, and when I open the fridge to get the milk there's a head in there. Human, obviously, and sometimes, in these dreams or recollections, wrapped in clingfilm. That's the dream, Head in the Fridge. And here is an acute instance of the experience that 'Head in the Fridge' is my convenient name for ...

I am woken by the sound of my new fridge humming, although it's actually been humming all night, so although that's what seems to have woken me it's probably just that it is the first thing I'm conscious of after I awake. Still with my eyes shut, the next thing I am conscious of is the feeling that something is wrong, and that feeling is quickly followed by the conviction that I've done something terrible. I've ruined everything. I open my eyes and I'm lying on the bed in my studio, facing the fridge. I throw myself across the room and flip the fridge door open. It's misty in there but I can see that all it contains is a plastic bottle, split because the water inside has expanded as it froze. I shouldn't have filled it right to the top. (Obviously I've got a headache and I feel sick.)

I stumble back onto the bed and begin to investigate this state of affairs. I give it some thought, but this yields nothing. How about the physical evidence? Well, let's see. I've fallen asleep in my studio and I'm in my underpants. I can't see the rest of my clothes. I make it to the en suite and there are my trousers, shoes and socks, but no shirt. I pause to see if that rings any bells ... Nope. Next, a body check. There's a mirror over the sink. I look OK, considering, but my chest and thighs have a slight sheen to them, a sort of coating. I feel it and it's sticky. And it has a smell. Oranges. There are little dark flecks of the orange's flesh dried onto my thighs.

It seems likely that I've done something to Emily. The smell of pulped orange causes a few snapshots and soundbites to scatter themselves on the table before my mind's eye, but nothing that really adds up – like a Scrabble tile, and a jigsaw piece, and another jigsaw piece from a different jigsaw; the rope from Cluedo, and the boot from Monopoly. Let us examine this stuff. What do we have? I've got an image of me knocking on Emily's door, a bottle of wine shoved into my hip pocket, and I'm holding a couple of glasses in one hand with the stems between my fingers. And then I think I've got Emily opening the door (after a lot of knocking) looking all sleepy and cross and adorable. That second bit I *think* I've got, but it could be just conjecture and fantasy. (What happens after you knock on Emily's door? Why Emily opens the door, of course.)

So there's that. I also have an image of me running down corridors, chasing someone. That could very easily be a dream, except although other people seem to have dreams in which they run along corridors (that's if the dream sequences in films are anything to go by), I've never had a dream like that. And this place does actually have a lot of identical corridors that you might run down. Something that makes me think it might be a dream is that I have an image of me turning a corner and seeing, halfway along the next corridor, a fox, with something nasty in its mouth. It's hard to say with this. The foxes do get everywhere, they've been spotted on the emergency stairs a few times, so it's not inconceivable that one got in here somehow and found the leftovers from a buffet lunch. It could even be living in the building. They're very adaptable. We'll leave a question mark over the fox. (Chasing a 'fox' into an orifice-like structure. And the thing in its mouth could be my cock. I don't think so. I gather from Ben that Freud is considered more of a literary figure than as any sort of scientist or clinical practitioner. He doesn't seem to have actually cured anyone. That doesn't mean that the notion of the unconscious is completely useless, though.)

61: consciousness – a digression

MOST OF WHAT THE BRAIN does is done unconsciously. Obviously, regulating all the somatic processes has to be unconscious. Your breathing, your heartbeat, digestion, releasing hormones, chewing without biting your tongue, and so on. And a lot of what you might think of as conscious activities, involving will or volition, have to be in large part unconscious. Walking, for example. You know you want to go over there, or wherever it is, and that you're going to be using your legs to get there, but you couldn't possibly be conscious of everything you're doing when you walk because each step involves a multitude of small adjustments of speed and direction and balance. You don't walk like a toy robot because few surfaces are flat enough to allow you to just set the process off and then forget about it. So walking is mostly unconscious even though it's a task requiring constant attention, on some level, and it is available to consciousness if need be. Say, if you were walking barefoot across a floor strewn with broken glass, or if you were learning to line-dance. But you don't want to be too conscious about it or it becomes difficult; like when you are walking 'naturally' in front of a copper, and you've got a pocketful of cocaine.

The unconscious is a resource which allows you to think, in the sense of making judgments and calculations, but which allows you to carry out other cognitive tasks simultaneously. Walk and chew gum. It is not the repository of a lot of stuff you can't face, like a cesspit that backs up occasionally and floods your conscious mind with filth, the image of your mum and dad fucking for example.

It's actually very difficult to draw a neat line between mental processes that are unconscious and those that are conscious. You'd think thinking was a conscious process, but trying to catch yourself in the act of thinking is impossible. It's like that children's party game, Grandmother's Footsteps, where everyone has to freeze the moment you turn around to look. You're aware there's been some activity going on behind you, you sense movement, and when you turn to look everything's different from last time you looked, but you never actually see anyone move.

Introspection is actually a very poor tool for examining the activity of thinking. I've tried to observe myself doing a sum in my head. A very slow process this, involving not only grey matter but all my fingers and toes. Watching me from outside, any observer would be able to see that I was thinking; eyes turned to the ceiling, lips moving, my forehead compressed, checking off the digits manually. All that hard, slow work ought to be the ideal object for introspective observation, but when I try it all that gets yielded to consciousness is a glimpse of the stages of the process. I have 3 and I have 4 – and then I have 7. What I don't seem to be able to watch, to perceive inwardly, is how I got from 3 and 4 to 7. So maybe consciousness in this instance is just a progress report. It's saying, 'We haven't got anything for you yet but we're working on it, and here's what we've got so far.' So if I have to add 3 and 4, and then multiply the result by 3, I get 7, then I get 21, thrown up onto the screen of consciousness. The addition and multiplication happen unconsciously, even though they happen, in my case, quite slowly.

Feelings are conscious, obviously. But that's because that's what feelings are, almost by definition. Not just feeling happy or sad or guilty. The feeling of touching things or seeing them; the feeling of running for the bus, or biting your tongue. My own feeling of guilt is the conscious register of something I've done that I know I shouldn't have done. The fact that I can't directly recall what that thing is, as a declarative memory, has nothing to do with any Freudian repression. It didn't shoulder its way into my consciousness only to be hastily shoved out again; locked in some dark cupboard and the key thrown away. It occupied my consciousness – I knew what I was doing while I was doing it – and then left, as all conscious experience will, but on this occasion without leaving a note.

I think that fox had part of a chicken carcass in its mouth.

62: head in the fridge (II)

I HAVE ANOTHER BIT OF EVIDENCE. My knob is really sore. I've definitely been doing something with it. I did have a dab of speed last night – I found it in that Pink Floyd CD case: no doubt I'd hidden it from myself – and speed does make me masturbate a lot. I've been on amphetamine binges that have left my cock in shreds. But I don't feel as if the wear and tear is caused by me continually pulling on it, this time. I suppose I feel that because there is now a barrier in my mind between Emily, what she means to me, and wanking.

The orange pulp is definitely a clue. I don't think I had any oranges on me when I knocked on her door, but I might have gone to the Day Room later and got some from the baskets by the coffee machine.

I can recall some kind of an agenda when I went to call on Emily. Two things I wanted to sort out. First, what sort of person did she used to be before she got sick? (I wanted to know; and it was something to talk about, what with me being so tongue-tied.) Second, has Stick fucked her? I'd have been planning to get on to that much later, after I'd got her to relax and open up a bit. And then this agenda would have had a final stage, having got those two things out of the way, which would be kissing her and so on. (I'm finding that all my fantasies about what I'd like to do with Emily are pre-watershed material. A kiss, and then fade ... Just use your imagination; you don't need a bloody diagram. A kiss and fade-out. This romanticism does not square with the state of my penis, but then whatever I've done to that has been done in the dark. Even I'm in the dark about it.)

Another material clue. There are no empties in my room, and I don't think I can have thrown them away. I generally sneak them out with me when I leave the building and put them in a skip by one of the construction sites. So, if they aren't here the only other likely place they could be is in Emily's room. This deduction causes a wave of fear and remorse so strong I almost pass out. I've carelessly left evidence just lying around. Wine bottles with my dabs all over them. What else have I left in there? Squashed oranges and semen. Bruises. I jump up from the bed and run into the bathroom again for another body check. No marks on my body at any rate; just the soreness. No marks on me decreases the likelihood of there being any on her, I reason. I'm not so strong that I could have used force without getting hurt myself. Unless I had a knife or something. No, no. Of course I couldn't have held a knife to her throat. Where would I get a knife? (An image now of me standing over her with a saw-backed survival knife. And this image immediately hustled from consciousness ... thrown out on its ear.)

But the strongest piece of evidence is this terrible sense of guilt and remorse. It's the worst I've ever had. Something must have caused this sense of catastrophe. It's a memory held in the form of affect because the facts, the declarative memories of that event, are too awful. (And if I feel like this now, then how am I going to feel when I *do* get the facts. The suspense is destroying me. It's a powerful feeling that's become uncoupled from its cause, and when that cause is brought to light it's going to flush me all away. I've got to know. It can't be any worse than how I feel now. How bad will this get?)

So, no strong-arm tactics. That makes sense actually, because I already had the means of getting what I wanted without having to resort to any threat of violence. I will have used her condition against her. Spun her a yarn. I probably told her I was her boyfriend. Didn't she remember how we used to juggle oranges together? (Splat!) Oh, and how I was never any good at it! We used to laugh about that Emily, before ... before all this ... .

I begin to see this course of events unfold – me sitting beside her on the bed; she hunched over her wine, holding the glass between the fingertips of both hands, fiddling with it, not really drinking. I place a hand on her shoulder and she looks down into the wine as if it were a crystal ball, and she's crying, softly. I squeeze the shoulder gently, reassuring but nothing too intimate yet. I've got a sad little smile on my face and every now and then she'll smile, too, about the things we used to do together, before she got ill.

A final thing that fits somewhere into this scene – me cajoling and entreating, and her not saying much. It's something I'm pretty sure she did say. Something about secrets – either 'I can keep a secret' or 'I'm good at secrets'; something like that. These words dovetail very nicely with my sense of culpability; the feeling that I have obtained something by deceit.

63: panic stations

SITTING ON THE EDGE of the bed in my underpants, all
sticky. I don't even know what the time is. It could still be
tonight. Or it could be the next day, and Emily's been discovered in a state, unable to say what's happened to her.
Jade and Dr Prabhakar and Ben are in her room, solemnly
acknowledging all the evidence. My shirt on the floor, and
the empties. Ben shaking his head now – 'He did seem very
very drunk when I left him last night, but I never would
have thought he'd ...'

I've got to get out of here. I clean myself up a bit whilst
considering how to get out with no shirt. I guess it won't
look too bad if I go out with my parka zipped all the way
up, even though it's not cold. It occurs to me to try and discover the time from the radio. After a tortured wait – they
say the time constantly when you don't want to know – I
find that it's only 8am.

Every little thing takes longer than you'd have thought
possible. Standing in the reception area, and the lift is coming. The security guy looking at me for a lot longer than he
would normally. Of course. My security pass is clipped to
my shirt (my fate sealed in the laminate). And I'm wearing
a parka zipped all the way to the neck. I look right at him
(it's the only way) and greet him cheerily, 'Awright?'

He greets me back, 'Awright, mate?' Probably he's seen
me before, with my funny hours and funny look.

Going down in the lift is fine. No chance of bumping into
anyone going down in the lift at this time, because anyone
I want to avoid is going to be going the other way, coming

up. But how about in the foyer? There's a very, very good chance at this time of bumping into someone, like Ben, or Prabhakar, or Jade, or anyone, coming into work. I actually manage to get lost going the short distance from the lifts to the main entrance – this is what a blind panic is – and I end up in the A&E department. Luckily there's been some kind of a major accident, and nobody pays me any attention as I blunder about with my hood up. All far too busy. I make it to the outside and feel much safer. Better but worse, because I now become very conscious of the way I am behaving. Hiding behind wheelie bins and skips and shrubs, sneaking place to place until I am safely out of the hospital's grounds. Oh dear. What have I done?

64: depression and remorse

THIS IS THE BEGINNING of a very bad time for me. I don't think I've ever been so depressed. Basically I just hole up like a fugitive. A fugitive with no imagination, because my bolthole was my flat. I was too lethargic to think of anywhere else. If they come for me, then let them. It's all over for me now. I've ruined everything.

Head in the Fridge is my pet name for what neurologists call transient global amnesia or TGA, and what most other people call a blackout. The temporary inability to form new memories, anterograde amnesia, accompanied by some retrograde amnesia for the period immediately preceding whatever occasioned the episode. For such a common and well-known phenomenon it is actually very poorly understood. The circumstances which engender the condition are obvious even to the layman – concussion, drink or drugs, etc. – but nobody really knows how these things cause TGA. They might be able to tell with a brain scan, but you'd have to be having a brain scan at the actual moment of the episode beginning, and the only way that's likely to happen is if they somehow induced the condition first. One theory is that it's caused by a brief cerebral ischemia, loss of blood flow, to the structures responsible for learning and memory.

Epileptics get TGA. A period of a few hours immediately prior to a fit can be lost to a kind of fugal state, where you look and behave quite normally but you're actually on autopilot, like a robot that's been programmed to do the kinds of thing you normally do, and say the kinds of thing you normally say. You seem fine. Nobody can tell you're not really there.

My so far fruitless attempts to remember what I did – hypothesising from clues, banging my temples with my fists – are likely to remain fruitless, because in neural terms there's nothing there to recover. It's not that you have something in your head that you can't access. There's no lost key to a secret drawer. During TGA you're not recording things. Stuff streams through consciousness without touching the sides. In one ear and out the other. Your ordinary memory is OK, allowing you to retrieve anything you'll need to function normally for a while – who you are, and what you do, and where you live – and your short-term memory is working fine, so that if you're in the middle of doing something you'll be able to hold all the relevant information in readiness. So you won't be halfway through changing a tyre and forget that that's what you're doing, or where you put the spanner just now. (Or at least you won't forget where you put the spanner just now any more than you usually do when you're doing something like that.) But none of this stuff is undergoing the process that keeps it for you when it's no longer the business at hand. The stream of consciousness leaves no sediment. No trace. Your brain isn't hitting SAVE. (A useful analogy this, so long as due caution about computer analogies is observed. They are just analogies: the brain is not a computer.)

What makes it so scary, and dangerous, is the unimpeded ability to act upon resolutions made just prior to the onset of the condition without any further thinking through. That's fine if all you'd decided to do before the thing hit you was to make a cup of tea and then phone the bank about something. You could be quite grateful for that being a lost-time episode; sitting there listening to that shitty music while your important call inches forward in the queue. But what if the onset of a fugal amnesiac episode catches you at the instant of having made a very bad decision? Something you would ordinarily have put from your mind immediately afterwards. I'm gonna fucking kill him. I'm gonna rape her. In this situation your body and your working memory – the kind of memory whose job it is to attend to the task at hand – are the slaves of your most aberrant, criminal drives. Your body carries on and does as it's told, with none of the countermanding regulations of decency or enlightened self-interest. This is why the drunken blackout is so dangerous. The amnesia takes away all prudence and inhibition just when you're feeling pretty imprudent and disinhibited anyway, because you're pissed. The epileptic amnesiac can find they've finished washing up, or watching the news, or even driving home, safely, as an automaton. The amnesia is not likely to get them just when they've made a bad decision. The drunkard's fugue is very likely to take his criminal self and set it in motion, like a robot stuck on KILL mode.

This is what I've done. A passing and shameful impulse has been taken by my robot self for an imperative. A task to be carried out as if there were no consequences. They've probably got CCTV footage of me. Not actually doing it, but on my way to Emily's room, all merry with my wine bottles. And then a few hours later waddling back with my trousers round my ankles, grinning. I've never seen any CCTV cameras in the Institute, but they must have them, probably ingeniously hidden, like the lighting. The architect who did that place would never have stood for anything as ugly as obvious surveillance equipment, ruining his nice lines and vistas. I spent, oh, about the first three or four days of my solitary confinement in my flat thinking about that footage. Adding details. Me marching up the hall with my cock out, bobbing along. Emily's door opening a crack after several minutes of drunken battering and hollering – silent histrionics because there's no sound recording – then the brute (me), after a few seconds of wheedling and leering, loses patience, and just shoves the door open with his shoulder, throwing her across the room; he slams it shut with a backwards bronco kick. The last thing we see is a glimpse of her terrified eyes just visible over his shoulder. What's he doing in there? What's he doing to her?

My standards about things got very basic during this time. I didn't wash and I ate only tinned soup. I drank all the time. I was poor because I'd been about due for another instalment of my fee from the Institute, and I economised by drinking only the cheapest drinks. Something called SUPA–XTRA, which is the cheapest kind of super-strength lager, retailing at about the same price as a tin of soup. (I've since found out how they make super-strength lager. It's not like those Belgian beers that are brewed longer for greater strength and depth of flavour. It's just ordinary lager, quickly brewed to normal strength, and then they add ethanol, straight out of the laboratory. They also add some sugary flavouring to mask the flavour of the alcohol. It's quite a different way of getting drunk. Not like the experience of finding your mental state is altering. You get a different mind. You exchange your own head for a crazy and damaged one.) I drank this horrible stuff, and fully exercised my aptitude for self-disgust, day after day, beginning at breakfast time and continuing until bedtime, except I never had breakfast or went to bed. I missed my studio and my books. I missed all my patients, not just Emily. The Blind Couple, Trevor, and Pauline. The A. Man. I wanted that look, like I'm nothing, I used to get from the receptionist. I wanted Ben to tell me things about the human brain. Its many mysteries. Its fantastic complexity and consequent vulnerability. All the stuff it does. How amazing it is that it manages to do all those things so well, all at the same time. All my brain's contents now sourly tinctured with remorse. Pound for pound it's the most complex thing in the Universe. Easily. Nothing else comes close.

Nobody came looking for me, and the Wednesday following my disgrace was spent sitting by the phone, hoping for and dreading a call from the Institute. They've probably decided it's not worth pursuing, with the only witness not able to give evidence beyond what a vaginal swab might show. I hadn't turned up that Wednesday, and that was enough. An admission of guilt and a resignation, both by default. Only when the evening came did I think to pick up the phone and check. Of course. Cut off. Pay the phone bill was one of those things, eleventh hour as usual, I'd been meaning to take care of when the next cheque came through (and did I say I've never had a mobile?).

Another few days of sodden purgatory while the last scraps of cash were pissed away, then I spent an entire day rifling my flat for coins – cavity-searching old pairs of trousers and overalls; a coat I used to wear; turning out drawers and looking under the bed, four times. I didn't look down the back of the sofa because I haven't got one. The search yielded enough money for ten cigarettes and three cans of SUPA–XTRA, plus two speed wraps, each with the makings of a line compacted in its corners. Not a bad haul. I am not embarrassed in the shop downstairs when I pay for my beer and fags all in one- and two-pence coins.

65: suicide solution

I SUPPOSE ONE OPTION that's open to me is I could kill myself. It *is* part of the mythology of the mad artist, but there's no reason for that, really. It's mainly just because of Van Gogh. I've known quite a few suicides, and only two of those were artists; it's not that rare. I've known a few borderline cases, where it's impossible to tell if someone's OD'd on purpose or not, but there was one guy I knew who must win the prize for determination. He *was* an artist, and he hanged himself, and the rope he used he'd actually made himself – people saw him making it in his studio, for months, and they just thought, I suppose, making rope was his new way of doing art.

Suicide always amazes me. Not just how people do it, but why. Being comparatively unsuccessful isn't so bad really. If what you really want to do is die, why not just wait? Your dream is bound to come true. You're certainly not going to be disappointed about that. You might think you've got a while to wait, but it's not that long. People think we're all going to live into our middle-hundreds because of the increase in life expectancy, but it doesn't work like that. Average life expectancy has increased, yes, but that's not the same as saying your chances for extreme longevity have increased. The average has increased because so few people die in infancy these days, and also the improvements in controlling infectious diseases have made a difference. Other medical advances like new treatments for heart disease and cancer have had a bit of an impact, but they only give us a couple of years extra on average. They don't affect the figures anything like as much as the near disappearance of infant mortality in the Western world. So, a lot more of us, on average, are going to live to be eighty or ninety odd, but there's not much scope for increases beyond that. Even if your heart is OK, and you don't get cancer, your brain is going to check out. There are no developments in the pipeline that are going to add many years to the tail end of life. Only things that help you get to the tail end.

I've never given suicide much serious thought personally, as an option, even when things are looking totally bleak and hopeless. That might just be laziness on my part. Suicides do seem to be quite proactive. Determination does seem to be an important factor. And planning – another weak area for me. I am not going to kill myself, because I can't be arsed.

66: another private view

THERE WAS NOTHING FOR IT NOW but to try and get some building or decorating work. I knew where to look. One of the functions of the gallery private view is to serve as an informal labour exchange. The groundwork for all kinds of career moves is laid down, almost invisibly, by people just here to see the show and see their friends, talking to other people here to do those things too. People talking about things with no obvious connection to any professional agenda. Going to private views is actually part of the job; being sure you're noticed and liked. And besides all the more sophisticated manoeuvring – aimed at landing an exhibition at So and So Gallery, or a job in the office at Such and Such, writing work for this magazine or that, a teaching job at Goldsmith's – there is the other labour market. This one a bit more straightforward. If you're looking for decorating or building jobs you don't need to be mealy-mouthed about it. You can just say to people, 'Do you know of any building or decorating jobs going?' You don't need to say, 'I loved your last building or decorating job. Fantastic.'

I knew of a private view that evening that was within walking distance. Nearly eight miles from where I live, but that would have to be walking distance because that's how poor I'd got. I didn't have the bus fare. I put some effort into making myself presentable because you never get offered anything if you look shit, not even a decorating job. I put on my private view outfit and walked eight miles, with frequent stops to check my whereabouts in the *A to Z*. Walking that far you can't afford any unscheduled detours.

Black Hole Gallery again, and a very welcome bottle of free beer. It's free because the show is sponsored by the beer company. The sponsorship takes the form of a few crates of beer, for which they get a mention on every bit of literature relating to the show. With my beer I take a copy of the press release, which features the beer company's logo so prominently I think they've taken the sponsorship to another level and named the art after the beer. (I will not name the beer because it tastes like piss. No. Piss has a flavour. It tastes like saliva, but beggars can't be choosers and a beer's a beer.) The artist's name is, if you hunt for it, on there somewhere, and it is not a name I recognise. Another new guy. His work is surprisingly diverse, with a very familiar traditionally modernistic feel to it, and he is prolific. There are paintings and sculptures and mobiles and collages all over the place, like an exhibition in the 1930s.

I saw my 'friend': unfortunate that his should be the first face I recognise tonight because he's doing very well at the moment, with his Bradford project. I decide to pretend to read the press release. In fact I just go ahead and read it. (I'm peering through my deep, deep gloom here. Really at a low ebb.) So, what have we got here? The reason this guy's work looks so familiar, and there's so much of it, and it all looks like generic modern art, is that he didn't do it himself. What he's showing here is actually all from film sets. When there's a scene in a Manhattan-style loft-apartment, or the headquarters of a sinister multinational corporation, or actually in an art gallery, the props department will knock up a lot of approximations of modern art objects. Wacky sculptural assemblages and splashy paintings (and it really hurts to note the resemblance of these to my own paintings). There are quite a few Op-Art stripes, and Pop Art objects – tin cans and whatnot. Some Picasso-like figuration: these dating from the early 'sixties when that was the idea of how contemporary art looks. A mad kinetic sculpture, like a huge jack-in-the-box with the head of Hitler slowly rising out of, and then slamming back into, the top of an upright piano. Quite a few all-white or all-black canvases.

The artist found all this stuff mouldering in a storeroom at Pinewood Studios, where his day job is, working as a model-maker. (I should have got into that myself instead of decorating. Long hours, but the pay is much better, so you only need to work a few months a year.) He found all these old props or bits of scenery, and when he asked around they said he could have them because they were only going to be chucked out anyway. Even the stuff from a James Bond. You'd think there'd be a market for that, not as art but as memorabilia.

Having drunk my beer as quick as I can I go back to the bar for another. Another two. I'll pretend I'm getting one for a friend. Here at the bar I find I am queuing behind Keith, who must know of some work going because he's come here straight from the job and he's covered in plaster. I'd worked with Keith quite a lot in the past. Even if there'd been any need for circumspection about asking for a job, I don't think I could have managed it. I didn't have the energy.

'Awright, Keith?'

He turned slowly. 'Awright.'

'Any work going?'

'No. Sorry, mate.' He turned back to talk to his companion. You can't crush me any more because I'm just powder now. I'm at rejection's furthest limit and well past caring. I follow them from the bar and then stand next to them. Just standing there. He's with a woman who's his client on this job. She's an artist who's doing very well at the moment, with her photographs of celebrities' thumbs, and she's got Keith converting her newly purchased industrial unit in Hoxton. Keith isn't just a moonlighting artist any more, doing the odd bit of work to make ends meet. He's a building contractor with his own team. Good move. I'm still not going until I get something. They can't ignore me if I stand here long enough. To my fantastic relief he turns and says something to me.

'I saw Arthur the other day. Says you owe him a lot of money. About ten grams' worth. He said he hasn't seen you for months.'

I guess I can make this into kind of a joke. 'That's why I need some quick money. You must know something going.'

'You can't come on this job. We don't need anyone. Unless you can do electrics … No?' He looked at me for a bit (I'm dying now, thinking how my pathetic supplicating face would have looked at this point) and came up with something for me. 'I know of somewhere that's looking for painters, but it's a shit job.'

I'll take the shit job.

67: a shit job

WE HAD TO TURN UP AT 7.45 for an 8 O'clock start, with two fifteen-minute tea breaks and half an hour for lunch. Knock off at five. I got up at 6 am, still the dead of night, and walked to Earl's Court (taking only one needless detour, because of there being a crucial page missing from my tattered *A to Z*). They needed a lot of painters to finish a big mansion-block flat conversion, and they were hiring right away because they were behind schedule. Just turn up tomorrow, Keith said, and they'll give you a job. I arrived to find a large group of men, my fellow lost souls, already waiting outside the building – me sweating and freezing; in no condition for a day's work.

What they were doing on this flat conversion was converting a number of spacious Edwardian flats into a much larger number of poky cells. Each large Edwardian apartment is divided into three with stud walls, and then these divisions are subdivided into cubicles – 'rooms' – with more stud walls. The function of each cubicle is then designated according to practical and economic criteria. We can easily feed the pipework for eight bathrooms through here, so here is where the bathrooms are for eight flats. And a similar logic for the kitchens. The remaining sections become either Bedroom, or Living Room, by default. Sometimes the Bathroom will have to separate the Bedroom and Living Room; or the Kitchen does, or both do, so that the cooker and toilet pan are neighbours. This place is a termite hill.

The day begins with shouting (and will continue with shouting). 'ANY NEW PAINTERS! NEW PAINTERS OVER

HERE. NEW ... You a new painter, mate? Alright, what's your name?'

Telling him your name doesn't make any difference because your name is 'mate' or 'you'. Nice they ask, though.

'Alright, mate, get your whites on. He'll tell you where to start.'

'I haven't got any whites with me.' I hadn't brought my overalls, which aren't white anyway.

'You can't work on this job without whites, mate. Looks unprofessional.'

I look around me, at the other human leftovers making up this workforce, and they all have their whites. 'Oh! My whites are in my bag. I'll just go and get them.'

I can't face walking home, that's all. Not ingenuity and determination. I know the painters already working here will have left their overalls somewhere inside, all in the same room probably. I just need to get in there, grab some overalls, and hope their owner doesn't spot me.

'Alright then, mate. NEW PAINTERS ...'

I run in after a likely-looking crew and they lead me to the room where they keep all their gear. Taking a big chance I walk in with them and, following a quick assessment, take a pair of overalls that are not too new-looking,

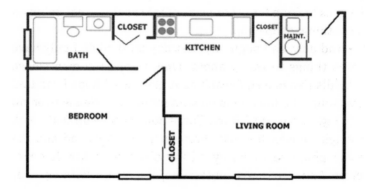

not too old. I take what look to be about the average type of overall, and then find another room to put them on. Standing in the centre of the room I can just about touch all four walls. That's how small these rooms were.

Now that I look the part I go in search of the man who's supposed to tell me where to start. Pretty hopeless, really. It is like an action scene on a WW2 battleship. Hundreds of men running around shouting like highly motivated film extras. There are men whose job is to run around with a ladder, shouting. Others, dangerously overloaded with paint tins, running and shouting. And there are the electricians, and the plumbers, and the dry-liners. The dry-lining blokes move at a more leisurely pace than everyone else, but still cover more ground because they're wearing special stilts with articulated feet, so that they can joint-fill the ceilings without having to scoot up and down a pair of steps all day.

I don't need to look for long. A big bald-headed geezer halts right by me. 'What you doing mate?'

'Me? Noth—'

'Right, in here, chop chop ...' I follow him, on the double.

'Right. You're in here with these two,' my workmates for today. 'Paint's there, rollers there, hit the walls and ceiling, then next door, and when you run out of walls you come and find me on the fourth floor—', this said over his shoulder as he goes looking for other pairs of idle hands to get going on something, chop chop.

And now, as I begin my first day on the job, I only have three things to worry about. One. I hope the man whose overalls I've nicked doesn't spot me. Two. I hope I can find someone who'll lend me enough money to tide me over till payday. Three. My failure. Three doesn't take up that much thought power. It's just there in the background and the atmosphere surrounding all my other thoughts, like tinnitus. And also there's my bad physical state, with my poor diet recently, and having to walk to work. Four. Just four things, then. Almost carefree, really.

The state I was in physically paid off in a way. Literally. It helped me out with problem number two. The two guys I was working that section with had been sent along by Brixton Jobcentre. They thought I was hilarious. They would get me to do any stuff that required you to climb a ladder, just so they could watch me haul myself up, with my paint kettle rattling against the frame, my face going alternately snow white and crimson, and swallowing constantly. They pissed themselves laughing the whole of the first two and a half hours until morning tea break. They asked me how I'd got myself into this state and I said I'd been on a bit of a bender, and I was now on the floor, financially, because of it. Even funnier that. I told them I'd had to walk to work this morning. They enjoyed that so much that they bunged me a few notes at lunchtime – 'Go and get yourself about twenty litres of Coke' – without me even asking; and they didn't come back after lunch. Probably they'd done enough to keep the Jobcentre off their backs for a week or two.

This, in turn, helped me out with problem number one. I returned after lunch, having downed a quarter-bottle of Scotch in a nearby churchyard, and was accosted by a youth as I went to my next job.

'Those are my overalls.'

'Fuck OFF!!!' I shouted it into his face and walked on. I couldn't have done that if I hadn't had that Scotch. He got the sack for not having his whites.

You get into a routine quite quickly with these things. One or two people get to know your name, and you find you've got your regular spot at tea breaks. There are these temporary base camps all over the building, picked for no particular reason from all the equally inhospitable and ugly rooms, as the place where you keep your stuff; where you sit on a paint tin at breaktime to have your tea and read the paper and twat around on your phone. (One lunchbreak my partner for that day points at an air vent. 'See that? Guess where that goes?' I don't know. 'It goes into next door's kitchen.' We happened to be having lunch in a toilet that day. Either the people using the toilet in here get next door's cooking smells, or next door's kitchen gets the smell of shit.)

Nobody says much about themselves. Certainly not me. At lunch break you'd talk about things in the paper mostly. Not all Red-Tops by any means. About fifty per cent. Nobody takes the piss if you read *The Guardian*, or a book. But most of the stuff that gets talked about is from the tabloids because there's not much time. The breaks are short because the job's behind. You'd sit on your paint tin at breaks, drinking your tea (I cut out the daytime boozing after the first day), and chewing a Mars bar, and someone would interrupt the slurping and munching – 'Seen this? Celebrity A has split from Celebrity B.' 'Did you hear about this …?' More celebrity stuff. But also world affairs, and science. 'Do you think we'll win the war, or the enemy will?' 'Oh look, they've cloned a Pekinese. Oh, no, it's 'Outrage about cloned Pekinese'. They might clone a Pekinese but they haven't actually done it yet.'

A lot of the science is Amazing Science, like 'By the year 3000 we'll all be living on Mars.' 'By the year 2500 the air on Earth will be so poisonous we'll have to live in biospheres on Mars and we'll be just a brain in a kind of floating pod powered by thought waves.' Sometimes contemporary art cropped up – 'Say's here there's a man who's done an art exhibition of his bogies' – and I would say nothing. Sometimes, quite often it seemed to me, amongst the bizarre deaths, and stories about massive expenditure on things you wouldn't think were worth it, there would be things to do with brains. 'Seen this? They've been removing the brains from dead babies without the parent's consent, for medical research.' Or 'They've been removing the brains from people who've committed suicide, without their consent.' 'How could they give their consent if they're dead?' 'You could leave a note.' 'It says here they reckon you can live actually outside your body in near-death experiences. You live in the form of a field of energy, and that's why you can look down on your body on the operating table.' 'How can you see if you're just a field of energy? You wouldn't have any eyes.' 'They've been doing these experiments on taxi drivers and they have a bigger hippocampus than other people.' 'What's the hippocampus?' 'Apparently it's the part of the brain that deals with directions.'

It shocked me to hear that word here, on site. As if someone had crept up behind me and whispered 'Emily' in my ear – out of nowhere, a propos of nothing.

68: cave in

ONE DAY, FRIDAY of my first week on the job. 'Seen this?' The man sitting on the paint tin next to mine holds out his paper to me, folded back on itself: 'Serve him right.' I take the paper from him and he turns to his other neighbour to swap sandwiches.

The insensitive headline reads, 'TRAGIC CAVE-IN CRUSTY'. A report from the inquest on a young man who has been killed in an accident while tunnelling under Gray's Hospital as part of a protest against 'The System'.

Typical. So Stick's real name is Duncan. Duncan Phelps. The caption for the blurred picture in which he is shown, amongst a group of basically identical white rastas standing round a bonfire, distinguishable only because of a ring they've put round his head, describes him as 'self-styled eco-warrior *Duncan Phelps*'. I suppose I'd give myself a nickname too if I was called something like that. He had been taken on as a volunteer on one of those archaeological digs at Gray's, and when everyone else had gone home he just kept digging, tunnelling towards the foundations of one of the more imposing hospital admin blocks. He was undermining the system. Only he didn't take the trouble to shore it up properly or anything. It collapsed after about seven metres, three and a half metres beneath a spot in the middle of one of those scrappy lawns they have there, between the buildings. What a way to go. And Colin is going to hate me now, isn't he. After all those things I said to Stick in the pub. So I suppose it's just as well I'm never going to see Colin again, really.

I'm kind of back where I started. I'm standing in the queue on a Friday afternoon, waiting to get paid by the twenty-two-year-old contractor. There are two big guys in clean whites standing either side of him.

'Painter?'

'Yep.'

'How many days you done, mate?'

'Five.' One of the henchmen nods. Yes, I'd done five, and my work was OK, so I don't get awarded the DCM (Don't Come Monday). If your work isn't up to scratch and you're not wanted back next week, then you won't get paid for *this* week, and you might want to make a bit of a fuss about that. This is why the contractor always has a bit of muscle by him on payday.

Less than three weeks since I'd last been to the Institute and I was beginning to think I'd imagined the whole thing. This is what I do. I do decorating jobs that no one else will do. I am available for work as a visiting lecturer at any out-of-the-way art school, if they need someone at short notice, and no one else will do it. In my spare time I do enormous abstract paintings that no one much likes the look of. My depression has evened out, and I am not in the depths of despair any more. Just ordinary chronic low-level despair, of a kind I can live with.

I began to adjust to this stable condition, putting my affairs back in order. I started nicking paint from work to do my own paintings. I got my phone reconnected and rang the landlord of my studio in Hackney, and I told him a long story. I have suffered a bereavement and things have got a bit behind, that's the downside, but on the upside I should be getting some money through quite soon, because of this bereavement. He gave me another month to start paying the rent, plus something towards the arrears. He probably does this because the property is almost impossible to let, and me staying on is marginally preferable to allowing it to remain empty. It'll be demolished soon anyway, when he gets planning permission for another building on the site. I had another week on the Earls Court job, then I'd ask around. There might be a day's teaching going somewhere. And there's always decorating. Maybe Keith will want me for his next job.

69: surprise phonecall

TUESDAY EVENING of my second week on the job I received a surprise phonecall. A surprise for two reasons. First, I hardly get any phonecalls and this was the first time it had rung since I'd got it reconnected. Second, it was Colin.

'Where you been hiding, then? You've been missing your Workshops. Ben asked me to give you a ring and see what's up. Where you been, Ay?'

'Agahurr ...'

'Hello?'

Following that initial vocalisation there had been a substantial pause, while I struggled to master a very complex array of anxieties. But, finally, I could say, 'Yes ... Oh, you know ... here and there' – the best I could manage, hearing this voice from, I had decided, the past. Since Colin had not immediately accused me of being a rapist I rallied a bit. How bad this could turn out to be had some limits, apparently. And why didn't he sound angry? Was it because he was grieving over his friend Stick? He sounded OK, though.

'Where've *you* been, Colin. You've missed a few weeks yourself.'

'I've been busy, haven't I? I thought I told you. I had my holidays in France, then when I came back it was Britain's bloodiest battle.'

'That rings a bell. I thought that was a political protest you were doing. With Stick. Before his ... accident.'

'Stick's had an accident?'

'I thought he was in an accident in a tunnel. Wasn't that Stick?'

'Ah, no. I know what you mean, Yes. One of the archae-ologists had a bad incident. I think he was a mate of Stick's, but not Stick. You know those characters love tunnelling; only this one didn't really know much about it and didn't realise there's more to it than just digging. He was called Duncan. Poor guy. Duncan something.'

'Phelps. I thought that might be Stick's real name.'

'No! Ha ha. Stick's real name is Stick. His mum and dad are hippies.'

'What is Britain's bloodiest battle, then?'

'It was in the Wars of the Roses. The Battle of Towton, in 1461. Me and my boys do it every year. It's a fortnight of re-enactments and war walks, and lectures. You should come next time. I could teach you medieval archery skills.'

'Cheers. And was it very bloody?'

'I'll say. They reckon about twenty-eight thousand dead! You thought that was a political protest, did you? You want to brush up on your listening skills, chum. So, anyway, I've come back and you've gone AWOL. You weren't in last week either. Ben got a bit concerned, 'cause you haven't rung in or anything.'

'I had a bereavement actually, Colin. My mum.' That's true in a way. My mum did die, about three years ago.

'Oh, I'm sorry to hear that, mate. You should have rung me. How you feeling now? Fancy a drink this evening?'

My brain isn't moving fast enough for this. I feel like just coming clean and saying I haven't been back to the Institute because I've raped, or at least sexually assaulted, Emily; and also, Colin, I thought you and I were no longer on speaking terms, about Stick. But I manage, 'Yes, alright then. Where?'

The Volunteer, again.

'OK. See you in about an hour.' I have to go or it will con-firm any suspicions he may have. This is probably a test.

Several times on the way there I almost turn back home. This has to be a trap. When I get there they'll be waiting for me with three policemen, one in plain clothes. Or I'll just be Tasered immediately by a SWAT team.

What'll happen, I decide more rationally, is that Colin and Ben will be there and they'll be polite and ordinary, offer me a dry-roasted peanut, and then, just when I think it's OK, they will turn their disgusted gaze upon me, the pair of them, and tell me that they know what I've done. We know what you've done to her, you bastard. We're not going to do anything about it because there's no real proof, and we won't sully ourselves by giving you the kicking you deserve. You're not worth it. We're just letting you know that WE KNOW. They'll both stand and walk out, their drinks left untouched on the table. They won't look back at my weak and shameful face, mouth open and starting to shake. I'm nothing now.

What prevents me from turning and running, even as I cross the threshold of the Canadian Volunteer, is an almost masochistic desire for some kind of resolution or closure – or justice. (I've been having a lot of bad nights lately. The days are OK generally, but the nights – particularly between about 3am and dawn.)

Colin didn't look entirely friendly, sitting there, in my favourite corner. But I wasn't looking so good either apparently. 'Hello,' Colin greeted me. 'You look like shit. What d'you want?' He went and got me a pint, another for himself, and carried them back to our table, two packets of crisps held between his teeth.

'Cheers, Colin.'

'Cheers. You look like shit.' This was good to hear, again, because it didn't seem like the kind of thing you would say to someone just before denouncing them as a sex case. Colin seemed a little reserved, but he was looking OK apart from that. Not like me. He proffered my beer and crisps as if giving broth to an invalid, which, I gathered, was what I was looking like.

I couldn't talk about Emily right away – is she even on the agenda for this evening? – so I broached the other subject.

'So – I didn't feel we left it in a good place when we were in here last time. Sorry I went off like that. I think I got a bit annoyed. I thought you were a bit annoyed, too.'

I was very relieved, and in fact grateful, to register the sudden softening of Colin's expression.

'I probably was a bit. I didn't think much of your attitude to be honest. I know Stick goes on, and it is all a bit far-fetched, but you just want to be more tolerant about other people's beliefs. Also, I know he's got it exaggerated, but there are some questionable things going on in the world, and we need people like Stick to help us keep our eyes and ears open. *Also*, mate, you want to understand he's got a condition. Of course he's going to get carried away! Any-how, we'd had a drink or three, and maybe tempers got frayed and things were said. That's all water under the bridge. So, you know, cheers! It's funny you thought he'd died. You must have felt awful!'

The provisional sense of relief I had begun to experience was becoming more secure with the decreasing likelihood that Colin knew or suspected anything about my conduct towards Emily. Obviously nothing even remotely like that was on Colin's mind, as he gave me a very full account of what he'd been getting up to lately: him and his two strap-ping sons, and their club, 'The Blokes of Bosworth Field', on its annual Battle of Towton fortnight. (I guess I tend to forget Colin has a life, and lots of interests – and, it turns out, a big family).

The reason Colin's club and a few others have opted for these slightly jokey names is to differentiate themselves from a side of the military re-enactment world they disapprove of. What Colin and his mates are interested in is what they call 'practical archaeology'. They research and reconstruct medieval martial arts and military tactics. They dress up in armour and have mock battles at summer fêtes and so on. They demonstrate medieval skills like fletching and cordwaining. They do jousting.

The other, rather more sinister, side of all this is the people who re-enact twentieth-century conflicts, generally those involving either the Green Berets or the Waffen-SS. Clubs called the Dogs of War, or Die Kameraden, or the Death Buddies. These are people, Colin tells me, who like to practise techniques for silently taking out a sentry with a knife or garrotting wire. Often they'll be doing this in their bedroom while their mum is downstairs doing the tea. These are the people who are secretly, though not that secretly, preparing for Armageddon – the collapse of Western civilisation.

And the reason he'd been annoyed with me was my evident lack of compassion and tolerance. I always forget the people I've been meeting here have conditions. They wouldn't be here otherwise, would they. We can't all be artists in residence. I'd just assumed he didn't really mind about his prosopagnosia, but he really *does* mind. 'Yer, it does bother me sometimes. I get my grandkids mixed up sometimes, whch I do find a bit upsetting. You can't understand what it's like not being able to see people's faces properly. You feel so isolated sometimes. I've always been a people person.'

70: borderline autistic

NOT LIKE ME. Sometimes I think I must be partially autistic. Actually I think a lot of men are partially autistic, or borderline sociopaths. One of the symptoms or defining characteristics of autism is the lack of a theory of mind. You can't impute subjectivity to others. You can't see it the other guy's way. There's a classic test. Sally has a basket, Anne has a box. Sally has a basket, and a marble. She puts her marble in her basket and then goes out for a walk, leaving the basket at home. While she's out, naughty Anne takes the marble out of Sally's basket and puts it in her box. When Sally comes back from her walk, where will she look for her marble? 'In the box,' says the autist. 'But where does Sally *think* the marble will be? Remember, she didn't see Anne take the marble from the basket and put it in her box.' Still 'In the box.'

And I'm a bit like that. If I know something, or feel something, I think everyone else must. And equally if someone is behaving in a way that characterises a particular feeling or belief, I just think they're being weird because I don't happen to share that feeling or belief. So that might be what it is with me. The lack of a real belief in the existence of minds other than my own. Which means that you lack compassion and empathy. It's not that you're heartless exactly. You wouldn't describe an autistic child as heartless.

You can find a similar lack of ability to empathise in the sociopathic personality, and here you *would* want to describe it as heartlessness. Actually there's a theory that the cause is neurobiological, having to do with the defective

267

functioning of a small organ in the temporal lobe of the brain, quite close to the hippocampus, called the amygdala. The amygdala seems to be responsible for the coupling of experience and affect. It matches the correct type and degree of emotion to the subject's experiences. If it works properly you will have an immediate and visceral response to the suffering of others. To watch someone being tortured is unbearable. Even if you see someone crying you'll want to do something about it. But if the amygdala isn't doing its job, you won't mind. You might even find it funny.

I'm not that bad, of course, but I do seem to be a bit removed. My mum's funeral, for example. It was a nightmare. I spent the whole thing trying to think what sort of face to pull. I wouldn't have been able to cry, not even if you paid me, but I couldn't just walk around with my normal expression on (whatever that is). After a bit of discreet experimentation behind my hymnbook I decided to hold my face in repose, but allow it to be disrupted every now and then by a sequence of rapid blinks, and then two or three big noticeable swallows. And then, if anyone happened to ask how I was, I was ready with 'I'm ... (blink blink, swallow) ... OK.' I wasn't sure I could carry that off, but luckily no one did ask.

If I'm honest I'm more worried about how what I've done to Emily has affected me than how it's affected her. But then again I'm sure she's OK really. She can't be traumatised because she can't remember a thing, probably.

71: Dien Bien Phu

ACTUALLY, I WAS STARTING to feel quite ill. I must really look shit if even Colin can tell. He must be able to see, even in his piecemeal, empirical fashion – an eye like a cicatrice; a crepey, patchily shaven cheek – that I'm not very well.

'I think I'm hungry, Colin. Can we go and get some food?'

'Yeah! Let's try that new Vietnamese place next door.' The Dien Bien Phu, right beside the Canadian Volunteer. By the time we'd got ourselves seated I was shaking like a leaf.

'You sure you're alright, mate? You're shaking like a leaf. You look in a right state.'

'I'll just have a starter. Some prawns with dipping sauce.'

'Don't worry. Have what you like. My treat.' He got the waiter over and ordered a big meal. 'And have you got any of that Vietnamese beer?' The beers arrived quickly, and Colin, very animated, was talking me through the little crisis I seemed to be having. How nice this place is, and the waiters, and it's amazing how they've come back from that war with no hard feelings. He didn't have to keep this up too long before the food arrived, the waiter with two dishes in each hand and a further pair balanced on each forearm. While he went back to fetch the rest, I nibbled at a king prawn in batter and realised I was starving. I cleared the plate in two minutes flat. Colin kept chatting, me going *nmmph ... efff ... schomp ... geck*. My Christ, I'm hungry. The effect of the food was almost immediate, like a shot of speed (probably the MSG). I began to feel quite chatty myself and I asked him (*Gulp – urp! Scuse me*) how things are at the Institute lately. How is it down at the old NNI?

'Ben thought you might have got wind of what's been going on lately and that's why you haven't turned up. It's all starting to come on top now, with Simon and Selina.' I shook my head (mouth full).

'Really? You haven't heard anything? Well, they're starting to apply a bit of pressure. They've got all these "observers" going round the place and going through all the paperwork and breathing down everybody's neck. It's supposed to be some kind of review, and an audit, but Ben reckons it's all about intimidation. When you didn't turn up the other week, Ben asked me to look after the Drawing Workshop because he was busy with all these snoopers nosing about. One of them was in the Activities Room the whole day during the Workshop, just sitting there. She was taking notes, and then she was whispering into her mobile while she was looking at us. Like the fucking KGB. Fucking Gestapo or something.'

'You looked after the Workshop for me? Thanks, Colin. I appreciate that.'

'No bother. Actually you've got it set up so it practically runs itself.' Have I really? Me? Well well.

'I think everyone's a bit bored with doing brains, though. Probably they'd like a bit more variety with the subject matter. You coming in tomorrow? Perhaps you could start thinking about some other drawing exercises. Some flowers would be nice. Or even a bit of abstract.'

Am I going in tomorrow? Colin doesn't know about what I've done, but Ben must do, surely. This must be an ambush. What happens when I see Emily again? They're hoping I'll break down and confess as soon as I see her.

'Yeah, sure.' It'll mean missing a day's work in Earls Court. 'Definitely. Yep. See you tomorrow.'

72: the Institute

I WAS READY, NEXT MORNING, to face whatever music there was to face. I felt compelled, actually. My guilt or remorse had a lot to do with the uncertainty about whether or not I was going to get caught. I was feeling none too good physically – terrible diarrhoea – but at least it was that keeping me awake all night and not the awful feeling of remorse. Whatever it was going to be like had to be better than the last couple of weeks. Even a spell in prison would be a relief after the way I've been feeling. I can't believe it's only been a few weeks. The 'me' that ran those Workshops is someone I don't even recognise now.

Approaching Gray's Tower I passed the spot where I'd seen Stick doing those archaeological digs, and where that poor guy Duncan Phelps died last month, a class war martyr; and looking up at the Tower I thought, not for the first time, that from down here the top floor doesn't seem big enough to contain everything I know it to contain. Its actual size seems incommensurate with how big it is on some other register of scale. A bit, actually, like the human brain. The Institute is like the brain of the building, and the rest is like the body. This would make more sense if the podiatry department was on the ground floor, and ear, nose and throat was second from the top – which of course they aren't. Still, the top floor could be the cranium, the Institute the brain, and the great balcony could be the eyes.

Stepping out of the lift (full of nerves and worried I might suddenly shit my trousers), I thought that the Institute's ambient light, from an invisible light source, could be the brain's consciousness. They've got a new receptionist. They've finally got rid of Miss Hair and Nails. For a moment I thought it was Michelle, but it was another woman who looked a lot like Michelle. Same type, with her functional dress sense, and glasses on a lanyard. I had to go and tell her who I was and why I was here.

'Where's your pass?'

My pass is with my shirt, and I don't know where my shirt is. Probably in a side drawer in Dr Prabhakar's desk, in a plastic bag marked 'Exhibit A'. I explained that I'd mislaid it, it's probably here in the building somewhere, and I was wishing they'd kept the old receptionist. At least she didn't give a fuck. Security had to be called on the phone to check that a security pass had been issued to someone of my name and answering my description. And then Michelle had to be called to confirm that.

'Have you got any other form of ID?' I had a cheque card. That was OK. At least that card's still good for something.

'I'm issuing you with a temporary security pass. Sign here … and here. Bring it back when you leave, and if you haven't found your official pass by the end of today we're going to have to report a pass missing.' That's how much needless trouble I've caused with my carelessness. They really are running a much tighter ship around here now, and it was doing my rumbling guts no good at all.

As I turned to go – permitted to go about my business – I nearly bumped into Dr Prabhakar. I caught a glimpse of her strained and impatient expression as she swerved past me, tutting, talking into her headset, reading a stapled document in a thick sheaf of documents, whilst walking fast, like a little machine.

Making my way to the Activities Room I saw a lot more of this kind of thing. A different kind of energy making itself felt around here. Strange people with their phones and files all doing something definite, like ants working in concert even though they seem unaware of each other's presence, Busy Busy Busy. Nothing like the leisurely passage of those funding people. The room with the MRI machine seemed to have become active for the first time in months. They'd put a row of chairs in the corridor outside and there were people sitting there and reading magazines and whatnot, all obviously waiting to do something in there. Participate in some test.

It was reassuring to see a few friendly faces in the Activities Room. Hello, A. Man. Hello, Blind Couple. Pauline. Colin – awright, mate? Emily. Emily was sitting stiffly at her usual place, and she had an envelope, looking at it as if she thought it might be a trick envelope that explodes sneezing powder in your face. When she saw me, she jumped up and, helped along by encouraging nods from Colin (because she might not have managed otherwise), she brought it across to me. They like to give her small tasks to keep her stimulated. 'This is for you, I think,' and she handed me the envelope. On the front was written 'EMILY. WHEN THE ARTIST ARRIVES COULD YOU GIVE HIM THIS NOTE?' and there followed a description of me. Not very flattering, but accurate enough to allow anyone to recognise me at a glance. Emily was looking as fresh as anything. Completely unsullied. If only she knew.

I opened the note, wanting to get it over with, my guts coming up to a nice rolling boil, and I expected to see something like this: SHE DOESN'T KNOW, BUT I DO – BEN. It actually said this, 'Sorry can't make it today (Audit!) My friend from neurology dept will be there today. Got some very interesting stuff re. synaesthesia which will interest you as an artist, Ben. p.s. R U OK? p.p.s. his name is Dr Daniel Bokassa'.

How funny. Ben writes notes like a posh schoolgirl. Dr Bokassa was sitting in a corner, apparently involved in some sort of conference with Hilary, from the Arts Council, or whatever it is she does. I went over to introduce myself but she cut me short: 'Excuse me, we're having an outputs meeting here. Could you not interrupt, please?'

Neither of her eyebrow piercings have settled down, both still very sore and painful looking, and she's got a new one in her upper lip which is badly swollen. I backed off and went to look at the drawings they'd done in the last two sessions. Nothing very surprising in terms of artwork. Just OK, I guess. I couldn't make out what Hilary was asking Dr Bokassa. When they were done he came straight across and said hello. His handshake was just like Ben's, full of surplus power.

'So you're the Artist,' he said, making it sound like there was only one artist in the world. Probably I'm the first artist he's ever met, but then he's only the second neurologist I've ever met.

'Dan … Hi, there. Ben tells me you've got a patient with synaesthesia to show me.'

'Not a patient. It's me. We thought we'd do a little experiment – just for fun. Ben suggested I could do some sketches of my "flavour shapes". With your expert guidance. I can't draw at all. I can't even draw a straight line.'

'Just use a ruler. What was Hilary after?'

'You know her, do you? Well, she was asking me about outputs from your Drawing Workshop, for her report. She's very on it, isn't she? I think I've escaped now. I hope. Don't worry, I was very complimentary about you. I'm from the neurology department downstairs. We hate you guys up here. You've been "borrowing" some of our patients. Ha ha.'

'Complimentary, huh? That's nice.'

'It has helped some of them. I told Hilary it's been quite useful with some patients. She wasn't sure if that meets her criteria for an "output", as such.'

When I got back from the toilet – the thing with diarrhoea is you always think that this has to be the last shit, surely – everyone was already sat down and working. Dan had found himself a place and laid out everything he needed for the little experiment he and Ben had devised. Or almost. He had paper and coloured felt tips.

'We need to get some snacks, too,' said Dan.

Snacks? 'Why? Why snacks?'

'For this little experiment I need to taste snacks. I thought you knew. Anyhow, look, I'll explain as we go. Could you just get something from downstairs actually? I'm supposed to stay here. Just get anything. Crisps and sweets and things. '

'Yuh. I am, actually, a bit strapped. For cash. Do you think ...?'

'Here's twenty.'

73: not feeling very well

TREVOR, UNFORTUNATELY, was right next to us during that exchange, and heard enough to make him think I had offered to get snacks for everybody. Especially him. I went down to the hospital foyer and loaded up with all the most filling snacks you can get for a few quid. Three Cornish pasties, a Camembert panini, a portion of fries. Another portion of fries (these portions are just a mouthful for Trevor), three bananas, two litres of Fanta, some Cheezee Savors, crisps and biscuits, a lemon (for Dan), and one *croque monsieur*, which was a terrible mistake.

The powerful fatty stench coming off those fries and that *croque monsieur*, coming up in the lift, was almost too much for me. Then having to put it all down on the reception desk while I rifled my pockets for my temporary pass because the receptionist demanded to see it. Her disgust at all these foodstuffs on her desk, and my sweaty green face (and she fucking *knows* I've got a pass, after all the fuss she made about issuing it). And then, back in the Activities Room, watching Trevor placidly consume all this terrible stuff. His mouth open and full, like shoving food into a front-loading washing machine, round and round. Bits of it getting everywhere, up his nose, down his front.

'I'm going to have to leave early today, Colin. I think I've got a bug. Tell that guy Dan, when he's free.' Dan was looking mildly panicked, cornered once more by Hilary, who had not, as it turned out, completely finished with him.

'It's probably a virus,' said Emily, who was sitting with Colin.

276

As I was standing in the reception area waiting for the lift (*just* standing), I felt a heavy hand clapped on my shoulder. Your reactions can be amazingly fast when you're not feeling well. Faster than normal even. I almost hit the ceiling. It was the receptionist.

'If you're leaving you'll have to return your pass.' I handed it to her. 'And where's your proper pass? You need to find it or we'll have to fill out a declaration for security.'

'I'll go and have a look.' She wasn't going to let me go. She was going to make me fill out forms and then probably stand and wait while she got on the phone to security, and to Michelle. I'll have to pretend to go and look for my pass. I'll go and have a lie down in my studio, Room 23. Staggering, actually staggering, to my room I was passed by two or three of these observers, or auditors, and noticed them noticing me, and making a note of it. That's something for Simon and Selina. They weren't sure how they could use it, but it's definitely something.

Tottering towards the bed, after another exhausted bowel evacuation in my en suite, I had a sudden intuition or insight, and instead of falling onto the bed, as planned, I looked underneath, and saw a filthy bundle under there. I pulled out, from under the bed, a bundle made from my puke-encrusted shirt, and it clinked. After some fiddly work untying a complicated system of knots, the shirt-tail tied to the sleeve and the other sleeve tied, somehow, to the collar, I found that the bundle contained five empty wine bottles and a couple of glasses. Around the necks of two of the bottles were the desiccated remains of oranges, in each case the orange shoved on like a collar and now shrunk tightly in place. Another bottle contained dozens of cigarette ends. I turned, still in a crouching position, to sit on the edge of the bed, and following a few moments' examination of all this, and some thought, experienced a rush of joyous clarity and relief. I still couldn't remember anything about what I did that night, but looking at all this evidence it was pretty obvious what had happened. I did go to Emily's room, pissed; but then I must have come back here, after going to the Day Room to take some oranges. Or possibly I'd collected them before going to Emily's room and then brought them here afterwards. Then I'd made a hole right through each of them (possibly I'd forced them over the taps in the bathroom to do this). Then, well, I suppose I must have fucked the oranges. No wonder my cock was so sore. Citric acid. A disgusting scenario, and not something I'd like to get out, but not criminal, or in any way harmful to Emily. No doubt, in my pissed-up and amphetamine-aroused state, I'd made some kind of connection between Emily and the orange. And I must have thought, 'if I can't have the real thing I'll settle for the symbol', which does share many of the original's properties – it's soft and moist and organic. Also, frankly, you'll fuck anything when you're on speed. It's not even all that perverse. There's that saying isn't there: a woman for duty, a boy for pleasure, a melon for ecstasy. This bundle would have been my idea of tidying up, following my lone sex and drugs and boozing orgy.

That terrible feeling of remorse was probably just a chemical thing. Add that to some fairly damning-looking circumstantial evidence, plus the gaps in my recall, and you've got all the ingredients for a false memory – a confabulated crime. And confabulations feel exactly like objectively accurate memories – so it's impossible to tell them apart.

I seem to be in the clear. Basically I've got myself into a right state over nothing. I may even have been the perfect gentleman when I went to see Emily; turning up like that, boldly unannounced, with a nice bottle of wine and (a little joke between us, this) some oranges. She wouldn't have got it exactly, but she'd have sensed that it meant something. She probably had quite a nice time really. What else is she going to do in the evenings around here? All on her own, listening to music or watching TV. So I spent some time with Emily and then went back to my room. I definitely remember her saying something about keeping a secret, but it wasn't a promise made under duress. I probably told her I shouldn't be in here like this, and she probably said it's OK – she could keep a secret. So it's all fine. But, let's be very clear, nothing like this must ever, *ever* happen again. I may not have done anything bad this time, but, terrifyingly, the capability is in me somewhere; otherwise I don't think I'd have believed I actually did do something bad. (An essential component of the false memory was my suspicion that I'm despicable.)

Cleaning the dried sick off my security pass, which I'd found still clipped onto my shirt, I felt marvellous. My bowels weren't griping or twitching any more at all. I felt completely cured. I'll show that bitch receptionist my pass, and laugh. Pausing a moment, I realised I still had to do something with those empty bottles. I couldn't carry them all out with me, so I rinsed them and arranged them in a neat row. I had to flush all the cigarette ends down the toilet, which wasn't easy because they float. Four flushes. It then struck me, tidying up and getting things ship-shape, that someone had been in here, looking through my books. I'd got it so that I knew where everything is in my room, and I could tell that someone had been in there moving things. Those observers sniffing around. Luckily they hadn't gone as far as looking under the bed, or they'd have seen my bundle, and they'd have had the bomb squad up here.

74: synaesthesia

THE RECEPTIONIST WASN'T HAPPY to see my pass, shoved triumphantly in front of her face. 'Well, we've already set the process in motion to report this as missing. I'll have to contact security now.' She phoned security. 'We'll have to call in a rescinding order on that missing pass alert ... yes, it's been re-found ... yes, that's a re-find.' And then she had to phone Michelle. A small victory for her here. 'Michelle wants to see you in her office.' A little smile on her face. Michelle would deal with me.

Turned out she only wanted to give me my cheque. 'I've had that sitting on my desk the last three weeks. I don't suppose you need it, with the amount you get paid for your modern art. Chopping up sharks. Probably been too busy going out with all your posh arty friends to come round here. You look as if you've been having some heavy nights.'

'Oh, hello!' said Dan. 'You OK? Someone told me you'd gone home.'

'I nearly did, but then I felt much better. Much, much better. All of a sudden. Here's the crisps and things. I'll pay you that twenty back next week if that's alright.'

Synaesthesia is a condition in which stimulation of one sense creates a kind of echo in another, so you can see sounds, hear colours, taste shapes, smell sounds, etc. Hearing colours is by far the most common form, while some combinations – hearing flavours, for example – are rare. But the condition itself, in all its varieties, is actually quite common. About four per cent of us are synaesthetes.

To call synaesthesia a 'condition' is slightly misleading because the term seems to imply a pathology, and really you could just as easily think of it as a special talent. Vladimir Nabokov was a synaesthete – his sensory 'leakings and drafts' – and it has been suggested that this may have added to the richness of his prose. He was a coloured hearer, particularly of words and letters (he hated music). So for him the letter *a* sounded like the tint of weathered wood. It only sounded like that in English. In French it was polished ebony. *f* was alder-leaf green and *w* was a dull green, with some violet. And so on. Rimbaud is also supposed to have been a synaesthete, but the evidence for this is just one poem – 'Voyelles' (Vowels):

'A Black, E White, I Red, U Green, O Blue;
some day I'll crack your nascent origins ...'

(That second line is probably better in French.)

It's certainly possible that Rimbaud was a synaesthete, but then again attempts to analyse artworks from a neurological point of view can be a bit literal-minded. Van Gogh gets a lot of this kind of thing. Obviously he had a lot of problems but that doesn't really justify the reduction of his particular style to a diagnostic tool. His paintings aren't symptoms, even if cutting his ear off probably was. The consensus on Van Gogh has settled on a whole raft of symptoms now held to be characteristic of Geschwind syndrome – an 'interictal' (i.e. between seizures) aspect of a form of temporal lobe epilepsy. It's a disorder which exhibits in hyper-religiosity, unstable sexual behaviour, clinginess and hypergraphia – compulsive and incredibly prolific writing, usually a diary or, as in Van Gogh's case, thousands and thousands of letters. This condition, along with manic depressive mood swings, is thought to have been exacerbated by absinthe, brandy, nicotine and turpentine. (The last inhaled accidentally. He probably didn't drink it.) The ultra-vividness of his paintings is thought to be associated with the heightened pre-seizure state experienced by some epileptics. But then he can't have been in that state every time he did a painting. And lots of painters, the Fauves in particular, adopted and even exceeded that ultra-vivid style, and they were all fine.

There have even been attempts to explain the multi-dimensional world-view of Cubism in terms of some kind of neurological condition. This sort of explanation of art tends to overlook the main thing about the subject, which is that it's art. The aesthetic version of reality is bound to be different from the consensus reality because that's what art is. It's all made up. Artists invent things. It's called creativity. Neuro-art criticism can be just as bad as the simple-minded application of pop-psychoanalytical thinking to art criticism, where you try and explain everything an artist does as the inevitable consequence of some formative experience. Art as autobiography.

It's not that neuroscience can't say anything about art. There's nothing in principle wrong with the idea, just as there's nothing in principle wrong with the idea of an artificial intelligence that's in every way like a human's – i.e. conscious. It's just that neuroscience isn't ready for that yet. It's still trying to figure out how it is you can eat without biting your tongue, whilst at the same time reading Nabokov, and maybe walking, too – and feeling sad. All using the same organ.

Wassily Kandinsky, one of the handful of artists who are generally credited with having invented abstraction in the visual arts, was very interested in his own synaesthesia. His abstract 'compositions' were, he thought, the visual equivalent of music, particularly in the sense that they were not representational in any straightforward way. He thought that abstract painting was the same as music, and music was the same as abstract painting. He even wrote an opera called The Yellow Sound. This was all tied up with his theosophical ideas about abstraction and spirituality. He believed in the spiritual value of unmediated experience – unmediated, that is, by language or representation of any kind. For him there was a clear line to be drawn between the ethereal higher forms of abstraction, and the corporeal, drearily mundane world of *things*, and verbal or pictorial representations of those *things*.

Kandinsky's abstract painting was supposed to be the means of access to a higher plane, and it seems quite sad the way his work has ended up. His visions of a higher plane of existence are now used as the default choice of picture for

decorating offices and chain restaurants. The sort of print you put on the wall if you think there should be one there but have no strong feelings about what it should be. It's a fate he shares with Miró, Klee and Monet. They're being used to add a bit of meaningless visual static wherever there's some wall space that needs filling at a Pizza Hut or a Harvester.

Ben and Dan's idea is for Dan to draw the shapes and colours he 'sees' as he tastes different things. He's had this thing all his life, but even though he's a neurologist he's never given it much thought; largely because it is only of anecdotal interest, not something that links in any obvious way to clinical practice, but also because he's found no easy way of describing these gustatory and colour/shape sensory links. (It doesn't work the other way, incidentally. He doesn't find himself 'tasting' forms and colours.)

They thought I might be able to help out here because Dan has never done any painting or drawing – not willingly anyway, and not since he was about six. He was amazingly awkward with it. Even the way he held a felt tip, as if he was holding it for someone else. We tried a few taste sensations, cheese and onion crisps to begin with, and then he was supposed to do a drawing of its visual and tactile analogue. (The shapes are somehow 'felt', as well as somehow 'seen'.) Crisps, he said, were kind of like a greenish pendulum which increases in weight as it swings. The apricot Danish was very flat, with a sort of bluey edge. He pointed at the handbag of one of the patients – 'that colour' – which I would have said was more of a viridian and cadmium yellow mix than a blue. Still. He tasted the lemon, and that, surprisingly, was like a very long smooth surface, a polished stone approaching a slope but not going up it, and brown- and red-striped. You'd have thought a lemon would be spiky and yellow. Lemon yellow, in fact. The synaesthetic analogue doesn't seem to bear any metaphorical or met-onymical relation to its source. Vinegar doesn't look sharp (salt and vinegar crisps), and oranges aren't orange. (Also the correspondences are not the same for all synaesthetes. My pork chop could be square while yours is triangular.)

We weren't getting any of this down on paper. Dan was unbelievably awkward with his drawing tools. He could barely describe the sensations in words, let alone draw them. This inability to describe a phenomenon is incred-ibly frustrating for a scientist like him, so it's no wonder he hasn't given his synaesthesia much thought in the past. Something so subjective and which, although quite com-mon, is experienced in a unique way in each case, is not a good subject for scientific analysis. It's too 'first person', and I can tell Dan hates that about it. It's like pain, which is probably a lot less interesting to a doctor than it is to the patient, who can't seem to think about anything else. (Say-ing 'I have a very bad pain' can never convey the urgency and the scope and the exhaustiveness of that experience. Even screaming doesn't do it all that well.)

Because Dan seemed practically incapable of even mak-ing a single mark on a piece of paper, we opted to do it the way the police used to get pictures of criminals before the days of Photofit and E-FIT. He would try and describe it and I'd try and make a drawing of the thing from his description – '... kind of long and thin, and it has a way of constantly flipping back on itself with the colour of a Telewest van flaring up, or pulsing.' This was an orange. It was almost as hopeless as trying to draw the flavour itself. Like trying to draw a scream as opposed to drawing someone screaming.

'Never mind,' said Dan. 'It was worth a try. I've got to get back downstairs now. Look after some "outputs". See ya!'

'See ya, Dan!' I went over to the others.

75: feeling much better

'HELLO, MATE. You've got your colour back. Feeling better now, are you?'

Yes, thanks, I'm feeling fine, Colin. Pretty good. A thorough purging can do you a lot of good, almost like doing detox. Everything pleasantly normal and orderly again (apart, that is, from the hovering presence of another of those goons; watching us, making notes). It's all normal again now, save for the fact that I'm walking on air, floating around the room, ministering to my people. Colin's doing a brain stem – 'Good work, Colin' – and Stick is doing a cerebellum – 'Smashing cerebellum, Stick!' Pauline's half a hypothalamus coming along nicely, and Trevor's apple. The Blind Man's enjoying himself even though he can't see what he's doing – it's just good to feel that you're doing something with your hands – and the Blind Woman is sitting next to him, not trying to do anything herself but happy that he's happy. There are some new faces, too, brought along this morning by Dr Bokassa and being looked after by Jade, who's just joined us. I give them a bit of advice and encouragement.

Emily. How's she getting along? She has the super-brain, one of Ben's most prized models, disassembled in front of her on the table. The entire complex model is scattered on the table in bits, so that if you didn't know it you'd never guess that all these parts could be fitted together to form the familiar 'boxing glove' shape of the human brain.

Emily did a strange thing then. She was working patiently and seriously, drawing each part one at a time, but then she stopped, and she put the model back together.

It only took her about a minute. She must have suddenly rediscovered some lost aptitude for doing puzzles, or model-making (and it occurred to me, once again, that her personality, prior to her illness, may have been quite a dull one). It is with a tremendous sense of relief that I am able to look her honestly in the eye and say, 'That's good, Emily. Excellent. You've done this before, haven't you?' Leaning over her to examine her work, and innocently sniffing her clean hair.

Some of them are beginning to dissent, though. Even some of the quieter ones are beginning to express some dissatisfaction. This lady here, for example: 'Can't we draw something else apart from brains?' She has brain damage in her occipital cortex following a nasty fall in the shower. 'I'd quite like to do a still life, like Trevor.'

The choice of subject is apt, because her particular deficit is the inability to perceive movement. One of the V areas in her visual cortex has been damaged, so she sees everything as a sequence of stills, like being stuck in a strobe-lit world. It's apt, but also odd that she has requested a still life, because she has generally shown an unwillingness to come to terms with her condition. She tries to act as if nothing's wrong and has to be prevented from trying to pour her own coffee at breaktimes. Because she's getting everything in snapshots, she invariably overfills the cup. One moment it's empty and the next she realises that it's spilling everywhere. She can't see the gradual filling of the cup. She's almost got herself run over on numerous occasions because she finds it impossible to judge oncoming traffic, and she won't be persuaded that she should ask someone for help when crossing the road. It's because she can't seem to get her head around the difference between blindness and a partial visual deficit. She's not blind and that's that.

I explained about the still life. 'We had to give Trevor things like the apples and the chair to draw because he has to have easily recognisable objects as he's learning how to see.' She would have no trouble seeing a brain clearly, so long as it stayed still. But then I gathered quite a few of the other patients felt the same way. I didn't want to give in on this because I was thinking about my exhibition – 'Brain Drawings by Brain Patients'. And who needs to see another poorly executed bowl of fruit or bunch of flowers or whatever? I said I'd see what I could do.

Now that I was back on track I felt it was time to get things moving with my exhibition idea. I had a small brainwave. I asked Colin to come to a private view at FRESH! Gallery that evening. Some Austrian artist, I think.

'Do we need invites?' asked Colin.

'No, you can just turn up. I'll introduce you to my dealer.'

'Do I need to change?'

'No, you're alright like that. Bring Stick along if you're worried. Then at least you'll know you're not the scruffiest person there.'

Actually I needed to offer this olive branch myself, personally.

'Hello, Stick. Hi.'

'Hi.'

'Look, I was sorry to hear about your friend. The one who had a tunnelling accident. That guy Duncan. I just wanted to say that.'

'That's alright. No skin off my nose. This is what happens when you get these amateurs involved in political protest. He shouldn't have been burrowing underground when he didn't know how to do it properly. He should have been protesting where it matters.'

Which, it turns out, is on the internet. In fact Stick's blogging campaign against NORMERON has been causing quite a stir amongst its followers. He knows this for sure because they are all known to him personally. Most of them live in the same house as him.

'Ah. Fair enough. The other thing, Stick, was do you want to come to a private view?'

76: another private view

THERE WEREN'T MANY PEOPLE THERE. You don't usually get much of a turnout for foreign artists, unless they're very well known. As we entered the gallery I noticed that Colin and Stick were both looking apprehensive, as if they thought they were going to be asked to leave. This made me feel, myself, very much at home. This is my world. It doesn't normally feel like that, but with those two here it was different. I went up to the bar and took a bottle of beer. Colin looked on uncertainly.

'It's OK, Colin. Just grab a beer. It's free. I'm just going to say hello to my dealer.' I left the pair of them watching the video. A stroke of luck, this. The video showed a young woman, presumably the artist herself – Heidi something – preparing breakfast naked.

I found my dealer in the office at the back of the gallery, and he was looking very unhappy. Another of the gallery's artists was there too, resting a hand lightly on the dealer's forearm, consoling him about something.

'What's up?'

'Oh ... Hi, there.' He raised his head from his hands.

'Something happen?'

'This show. It's a disaster.'

'Well, I know there aren't many people here, but you never get much of a turnout for foreign artists. I've brought some people.'

'People are going to be really upset. It's disgusting.' He shook his head slowly. The artist was nodding sympathetically, and he sighed.

'It's not so bad, I wouldn't have thought. A bit of nudity. A bit sexist, I suppose.'

'Do you know what coprophagy is?'

'I think I've heard the word. No. What is it?'

'Go and have a look.'

I went back to have a look.

Colin and Stick were in a small group huddled around the video monitor. Colin was smiling nervously, and Stick's mouth was hanging gormlessly open. The naked woman's breakfast preparations had taken a disturbing turn. She was squatting on the kitchen table and shitting onto a slice of toast. You could see her legs shaking as she did it, the way dogs' hindlegs shake when they defecate. It had all been filmed using the most basic equipment, probably without a cameraman, with the camera set up on a tripod by the woman herself and left switched on.

The kitchen was of a sort I imagine to be quite typical of the middle-class Viennese suburbs. It was a very neat and tidy kitchen; a tree visible through the window, a light drizzle outside, and muffled noises off – cars passing, and a dog's bark. That particular quality with low-tech sound recording where everything sounds too real, as if you had a migraine headache coming on. The woman climbed off the table, quite clumsily, sat down and started to eat the toast. None of us could look – but at the same time of course we couldn't help looking. Our heads were half turned away from the monitor screen, but then our horrified eyes swivelled back towards it again, so that we were all watching more or less sideways, devoting full attention to peripheral vision.

She can't be going to eat all of it. The point, surely, has been made – about drudgery and self-hatred I guessed – and she can stop now. The crunching of the toast made it so much worse somehow.

'Continental breakfast,' said Colin. Good try, but joking didn't make it any less appalling as an experience. So he added: 'She's going to make herself sick, doing that.' 'This is CGI, isn't it?', someone murmured hopefully. No it isn't. It's all for real, filmed in real time.

I went back to the gallery office. 'I see what you mean,' I said. 'It is disgusting.'

The reason she hasn't come over for the opening of her show, her first in London, is she's in hospital.

And the reason FRESH! has ended up agreeing to show this stuff, sight unseen, is because of a reciprocal artist-exchange agreement with Heidi's gallery in Vienna. Two galleries, usually in different countries, agree to show each other's artists in a straight swap. This is to help promote artists abroad, and open up new markets for their work. We'll show your artist X, if you'll show our artist Y.

Did he have no idea what the content of Heidi's show was going to be?

'They said it was going to be controversial work ... *challenging* work.'

'Is it not?'

'Dave's work is controversial and challenging. This is just disgusting.'

Dave is the artist in attendance here, consoling. He's the London half of this exchange deal with Vienna. His controversial 'FUCK U' series has been a big hit. The heads of well-known cultural and historical figures collaged with Photoshop onto the bodies of porn actors and models – Van Gogh being fisted by Nixon; Gandhi giving Keats a blowjob.

('Some people will do anything for attention,' muttered Dave, shaking his head sadly.)

'Couldn't you have refused to show it?'

'No. They've already shown Dave's work in Vienna and it was a sell-out show. So now I'm supposed to show Heidi's work to all my best clients. It's a disaster. They'll never come back.' Now may not be a great time for me to broach the subject of my exhibition idea – but then again it could be just the right time. Give him something else to think about. Take his mind off Heidi's self-abasement.

'Listen, I've brought some people along to meet you. From the Institute.'

'Sure,' he said. 'Bring them in.'

I only caught a glimpse of what Heidi was up to when I went to fetch Colin and Stick. There was the sound of retching and crockery exploding against a wall as I dragged the shell-shocked pair along to the office.

The meeting went OK. Stick, probably because of his medication, stayed very quiet, and Colin started to go on about Monet in a slightly embarrassing way. The pair of them both obviously intimidated by their surroundings. So, this is the Art World. My dealer was very polite to them in a way I found actually quite touching, but you could see the question he was dying to ask, somewhere in there behind the eyes: 'They seem OK to me. So what's, actually, wrong with them?' Like meeting someone who's just got out of prison and you're dying to ask them what they did. Beyond the curiosity is a little bit of concern – they're not going to, like, *do* anything, are they?

Later in the pub, a thin crowd, particularly with the artist herself not well enough to be present, and I was able to get some kind of a provisional agreement out of him. We left it that I would bring in the drawings I'd been talking about, the Brain Drawings by Brain Patients, and then we'd kick a few ideas around about how to do the show. Stick left almost immediately. When I decided to leave myself – suddenly completely exhausted – Colin was being entertaining at the bar with Dave and his girlfriend.

77: a better day

IN THE LIFT ON OUR WAY UP to the top floor were me and a delivery man. He had the name of his firm embroidered on the left breast of his sweatshirt. I knew the name but couldn't place it.

'Awright?'

'Awright?'

I was feeling rather good today after a week spent mostly in bed, not having to go to Earls Court, and I was looking forward to my Workshop. I was just about to disappear into a corridor, having flashed my pass at the receptionist, when she called me back. What now?

'You know the way to the MRI suite.' I know it's here, I guess. Yes, I suppose I do.

'If you wouldn't mind showing this gentleman there. If you don't mind.'

He seemed OK with that big trolley loaded with boxes, so it wouldn't matter if we went a bit of a long way; and I couldn't say, in front of her, that I wasn't confident about getting us there via the most direct route. So alright then.

A very slight detour, not bad at all by my standards, lengthened our journey just enough to require me to make conversation. Otherwise the sound of our footsteps and the slight squeak of the trolley would have been too loud.

'So ... what you got there, then? Spare parts, is it?'

'Biscuits.'

I knew I recognised that company name on his shirt, and on the boxes I now notice. A foodstuffs corporation that's been in the press a bit lately. There's been a bit of controversy about them aggressively marketing unsuitable dairy products to nursing mothers in the Third World. One of Conrad Norman's concerns, I think.

'Here we are.'

As I hurried off towards the Activities Room, a bit late now because of that, I caught a glimpse of some technicians helping him unload the boxes onto an already gigantic pile of boxes of snack foods and drinks.

Everyone was already there and settled, apart from Ben. And there were no brains out.

'Where's the brains, Colin?' They seem to have pre-empted my decision about the subject matter for our drawings. I had been going to concede them a few more traditional still lifes in the coming weeks, and I even thought we might get a life model in at some point. But they seem to have taken matters into their own hands, and were sitting there with various fruits and pieces of crockery borrowed from the Day Room. Some of them had even started to do drawings of this stuff. Trevor looked in his element. He's an experienced fruit draughtsman now. Emily looked as if she was concentrating hard, but not actually drawing yet. Colin had made a start. And Stick.

'I thought we'd better improvise,' said Colin. 'We can't use the brains today. Matter of fact we can't use them again at all. Ben's just packing them.'

'Packing? He's leaving?'

'Yeah, I know. I'm going to miss him. Actually, I think he wanted a word. We'll just carry on, shall we?'

78: packing

THE DOOR TO BEN'S OFFICE was jammed open with a cardboard box full of books and brains.

'Ben! You're leaving, then.' He was in the middle of a quite detailed bit of packing, individually wrapping each part of his biggest brain in pink tissue paper, and then pushing them gently into a box full of those polystyrene things like corn snacks.

'Hi there!' He's in a very good mood. 'Actually I wouldn't mind a hand, if you're free.'

I'm quite good at packing because I worked for an art gallery for a while, and that's one of the main things I had to do. Preparing costly artworks for transport. They'd go mad if anything got damaged, or even got a fingerprint, other than the artist's own fingerprints. I could see Ben really needed some help with all this stuff – thousands of books and brains, and other bits and pieces. I got him a bit more organised with it, sorting things into categories and sizes, and making sure all the boxes had their contents written on them before they were taped up.

We talked as we worked. First of all: 'Where are you going, then? What are you going to do?'

'Owen Madden's offered me a job with his new biochem firm. Researching neurogenesis in Santa Barbara. Great money.'

'Isn't it all a bit … sudden?' This came out sounding hurt.

'No, not really. Actually, we've been planning it for months, but we both thought it'd be best if I finish what I had to do here.'

'Sorting out the funding.'

'Yeah. And a few other things.'

'Like Emily.' I hadn't meant anything in particular by that but he looked a bit uncomfortable for a second. I fucking knew it. He does fancy her.

We'd done the brains first, instead of mixing the brains and the books together like he'd been doing, and I made a start at sorting the books out.

'Shall we do this according to subject matter, or colour maybe? Or usefulness? You don't want the books you never look at mixed in with the ones you use all the time. How about these?' I took one from the top of a pile of scruffy-looking notebooks, and absently flipped the pages as I spoke. When he noticed what I'd got hold of he reacted as if I'd stumbled upon his secret porn stash or something. He kind of lunged at me and snatched it from my hands – 'N ... not that!' Jeezus. I was only asking. He looked embarrassed then, and had a bit of a think.

'Oh ... I don't suppose it matters now. Go on. Have a look if you like.' I wouldn't have had any strong feelings about looking or not looking, but if he felt it meant something, of course, I was very curious.

It was fascinating actually. The pages of this notebook were so densely written, in a variety of coloured inks, that the pages were actually heavy with the ink, and curved by its weight. The writer had exerted so much pressure that the point of the pen had embossed the paper, and you could see the writing in relief on the reverse of each sheet, like Braille. You couldn't actually read any of it, though. You could hardly distinguish individual letters, even where they were done in different colours, let alone make out words. Each page looked like an abstract drawing. I glanced through a few of the other notebooks in the stack, dozens of them, and they were all the same. Actually you could just make out what seemed to be dates at the head of some pages, like a diary.

'Is this someone's diary, Ben?'

'It's Emily's diary. She's always kept diaries. These are from before her illness.'

'*Before?* They look mental.'

'They *are* mental. She was bipolar. Manic depressive.'

'Shit! Out of the frying pan and right into the fire, huh?'

'That page you've got there is the sort of thing she'd produce at the height of a manic episode. It's called hypergraphia. They just write and write and write. And this ...' he took the notebook from me and found another page, 'is Emily depressed.' Blank, apart from the word 'NO' feebly traced at the head of the page. Several pages like that, until she couldn't even be bothered to write 'NO'.

Here's what Ben told me. (And even now I can't quite get my head around the fact that he'd been lying to me. Not lying exactly. Not being entirely frank. I can't get my head around it just because, and this is probably going to sound silly, he doesn't seem the type. And I thought we'd established a rapport. Of course it wasn't really any of my business. And we do seem to be in an unusual area here – where both the medical practitioner's confidentiality, and the discretion required of employees in a competitive field like commercial biochemistry, are being observed. They overlap, and so the demand for secrecy is doubled. I understand all that, but even so ...)

Emily's condition is actually something she's done to herself. At first they'd thought it might be a suicide attempt, but really it's the result of a suicidally reckless experiment, using herself as the subject. While she was working for NORMERON, in Belize. The free clinic for local people had been pretty much all her idea, and she did most of the work there. It was, it now seems clear, an outlet for all that

surplus manic energy, even though she was already working very long hours doing research in the labs – she was in
charge of conducting pioneering studies on neurogenesis in
monkeys. (The availability of monkeys, incidentally, was an
important consideration in choosing Belize as a location for
the NORMERON research facility. Lots of monkeys and no
animal rights activists to cause problems.)

The bulk of the research involved the testing of various
compounds for their capacity to promote neurogenesis.
First the monkeys' hippocampi would be removed, either
surgically, or by infecting them with a virus, directly injec-
ted into the temporal lobes to cause devastating focal
brain damage to the hippocampi and associated structures.
This would create a kind of tabula rasa against which the
regrowth of new brain tissue would be easy to detect. Following this procedure the monkeys would be treated with
neural stem cells and varying types and dosages of drugs,
and then tested for signs of regrowth. You can do this in
several ways, including aptitude tests on live monkeys, but
given the sheer numbers involved their preferred method
for detecting neurogenesis was to kill the monkey and look
at its brain. In this way they discovered, by examining
thin slivers of brain tissue, that although the results were
mostly disappointing they were on the right track with
some drugs. Isoxazole-9 looked good.

And Emily did to herself more or less what she'd been
doing to those capuchin monkeys. What she did was an
experiment, with very high, but calculated risks. Here were
four possible results:

(1) She dies.

(2) She lives, but she's a vegetable. (These two are by
far the most likely results of injecting yourself, directly

into the temporal lobe, with a virus: and then, probably about a week later, just prior to the first symptoms of encephalitis emerging, self-administering a cocktail of stem cells and experimental drugs, in the same horrific and painful way.)

(3) She lives, but with severe anterograde amnesia. (This could have the effect of a sort of drastic 'cure' for her bipolarity, simply by destroying the self that suffers the condition. Like curing athlete's foot by chopping your legs off. So, for example, you won't make crazy plans if you can't make plans at all.)

(4) She succeeds in destroying and then regrowing both hippocampi. A new and total cure for any number of conditions, including bipolar disorder.

This last would be the least likely result. 'About a gazillion to one,' says Ben, 'but not actually impossible.' But Emily would have been, at the height of a manic episode, extremely confident about achieving a positive outcome from this experiment (and the thrilling possibility of success will have shone very bright against the dark background of depression).

And actually, it seems crazy, but her confidence about this was not completely irrational. She was, apparently, absolutely brilliant; a prodigy, in fact. And obviously she knew this about herself. She had sound reasons to trust her own judgment. (I now realise that part of the reason she struck such a chord with me, as if I had known her in another life, is because I'd seen her on television when she was about twelve. She'd just started at university. Most of her education to that point had been conducted at home, and the interview was clearly being monitored by her vigilant parents, with their tight smiles. I can remember her obvious discomfort at being questioned about missing out on all the normal things children do, and who was her favourite pop star? She didn't know any.) Her decision was the product of a mind used to dealing in extremes. The payoff, in the event of it working, would have been epoch-making. The 'clean-slate' cure for depression.

There is a lot of interest in researching depression because it's so widespread and costly, causing billions of dollars' worth of absenteeism. The drugs used to treat it can be very effective, but in many cases they are mere palliatives, offering only temporary relief. No one has any real clue what, ultimately, causes it, but it is now thought, like schizophrenia, to be a 'polygenic' condition. That is, there will be several causes – a mixture of social, genetic and biological things. And Emily's extreme course of action will have been to do with the fact that the hippocampus is now thought to be strongly associated with the depressive illnesses – unipolar (just depressed) and bipolar (manic depressed). The hippocampi of chronically depressed patients actually shrink! So, if Emily's pain during the depressive phases of her condition had a *physical* site, then she had good reason to suppose that that was most probably it. The possibility of destroying that organ and replacing it with a better one will have seemed very well worth the risks. Assessing all the possible outcomes, it would actually have looked like a 'win-win' situation to her.

79: coping strategies

OF COURSE THERE WAS A HELL of a flap at NORMERON
when they realised, more or less, what she'd done. It was
touch and go for a bit, but she lived, and then there was
the problem of what to do with her. Nancy Prabhakar was
Emily's boss, and so it had ended up being her problem –
particularly since she felt, rightly, that she ought to have
been keeping a closer eye on things. She responded very
energetically to Emily's medical emergency, using all the
considerable resources at her disposal to take care of every
aspect of her care and her safe return to the UK.

Emily had been quite good at keeping her medical history
a secret (and her naturally secretive disposition had been
one of the things they liked about her), but Dr Prabhakar had
always suspected something was up. All those mysterious
gaps in Emily's CV. But the missing months in her history
were easily overlooked, sandwiched as they were between
periods of astonishing creativity and achievement in
neuroscience. They even overlooked her occasional
absences from work, periods of up to a week spent either in
her room or at her free clinic, because her productivity still
outstripped that of any other researcher. There was some
concern about her astonishing promiscuity – her lovers,
rumour had it, including several of her Mayan patients at the
clinic – but this behaviour was put down to the need to let off
steam, and have a bit of R and R; completely understandable
in someone with such a heavy workload.

The consequences of Norman's recently diagnosed
Alzheimer's were not yet clear, and the possibility that

Nancy's plans could be derailed when it got out about Emily, and what she'd been up to, will have been the cause of some sleepless nights. Norman might well have withdrawn his funding, for all anyone knew. In the event what that diagnosis actually made Norman want to do was to get on with it, and within a very few months the London institute was all ready and equipped to the highest standards. It just needed some staff, and patients. Here, as it turned out, was the solution for Emily, and for Nancy's problem with Emily – what to do with her; and, more importantly from a professional point of view, how to, as it were, debrief her. (There's an irony here, because it was Nancy's preoccupation with setting up the NNI that caused her to overlook the signs of excessive stress in Emily. And Emily was to become their first ever patient.)

The problem of explaining what had happened was not much of a problem at all, because there turned out to be hardly anyone who'd want to know. Emily had had literally hundreds of lovers but no steady relationships. She didn't seem to have any friends, and she hadn't spoken to her parents for years – probably because, having been educated at home up to the age of twelve, and never allowed any contact with other children, she must have felt that she'd had enough of them. She hadn't seen her parents since she was nineteen, and she was twenty-eight when all this happened. (Twenty-eight. That makes her … quite close to being my age now. Amazing. You'd never think it to look at her.)

80: a new dawn

EXCEPTING THE TRAGIC CIRCUMSTANCES, it all worked out quite well. Perfect timing. Emily was the ideal patient to kick off the Institute's unique inpatient program, with Ben joining the staff not long after the place was opened. Ben, it turns out, is another bright star. Not in Emily's league, but a very promising young man, ideal for the task of oversee-ing Emily's care and debriefing. This was quite a sensitive thing. Emily knew a lot of very important stuff, even within the remit of her normal responsibilities at NORMERON. It wouldn't have been good if her condition had impaired her ability to be discreet. And apart from that, what of her own supererogatory researches at the clinic? It's *just* possible that her experiment wasn't as mad as it seems.

It took nearly two years of regular and frequent one-to-one sessions with Ben (and with Nancy Prabhakar when she could find the time), close observation, and repeated failed attempts to make sense of Emily's diaries, all three hundred of them, before it was reluctantly agreed that she would never show any marked recovery from the virus. And that there was nothing useful in the diaries. The only reason he'd stuck with it for so long is that Emily seemed to have recovered some ability to retain new spatial memor-ies. She had learned her way around the Institute even though the scans they'd been doing continued to confirm that she still had gaps in her head where the hippocampi ought to be. This ability, it was eventually decided, had to be labelled, unsatisfyingly, as 'anomalous'. One of the things that doesn't square with any current understanding of how the brain works, but which does exist. Perhaps the effect of some kind of neural plasticity. Its difficult to theorise by extrapolating from a one-off case like hers.

Ben had long since given up the most obvious method of pursuing his research into Emily's condition, which was just to ask her which virus (there are very many she could have used for this, including the cold sore virus), and how much? Often, patients with anterograde amnesia will also have lost some of their memory of the time immediately preceding the affliction, but it was worth a try – who knows how long she'd been planning this? Or what effect the drugs may have had in qualifying that memory loss? It would have been no good persisting with his questions – besides her apparent inability to answer questions about her past, Emily clearly did not like being asked about herself. No doubt this was out of habit, she having decided to keep her fragile mental health a secret. All her relationships seem to have been kept as perfunctory and expeditious as possible. No friends or boyfriends, and estranged by choice from her family. In fact, her diary seems to be the only thing she was at all close to ... and that's not telling.

I had another go at the diary myself. Surely no one can write that much and absolutely *none* of it be comprehensible. There was the odd passage that you could just about make out. One bit I recognised, despite the incredibly dense and jangly handwriting: 'This is the first time I've ever been here. I am alive for the very first time. I am sitting in this room ...' and so on. This apparently written at the beginning of a particularly inspired manic episode.

What Ben has been concentrating on is the stuff that seems to be research notes. Research scientists are always making handwritten notes. It becomes like second nature after a while. Ben is one of the few people capable of making sense of any notes to do with possible lines of enquiry Emily may have been following, but he hasn't got very far. He can tell, just about, that there is material in the diaries that resembles the kind of notes you'd make of an experiment, but he can't understand enough of it to be able to tell if it's an illegible record of a real experiment or just gibberish. She seems to have employed several codes, each of which on its own would be a fairly simple matter to break, but changed from one code to another at random, or according to some system in her head and not contained in the text. She may have changed codes actually in the middle of words. The different-coloured pens are clearly significant, but their significance seems to be different in different places. (One very beautiful page has a different colour for each letter or figure. Another page is half green and half red. The one after that, red and green alternately. And so on and so on.)

It's just possible that a very gifted cryptographer would be able to get somewhere with it, were it not for the incredibly arcane content. The cryptographer would also need to be a neuroscientist. Ben's given up. He's had to concede that Emily's heroic decision to experiment on herself – an experiment which, if successful, might have heralded a new age in which the defective parts of a human brain could simply be removed and regrown, like a starfish growing a new leg, an end to all kinds of neurological conditions, from Alzheimer's to Parkinson's, from stroke to trauma, depression and schizophrenia (and who knows what potential improvements to the already functioning healthy brain?) – that that experiment has not, unfortunately, produced worthwhile results.

Owen Madden had been urging Ben to join him in Santa Barbara, but he made the decision to put his career on hold while there was still even the remotest chance of Emily having really done something. He admits that at times he has been quite intoxicated with the possibilities of being involved in a quick and gigantic scientific breakthrough – because it's all possible.

81: Dr Nancy Prabhakar

THE INSTITUTE'S FUTURE is a little uncertain at the moment, but if it does have to close Nancy will make sure that Emily is properly looked after. They have had a few successes with alternative funding, enough at least to keep the thing afloat for a while. Ben says they've been pleased with the way my Workshop has been going, so they'll want me to stay around. Everything was in boxes now.

'All done then,' I said.

'Yeah,' said Ben. 'Thanks for all your help. You're good at packing, aren't you.'

'Glad to help. Actually, Ben, I was just wondering. These diaries. Do you think I could have one?' He didn't say anything. He just gave me a look. No fucking way. Shame really. I would have loved to have kept one. They're fascinating things even if you can hardly make out a word. I could look at them for hours.

'Right, then! I might not see you again. Good luck. Have a nice time in California.'

He smiled. 'Yeah thanks, you too. And oh ... I think Dr Prabhakar would like a word if you've got time. See you.'

'See you, Ben.'

I don't mind admitting I'm scared of Nancy Prabhakar. I do mind actually, but there it is. Having felt for so long that I was a fraud, and that I'd been getting away with something (even, at one stage, a serious criminal offence) and having found that I really didn't need to worry so much about all that, I felt as I searched for her office that now I was, after all, about to be exposed as a phoney. But I think a lot of people feel that way around Dr Prabhakar. It was actually all OK.

Her office suited her. A definite air of authority, but nothing put there with the deliberate intention of intimidating people. No wing-backed James Bond villain chairs – she'd be lost in a thing that size anyway – or Albert Speer desks. Some leather upholstery, but brown, not black. She only has one picture on the wall. One of de Kooning's powerful mid-period figure paintings, *Woman (I)*. Good choice.

Mainly she wanted to tell me that they were quite pleased with my work at the Institute. (She didn't look pleased because she never smiles.) The patients seem to have got a lot out of my Workshops, and the Institute has derived some benefit from them too. I took it this meant benefits in terms of funding, attracted in part by the good impression the Workshop gives. That and various other outreach initiatives. Seminars on living with Alzheimer's, for sufferers and their relatives, or living with autism, or stroke or Parkinson's, or epilepsy, or depression. Also demonstrations of the Institute's willingness to embrace the commercial applications of neuroscientific research – biscuits in the MRI suite and so on.

Simon and Selina Norman's litigious bid to seize all the Institute's assets has not been resolved. It's going to take a while. Most probably it will end in a compromise satisfactory neither to them nor to Dr Prabhakar. The Institute will carry on, but not in anything like the form she had envisaged. I began to feel quite sorry for her. She's stuck here now, administrating the aftermath of her bold, and now fatally compromised, experiment. She had hoped by now to be marshalling all the knowledge and resources of neuroscience's vanguard, redefining the cutting edge. Not talking to me about my Drawing Workshop.

She took me a bit by surprise, asking how I felt my training had gone with Ben. I suppose it *was* training, really, in a way. So I said 'fine'. And she had a bit of good news for me about my fee. They'd had to do a bit of juggling with the finances around the time of my appointment. Some of this juggling involved the funding package that had brought me, as artist in residence, and a writer in residence, to the Institute. Matter of fact, they'd been saying, if anyone asked, that I was the writer in residence, and using the spare cash to cover some other staff costs, reception mainly. Nancy felt bad about that, and from now on I'm to be paid for both posts. I might like to think, she suggested, about doing some kind of creative writing workshop, Thursdays. They'd been impressed by my ability to work with limited resources, like just a pen and paper.

She had a couple more things before I went. Ben had told her about my idea for an exhibition of patients' drawings. That's something we could develop. Perhaps we could hold the exhibition here, in the gallery. She'd let me know about a meeting because there were a few other people she'd like present. (What people? What gallery? And when did I tell Ben about my plan? Obviously when I was pissed, but *when* exactly when I was pissed?) Also, one other thing – 'I notice you've been having lunchbreaks in the Day Room lately. I should carry on with that.' I understand. Do NOT come in in the afternoons pissed.

82: colour constancy

WHEN I GOT BACK to the Activities Room it was nearly time to knock off. They all seemed to have been enjoying themselves doing their still lifes of oranges and croissants and coffee cups, all crap. I didn't mind about that, though, because I already had plenty of material for my exhibition – 'Brain Drawings by Brain Patients'. I hadn't told any of them about it because I needed to resolve a few issues about authorship. For example, what if the exhibition got sold? I'd conceived of it as a single, whole piece, an installation if you like, and not as lot of individual works. As individual pieces, by amateurs, the brain drawings were worthless. This has rather been taken out my hands now that Ben (thinking, I suppose, he was doing me a favour) has told Nancy about it. It was supposed to be a project for FRESH! A solo project – by me. The patients would never have found out if I'd done the show without telling them; I very much doubt any of them reads the art press, and it *is* my idea.

Now that Colin was bound to find out about it anyway, I thought I'd better bring him up to strength. I'll tell him about it as if I only just thought of it. And perhaps we could discuss issues of authorship, should any of it actually come to be sold. (Actually it's for the best that FRESH! won't be involved now, because it means I don't have to give them their fifty per cent cut. Excellent.)

It was a nice day, so me and Colin decided to get some coffees in the Tower's foyer and drink them outside in the sun, in one of the hospital's garden areas. We went to the newest

311

one, a 'Peace Garden', which they hadn't quite finished landscaping yet, but which was more usable than any of the others. There's no budget for maintenance, so most of the gardens get covered in nettles and beer cans quite quickly.

We sat on one of the newly installed benches and watched the landscapers at work, me trying to think of a way of broaching the subject of my exhibition. I couldn't think of one so we sat in silence, watching, and enjoying the sunshine. There was a man putting the finishing touches to a small pond, standing in the middle in his waders and pushing young plants into the mud around the edges. Colin called out to him, 'You putting any waterlilies in?' The man looked up for a moment, didn't say anything, then carried on. Colin tried again. 'Oy, mate. WATERLILIES!'

'He's ignoring you, Colin.'

'Yer, I know. They don't care, do they? This'll be all nice for about ten minutes. Six months from now it'll be a shit hole like all the others.'

We watched another guy who was painting a wall behind one of the raised beds. White, to set off the colours of the azaleas. That wall had already been painted white, but some time ago. 'You don't notice white things getting

discoloured till you paint it again, do you? I was doing some of the woodwork at home the other day. The kitchen door's the worst. You don't notice how yellow it's got,' said Colin.

'That's called "colour constancy".'

'Oh yes?'

'It's an optical illusion that causes you to see a white thing as white all the time, no matter what the lighting conditions. A white sheet of paper is actually changing colours all the time. It goes from white to blue to yellow to pink. Colour constancy is the fact that you tend to see things as being the colour you know them to be. Your brain deals in average colour values. It says, "This is WHITE and that's that." Otherwise it'd be confusing and use up a lot of energy to see things constantly changing colour – like living in a kaleidoscope. It's quicker to jump to conclusions about what's there, based on what you already know.'

'What about those marvellous Monets, though? Those paintings of Notre Dame, and the haystacks, where he paints it over and over again and it's different every time?'

'I know, that's what I'm saying. If you ask anyone what colour a stone building is, they'll say it's grey, even though it's only grey some of the time. Sometimes it's pink.'

'How come, then,' Colin wanted to know, 'Monet didn't see Notre Dame as just grey? I thought with optical illusions they always work even when you know it's an illusion.'

'That's true with most of them,' and Ben would probably disagree, 'but with this one you can decide to ignore it. It makes things a bit confusing but it's much prettier. Pub?'

We passed Emily as we were on our way to the Canadian Volunteer. She was sitting on the next bench with Stick and an elderly couple – her parents, I think. Colin said hello to them but I didn't because I was still trying to think of a way of telling him about my exhibition.

83: orange juice?

'ORANGE JUICE? Are you kidding me?' said Colin.

'Well, I've been losing my edge a bit lately. And also Dr Prabhakar's had a little word in my ear about it.'

'Alright, then. Two oranges, then.' The thing is, Colin is your actual social drinker. It's the society of others he's after. The drinking part he can take or leave. He was chuckling when he brought the glasses over.

'Your "edge", ay? Well well well.'

'Yeah, I know, very humorous. Listen, though – there's something I wanted to talk to you about.'

It didn't take very long for me to explain my idea for an installation utilising the drawings from my Drawing Workshop. Hardly any time at all really, which was a bit discouraging because it had seemed as if there was more to it before I'd described it out loud. (But then that side of things is new to me. I would need a proper press release to bulk it out, conceptually. Something a young curator might write.)

Colin considered, impassively, and then delivered his verdict. 'Well, obviously I'm no expert, but it sounds to me as if you're planning to take credit for the hard work of others. That doesn't seem like much of a concept to me. To be honest it sounds a bit dishonest.'

'Yes, but the whole notion of authorship is in transition. Most artists get their work fabricated these days. Or there's "appropriation art", where you do something that looks like pastiche, or plagiarism, or forgery, but which isn't any of those because you're declaring the lack of originality, and it becomes a kind of critique.'

Colin was facing straight ahead, mouth pushed up, eyes narrowed. I tried a different tack. 'Did you know, Colin, that Henry Moore made hardly any of his own sculptures? It wouldn't have been possible, anyway. He had assistants. The thing is, it's the idea that's important in a lot of art these days.'

'OK, but suppose it's not a very clever idea. Or suppose there's a bit more to doing it than just thinking of it. Suppose I wanted to do a five-hundred-foot jewel-encrusted statue of Madonna that flies to the fucking moon. Thinking of it wouldn't be the most difficult part of the whole thing, would it? I mean, I've just thought of it now, haven't I? That would be job done as far as you're concerned.'

'Well, you've come up with quite an extreme example there, but I suppose you could do it if you had the resources. But you're being a bit sarcastic. There are ideas and ideas.'

'Yer. What I'm getting at is it doesn't seem right, on a very basic level. It seems rather unprofessional to me. There's been a couple of times I've been meaning to have a little word with you about your professionalism. For example, I don't think your attitude to Emily has been very professional.' Oh dear. 'I know she's a very attractive young lady but I've seen you looking at her, and most people probably wouldn't notice, but you looked to me as if you fancied her something rotten. And that's just not on for a man in your position.'

This is amazing. First of all I'm definitely in the clear, because, as Colin has rightly surmised, I've done nothing wrong, even if my attitude was definitely wrong there. I've sinned in thought, and someone working in a place like this oughtn't to do that. Second, though, how can he tell? His deficit affects precisely the ability to tell a leer from a smile, or a pout from a grimace.

'I know,' I said. 'Yeah ... Well, I'll be honest, you're dead right, I did find Emily very attractive, but I'm past all that now.' Which is true actually. Now I know she's a genius, or *was* a genius, I've gone off her. That's a bit disappointing, really. I had felt as if my feelings were deep, and they were shallow. Or, at any rate, contingent: my love for Emily was reliant on the obviously unrealistic possibility of her being some impossible creature of my dreams. The hopelessness of romantic love is well-known, and mine would just be an exemplary and extreme case of that. 'But how could you tell? How could you see I had ... um, feelings towards her?'

'It's a bit like being blind. You learn to read the other signs better. It's not much good if you weren't particularly perceptive in the first place, but I've always had a feeling for people. I could tell just from your posture, and how your voice went all funny every time you spoke to her, or whenever she was mentioned. You've stopped doing it now. Listen, it's bleeding gloomy in here on a nice sunny day like today. D'you want to sit outside again for a bit?'

Colin seemed to be giving my exhibition idea some serious consideration as we strolled across the new lawn to the new benches.

'Look,' he said, 'I've still got some doubts about this idea of yours but I think you're basically a decent fella, so you're welcome to use my work and any other help I can offer. I've done trade fair installation so it can't be that different from putting up an exhibition. It should do well now that there are all these other people interested in our Workshop.'

'What other people?'

'That's right. They came round when you were AWOL a few weeks back. You know that woman Hilary? She came round with Dr Prabhakar and some people from a museum.'

'Museum?'

'Museum wossnames. Oooh … what do they call them ..?'
'Curators.'

'That's it. Museum curators. Although I don't think they were from a museum.'

'Did you catch any of their names.'

'Yes. There was one lovely girl I had a long chat with called Susan. Conrad introduced her to us. Why? D'you know her?'

84: let's have a meeting

I WAS SPRAWLED, SULKILY, on a chair by the large oval conference table, in what may have been the conference room in which I was first interviewed for this thing. The habits born of many years trying to disguise my drunkenness are in evidence here, because I'm way too early for this meeting. Perhaps, I think, I should stop sulking and sit up straight, like an adult. After all, I can't really claim that the idea of showing the drawings of a group of patients is an entirely original idea of mine. It belongs to an established genre or school called 'Outsider Art'. And appropriating somebody else's handiwork to my own oeuvre isn't an original idea either. It's a postmodern staple. Everyone's at it. I'm not sure how I'd have handled it if my original plan had gone through and I'd shown the stuff at FRESH! Would I have asked the patients to the private view? And would they have got a cut if the piece had sold? No. Not if I could have got away with it. So, basically, I haven't got the slightest justification for being all sulky.

I sat up straight. Actually, given all that deviousness on my part, I'm lucky to be here at all. They'd have been within their rights to have excluded me from any further involvement with the project, if they'd known. Which, of course, they can't have done. I feel OK now. Rather good, in fact. Having given this state of well-being some thought, I decide it must be connected to my not having a hangover, and isn't the result of some change in the mood of the entire world.

Dr Prabhakar came in with Hilary (from the Arts Council, or whatever). They nodded in my direction, took seats at the far end of the table, opened their laptops, and began a sort of pre-meeting meeting. Susan came in and said bright 'hellos' to Nancy and Hilary, then, seeing me all the way at the other end of the table, gave me a huge and guileless smile. She sat down, opened her laptop, and joined in the pre-meeting meeting. So, I'll just sit up here, then. I'll be over here if you want me. (I wish I owned a computer.) Colin came in, saw the women working, and seemed to be a bit unsure of himself until he saw me at the other end of the table and came over. (I feel as if we're about twelve years old and this is the back end of the coach on a coach trip.) Two of those creepy-looking types I've been seeing around here lately turned up next. Colin leaned over and told me that one of them was the woman who'd sat and watched an entire Workshop without saying a thing, just taking notes and giving everyone the creeps.

Is that all of us? Apparently there's someone else we have to wait for before we can begin. We waited another three quarters of an hour, with me and Colin getting bored and the others at the other end getting a lot done in their pre-meeting meeting.

Simon and Selina finally entered, causing a self-conscious ripple of semi-formal behaviour – hand shakes and murmured introductions. Me and Colin sidled to the other end of the table, where we were introduced to Simon and Selina as 'our star patient, and quite an artist' (Colin obviously) and 'our artist in residence'. I felt important again then, because of the way Nancy said it. Nobody took much notice of Conrad, who seemed to be moving in Simon and Selina's wake rather than under his own steam.

We all sat down and Nancy opened the meeting. 'First of all I'd very much like to thank all of you for coming this morning' (my pleasure, I thought, don't mention it), 'and since most of the details regarding funding and publicity and so on have been dealt with, I see no reason why we shouldn't press on with viewing the art gallery.' She glanced at Susan and remembered the more professional-sounding term. 'The "space", in fact.'

We'd only just sat down, and we were all looking from side to side, waiting for someone else to move first. Nancy snapped her laptop shut, which caused us all to stir, and making a noisy fuss with chairs and paperwork and doors we managed to get ourselves out into the hallway. Michelle, waiting for us, clicked on her walkie-talkie: 'Reception? Yes, we're moving towards the art gallery now. Over.'

As she said this she began moving quickly alongside Dr Prabhakar, both of them swinging one arm quick time to set the pace. We'd got to the first corner when we found that Simon and Selina and Conrad were not with us, and looking back we could see they were making no attempt whatsoever to stay with the group. We had to wait quite a long time for them to catch up, and then proceeded at the pace they obviously preferred – about the speed of heavily laden refugees.

We were in transit so long that Michelle needed to contact base camp, i.e. the reception desk, twice, to tell them we weren't there yet. Finally, we seemed to have got there, and I recognised it. It was the same corridor I'd gone to with Ben a month or so back, just before I had my little nervous breakdown. We were standing by a door on the opposite side of the corridor from Miss Havisham's laboratory.

'Alright now,' said Michelle, 'let's hope this is it.' She opened the door, and we stepped into a very up-to-date, purpose-built exhibition space. A white cube, in fact. Those architects really had thought of everything. I caught Susan's eye, and she was nodding slowly with her chin pushed in and her eyebrows raised. Nice! *Very* nice.

85: installation

NORMALLY WHEN YOU INSTALL an exhibition of contemporary art, the first job is to paint the gallery white, even though it's white already. Some art galleries have been painted so many times that features like air-vents and power-points have got lost under all the layers of paint. We didn't need to do this here because, like everything else in the Institute, this perfectly square room was kept constantly fresh. It was repainted every six months, which is plenty considering it's never been used. The exact thinking behind the decision to have an art gallery here has got lost somewhere, but it's in keeping with the lavishness that characterises the whole enterprise (there's a sauna and Jacuzzi somewhere in the Institute that never gets used).

Before going ahead with the installation we were obliged to consult with the patients about how we all thought the show should look.

'Can't we have them in nice frames?' asked Pauline the hemi-neglecter. Susan explained why that wasn't a good idea. 'Aside from the cost, there's the issue of selection. If we had them framed we wouldn't be able to show nearly as many, and we'd be in the position of having to reject a lot of people's work, and I don't think any of us want that.' We had the moral high ground here. Another reason for showing absolutely all of the drawings was that, whilst giving the impression of being to do with a kind of aesthetic democracy, in which all people's work is of equal value, it had the effect of homogenising the work and thereby transferring authorial credit to the organisers – me and

Susan. Pauline wasn't the only one who wanted frames – actually they all did, but Susan was able to convince them that framing would introduce a hierarchy of value judgments, and this wouldn't be fair to some of the less able amongst us: like the Blind Couple for instance. Susan is bloody good at this. She doesn't even know when she's bullshitting, she just does it. And I didn't feel bad about it because they were all having fun, and I think I deserve my bit of credit.

The real fun started when we began to hang the drawings. This took some organising because there were thousands of them, and they all had to be tacked to the wall. Colin did some sums (I'm hopeless at arithmetic) and found that, amazingly, if we used every drawing we had, pinned right up next to each other, we would be able to exactly fill all four walls, floor to ceiling. Or almost. We were short by one drawing. Amazing.

We wanted to involve as many people as possible, so we got four stepladders, one set for each wall, and organised the patients into teams of two. We started working from the top left-hand corners, with one person up the ladders and the

other handing them drawings from a big pile in the middle of the room. A bit like wallpapering really. Obviously not everyone was capable of joining in fully because of their various deficits, but everyone was there anyway, just to feel involved. Trevor, for example, couldn't really make it up the ladders because of his size, but he was fine once the top rows had been done. He and Jade worked together. She seems to have taken a bit of a shine to him. The Phineas Gage guy started working with the Scratching Man, but he got pricked slightly by a drawing pin and stormed off in an incredible rage. Oh well. Pauline and Colin were working steadily on one wall, her evidently able to align the edges of drawings within the perceptible half of her world, and Emily and Stick were going like the clappers on the wall next to them. These two were going so fast because Stick, besides positioning each of the drawings Emily handed him, was scooting down the ladder each time to get another one. He was a blur, and Emily was fine because she's very good with simple repetitive tasks like this. She seemed to find it enormously satisfying.

We had a few days to get the whole thing done, and work was going very well, so tea and lunch and snack breaks tended to be quite extended, sociable affairs. We'd sit in a scruffy circle on the floor in the middle of the gallery, eating oranges and croissants and *croques monsieurs* and apricot Danishes and Cheddar paninis, or trying some of the sandwiches that the A. Man would bring in. He'd turn up every day with an enormous Tupperware container, and some of his sandwiches weren't bad actually.

About mid-morning on the third day I was working with Susan, getting close to finishing the wall that Stick and Emily had started, and Dr Prabhakar came in with Hilary and some of those audit goons. They took a turn about the room, stopping and chatting to people as they went (in that way that always makes me think of the Queen) and, having given everything a good look, they came over to me and Susan.

'Can I just check, just quickly ...' said Hilary, '... some of the figures? Just a quick breakdown. Can you give us a number of people *benefiting* from this activity?' The obviously new tablet she proudly held was doing a lot for her sense of authority. I said a number and she added it to her records. 'And can you give me age groups, please? Children under five? Children five to eleven? Young people twelve to fifteen ...?' I gave more figures (Susan had told me what to say, and what you were supposed to pretend you knew). 'That's lovely,' said Hilary. 'Now – Asian or British Asian? Black or British black? Chinese or ...' I did not laugh right in her face when she asked me next, standing in a hospital, if there were any beneficiaries with disabilities? and how, and if, these disabilities affected the character and the degree of this benefit? I just answered, along the lines in which Susan had coached me.

'This all looks very impressive,' said Nancy Prabhakar. 'Well done!' She was being, by her standards, extremely warm towards us, but that's not surprising considering it was us who were mainly responsible for getting Simon and Selina off her back, and out of her cropped grey hair. Conrad had told her about his idea of having an exhibition of patients' drawings (having, most probably, forgotten that it was Ben who'd told him about *my* idea), and not long after that she'd been approached by resourceful Susan – with the same idea, or 'proposal'. When the possibility of being involved in an important contemporary art exhibition was skilfully presented to Simon and Selina, they were thrilled.

Of course, Colin, perceptive as ever, understood exactly why they changed their tune so radically. 'See, they just wanted a bit of attention.' The billionaire kid's combination of lavish material privilege and emotional deprivation can create some uniquely troublesome individuals. All Susan had had to do to bring about this change of heart (and persuade them, by the way, to set up the SIMON AND SELINA NORMAN FOUNDATION FOR CONTEMPORARY ART) was to show them the social pages from a few magazines: dozens and dozens of photographs of celebrities hugging artists and art collectors and gallerists at private views – holding a glass of Champagne in their free hand, and smiling.

The whole court case thing hasn't exactly been called off, but apparently these things need constant feeding with cash, and if the cash stops flowing they just die a natural death. Nancy is very pleased indeed. If only she'd realised it would be so easy! It simply would never have occurred to her to treat the Norman children – all of whom are in their forties – like children.

Since she seemed to be so keen on me now, I decided to ask her a sort of favour. I needed her permission for a particular addition to the show. OK, she said, so long as it's OK with Ben. I rang Ben and he said it was OK with him so long as it was OK with Dr Prabhakar. That settled, I needed to get something from the hospital's storage. They used to have a medical museum at Gray's, and although a lot of the stuff was sold or thrown out, I was hoping they'd kept some of it because there was a particular kind of display cabinet I needed. Michelle put me in touch with one of the building managers, and he said it would be fine for me to go down to the basement and have a look. There, amongst an enormous quantity of obsolete equipment and furniture, was exactly the thing I was after. Some handsome Victorian glass-topped display cabinets of the type they use in the British Museum to show autograph manuscripts – the handwritten originals of famous works of literature.

It took me and Colin quite a while to bring up five of these things, one by one in the lift, and by the time we'd done it the picture hanging was about finished. This huge, high-ceilinged room entirely covered with thousands of variously competent drawings of the human brain. *Almost* entirely. There was enough space left for one drawing – and no more brain drawings left.

'I'll do one now,' said Stick.

'Hang on,' I said. 'I've got another idea.' I went to the Activities Room and came back with a drawing from the last still-life session we'd had. I pinned it in the gap – There! All done.

'Isn't that Pauline's croissant?' said Colin.

86: another private view

WE WERE STANDING in the gallery waiting for Ben, and Colin picked up a press release from the desk. It was getting on for six o'clock, and Ben still hadn't turned up with those diaries. If I'd had a watch I'd have been looking at it all the time; instead I was constantly leaning down and twisting my head to look at Colin's expensive watch. He was reading our press release and didn't seem to be enjoying it. Next to the desk our caterers were about done putting white tablecloths on a pair of trestle tables, and they were setting out bottles of Champagne and hundreds of glass flutes.

'You seen this?' said Colin. I'd actually stayed well away from the writing of the press release; that's Susan's area.

'No,' I said. 'Why?'

'I don't understand a blind word of it. What's "relational aesthetics" when it's at home?' He held the sheet of A4 as if it were an X-ray, and he was scrutinising it for evidence of some terrible illness. 'Here's another one – "performativity". And what's "the voice of the other"?'

I could have explained that the purpose of this kind of writing – this kind of 'text' – is magical. It's not there to give information or guidance; it's there to invoke the spirit of contemporary art. It's not supposed to be clear, because it's a kind of spell – an accepted form of gibberish. And besides, who am I to mock and criticise? Left to me, none of this would have happened. My 'plan' consisted of nothing more than telling my dealer about my big idea, while both of us were drunk. Granted there isn't much information in this press release, but there is *some* – my name, and the 'NNI Drawing Workshop'. I changed the subject slightly.

'What do you think of the invite card, though, eh? I think it's really nice.'

We'd gone with 'BRAINS' as the title for the show. One side of the card had an old black and white photograph of a brain we'd found online somewhere, with the word 'BRAINS' running diagonally across it in stark white, and on the reverse we'd put the names of everyone who'd been involved, in whatever capacity. The names were printed in alphabetical order and without spacing, so that at first glance it just looked like a block of randomly selected letters. No one was overlooked and no one was singled out – in theory.

'Yer. Very nice.' Contemporary graphic design isn't really Colin's cup of tea, but he's willing to defer to my superior knowledge on this. 'Shall I give Ben a ring?' he said. 'See where he's got to?' He made a call, and then, closing his phone, told me, 'He's here. He's down in the foyer. He wants us to go down and give him a hand.'

We found Ben standing in the middle of the decrepit foyer with his foot on one of three large cardboard boxes.

'Hang on, guys,' I said. 'There's just one thing I need to do before we take these upstairs.' Without asking anyone's permission (because it's hard to tell who's in charge down here), I Blutacked a few 'BRAINS' posters about the place, trying not to cover anything important, like the directions to A&E for example.

'OK,' I said. And then 'Ooooff!', because these boxes were incredibly heavy. Standing in the lift, each of us leaning back to counter the weight of the boxes we were holding, I asked Ben about his move to Santa Barbara. 'When you off?'

'Tomorrow morning, actually. I'm not really done packing yet, so I can't stay long this evening.'

'You'll stay for a drink, though.'

'Oh yeah.'

Once we'd got to the gallery I gratefully plonked my box by a display cabinet. We'd arranged them in a line spaced diagonally across the room from corner to corner, making a nice fusty Victorian counterpoint to the ultra-modern surroundings. Colin opened his box and took a look.

'What are these?' he asked, leafing through one of Emily's deranged hypergraphic diaries, with his mouth open. 'This looks mental.' The sheer graphic density of them is astonishing – the thousands of frantic hours. Ben gave Colin a rather bowdlerised account of the background to Emily's condition – the bipolarity and the 'suicide attempt' and so on.

'Emily's a doctor?!' said Colin. 'Well ... I'll be jiggered. Well I never.' He picked up another diary and examined it, moving his head slowly from side to side, and tutting. 'Oh dear,' he said. I was going to explain that I wanted Emily's hypergraphic diaries in the show because, beside the fact that they have an unnerving beauty, the way they blur the distinction between symptom and self-expression is, I believe, instructive, and profound. I didn't, though.

Obviously there were far too many diaries to show them all, so we thought, given the size of the diaries and the size of the display cases, that it would be best to just show five diaries in each case; twenty-five altogether. God knows there's enough to look at. Even a single page is too much. The choice was made easy by the simple criterion of displaying those that stayed open whilst laid flat, and the choice of page was similarly simplified – they were left open at the page they stayed open at. While Colin was carefully arranging a cabinet at one corner of the gallery, me and Ben were doing the same on the other side.

I asked Ben about something that could have been a problem, potentially. 'How do you think Emily will react when she sees them? You know she's coming this evening.'

'Oh, she's seen them. Of course she has. Me and Nancy have spent quite a lot of time going through them with her to see if they mean anything. Emily can't even read them; or she can't make out any more than anyone else can. Just the odd word or phrase. She does know she did them, but they don't mean anything to her now. The reason me and Nancy agreed to let you use them is we're quite certain the only meaning they've ever had was the meaning they had for her while she was doing them. They're the record of a state of mind. That's all. We'll continue to keep an eye on her, of course. Certainly Nancy will. She's just finalising the process of becoming Emily's legal guardian, and she's organised special provision for her to stay here at the Institute, where everybody understands her needs. Her folks can come and see her anytime. They're getting on a bit, so they can't really look after her themselves, but they can visit – I think all the bad blood between them is gone now.'

'Ah ... Jesus! What's the time?'

Ben looked at his expensive watch (they all look expensive to me). 'Six.'

'That means we're officially open.' We looked across at the doors, expecting some instant change there. One of the bow-tied waiters, standing by the bar with his hands loosely clasped in front, leaned over and said something to a tiny waitress in an A-line skirt that matched his tie and trousers, and she nodded. They both went back to staring ahead and not doing anything.

Susan came in. 'Could someone please put up some signs to guide people from the lift? Everyone's going to get lost otherwise. Colin. Would you mind?' She knew not to ask me to do it.

It took a moment for him to respond, because he'd become engrossed in Emily's diaries. 'Hmmn? Oh, yeah, course I will.'

Nancy appeared, all in grey as usual, accompanied by her usual posse of funding bodies and audit goons, most of them also in grey. The small amount of sound they were generating made me very conscious of the room's hollow acoustic qualities. Given the enormous quantity of artwork to be seen, you'd think they'd spread out and take a look. Instead they seemed to prefer staying all bunched up together as they moved about. Exactly like sheep, in fact.

'It's always like this at the beginning of a private view,' I said to Ben, whispering for some reason. 'The quiet before the storm.'

'Ah,' he said, 'OK,' and took a glass of Champagne. I took a glass of orange juice because I didn't want to get pissed too early. Not with Nancy there keeping her eye on me. Her little group had found a spot where they felt comfortable stopping – about equidistant from every wall and object, and other person, in the room. Some sort of consensus had it that this was a good spot to stand, and murmur. A waiter took them some drinks.

The patients were arriving now, most of them entering only after having poked their heads round the door to see if this was the right place, even though they all knew it was, because they'd hung the show in the first place. I wondered why this was, then realised it's because they're awestruck. They're excited and nervous because they're in an art exhibition. An art exhibition *that they're in*! Very likely nobody will turn up tonight, but at the very least I've helped to give them this, and that's something. That's an achievement right there, just on its own. I'm not ashamed (even though I am a bit surprised) to say that I am touched by this. The look on their faces! If only Colin could see it. In fact, look at the look on Colin's face. He's thrilled.

Almost every patient who had a glass of Champagne had asked if it was OK before they took one – the A. Man did; Pauline and Trevor and the Scratching Man did; even the Phineas Gage guy and Stick the rebel did. They were keeping their voices down as they moved about in tight little groups, looking and nodding and smiling, all hunched and reverent. (But it's your own stuff! I was thinking. There's no need to be intimidated, just because it's art.) The guys in grey suits stayed together, and the patients eventually congregated around the few wheelchair users present, so that they began to resemble a band of settlers stranded on the Western prairie – all together there, in the middle of that gigantic, echoing room.

It stayed like this until 7.30. We all became aware that something was heading our way at about the same time, and before anything was audible. Conversations halted, and shrewd glances were exchanged as we cocked our ears. Can you—? Was that—? There are people coming this way. It sounds like a *lot*. The gradually increasing clamour, moving smoothly up the scale from the barely discernible to the unignorable, suddenly leaped a dozen notches as the column swung across the threshold and swelled into the room, filling it completely in less than ten minutes. For some reason this always happens at private views. People must time it this way. It must be to do with everybody trying to be the last to arrive, but still wanting to get there before all the drink runs out.

The idling bar staff were now under siege, and Susan seemed to be everywhere, thoroughly galvanised by the success she had engineered. I looked at Ben and Colin, both of them silently registering disbelief. 'THIS', I shouted, 'IS THE ART WORLD.'

Of course, Ben and Colin had both had some exposure to aspects of the art world before, but not to a massed showing like this. Susan must have got the best mailing list in the world. Everybody was there – artists, gallerists, collectors, celebrities; the fucking lot. While she energetically worked the room, I decided to relax and let the room work me. I took a well-earned glass of Champagne from a passing waiter, and remembered, after a sip or two, that it's one of the few alcoholic drinks I absolutely cannot stand. In the past I'd have drunk it anyway, but I decided to try something new today, and *not* drink it.

'Hey, Trevor. Do you want to finish my drink for me? Save you another trip to the bar?' Trevor was having himself a high old time. Cheers, Trevor! I too was very much enjoying things by now, because, almost for the first time ever, I was at a private view and people were actively seeking my company. Here's my dealer (from FRESH!), for example.

'GREAT SHOW!' he shouts.

'THANKS!' I shout back.

And now here's my 'friend': the guy who told me about the residency here in the first place, and then was too snooty to bother applying for it himself.

'Hi there,' he says. 'Great show. Listen, do you, by any chance, know when they're advertising the next residency? Only I was thinking I might apply. What d'you reckon?' He was hoping I'd put in a good word for him. I might do. In the time it had taken him to say that, I had seen three well-known celebrities go past, and Simon and Selina actually running after them. (I think I preferred those two not smiling. It's a revolting spectacle.)

I was just chatting to Dr Bokassa about Wilder Penfield (our hero) when I became aware of a minor commotion over at the door. I couldn't hear what they were saying because of all the racket in here, but the new receptionist was obviously very angry about something, and Susan was doing her best to calm her down. An uncomfortable-looking security guard was standing just behind the highly animated receptionist, and hoping, I guessed, that he wouldn't be called upon to intervene. Of course! I know what this is about. They've run out of security passes, and they're having to allow people in without them. That's the sort of thing she hates. She was really incredibly angry, and Susan was looking as if she couldn't cope, but then Conrad came to her rescue – dealing with it, I must say, with great aplomb. The receptionist was sent away with a flea in her ear, and Conrad made his triumphant way back to his girlfriend, who handed him a glass of Champagne as if it were a sports trophy. Very likely she'll be getting her old job back now. (Not a bad thing, this. She's a shit receptionist, but at least she isn't a nuisance.)

I was soberly and scientifically observing the effects of lots and lots of free Champagne on a diverse crowd – the main effect is that the diversity is overcome, and artists, for example, will mix freely with neurology patients – when I saw Emily looking unnaturally and worryingly immobile as she leaned over a display case. It took a while to reach her, pushing and squeezing through, and trying not to be rude to anyone – 'Hi, Zeinab! How're you?' – but when I got there I saw that she was just trying very hard to read what it said in her diary. As if it was some sort of test or puzzle.

'Hello Emily.'

'Oh – hello.' She smiled at me. A great big smile. 'Have you seen my writing? I can't make head nor tale of it!' I smiled back and nodded, feeling embarrassed, and very sad all of a sudden. Her bewildered parents looked on, still puzzled by the sunny disposition she has achieved at such cost, and Stick came up behind them, placing large reassuring hands on narrow shoulders. He leaned down to murmur a suggestion, and both were visibly relieved as they nodded their assent – *Yes, that's probably enough excitement for today. Let's go somewhere a bit quieter now. Let's go for a nice sit down.* Bye bye, Emily. Bye bye, my love …

Ben had to go now, too. 'Thanks a lot. It's been brilliant. I think the patients have really benefited a lot. They look like they're having a brilliant time. I'll see you soon, though.'

'Well – thank you, too! Thanks for bringing those diaries along. They're the best thing in the show, I reckon. See you soon? Aren't you off to California?'

'Yeah, but I'll be coming back every few months. In fact, now that the situation is looking more promising around here I may well be back here for good after I've spent a couple of years abroad. I've just been chatting with Nancy, by the way, and she's thinking of creating a permanent post for you. "Neuroaesthetics".'

'Excellent! That's bloody brilliant! You've met my ex, haven't you?' Susan gave Ben a distracted nod, and then beckoned for me to follow her out into the corridor.

'We've got a problem. Conrad wants to buy the show.'

'That's good, isn't it? We haven't really sorted out how we should split the money yet, but that shouldn't be too difficult. Should it?'

'He says that as the curator he wants to pay the patients fifty per cent and himself the rest. He's claiming it was his idea. I think he actually believes that.'

'It was *my* idea!'

'Hang on – there's more. Simon and Selina are saying that he can buy it *from them*. Because it's to do with their Contemporary Art Foundation they reckon. They're all on the phone to their lawyers already. Right now.'

'Awright people?' said Colin as he was passing. 'I'm well overdue for a sprinkle.' Then he stopped and turned to take a proper look at us. 'What's the matter with you two?' he said. 'Why the long faces?'

list of images

p.27 Willem de Kooning: *Morning: The Springs*, 1983 (GettyImages/Stedelijk Museum).

p.64 Ventral view of the brain by Vesalius, 1543.

p.119 Hippocampus pyramidal cells, Cuntz et al. (WikiCommons).

p.143 Monet: *Waterlilies*, 1906, Art Institute of Chicago.

p.175 Drawing of a clock by a neglect patient with allocheiria (WikiCommons).

p.186 Crop circle, Wiltshire, 1990s.

p.194 Hogarth: *Credulity, Superstition and Fanaticism*, 1762.

p.208 Cortical homunculus.

p.221 Map of Belize.

p.254 Flat floorplan, 2015.

p.283 Wassily Kandinsky: *On White II*, 1923.

p.312 Shades of white.

p.322 Croissant.